# HOME WRECKER

## JODY KAYE

Special Edition Paperback

First Print: January 2024

www.JodyKaye.com

Splinter of Hope
Shred of Decency
Sliver of Truth
Holding Onto Hope
Home Wrecker
Deep Gap
Bleeding Heart
Shattered Soul

She's stolen my heart,

and I'm set on

winning hers over.

For every mom who is positive they are doing
it all wrong. Me too, friend.

But at least it's good we're confident about
something.

*Cary*

"Hand me the wrench, Bhodi."

I'm underneath the hood of a 1964 Mercury Colony Park. I'd been on the lookout for a Chevelle wagon, but after seeing the potential in this classic California surfer wagon, I was hooked. Nowadays, the silver-blue finish is cringe-worthy, but the teal is spot on for the era, and the wood panel appliqué was in fantastic condition for a car sitting in a musty barn in the Sandhills of North Carolina for decades.

"Which one?"

I glance up confused and chuckle. The kid's holding two wrenches to his face, peering through the holes like glasses. The silver tools combined with his shaggy brown hair make Bhodi Carrington look like Daniel Radcliffe about to have the sorting hat placed on his head. Underneath his grease-stained navy coveralls though the Vans store exploded on my fourth-grade apprentice. He's even got the checkerboard slip-on shoes that he's quick to cover whenever we enter the garage to restore this car.

When the local big brother program paired us together, I was sure they'd made a mistake. However, I've learned Bhodi's neat as a pin appearance has more to do with having a shit-ton more respect for what he has than I ever had growing up. Bhodi's no dweeb.

He is a quick learner, handing me the five-eighths, which is the exact one I need.

"You're awesome." The tone of my verbal complement reflects the way my grandfather had ruffled his hand through my hair when I was a kid.

I brought Bhodi into the service bay on a lark. We had an hour to kill after a movie we'd gone to see ended early, and the head mechanic texted this beauty was on a flatbed outside the dealership. We watched its low, bald tires slide down onto the asphalt, and a bunch of us, Bhodi included, pushed it into the service area where it sits now. When he started asking questions, I took him into the showroom. This location alone has six restored cars on hand. It's sort of our hallmark. One of my favorite things is how amazed customers coming into the dealerships, ready to buy brand new off of the lot, are when we're able to start the classics up.

The first time I'd helped my grandfather under the hood of a car, I wasn't much older than Bhodi. I caught the bug from there. To my chagrin, the asshat in charge of this place diverted a lot of Grandad's attention elsewhere. I hadn't honed any true mechanical skill until I was college bound and the technicians took pity on me. Over the majority of the past eight years, the side benefit of this has been the more time I spent in the service center rather than the corporate offices, the more it pissed off the CEO. A man who gave me his last name.

I finish tightening the bolt and, after handing the wrench back to the kid, wipe my hands on a rag and check my watch.

"I think we're done."

Bhodi's shoulders slump as he puts the tools back in order. I pat him on the back.

"Dude, make sure you thank your mom for letting you come in this afternoon."

It's normal for me to take Bhodi on the weekend. Over the course of helping out, he's gotten to a point where he's capable of doing a few of the tasks on his own, so yesterday I got permission from Holly to switch days and pick him up after school.

We shrug off the coveralls. The mechanics keep it light and joke around with Bhodi while he washes up. Something I appreciate. A few of them, with kids of their own, compare the black under their fingernails to his. One of the older fellas sends Bhodi back to the sink to try again while I snag the keys to a test drive vehicle with dealer plates on it. I like that the service center mechanics look out for him.

I signed up for the big brother program a few months ago to fix me, not realizing in the process I'd feel more responsible for this kid than I have for anyone. Is that crappy and self-centered of me to admit? Because I thought this was going to be like when my prep school forced us to volunteer for a stupid service project at the local pound. You couldn't get attached to those animals because they came in and out of a revolving door of surrenders and adoptions. Before now, the idea of having kids around was foreign. If having any of my own didn't seem like a game of Russian Roulette and I wound up with one like him, I could see myself doing it someday.

That's not to say Bhodi doesn't have his quirks.

He climbs into the passenger side next to me and starts fiddling with the radio.

"Back seat." I throw my thumb behind me.

"Why?" He whines.

"We've talked about this. It's safer back there for pint-sized people."

"It's boring back there. There's not even a TV in this car."

"You're going to waste the last fifteen minutes with me watching television?" I place my hand over my chest. "I'm wounded."

"No, you aren't."

"No, I'm not. Now get."

Bhodi's shoe lands on the console, leaving a dusty print on the leather as he slips between the seats. I wipe it away and then adjust the mirrors, pretending not to watch him buckle up in the center. He leans forward, still trying to change the station on the dash.

"You know this is stupid, right? The station wagon we're working on doesn't have *any* seatbelts. If you stick to the rules, how am I supposed to ride in it when we're done?"

I'm not telling the kid that I'm going to retrofit them. I've never done that on a showroom restoration before, but it's a compromise I'm willing to make.

"Sit back." I push him by the forehead, shift into drive, and fiddle with the tuner trying to find the station he likes.

"Stop!" Bhodi yells.

I jam the brake, jerking us to a halt, and swing my head back-and-forth like a moron, wondering what I'm about to plow into.

"Right there!" He points at the dash's digital display.

"You just gave me a heart attack because of the *Arthur* theme song?"

"It's a good song. My mom sings it."

I try to focus on Bhodi when we're together rather than his mother. Holly Carrington is a looker, and it's unfair to the kid that I enjoy dropping him off as much as I do picking him up.

Shit, did that come out wrong?

What I mean is, his hot mom aside, the kid is my priority and I have fun with him.

At the sax part, he's blowing into a fake instrument, wiggling his fingers in the air. I can't help laughing. When the song ends, he's cool with my choice of something a little more modern and hard. But when I pull up to his condo and we get to the steps with his backpack, I can hear the thump of eighties music vibrating through the door.

I knock as a warning before Bhodi barrels inside. The Tom Petty blasting in the kitchen gets turned down to a manageable level, and I hear Holly's sweet voice welcome her son home.

She finishes hugging him and the kid whips his bag across the floor, scampering away so she can't tell him to empty his lunchbox.

"Right on time, thanks. I really wanted a chance to see Bhodi before I left. Friday's are Crazytown at work." Holly smiles, moving toward the sink and turning on the tap.

She puts a watering can below the spigot to fill up. Some water splashes up as she does, turning me into a hound dog waiting for the droplets to soak into her top.

Holly has a rockabilly style with pin curls when her hair is down, and these blonde sexy-cool gravity-defying swirls when it's up in a kerchief. Today, she's got on black high-top Chucks. Her tattoo which starts below the cuff of her bobby socks has my eyes trailing up to her pert ass. The swell of it hangs out of the bottom of a deep green pair of cut-offs. The ink doesn't show at her collar line, but a faint color seeps through from underneath a white t-shirt, so it may stop around her small braless tit. Both of those rosebuds dare me to look each time I see Holly. I can't not sneak a peek before meeting her brown eyes.

When we were introduced, it was obvious based on her appearance Holly had an interesting job. Then one time when she mentioned it was her day off—still dressed in short shorts and cropped tops tied at her middle—I recognized this was her personal style. Although, you could've bowled me over when I walked into Sweet Caroline's, looking for Jake Ballentine, and Holly was tending bar. The last place I'd expect to encounter my mentee's mother was at Brighton's notorious strip club, and if that doesn't qualify as a complication to an already problematic situation, I'm not sure what does.

One thing is for sure, for a woman whom I've never seen naked, I have an uncanny awareness of her body. Holly's at minimum ten years my senior. I've always had a thing for older women. I like the confidence they have when they ask you for sexual favors. Not sure if the cause is nature or nurture. Less certain I care either way. She's Bhodi's mom. I wish my dick understood that.

"Bhodi's enjoying working on the car with you." Holly tilts the watering can, sprinkling some houseplants sitting on an overcrowded window sill.

*Bhodi. Yup, he's why I'm here.* I nod, doing my best to roll my tongue back into my mouth. She's hot and I'm a perv.

"Before he left this morning, he begged me to let him go on a school day again next week," Holly continues, covering a yawn as I try to get my wits about me.

I hadn't thought that far ahead. "What we fixed today was simple stuff. He's a capable kid. I might need to find him a challenge." If Bhodi's having enough fun that he wants to come back to the service center, I'll have to put in hours by myself after work to prep the next part for him. We're close to finishing. "I can take him more often if it makes it easier on you."

I'm the kid's weekend entertainment. About once a month the organizers plan a big meet-up, so it's not always one-on-one. He gets to interact with other boys his age, and the adults share ideas of how to keep them occupied. We're scheduled to go to a history museum and are even talking about coordinating a camping trip.

With her back to me, Holly makes a noncommittal sound. I should show myself out and text her the details whenever I have something to share. Instead, I stuff my hands in my pockets and bumble for a reason to stay.

"Do you like flowers?" Hell, I sound like a three-year-old. *Does she like flowers?* Duh, she's got something of every shape and variety crammed into the bright space. No wonder this woman isn't the type to take me seriously. She must think I have a supernatural ability to look past the obvious.

Her fingers travel over one plant, crunching dried petals between the tips. The action has a scent permeating the room. Her nose twitches and the corner of her mouth lifts, like that Samantha chick on *Bewitched* reruns.

"I had a garden when I was—um, a few years back. A little one, but still enough space to dig in." She bites her red-stained lip when she turns her attention back to me and I'm a fucking goner.

"My, ugh," I cough and scratch my short beard. "My mother loved gardening. She had tons of plants until her arthritis got in the way. Maintaining it is too much for her now."

I leave out that her "arthritis" is "disinterest" and a landscaping crew takes care of it. The latter more so I don't come off as conceited.

"That's so sad." Her frown lasts a moment, and Holly cocks her head before scenting a potted plumeria. "I hope to get another garden before I'm too old to enjoy it."

"I'm sure you will." Platitudes. Nice.

Why do I want this woman to like me when I can have one that's unencumbered? I even googled what the fuck a plumeria was since the condo smells like a trip to Hawaii and resembles the set of a fifties movie.

"Mom!"

Oh yeah, her kid, that's why. Bhodi needs a role model, and I've volunteered to pretend I'm an upstanding citizen. Little does anyone fucking know I'm as messed up in the head as the next guy. My issues are easier to hide.

Holly's line of vision bounces to the stairwell. She gives me a weak smile and I take it as my cue to go.

# Chapter Two

*Holly*

If there is a God, he smiled on me when Bhodi called from upstairs. Lord knows Cary Cass has an ass you can bounce a quarter off of.

Like a lech, my body leans as Cary turns the corner so I can get a better view watching him leave. I roll my eyes at my lasciviousness. It's not ladylike. How would I feel if my son acted towards a woman the way I just have with that young man?

God, he's so fucking young.

At twenty-five, Cary hides his baby face behind trimmed facial hair. There's not a damn trace of crow's feet around his expressive hazel eyes and his cropped brown hair never gets shaggy, proving his standing appointment with the local barber. It's the kind of perfect a girl would kill to run her fingers through. Not this girl, but *a* girl. One younger than me.

My attention to his appearance is all wrong. Thank fuck I'm not quite old enough to be his mother.

"Moooom!" Speaking of...

"On my way, Bhod!"

I reach for a few of Emory's toys to bring upstairs with me to keep the house tidy. My son and I live in my sister, Laurel's, three-bedroom condo with her and her daughter. It wasn't that either of us wasn't capable on our own. I make decent money assistant managing and from tips tending bar. Laurel and I simply realized combining forces made both our lives easier and cut a few unnecessary expenses; Daycare for her and an overnight sitter for me.

My ten-hour shift at Sweet Caroline's ends in the predawn hours. Laurel's amazing the nights I work. She helps Bhodi with homework and tucks him into bed. She even makes the coffee and gets the kids up and ready before leaving for the day, allowing me a few extra hours of sleep. Then my niece, Emory, and I walk Bhodi to the bus stop and it's my turn to take care of my sister's kiddo.

I'd thought Bhodi would have siblings. I loved every minute of being pregnant with him and couldn't wait to do it again. The joke was on me when William broke my heart. In a sense with Emory, who is four, I've gotten to do all those little things over again that I'll miss out on.

I jog up the steps, ducking my head into the large master Laurel and Emory share. My niece is happy, chatting to the figurines in her pink dollhouse. I stroll into Bhodi's.

"What's up?"

He stands there, all five digits on each hand emphasize the small brown speck on his shirt. "What do I do?"

"Put it in the laundry?"

"What if it stains?"

"Chill, Bhodi. I'll spray remover on it." I gag when he pulls the tee over his head. Having the olfactory senses of a bloodhound can be a blessing and a curse.

"Why don't you shower?" I suggest.

"I don't want to shower."

"Okay, then." My hand rests on my hip. "I have a bit till I have to leave. Let's see what you have to do for math over the weekend."

"I'll shower."

"Good choice."

English was my strong suit. On my last day off, I had to watch a twenty-minute online tutorial on fractions to help with ten minutes of homework. While I want Bhodi to do well, I also wonder how much of what he's learning in school applies in real life once he's grown.

I check one more time on Emory before heading back downstairs. Laurel is breezing into the house.

"Did I miss him?" Laurel places grocery sacks on the counter and smooths her pencil skirt.

I notice the silk scarf she wears tied at her neck is missing and an extra button on her blouse has come undone. I slip it back through the hole and pat the silky fabric at the collar.

"If you need to get laid, there are plenty of clients at-da-cub." My sister has slipped her palm over my mouth, muffling my last words.

"I'm not that desperate."

"Yet," I tease.

I swear since her divorce, Laurel's harder up than I ever was. It has me worried about her because I've been there. In a moment of weakness—after my so-called engagement crumbled—I considered stooping to sleeping with my boss's boss.

Her lips twist and Laurel raises a brow, but we share a laugh.

"Cary is easy on the eyes, and it's nice to have something to look at now that Dusty isn't around as much," Laurel muses.

My best guy friend started dating one of my best

girl friends this winter. I'd seen the writing on the walls early on, and where Dusty was the closest thing to a father figure Bhodi had, I put in an application with the big brother program. The coordinator matched my son with Cary Cass of all people. Thankfully, they hit it off during a group outing to a Triple-A baseball stadium for a behind-the-scenes tour before the players reported for spring training.

"At least, tell me you gave him a hug."

"A hug? Why? Oh, crap on a cracker!" Dropping a box of rice I pulled from a reusable sack, I smack my forehead with both hands.

"You forgot. You had one chance to express your condolences—and cop a feel—and you blew it." Her lips twist and her finger waggles in the air. "Bless your silly little heart, what were you thinking letting an opportunity like that pass by?"

Laurel and I dance around one another, placing the groceries in the appropriate spots on shelves and in the fridge.

"I had just woken up from a catnap, and I was doing the same thing I always do; trying not to look. Oh God, Laurel, I must seem like such a—" Laurel makes me defensive. Still not being alert enough to be compassionate toward Cary is distressing.

"Cunt. Bitch. Floozy. Dipstick. Natural blonde instead of the bottle-headed bimbo your friends think you are?" She gives it to me the way only a sister can.

"Hey!" I shove her with a can of beans in my grip.

"I had one chance to live vicariously through you tonight and you blew it."

"I did, didn't I?"

I feel awful. Not only for the fact that my sister sees my pathetic life as enviable, but that I hadn't the common courtesy to offer Cary my condolences for the second time in person.

He'd called last night asking to switch Saturday for

Friday. Cary wanted to hang out with Bhodi at the dealership to get his mind off of his dad's death. I hadn't expected he would contact me at all this week, and when he did, the last thing I considered was refusing.

Laurel and I have lost both of our parents, and I remember those emotions keenly. It was hard not to wade through the memories when I saw Mr. Stanton's obituary featured on the news. He'd been a big-to-do business executive in the area long before the Cass-Stanton Group began buying their competition and became a conglomerate. However, Bhodi was so excited to see Cary that he darted outside as soon as Cary pulled up in front of the condo. By the time they got home, it slipped my mind.

Laurel opens her arms and gives me a big hug. "It's okay, sis. When Cary comes to pick up Bhodi next weekend, explain you didn't bring it up because you hadn't wanted to upset him. I mean, you never know how a man is going to react over his own father's funeral."

I let go, closing my eyes. Guilt washes over me and then I'm hit with the scent of bergamot and citrus from the only soap powerful enough to erase the scent of my prepubescent son's pits and stinky sweat socks.

"I'm hungry, Aunt Laurel." He turns to me. Water droplets drip from his sopping hair, wetting his pajama top. "Why are you still here?"

"Oh my God, I'm late!" I grab my purse and Bhodi by the cheeks to plant a fat red kiss on the top of his head. "Later, tater. I love you. Be good. Show Aunt Laurel your homework! I know it's Friday, but go to bed at a decent time!" My instructions get louder as I run for the door.

Thank goodness Sweet Caroline's isn't far from

where we live. I'm parking in the club's lot as the two zeros appear after the hour on the dashboard clock.

The early crowd who came for happy hour is leaving the building. The bouncer holds the door open as I slip in. Kimber is double-checking to ensure we're stocked with ice and mixers. Her husband, Trig, has been planted in his favorite spot at the end of the bar for months. His presence doesn't pique my interest until a half an hour later when Jake, the owner, shows up out of the blue.

Sweet Caroline's is a well-oiled machine on evenings Jake isn't around. Kimber's taught me how to stay on his good side. I'm comfortable going to him if there is a problem, but I'd rather not. We're given the autonomy to keep those pesky issues that crop up to a minimum. Jake doesn't like the daily workings of his own business bothering him. He's a bottom-line guy. And by that I mean he cares about how the newest dancer's bottom looks in a g-string and if it draws in a big crowd to make him money.

Trig runs a surveillance company—which came in pretty handy when he offered to find out more about my son's "big brother"—and between the cameras and his permanent butt print in the stool, watching over his wife, I'm certain Jake figures Trig's got everything under control.

"What's up, fucker? I had plans tonight." Jake slaps Trig on the back.

I've already got the tumbler filled with ice for Jake's drink. Kimber takes it from me and is heavy-handed with the shots. Not her norm. Kimber doesn't mind serving, but she's also conscientious when it comes to the staff. Many are recovering addicts and she's the queen of concocting non-alcoholic drinks so they can have an inconspicuous glass in their hand along with everyone else.

"Change of plans. My Love and I need a word with

you."

Kimber slides Jake's beverage over the glossy wood.

Jake catches it. His lips flatten a line and his brows pop at the first taste. "Sounds serious."

He turns on his heel toward his office without inviting Trig and Kimber to come along. After he disappears, Trig gets up and Kimber hands me the rag she's used to dry the water spots.

"Everything okay, dearest?" I wrinkle my nose.

"It will be. I saw Morgan at the mill and asked him to drop in to cover for you for a few minutes. When he gets here, come knock on the door."

I'm surprised to hear I need coverage but, "You couldn't pay me enough to waltz into that office without knocking first." The place reeks of leather and sex.

"No kidding." Kimber laughs. She glances up the hall, then back at me and sentimentality replaces glee.

I snag her wrist. "You'd tell me if it was bad." Unless it's an emergency, meetings go down here when audiences aren't around. I prefer it remains that way. I don't have a desire to be complicit in any of the other crap it's rumored the men around here are involved in. Uncertainty keeps freaking Pandora's box locked tight. I have Bhodi to care for.

"I swear it's good, Holly. Really, really, good."

Doubling her adverb sets me at ease and, like Kimber asked, I have Morgan take over after he's squared away behind the register. The guys who work across the street know the ropes around here and are second to none at helping in a pinch.

I rap on the door and wait for Trig to tell me to enter before twisting the handle.

"You can't do this to me!" Jake balks. "You... You bastard. I should go after you like her father on the porch with a shotgun."

"We already have one kid together, so you're a little late," Trig responds sardonically.

"Your pregnant?" My jaw drops and the door snicks shut behind me.

Kimber lifts a finger to her mouth. Besides Jake, I've got to be the first in on the secret. She blushes, and as she moves it away, a second finger pops up making a vee.

It takes me a minute for the silent message to sink in. "You're having twins?"

"I'm getting promoted to full-time mom." She gushes with excitement. "You won't have to put up with my decaffeinated antics too long this time. Congratulations!"

"I'm supposed to be the one saying that!" I give her the biggest hug, adding how excited I am for her.

"You know, just to be a complete ass, my new manager is getting your salary as a bonus on top of hers." Jake barks at Kimber. He grabs my shoulders, pinching me as if I'm a possession Trig can't have.

I'm unsure if the "huh?" of confusion is uttered or imagined until Kimber winks. "Break a leg, Holly. Looks like you are officially in charge of Sweet Caroline's."

# Chapter Three

*Cary*

The showroom is open until nine, but I don't bother stopping back at the dealership to exchange cars. After skipping out of the management offices early to hang with Bhodi, someone working late is bound to want my attention. I've still got my mother, Davina, to deal with tonight.

In the driveway, I cut the ignition and stare out the windshield. The moon is rising over the massive brick colonial. My parents built it two decades ago when an increasing number of professionals from up north decided the standard of living was better in the south and took up the job relocation offers big companies were doling out en masse. My start-the-day-perkin' grande at Baked Beans sets me back a pretty penny, so I'm not sure that's the truth anymore. Yet, since the family business is selling cars, as long as the economy is doing well, the massive population increase benefits the dealerships.

Passing the hedgerow on the way inside, there's a withering bloom on a tall magnolia. They only last a few days before the white tips turn brown. I think of the way Holly pressed the crushed petals between her fingers and sigh.

Davina Cass-Stanton gardened to keep herself out of the house while her husband was inside. Although, since before the doctors admitted Rex to the hospital, gardening hasn't held her interest the way it had when I was a kid. More recently, Davina had been apt to hide out in the Outer Banks when Rex hadn't insisted she was in Brighton. I guess some hobbies are born of necessity and others from genuine passion.

My father suffered a stroke on the back nine after a heated discussion outside the golf club's lounge with none other than the owner of Sweet Caroline's, Jake Ballentine. I haven't felt any devotion toward Rex Stanton in I can't remember when. I may never have at all. However, the one piece of worthwhile advice Rex gave me was during a company golf tournament and it was to steer clear of Ballentine. By then I'd learned to question my father's motives. Rexy's willingness to share how Jake extorted money from one of the dealerships top exec's to hide a sex scandal meant there was a layer of self-preservation he was maintaining.

One of my father's golf cronies mentioned a private, and heated, discussion between Rex and Jake before Rex and his companions hit the green. When the golf buddy asked Rex about it, my father snapped at him. I couldn't help the gnawing in my gut that Ballentine had something to do with Rex's hospital stay. It took me days to track the fucker down since Jake only goes into his own club when it's closed. I confronted him and he acted like I was nuts. The funny thing? I wasn't there to defend the family honor. Rex had apparently forsaken that decades ago. I just didn't want Jake's bullshit raining down on me.

The confrontation with Jake was in the forefront of my mind for weeks. Ballentine smirked with sharp teeth, placating me with false sympathy and concern for Rex's health, but not uttering a peep about what they'd discussed. I know Jake would've caved had I lined his pockets. And I also understand it would lead to me doing the same in the future.

There's nothing to worry about anymore. Rex put my mother and I out of our suffering earlier this week.

Or so I'd thought.

My mother is sprawled on an overstuffed chair. It's dinnertime and she has on silk pajamas and a matching peach robe. I wonder when Davina rolled out of bed, if this is as dressed as she's gotten today, or if she followed through with the grieving widow act, went to the mortuary, and is turning in early with the funeral happening tomorrow. Darkness forces its weight on my shoulders like Atlas carrying the world. My curiosity seems like a fuck ton more consideration than she spared for me.

"You're home." Her voice hitches, though my coiffed socialite mother has used the same phrase every evening since I moved back in.

"I live here. Why are you surprised?"

When it became apparent the prognosis was that my dad wasn't likely to recover after his stroke, I'd broken the lease on my apartment and packed my shit into a storage facility. A year in therapy, battling the demons I knew about before yesterday, had me afraid of what my mother might do left to her own devices. Now, my anger toward her makes me uncertain why it mattered.

Davina clicks on a lamp, flooding the formal living room's pink walls with golden light. With a still-full squat goblet of Rex's best Scotch in her opposite hand, my best guess is she's about to self-medicate whereas I'd had an emergency appointment with my shrink today. She wipes under her eyelid, removing any trace of remorse from her face, and touches her upswept brown hair.

"You didn't come to the calling hours for your father this afternoon."

I find it interesting she did, and that she expected me to show after dropping her little H-bomb.

Fuck if I'd ever imagined I was the Cass-Stanton family's dirty little secret.

"For who?" I fold an ear over, pretending I didn't catch what she said.

"I deserved that."

She does, but I won't rub it in. One of the reasons I opted for counseling was to figure out why walking around on eggshells is normal for my mother and me. There has to be a better way to deal with our mess of a relationship. It wasn't until my therapist brought up the man she married had conditioned us to act this way that I was willing to see her side and how Rex's behavior affected both of us.

However, Davina hadn't copped to the reason behind Rex Stanton's perverted brand of viciousness until the asshole's body finally gave out. And I've had less than twenty-four hours to process her betrayal.

There's a point in every kid's life when they look at their parents and think, *"I've gotta be adopted."* Or moreover, *"How the hell did I wind up with these two imbeciles?"* I'm no exception. I'm pretty sure that fleeting feeling went away for the rest of my friends around the time we got through puberty.

It didn't for me.

Turning into a man became a test of endurance. A challenge dear 'ol Rexy took upon himself… to break me. He was the first to hand me a Playboy when I was fourteen. An easy grand followed a year later on our family vacation to New Orleans during Mardi gras for a topless prostitute in a back alley in the French Quarter to suck my dick. Ever after, when it came to women, I—as a minor, no less—was flush with singles and placated with booze.

These were normal occurrences in my life. So why did my intuition question it? Why was my reaction to tamp down those gnawings? Pushing them to the side.

The kids I hung out with were rich too. Their parents seemed to love one another and many were social with Rex and Davina, going places to see and be seen. Therefore, I didn't think much of my dad's behavior until I was eighteen.

Davina turned a blind eye, playing along with Dad's lax rules. The only exceptions were the times I led whichever current girlfriend I was doing up to my bedroom. My mother would try to stop it. My dad spat condemnation at her. And once my door was shut and locked? I'd take my aggression out on a teenage girl's lovely pussy, slamming the headboard against the wall and making her moan loud enough the whole house knew when she came. Never once realizing I was playing right into Dad's hands.

Looking back at all the available, attractive, and willing women, the most remarkable thing is Rex's intent wasn't to prove to me our status in the community entitled me to whatever cunt I wanted. No, my father took sadistic pleasure in it for his own selfish reasons.

Because he wasn't my father at all.

"We should talk about this before the service." Davina swallows hard.

"Why? Are you worried I'll make a scene?" I scrub my beard, pinching the short splinter-like hairs between my fingertips in frustration.

"Will you even be there?"

If only Davina and I know the truth, staying away

is unwarranted. I'd rather hold my head high and hadn't considered failing to show up for the sake of the business Grandad started. My mother inherited a small franchise of car dealerships from my grandfather. Rex grew it to one of the largest auto conglomerates in the country. With few exceptions, we've got access to near every new make and model. The market is ever changing, but I don't foresee anyone not needing a vehicle. Over the next twenty years, I have a chance to leave a mark. If taking charge of a company my dad probably didn't want me to have and building it bigger is the only way I can dance on Rex's grave, then so be it.

I don't know what Rexy waited all those months on a ventilator for other than to prove even without his faculties he was capable of sticking the knife in a little further and causing us grief. That right there is fucked up. The more I've mulled it over, I'm positive —not sticking around to defend his actions—Rex earned his wings masquerading as the innocent party.

At this point, publicly revealing the man for who he is to me means his number one weapon hammers the nails into Davina's coffin. Rex is using me as a tool to ostracize her. I'm not sure where my sympathy for Davina stems from, except my shrink is sure my mother spent more years being gaslit than I have. I'm done playing victim to Rexy's selfishness. Davina can make whatever choices she wants.

"I'm showing up to make sure they put the right man six-feet under, and I'm cutting the string on his damn bell at the cemetery."

My mother's pastel manicured fingertips cover her mouth and her eyes water. "Don't be cruel. You're not like your father."

"Apparently," I mock back.

Mom reaches out to grasp my hand. "I'm sorry, Cary. Rex swore me to secrecy, and I didn't understand the bargain I was making. All I wanted was for you to have a good home. Two parents. Stability. I love you. I wanted to tell you."

"But you didn't. You let him hold power over us. You watched while he made a mockery of me to keep you in line. And I suppose you'll want to explain next that you never cheated on Rexy again."

"I didn't."

"Why the hell not? You had nothing to lose." I peg her with a hard stare. "You could have left the way *your* mother did." Grandma skipped out on Grandad.

"I would have had to leave you behind or risk the dealerships."

"How stupid do you think I am?"

"In this case, about as stupid as you think I am for staying. Rex conned me, Cary. I was nineteen and foolish, for heaven's sake, and Rex wanted your grandaddy's company any way he could get it. I'm not too proud to admit I was as quick to jump into bed with a sweet-talking man as you are with any woman."

My fist clenches because this verbal sparring is as close to duking it out as we've ever gotten. "It's a good thing Grandad taught me it was wrong to hit women." I wouldn't punch her. I don't get any masochistic sense of relief putting women in their place.

"Listening proves you aren't your dad's son, now doesn't it?"

"He did a damn good job of poisoning me whether or not his blood runs through my veins."

"Yet, you stand here looking for the best in a person, forgetting that your grandfather's been gone longer than he was around to teach you better. Spit roast me all you want, but when it comes down to it, I was faithful to my marriage when it mattered."

"You mean when it suited you. Do you even care

Rex is dead?"

Mom cocks her chin to the side and looks up at me. "In silence, I grieved during the years beforehand, trying to keep my son and get back what he rightfully deserved. After the funeral, it's time to put the past to rest and move on."

I roll my eyes, glancing toward the staircase. "How great for you having my entire lifetime to become self-aware! Maybe after I've had a quick shower I'll as easily compartmentalize how my mother spent twenty-six years pretending she hadn't fucked someone else." The lingering scent of grease and motor oil permeates my nose, and tomorrow I have to play the grieving son. Perpetuating the lie to my employees and the people who know us best makes me feel dirty.

Davina is hot on my heels as I stalk to the steps, trying to get away from her and make sense of my life.

Mom grips the oak banister. "Cary, don't you have questions about *him*?" I can tell from her tone she means the man who contributed to my DNA.

"What difference does it make? You told me the guy's dead too." I'm half-way up.

"He has a daughter. She lives in New York."

"Whoop-dee-doo." I spin my index finger near my head. "Like you said, it's time to put the past behind us."

## Chapter Four

*Holly*

I'm slouched on the sofa, staring at the long dresser we've used as a television stand and the stepladder next to it. Found at an estate sale, Laurel and I dragged it home and into the backyard where we took black paint to the frame and three different colors of pastel to the six flat-faced drawers. Each row is a different shade and it fits our retro theme to a tee. The high-definition TV is off and unplugged, waiting for Dusty to come work his magic this evening and hook it up for us.

Laurel scoots in after work while I'm studying the atomic black cat prints with teal backgrounds bought off of Etsy. I had them framed at a shop on the main drag in Brighton's old downtown area near Baked Beans and Paisley's, an upscale boutique my girlfriends like to shop at.

"How was traffic?"

"Do you mean the cars on the road or the planes the controllers kept circling in the air during the deluge this morning?" My sister whips the silk from her neck, wrapping it over her head babushka-style.

"That bad?"

"The delayed departures all got off the ground." Laurel sighs, flopping next to me.

Angry travelers come part and parcel with Laurel's position at the airport. Although, her contentment given a long shift proves she witnessed a few sweet reunions.

Both of us were flight attendants about a bazillion and twelve years ago. Neither of us has flown the friendly skies after having babies. Laurel wasn't ready to give up the airlines altogether. She says it's a lot easier to deal with customers from behind the ticket counter than being trapped for hours thirty-thousand feet in the air with someone with an ax to grind. But I know it's wholly different and she misses flying.

"Any news about when Kimber's last day is?"

I shrug, forking a tomato from the salad I'm snacking on, popping it in my mouth, and chewing. I'm not on the schedule at Sweet Caroline's tonight, so my day of wallowing and playing dolls with Emory wasn't near as tough as Laurel's. I don't want to bring her down. Besides, Dusty and Cece will be here soon with Sylvie Rhys. It's not great timing for a heart-to-heart.

"For someone who scored a promotion and a big fat raise, you're less than enthusiastic." Laurel flicks the bow on my wide red headband.

She pulls the bowl of lettuce from my grip. Placing it on the mosaic-tiled coffee table, she leans against the low-backed square couch cushions and rests her head where my off-the-shoulder striped blouse exposes my bare skin.

"Drowning your sorrows in salad dressing meant for our company tonight isn't quite as effective as chocolate sauce. I'd take you for ice cream, but..." Laurel points to the ceiling. Emory is upstairs obsessing over her dollhouse. Bhodi is off with Cary, who has promised to have him home at a decent hour after their second after-school mechanics lesson in the past two days.

I wipe olive oil off my lip, cross my arms over my stomach, and let out a heavy groan.

My sister snuggles in, giving me a half hug. "Talking about it will make you feel better."

"I wish I'd worked for it," I say.

This elicits a sadistic cackle from my sister. She tosses her fist in the air gyrating it like a lasso and wiggles her hips in the tight uniform skirt she has on.

I'm woman enough to take the good-natured ribbing Laurel gives me. I'm not a stripper, though many of my closest friends have been and they were quite good at it.

"What I mean is, Kimber leaving seems like I became the manager by default."

I've fallen for beautiful lies once in my life and learned nothing is guaranteed. That includes the things you earn.

"Seriously, Holly, how else did you see Kimber exiting the club? She was a dancer, then the manager, and now she's planning to enjoy her family. Did you think Jake would can Kimber or that she'd never leave? Did you plan on being the assistant manager forever?"

"Is 'sort of' a pathetic answer?" My brow and lip quirk in time with the question. "Not to the firing, though. What if I'm not as good as she was, and I fail at keeping all of the silly stuff Jake can't stand out of his hair?"

"Hol, is it so hard to believe some people leave for all the *right* reasons and, in this case, with the faith in you that it'll be even better once they're gone?" A soft smile plays on Laurel's face. She caresses my cheek the way our mom did drying our tears.

I'm able to read between the lines. Bhodi's father, William, did me dirty. I thought the love we shared was invincible, but for William's part, it was more like invisible. I wish his middle-aged motives had been as transparent. I truly believed he'd laid every last dream I had at my feet. Besides my son, the only picture-perfect things I have to hold onto are the vintage A-line dresses in my closet.

My lifestyle isn't an attempt to recapture what I lost. Laurel and I wore clothes like this on occasion for fun before I met William Mayer. Now, we both wear them because there's no one around to criticize or tell us not to. William taught me all handouts come with a price, and I'm not buying into the Prince Charming bullshit again. The dude didn't even recognize his true love without the heels. How does that prove the "love is blind" nonsense?

"Maybe I am projecting." It's hard for me to accept things I haven't earned and even more difficult to convince myself any effort I've put toward success has paid off.

"I understand you never want to be dependent again, but independent women clap for their damn selves and you're slumped on the couch hostessing a pity party. Aren't you the sister who convinced me after my divorce that I was stronger than to let the past get in the way of my future?"

"Are you spoon-feeding me my own advice?"

"Sure as shit, I am." She reaches into her pocket, pulling out a tube and compact. "Now, fix your lipstick and show 'em who's boss."

Laurel hands over the fire-engine red once she's applied it herself and puckers fishy-faced, waiting for me to paint my own in the mirror. Afterward, Laurel heads upstairs to change out of her uniform.

I rinse my bowl and tidy up so she doesn't have to. Laurel is the head chef tonight and I'm the side cook and busboy. My sister should enter one of those TV pitmaster competitions because she'd win with both hands tied behind her back.

Laurel promised Dusty southern barbecue a while back when he helped her spray the modern white kitchen appliances with a smooth coating of cotton candy pink to match the Lady Kenmore she saw in a nineteen-fifty-eight Sears catalog. We normally pay Dust for everything he does for us—and he does quite a bit—but when someone of Dusty's stature plants his feet, it's better to compromise than try to make him budge.

A Boston Butt roast has been in the smoker all day. I'm no hack when it comes to food, but Laurel left me strict instructions for when to do what. I hope I didn't mess up the meal when I poured the hot sauce over the meat and wrapped it in foil to seal in the juices.

Our company arrives in the casually late window, something I appreciate being the type of person who is gloriously bad at being on time for anything except work, and that's often by the skin of my teeth.

Dusty's daughter, Sylvie Rhys, hugs my knees. Finding out Emory is upstairs, Sylvie bolts for the steps to show off the latest in her ever-growing sticker book collection.

Dusty and I met at Sweet Caroline's. He was the handyman there and across the street at the mill building where Celine lived while she danced her way to a medical degree. Right after Christmas, Cece graduated, became a physician's assistant, and they'd begun dating. Much to my dismay, Dusty hung out a shingle and started his own business this spring. I lost two great coworkers at the club within weeks of each other. Actually, three since Celine's brother, Morgan, the guy who covered for me at the club yesterday, had only stuck around out of an insane amount of concern for her welfare and quit too. With Kimber leaving, it's like I've lost family members. After so many years, not having the faces I've relied on for so long around every day is difficult. I'm just glad Dusty and Cece come over to hang out with us whenever they can.

Standing crammed in the slim hallway by my bedroom, Dusty's brow creases and Cece rubs his bicep, saying what he's thinking. "No Bhodi?"

"He'll be home soon. He had the big brother program this afternoon."

"How's it going?" My best guy friend's enormous frame radiates concern.

I'm ready to drag them the rest of the way into the condo and crack the top on a few beers when the bell rings and the front door simultaneously pops open.

"It's here!" Bhodi jumps up and down like he's on a pogo stick.

Cary's holding his backpack.

"I don't know what that is, but it's impressive." He looks back as I beckon him inside from the stoop.

My nose wiggles, filling with the lingering odor of motor oil and shop grease. It does little to cover the spice of Cary's aftershave, a scent I'm intimately familiar with thinking about him when I'm all alone.

"C-could use a hand if you don't mind?" Dusty motions outside.

"Not at all," Cary replies. A little piece of my heart swelled when he ignored Dusty's stutter.

The guys introduce themselves, shake hands, and are out unstrapping the ratchet system holding the load in Dusty's truck upright and steady.

I'm three steps behind everyone else when Celine and my sister gang up on me.

"She's blushing." Cece mocks low to Laurel.

"She does when he speaks too. And she pretends not to look at his ass."

"Oh, Dust has the tightest glutes, but that's a fine ass too."

"Sure is." Laurel hums in agreement.

I'm aghast, shushing the pair as they lean against each other, conspiring to embarrass the crap out of me.

We shift into my room, allowing the guys ample space to heft the massive box through the hallway and into the living room. They set it in front of the unplugged TV on the dresser. Bhodi follows with Dusty's tools. The trio gets to work, mounting the television on wall brackets and triple-checking measurements before drilling holes into the sheetrock. It's amazing how little talking happens and I see the complement of Dusty's maintenance man skills and Cary's mechanical skills overlap with the tasks they give my son.

"You seem a little peaked, Hol. Do you need to sit down?" Cece puts the back of her hand to my forehead.

Laurel snorts when I slap it away and the commotion has Cary glancing at me, making more heat rise from my neck.

Dusty pulls a silver dome antenna out of his toolbox and steps up on the ladder one last time. Removing the paper from a double-sided adhesive, he sticks it to the top of the box.

"I love it!" Laurel claps.

"I can't even believe you built this. It's perfect," Cary has both hands on Bhodi's shoulders and has already thanked him for being a great assistant.

My son looks at the wall, proud of our overt weirdness.

The simple wide box Dusty built surrounds the modern TV. It has an oblong hole cut out for the screen and the false rabbit ears on top. From what Cece's told me, he had paused the scene from *Back to the Future,* where Marty is with his mother's family trying to explain reruns, while designing and painting it to resemble an old RCA.

Dusty accepts hugs, blowing off our appreciation for a job well done. I see him pocket the check Laurel gives him and that makes it worthwhile.

My sister insists Cary stay for dinner. I can't overrule the chef, and I won't take credit when she unwraps the roast, slicing into the flaky meat. After being called to the table, the kids only stick around long enough to fill their bellies and disappear in a foot-race up the stairs. In charge of clearing, I fall into my barmaid role and refill everyone's drinks while they sit and chat.

"Thought you had a thing against younger men." Dusty's voice is a low rumble passing behind me to deliver a wayward dish to the sink.

"Cary?" I bat my hand in the air, accidentally letting go of the plastic wrap I'm trying to get off the roll to cover the leftovers. It wrinkles, and I'm picking at the edges to unstick the film. "He's Bhod's big brother," I remark as if Cary's presence is insignificant and my nipples haven't been hard dots, poking underneath the fabric of my shirt since he returned with my son.

"Then stop undr-ressing him with your eyes like he's on stage at the club." His voice remains at a whisper.

"You're one to talk, Big Guy." I scoff.

"Know exactly what I'm talking about. Need me to take the kid to do something more often? Cees won't mind."

"Cece won't mind *once*. Your girlfriend doesn't need to be responsible for another child while she and Sylvie Rhys are still getting to know one another."

"Offer's open. Sylvie loves hanging around with Bhodi."

"Thanks." I squeeze his massive bicep and glance across the room at the table. Laurel and Cece are deep in discussion. Cary's listening to what they're saying, but his intense scowl makes it obvious he's been studying our interactions.

# Chapter Five

*Cary*

My jaw clenches when Holly puts her hand on Dusty's bicep. All of a sudden, it doesn't make a difference how well Dusty and I have gotten along this evening. My instincts ignore his attentiveness to his girlfriend, and the genuine affection they shared when Cece congratulated him for how great the retro frame for the television came out.

By the slight way her soft lips part and she turns from me, I know Holly's seen my reaction. She draws her hand away, pretending she's engrossed in packing up the leftovers.

These are friends Holly and Bhodi rely on. However, the small amount of tenderness Holly's shown to Dusty makes my blood boil.

I'm having a problem turning my internal burner down to a simmer, and I need to get the hell out of here.

Stumbling through thanking Laurel for dinner, and telling the others it was great to meet them, I excuse myself from the table. On the way to the door, Holly agrees to say goodbye to Bhodi for me and to remind him that I'll see him again tomorrow.

It's a dick move, but I've been playing on everyone's sympathy—including Holly's—since enduring my father's memorial service. Bailing on what's expected of me in the corporate offices and avoiding the lawyers' transition paperwork isn't right. But I haven't taken an actual bereavement leave. Aren't I owed a few hours to work through my shit and I don't know, forget? The only place I want to be is back in the garage.

I'd called suggesting Bhodi and I work a few afternoons to get the Mercury ready for the upcoming field trip. There was a hesitancy in Holly's voice accepting my offer to pick up her son from school again. While I'll cop to wanting to see this gorgeous woman too—and it makes me feel like I'm taking advantage of Holly's generosity—making the kid happy is the actual bright spot.

Except, she'd left for Sweet Caroline's by the time I'd gotten Bhodi home yesterday.

"I appreciate you letting me have him a few extra days this week. We're having fun." It's the truth. "If you aren't here when I drop him off, I'll pick him up on Saturday at eight for the group field trip," I tell her, hoping there are no issues with the car parts tomorrow. I want to see her face when Bhodi tells her we're done.

"He's really excited to take the Mercury out for a spin. I can't wait to see it in person."

I decide then and there we'll drive it so she can share in the accomplishment.

Up close I notice after eating she still has flawless red lips, emphasizing the crisp, heavy liner surrounding her expressive brown eyes. Eyes that are as filled with concern about my hasty departure as my insides are confounded by my jealousy.

"Thanks again for feeding me." I cross my arms while we stand talking on the porch. This is the longest face-to-face discussion we've had.

"It's the least we could do for helping out. If you aren't careful, we're going to start relying on you as much as we did Dusty."

"Not a problem." I mean it.

Her hesitant smile fades and a moment of awkward silence ensues. Why does this always happen? What the hell is wrong that I lose my tongue around her? I have plenty I want to say, ask. Albeit some of my curiosity is dirty as fuck.

Holly blinks at me a few times. She's tentative lifting her hand. Her fingertips dance against the skin of my forearms. Little sparks cause the fine hair to stand on end. Her breath catches. She swallows hard and I know she felt whatever passed between us too.

"It's awful of me to bring up a sore subject after a nice night, but I forgot to mention the last time I saw you how sorry I was to hear about your father's passing. I hope the funeral gave you a little closure. I'm sure it was beautiful, with so many there who loved and knew what a great man your father was." Her proud chin has tipped up.

I may be younger, but I'm not dense. Her reaction is abnormal for a friendly expression of sympathy. I fight the urge to put my hand over hers and stay longer. Instead, I leave before making a class-A fool out of myself.

I don't want Holly's condolences. Rex Stanton was a lousy prick and doesn't deserve to be a part of the conversation anymore. Her goddamn boss can take a flying leap too. However, in the moment, Holly gave me the impression she'd been struggling with her faux pas since the last time we'd seen one another. Knowing I've consumed her thoughts boosts my ego.

Unable to stop the mental imagery of Holly

touching me from replaying in my mind, I stay up late scrolling my phone's   feed as a distraction. At some point, my lids glue themselves shut. When the alarm goes off the next morning, my screen is still playing snippets of comedy show monologues.

I have a hard time rubbing the sleep away. I'm tired as fuck and have a full afternoon of business meetings after counseling. I always book my appointments early. That way I can get engrossed in work if it messes with my mind.

"So let's discuss your last date," my therapist says, changing the subject. He's sick of hearing me pining on about leaving Holly's after dinner last night.

My folded thumbs are flicking back and forth. I've been trying over the past hours to recapture the tingle I felt when Holly had placed her hand over mine.

Frankly, I'm a little exhausted trying to make sense of it too. I'm glad for this session and hope it screws my head on straight. Today I hate everything about myself.

For as messed up as I am, I don't believe there's some magical age when you learn to keep your dick in your pants and fall in line with the committed relationship scenario. However, that's sort of why I'm here. Most women don't hold my interest. I'm not sure if that's on my mom and grandma Cass and who I was supposed to be or if it's Stanton cruelty.

It was years ago when I stepped foot in Pinewood College's dorms. The first thing that came into focus was the number of friends who had lost their virginity with a high school sweetheart far surmounted the number whose dads handed over cash for whores. They clung to the value in those relationships. In comparison, the abundance of nameless partners I had was abnormal. I learned to keep my yap shut about it long past when my fellow freshmen considered a spiteful one-nighter with a rebound-girl to ease the pain of a broken heart.

Not that my friends hadn't assumed I was out for a good time when it came to the ladies. Moving out from under Rexy's roof just made his handiwork abundantly clear to me. I was on my way to being a stereotypical bachelor who'd never settle down.

Unfortunately, it took me a few more years to possess the wherewithal to address the root of the problem and go the psych route. The more sessions I have, the more apparent it becomes that Rex wanted me to be lonely the rest of my life; Living in a sort of purgatory the same way my mother claims she was. I hate the man who she decided I should call "Dad."

Hunched forward on the couch, my stomach clenches on the same visceral level I'd experienced when Holly paused cleaning up from dinner.

"My last date was, uh—" My hands fall apart and I push a thumb and forefinger into my eye sockets, trying to rub the gritty feeling away.

*How was my last date?*

At my therapist's urging to consider available ladies who are on more than online sites, I have had several.

"Not being able to remember her face or name off of the top of my head makes it pretty memorable," I remark facetiously. "I may have given her a hug at the end of the night?" I question my memory.

"No intercourse?"

I shake my head. I've had plenty of female friends since college. None of whom I ever crossed the line with. I'd set out to treat my date the same as I do them.

"Did you hold her hand?"

"Not that I can… No, I didn't." I spread my arms wide, shrugging. "I thought that was the point of this."

"I never mentioned applying for sainthood." He pauses and puts down the pen he's been using to take notes on a clipboard and sets both aside. "Pretend you have three buckets, Cary. In the first bucket your mind places your friends who are women. In the next, women who you sleep with. In the last are the ones who are, for lack of a better term, off-limits. For instance, the wife of an employee. Is it possible, given what you've told me before about your female friendships, that when you made a concerted effort not to engage in sexual activities, subconsciously you moved your date from the second bucket to the first?"

"I guess."

"So perhaps, using the bucket analogy, you should concentrate on creating a fourth."

"That's a lot of buckets. But where you're married," and I'm paying him by the hour to help me fix my philandering, "I'll give it a go. What's this bucket got in it?"

I doubt it's a growler filled with ice and beer.

"Women who you don't immediately engage in sexual activities with, who are still possibilities."

"But not Holly."

"No different from your date, you've already assigned Ms. Carrington to a bucket; You relegated her to off-limits."

"So, you think whatever I felt when she touched me was some sort of fucked up chemical imbalance? Like my dick made a bigger deal of it than it actually is?"

"There's a definite taboo engaging in a sexual relationship with the mother of a child whom you're mentoring. You've expressed before that the majority of your early experimentation was with older women."

"Know what I hate about therapy?" I scrub my

beard.

"What's that?"

"That you don't give me a straight answer."

My counselor laughs. "I can't give you the answers, Cary. It's up to you to determine what's right for you."

I'm not sure if the awkward silence is because he wants the statement to sink in or just what. I do know based on the clock on his desk that there are ten minutes until we're finished.

He clears his throat. "Concern over your mother living alone when Rex became ill prompted you to move home. How have things been between the two of you since the funeral?"

"You mean since I came here about her bombshell? She bought paint for the living room, spilled it all over the hardwood flooring, paid one company to fix the mess on the walls and another to replace the flooring. She leaves me alone. Until she doesn't and then she brings up the DNA donor and presses me about meeting my biological sister." I word vomit.

"Have you considered moving out again? Finding your own place locally?" It's a trick question.

"No, she took off to the beach."

While the aforementioned shit show was taken care of and after I yelled about letting sleeping dogs lie.

I don't give a shit about Rex's reputation. There's a modicum of satisfaction knowing I'm not his kid. But hell if I'm going to go off half-cocked, announce to everyone in Brighton I'm a bastard, and blow my chance by dragging my grandad's company through the mud.

"We could work it so we switched off. I'd never have to see her," I joke, disparaging the lack of communication.

"Or you could see if Davina has any interest in

going to dinner. In a neutral space, it may be easier to discuss how you're both coping with Rex's death, and how you see yourselves moving forward."

"I'm not dating my mom." I sneer.

"Do you believe her about the role she played in keeping your parentage hush-hush."

This isn't something I want to talk about. Con-job or not, I haven't finished being mad that she signed them. Although after seeing the documents, I fired our family's—and by that I mean Rex's—longtime personal attorney.

"Hey, I don't mean to cut this short, but I have a full day ahead of me, and I need to get to work soon." I hear myself becoming combative.

I had it in my head to figure out the Holly situation. So, no thanks to dredging the rest of my emotional swamp. It's the same level of agitation I end up with when I come in here in a great mood. I hate leaving after he's wanted me to explore some screwed-up adolescent memory. Annoyed that he doesn't want to help, I've stopped listening.

*Cary*

The guys who I've connected with in the big brother program are in various stages of life. I know the short version of most of their stories, but we don't delve too deep into why any of us do this. There's no box to check on the mentorship application stating you have to have fought your own demons to make a difference in a kid's life, only the willingness to want to see them happy.

"Do we have to?" One of the boys takes up the groaning we've been listening to for the last forty minutes.

It may have been Glen's charge. I'm not keeping tabs anymore on which kids have complained and which ones are dragging their feet over the cobblestones, tripping from one antiquated national landmark to the next.

This trip was Glen's idea. He teaches high school history. Square as a carriage bolt, all he lacks is glasses and a pocket protector and he'd hit every mark to be called a Poindexter. He hasn't even unbuttoned his shirtsleeves like the rest of us and it is blazing hot walking on the sidewalks in the sun. Another reason the kids are a mess.

Aside from not getting how bored the kids are, Glen does know his nerdy shit about the historic little town and has answered my dumb questions faster than the docents. I guess some women are attracted to those kinds of eccentricities since he has a fiancée too.

The other mentors are taking notes on where the boys want to go on the next group outing. So far, the most votes have been for an amusement park down past Charlotte and an adventure park near Raleigh with bumper boats and an arcade.

"Hey, if I haven't said thank you for taking care of the admission fees for everyone—" Glen's shaken with excitement each time he's brought it up.

"No big deal," I cut him off. "You arranged the group rate and The Cass-Stanton Group has got specific outreach programs for this type of thing."

I have a little guilt that it paid for me. However, the dealerships have given far more to local Brighton and Triangle Area charity organizations than to penny-pinch over a dozen entrance fees to a living history non-profit.

"It's great to see young minds sucking up culture." Glen has his hands out parallel, they move up and down like a toy soldier as he explains his elation. "Having experiences up-close that others can only read about in books. It leaves an impression. I think they're really going to remember this."

Bhodi nudges my elbow. I ruffle his hair. It's still sweaty from when we gave the kids a chance to run around under some big oaks in the quaint town's park.

"I'm sure they will." I wink, sharing an inside joke with Bhodi.

I doubt the boys will forget today, but there's the distinct possibility it's not for the reasons Glen wants them to.

Our final stop is the apothecary. Glen marches in with gusto. Meanwhile, while one of the other mentors snickers to a guy beside him that he hopes the reenactor inside this building who plays the doctor has something to put us out of our misery.

I hold the door, laughing under my breath. Glen's a good man who has forgotten what a grown-up finds fascinating is loads different from a bunch of boys who haven't made it out of elementary school. This place may be mildly more interesting to me if it were adults only.

And there was a beer tent.

Bhodi waits at my side with raised eyebrows and a furrowed forehead.

*Or maybe not,* I think.

If the kid who got his groove on to Billy Ocean while we put the finishing touches on the Colony Park so we could drive it here today is bored, it's probably a sign. And, while we're on the subject, what the fuck does Holly keep on her playlists that Bhodi has those lyrics memorized? I'm glad we weren't detailing a red Corvette.

A chorus of "Woah!" fills the musty space and my half-pint darts in to see what his friends are interested in.

Kids cram around a butcher block counter in the humid room while a man in period costume and a white apron explains herbs to them.

"But what are the slugs for?" A boy pipes up.

"They are leeches and we'll get to that in a moment." The older man cautions.

The same boy makes his fingers walk like a spider up Bhodi's arm. I see Bhodi's body make a slight shiver and he leans away, lip snarled.

The old "apothecary" makes the boys sit on the wooden floor and starts his rehearsed spiel about the rigors of life in the eighteen hundreds. The boy's eyes glaze over. They won't answer the questions he poses. The reenactor understands his audience is all about the creepy crawlies and cuts to the chase.

"Leaching," he marks with gusto, "was a common practice to help with humors."

Three minutes into the speech, I can tell Bhodi doesn't find it the least bit funny. He's turning green and swallows with urgency.

"Hey, Glen, I'm taking Bhodi outside for a few minutes."

"Good call," he replies, watching Bhodi scoot back against a cabinet.

Bhodi has tucked his knees up to his chest, resting his forehead on them. I have to squat and duck-walk across the floor to get his attention. His eyes are wide and there's perspiration on his upper lip. I clasp his hand, pulling him after me, hoping I've gotten there in the nick of time. Lord knows I don't want the kid to get embarrassed by puking in front of his buddies.

Outside, I sit the half-pint down on the cool granite slab atop the entry stairs, letting him get his bearings. It's only a fractional degree cooler than the stuffy room, but the air does him good as he hangs his head between his knees, taking deep breaths.

"That was pretty gross stuff they used to do back then," I say to break the ice. "How about while they're finishing up we go see if the gift shop has any water or if there's a vending machine nearby?"

He peers toward the apothecary window. "How will they find us?"

"I've got my phone and Glen's got my number." We're his ride home and he'd already mentioned texting me if we got separated.

Bhodi sluggishly ventures across the road with me.

I take his hand out of an abundance of caution. Holly will kill me if I call her with the news her son has passed out in the middle of a street.

Thank goodness we're hit by a cool blast of air conditioning as we enter the little shop down the block since I'm peeved at the person who decided a Pepsi machine outside would break the ambiance of this place. I pay cash for an overpriced bottle of water. Unscrewing the cap, I move to the side so the cashier can ring the next person in line out.

"Sip on this."

Bhodi takes the bottle and chugs the water down, collapsing the plastic.

"Slow down, Half-pint."

"Want some?" he asks, droplets dripping down his chin. The bottle is half empty.

"All yours." I'm not into backwash. "Feeling better?"

"Yeah." He tucks his chin, using the short sleeve of his shirt to wipe his face.

"Missed a spot." I grab the hem, pulling it up over his forehead, and attach my hand to his face like an octopus.

"*Gah*—Stop!" He cracks up, recovering his stomach when I let go.

I pat him on the back, and we share a laugh.

"Wanna look around while we're here?" I toss my chin to the rear of the shop.

There's not much in here that interests me, but they've got a small children's section in the back and it's a good way to kill time.

I stay a step behind Bhodi until he finds one of those old-fashioned peg board games where you jump your opponent with a golf tee. We play a few rounds. He wins one and I win another.

As we're leaving to meet up with his buddies, Bhodi stops to inspect a Christmas tree display.

"Little early for Santa there, dude."

"This is cool." He holds up a paper star-shaped ornament at the same time another larger one made from metal and hanging from the ceiling catches his attention. "Wow! My mom would love this." He reaches up.

I beat him to the price tag because he's right. The black tin and angles are totally something Holly would enjoy. Bhodi has pocket change, but it's not going to cover the hundred bucks the lamp he wants to bring his mom costs.

"How much is that one?" I ask about the ornament he still has in his hands.

It's white and not as impressive as the big one, but it's still got extra designs to the flat areas with parts that have been punched out so you can see through it. This one is delicate where the other is rugged. I honestly think she'd like either and flip the tag. Of course, it's more than the twenty Holly slipped Bhodi to get himself a souvenir. Since he's not gunning to buy anything for himself, I offer to float him the extra.

After making the second purchase, we discover the rest of our group congregating outside. The other kids mill in and out of the shop. I don't hear any of them wonder aloud to Bhodi why we left, which is good. I don't want him teased about having a weak stomach.

A few jet off for the restrooms before the adults agree it's time to leave. Approaching the car, I realize how useless it was parking beneath a tree considering the unexpected heat today. The sun has been beating through the wagon's windows.

I turn the vents on full blast and Glen and I shoot the shit, waiting a few minutes for the interior to cool down before we let the boys get in. Since it's coming up on dinnertime, we decide to stop for burgers instead of trekking the two hours back to Brighton right away. Despite the complaints, Bhodi and his friend were good sports about being on their best behavior. It scored them points.

It's the smartest decision we make, alongside not asking the kids to dump their sodas in the trash as we leave the fast-food joint.

"I hate to eat up more time, but need to fill up before we hit the highway."

"Gas guzzler?" Glen quips, following it up with "No problem."

I put the key in the ignition and twist. The engine clicks. Not a good sign when cars of this era make an abundance of noise when they roar to life. Flicking the switch, the headlamps faintly illuminate a tree a few yards away. My instincts are right. It's not the battery.

"Fu—damn," I mutter, remembering at the last second I have kids in the car.

"What's wrong?" Bhodi pipes up from the backseat.

I'm already around the front bumper, popping the hood.

"I'm almost certain we've got a bum starter." Wiggling the connection, I tell Glen to try the key again.

"No luck," he replies. "Too bad we don't have a hammer to bang on it with."

I pull out my cell, hitting the number for the towing service. "Fortunately, I know a guy with the right connections."

Unfortunately, we're stuck here until the truck arrives.

# Cary

It's almost midnight when Bhodi pounds on the door to their condo. The lock flips and Holly opens it, quick to wrap her arms around her son, and drags us inside.

Slinging his gear onto the foyer floor, I happen to notice the bottle of whisky in her grip before she puts it on the entry table along with a shot glass.

Both Glen and I made it a point to call, letting the kid's mothers know we'd had car trouble and we'd texted them frequent updates. I'd thought Holly took it in stride. Guess I was wrong.

She cups Bhodi's cheek. "Tired, Bugaboo?"

He nods, leaning against her stomach for another hug, and then scoots down the hall. We both call goodnight after him and he waves his hand behind his back as if saying the words back is too much effort.

"He doesn't need you to tuck him in?"

"He's grown up," she says with dramatic air quotes. "Mind you, the first bump in the night or bad dream he's climbing into my bed." She gestures to a room to my right with a side lamp on.

In any other row house it's supposed to be used as an office. The panes of the single French door are painted black so no light can shine through.

Holly sighs heavily, drawing my attention away from her personal space.

"Oh, I forgot. He bought you something." I hand over the brown paper shopping bag with the ornament in it. "You may want to wait to open it. He seemed excited to get it for you."

She sets the bag to the side and asks me about the trip, screwing the top off of the bottle as she does.

I run a hand through my hair, apologizing for how late we've gotten back "It took longer than expected for the tow truck driver to show. It was easy to get a rental, but the closest location was closed." We wound up getting an Uber to a small airport that happened to have flights arriving later and a national car agency in the terminal. "And then we dropped off Glen, and now we're here." I spread my arms wide, ready to take a bow.

"Impressive." Holly downs another shot. "You must be tired."

"I was until we pulled in and got out of the car. Sort of a second wind, I guess." I admit leaving out how the alcohol makes me nervous that she's going to hand me my ass for keeping her kid out so late. "You been drinking all night?"

"This is my first one. Uh, two." She gulps another shot. "Make that three." Holly clears her throat. "I waited until Bhodi got home and it's time to make up for lost time. Wanna join me?" She pours the amber liquid into the tiny glass.

"What are we drinking to?"

"Shitty exes."

I salute her with the cup.

"Come on, it's no fun drinking alone, and I've got a second wind now too." Holly spins on her toes.

I follow Holly into her bedroom, watching her ponytail swish because for once her shirt covers her ass.

That tattoo though? It swirls down her ankle with a flourish over the top of her foot, making me even more curious where the other vines and petals grow.

She closes the door and tucks into a coral high-backed wing chair near the bed. Her baggy and wrinkled t-shirt creeps up, revealing a pair of boxers.

With no place else to sit, I lower myself to the mattress. The headboard and footboard are made from woven rattan, and the way they curve together is like being cradled in a basket. The room would be a decent size if it weren't stuffed with furniture. She's got a vanity table, wardrobe, and large flatscreen TV playing soundlessly on a dresser. I notice the mute symbol at the top corner. The remote's next to me, and I let the commercial announcer's voice fill the silence before it becomes uncomfortable.

"Want to talk about it?" I offer.

Giving up on decorum, Holly swigs from the spout. "God, no. Bhodi's father is a loser among losers. I won't waste my breath on him."

"You got a great kid out of it. He was calm and didn't complain—well, not much anyway—during the whole ordeal today." I wiggle my fingers in a gimme motion and toss back another swallow when she passes me the whiskey.

"Last time you bring a bunch of kids on a field trip?"

I wrinkle my chin, disagreeing. History might not have been the boys' first choice, however, I hadn't considered not doing it again.

"Shit happens. Big fucking deal. Today was sort of an adventure. Anyway, I won't be taking the station wagon that far again. It's a cool car, but not all that reliable."

I'd done it so Bhodi could show off his handiwork, then took the heat for the bad starter and bought the four of us dessert.

"I'll lend you my Honda, but obviously..." She doesn't need to finish the statement by saying I have my pick of anything *reliable* on the lot.

"Thanks." My jaw cracks when I yawn. I kick my shoes off and my feet up. It's cute that she wants to trade vehicles. I look at Holly as she covers her mouth, hiding her tiredness. Then I shimmy over to one side and pat the mattress.

"Hands above the covers," we say at the same time.

I "jinx" it first, feeling all of twelve-years-old when I do. She gives me a glassy-eyed smile and we lean against the uncomfortable holes in the headboard, passing the bottle and joking about whose generation was more mature in junior high.

An hour goes by and we've slunk down so that our heads are on the pillows and we're making fun of random people on television. Not in a mean way. We're just fumbling on the edge of drunkenness and everything has a hysterical tinge to it. We've also both shushed each other once or twice when the fits of laughter have gotten loud.

Our lower limbs tangle together and neither of us bothers moving after the second time we accidentally touch. I'm not sure about how Holly feels or if it's the alcohol talking, but goofing off with her seems right.

She's laying on her back, snapping the ponytail holder on her wrist to keep herself from dozing off. Her eyes have dipped closed.

"I'm still awake," she reassures me with her long hair spilling over the pillowcases.

"Sure you are." My fingers tickle the inside of her

thigh to wake her up. The last thing I expect is for Holly to rest that knee against mine.

She turns her head on the pillow. The tip of her tongue peeks out and Holly bites her lower lip as she opens her sleepy eyes.

"I should go," I say. She's the mother of my little brother.

I'm not going to lie and say I've never thought about fucking Holly, but crossing that line seemed lewd and like something the lecherous kind of man Rex was intent on turning me into would do.

"Yeah, you should," she replies with absolutely no conviction.

My fingers trail up the skin of her inner thigh. "God, you're so soft."

She wiggles closer. I've turned to my side and the lace of her thong under those boxers is scratchy compared to the silk of her skin. Neither stays on long. My fingertips find her wet folds as our lips fuse, catching Holly's whimper as she tightens around them.

Her hands tangle in my hair, and I sneak my other hand up her shirt, pinching her nipple. Her breasts are perfect. Exactly the right size to palm and thrum my thumb against the tight peaks. She's heaven underneath me, and I'm dying to know what it's like to be inside her.

Holly's hand slides down, popping the button on my jeans. The other's guiding, making sure my mouth won't quit. Yet, as my lips trail down her neck, we have to part because I'm salivating, waiting to get one of those tits in my mouth to suck on. Thankfully, all the moving we've done on the mattress has her baggy top riding up.

Taking her lead, we both whip off our shirts in unison, and finally I'm rewarded with the sight of the petals and vines that decorate the skin of her right breast.

I'm on my knees between Holly's legs. My pants are half off and my eyes alternate staring at the bright color contrast between her tattooed tit and the spartan side, and the way she's palming my cock. I swear I could come right now and it would be better than the fantasy fuck I'd given her last week all alone in my shower.

"Condom." It's not a question or a demand from Holly. Though I'm aware if one of us can't produce one, she'll put the brakes on what's happening.

There's no graceful way to get my pants off and the protection out of my wallet. Holly doesn't seem to care as she sheds the rest of her clothes. It makes me slightly less ashamed that I'd made a pact with myself not to sleep with random women because it played into the image of the man someone else was set on turning me into.

But Holly's not an indiscriminate fuck like the women you'd hook up with online or bring back to your place after only knowing them a few hours. I've thought about this, replaying the little figments my imagination has set in my brain over the past few months. Being with her is a chance I never thought I'd have to take. And, Goddamn, if all she wants is a casual, alcohol-induced screw, I'll give her a night she won't forget that replaces everything troubling her.

Her fingers stay close as I roll on the rubber. She's not bewildered by my touching myself the way I've seen women closer to my age get embarrassed as soon as the subject is brought up.

Hell, she's the one who brought it up and I don't like that it might mean she's got more practical experience when it comes to sex. Yet something about the lack of inhibition and going after what she wants in the bedroom makes Holly sexier.

She guides me to her entrance, and I watch our

bodies connect. The head of my cock disappears. My shaft, as I push her knees outward. She's conscious of it too. Her lips part and she calls my name, beckoning me forward. I cover my body with hers, caging her head between my forearms as I steal a long kiss.

With every thrust, Holly fights back a strangled moan. Her nails dig into my backside, urging my ass forward each time my cock retreats from her center. Proving how into this she is. Stunning me with how much pent-up desire she has. In the meantime, we'd never spoken the words.

The weight of my silent frustrations now out in the open is about to kill me. I'm fighting not to let go before she does.

"You're so tight." I grab around her thigh, opening her up more. Rocking against the spot that has her closing her eyes and biting her lower lip each time I hit it.

This is the first time I've given a rat's ass about whether talking dirty turns my partner on. Normally, it's what does it for me, so who gives a shit?

I get a needy whimper in return, followed by that all-too-familiar flutter sending a shockwave into my system as my orgasm follows hers.

Still cocooned inside of her, I trail my tongue down her neck, then move back up to kiss her again.

"I don't do things like this a lot." I'm aware by the way her nails lightly tickle my back she's responding to the last thing I said to her. Holly doesn't want me believing she's a prude or a slut.

Over the past few hours, I haven't thought of her as Bhodi's mom or the reasons why I came to meet the two of them. It's only been us, enjoying one another's company; Clothed and naked, consenting adults.

"Hadn't crossed my mind." I white lie. I don't want the men she'll bring to this bed after me ruining the here and now when it's at an end.

I cross the hall to the restroom, dispose of the condom, and clean up. Holly's eyes are closed and her face is relaxed when I walk back into her room. She's gorgeous, but with that just-laid contented expression—the one I put there—she's stunning.

I snag my jeans off the floor, cautious as I sit on the mattress to pull them on. I stand, losing my footing and she cracks a lid.

"Are you okay to drive?"

"Probably." *Not.*

I'm not a lightweight. I can handle my booze. But Holly's a bartender and she sees through the bullshit.

"Lie back down for an hour. I couldn't live with myself if, you know." She pushes the blanket to the side, uncovering a glimpse of her soft curves and the warm, welcoming sheets.

I'm not stupid. This is over when I leave, so what difference will adding sixty more minutes make to a lifetime of regrets?

I climb in with my pants on and skim the bell of Holly's hip with my palm. Her breath evens out, and I drop off to sleep.

# Chapter Eight

*Holly*

"Bhod, turn that down, please."

I touch the center of my forehead and the volume of the manga kid's cartoon on the television lowers. My eyes flutter open to a view of my t-shirt tented on the floor. It takes a second for me to realize the bottle from last night is underneath. At about the same time, the tingle between my thighs reminds me of what I did with Cary. I hear him mutter an expletive underneath his breath.

He's still here and, like every uncomfortable parenting moment since the dawn of time that's landed a mom flat on her back, I'm thinking on my toes.

Clutching the sheets to my chest, I roll toward the center of the bed. Bhodi has wedged himself between us. He's intent on the high-pitched voices competing over red and white balls with alien-like animals inside.

Cary is stock still, reclining in my bed. His hand is over his brow. I don't think it's because he has a hangover, more like he's wondering how the fuck he got himself into this.

Right there with ya, buddy.

"Why'd you guys have a sleepover without me?" Bhodi places one hand on my thigh and the match on Cary's.

Oh Sweet Jesus, thank you for the easy opening!

"After you went to bed, Cary was telling me about the fun you had before the car problems. It was late, and he was tired. I didn't want him to have an accident on the way home."

So, that last part wasn't a lie. And Cary had shared what they'd done with the boys; how they'd eaten ice cream sundaes out on the curb while waiting on the tow truck.

Bhodi's focus is on me. He doesn't recognize Cary's attempt to find the rest of his clothes and make a hasty retreat. He takes my explanation at face value.

"Now that you're up, can we have pancakes? I'm starving."

"Sure thing. Can you go tell Aunt Laurel we're making breakfast and see if she and Emory have eaten?"

"Yup. Are you staying, Cary? Did the car get fixed yet?" he asks with a measure of excitement laced with trepidation.

"Uh." Pulling his shirt over his head, Cary freezes like a deer in headlights. "We have to order the part. Do you want me to stay?"

"After we eat, we can go fix it together."

I can't help smiling at how sweet my son is in comparison to how mortifying this scenario will be for him years from now when Bhodi figures out his mom had a one-night-stand with the guy from the big brother program.

"It'll take a few days for it to come in, but I'll wait

so you can help," Cary replies.

"Cool."

Bhodi skips out of my room and Cary is quick to close the door my son left ajar. The painted over panes rattle at the hard jostle, reminding me of the way the headboard hit the wall while we'd gone at it. This is not one of my finer moments.

"How the hell did you con him into believing—" Visibly shaken, I can't tell if Cary's mad at me or himself.

"If you make it sound normal, they accept it."

Cary regards me pensively. "How the hell does that trick not come back to bite you in the ass when it's an adult convincing him something wrong is right?" His jaw squares and I can feel a thrum of antagonism coming from his side of the room.

"My son knows if he needs to talk it out, I'm here for him. I answer his questions as honestly as I can, Cary. Do you want to tell him what we did in private? Explain to a nine-year-old why you woke up in his mother's bed and lead him to believe there's anything romantic going on between us?"

"You're right." He scrubs his scalp and his shirt inches above his waistband, revealing the toned abs I had my hands all over a few hours ago. "It's sort of embarrassing. I meant to go before he was awake. Maybe I'm overreacting. I've never been in this situation before."

"That makes two of us."

"So, now what?"

"I got the eggs out. Are you coming!" An impatient Bhodi yells down the hall.

I slip past Cary—our bodies so close I want to tuck my fingers up under his shirt and touch his taut stomach for the sake of the memory—and crack the door back open. "We're on our way." I look back at the much-too-young-for-me man who made my evening a little less disappointing, and who my son thinks hung the moon. "Now?" I repeat. "We have pancakes."

"I'll be there in a minute," is his tentative response.

Cary follows me out of my bedroom and enters the bathroom across the hall. I hope he's a better man than to make a mad dash to his rental, or whatever the heck he's driven here, when my back is turned. Explaining why his "big brother" skipped out will be harder than indulging my son's curiosity over us sleeping in the same bed.

In the kitchen, my sister pounces. "Cary's here? Why's he here?" She glances at the kids. They're distracted, swinging the fridge door the way we get angry with them for, and letting all the cold air out. "I heard the thumps in the wall but thought you and BOB were having a wild night. Are you kidding me? You…" Laurel's voice dissipates and she mouths the letters F-U-C-K-E getting cut off before the D when Cary clears his throat behind me.

"Good morning, Laurel." Doing the least expected thing, Cary places a warm palm on my neck that smells a lot like the soap by the hall bathroom sink. "I hope you don't mind me staying for breakfast. Somebody said something about pancakes and I couldn't pass that up."

My sister can't see, Cary's fingers massage the base of my neck. Unlike all the bumbling conversations we had before last night, there's nothing awkward about the warmth of his hand. I relax into his touch.

"No, not at all. Only a fool would pass up pancakes." She gives me a conspiratorial wink.

# Cary

Holly scoots me out of the way when I offer to stir the pancake mix and adds vanilla to the batter. Making breakfast is abnormally normal... If two single moms, bopping around the kitchen to an eclectic mix of fifties rockabilly through eighties show tunes with a little nineties grunge mixed in for good measure is commonplace.

The kids stuff their chipmunk cheeks and are giggling and dancing in their pajamas. I'm able to relax supposing their contagious happiness is what matters. I even stop to belt out a refrain from a Weezer throwback cover. When a slower ballad comes on as we're clearing plates to the sink, I scoop up Laurel's daughter, Emory, swaying with her. After a spin, I put the little girl down. The soft smile playing on Holly's washed face hits me like a ton of bricks. If I'd seen it sooner, I wouldn't have stopped dancing with her niece. It fades too soon and we all return to the chore of getting the kitchen in ship shape.

When we're finished, I follow Holly back to her room to thank her for saving my ass with her kid.

Using the john before, I hadn't considered skipping out. I was wound tight worrying about Laurel's reaction to the news I was in her home this morning, and what Bhodi would think of me. That's how I fumbled putting my hand on Holly's neck. After that I tried to play it cool. I'm not sure what I'll do if Bhodi puts it together that I did his mom, and Holly asks the mentorship program to assign him a new big brother.

"Listen, I uh, I'm. What happened—"

"The fucking." She pulls fresh clothes from a scuffed antique mahogany dresser that's been around the block more times than I have.

"Yeah," I scoff, feeling heat rise from my collar. I'm not sure what's making it difficult for me to ask. I rub the back of my neck, enjoying the way the hair regrowth prickles my skin, prodding on. "Like what went down is cool. I'm not freaking out about staying to smooth things over for Bhodi anymore."

I reach for a pillow that's fallen to the floor and toss it onto the mattress.

"But you want to know why," Holly says astutely, putting the shirt and pedal pushers on the haphazard comforter.

"Yeah, I do. Why were we toasting to your shitty ex last night?" I'm not leaving until she's honest with me.

"William is contesting his child support payment on the grounds that I make enough to take care of Bhodi on my own."

"Are you kidding?"

From what little I know Bhodi's father isn't in his life other than in name. I don't get it. The kid is great. William's loss is my gain.

Holly slumps down on the bed. "A part of me gets it, except I don't understand why William doesn't ask for his parental rights to be revoked. He hasn't even seen Bhodi since he was a baby, and that statement makes it seem a lot more sunshine and lollipops than the visit was. I guess I don't appreciate the way he went about reducing his payments either time."

"This has happened more than once?"

"Yes, Jake posts headshots on Sweet Caroline's website of all the female employees to attract clients.

He also likes that having a woman in charge makes it seem like there's a legacy to Caroline's balls-to-the-wall style. It allows him to fade into the background. Anyway, an unfortunate side effect is it allows William Mayer to internet stalk me. At first, I worried he'd use my job there to argue I was unfit and file for custody of Bhodi. Instead, he waited until I became the assistant manager and filed in court to have his portion cut."

"Did they?"

"No, but he never sends the amount he's supposed to either."

What an asshole. Be it monetary or basic human decency, I'll never understand why anyone has a kid they don't want to be responsible for.

"Can't you fight it?" I sit next to her and fold my hands in my lap.

"Lawyers cost money I hadn't had to spare, and I ran the risk of him not paying at all. Not that it matters in the long run. Jake was livid at Trig when Kimber quit. He doubled my salary to be a jerk and it backfired… on me."

"Okay, but if this William guy isn't around for Bhodi anyhow, I can't see how your raise makes it bad. Is it enough to cover what he's trying to get out of paying? I don't mind helping if you need a loan for the court costs."

"You're sweet, Cary." She pats my leg. "But yeah, my salary now is enough. I'll even be able to pay off a few bills."

"I guess I don't understand then how it wound up that we…" My voice trails.

Holly rolls her lips between her teeth. "It was the principle of it. I was wallowing in every poor choice I made when it came to William. I got hyper-focused on how much I love my son and wondering why his father can't love him back. Why the person I thought

I was creating a life with—a whole life, not just a human one—took. And not only the good parts. He actually left some of those because I got to be a mom; Bhodi makes everything right in my world. But each time William shows up, he uses our child to pick away again at the shell of a person he'd tried turning me into." She covers my hand with hers as if she's letting me down easy. "Thank you for being there."

"But it's better if it doesn't happen again." I complete her thought. "Don't worry, I get it. And I have zero regrets being the person you leaned on, Holly."

I lean in to kiss her cheek, comfortable with the idea that we are sticking to a cordial friendship for Bhodi's sake. The two of us having sex shouldn't be the reason she decides I can't hang with the kid anymore.

The situation is precarious. My feet are set on a rung not much higher on the womanizing ladder than William's. However, I've made it a goal to change, and from what she's told me, that's more than I can say for Holly's ex.

I want Holly to understand I respect her choice. Bhodi needs someone to look up to who won't flake and bail. I plan to be that person.

Though as my lips graze her soft skin, our eyes connect. I fight the pull to bring my palm up, tilt her chin, and delve into the sweetness of her mouth, sucking her tongue into mine. I could lie Holly down, make her regret her words, and change her mind.

"Cary," she whispers. Her reactions are proof Holly's mind has gone in the same direction.

"I'm going to get moving."

"Sure thing." Our faces are still inches apart.

"We're good?" I stop my voice from cracking.

Like being hit on the head by a coconut falling from a palm tree, the absurd notion strikes me that giving up on whatever happened between me and Holly is anything *but* good. However, it's worth losing out on for Bhodi's sake.

Her tongue darts out, unsure. But she nods in agreement.

Chapter Nine
_______________

*Holly*

"Stop that now, Miss Holly. You're gonna be puttin' me out of business by makin' me look bad."

Mr. Johnston chuckles when I snatch my hand away from the lone brown leaf on the potted flower in his stall.

My lips purse together. "You caught me… Again."

"You're a hard woman to miss," he remarks, tugging the brim of his navy USS Battleship North Carolina ball cap to shade his grizzled face from the sun.

I stand out like a sore thumb in crowds, but Mr. Johnston has been telling me for years he much prefers the way I dress to the "get-ups" he sees at the Farmers Market. He once complimented me on a dress, saying his wife had a similar one when they dated. Though the time we compared the colorful lines on my leg from my tattoo to the fading wisps of blue diffusing into his forearm after over half a century, Mr. Johnston told me for as beautiful as the flowers were, he worried for the soul of any woman who needed as much ink as I've adorned my body with. *My, how times have changed,* I thought.

"Come along." He holds out his weathered hand, holding mine daintily when I accept.

Poor Mrs. Johnston, Mr. Johnston had to have been quite the charmer in his day.

"I'm around the bend," I say to Bhodi, pointing beyond the next row of hanging plants.

My son is counting blooms on a squat table brimming with pots of phlox, Shasta daisies, and coneflowers. A few feet away, Mrs. Johnston sits in the shade of the warehouse building. There's an oxygen tank attached to her wheelchair. She has a bright floral top on, a blanket spread over her lap, and a large red umbrella already open behind her for when the direction of the sun changes later in the afternoon. Her face moves a fraction and I catch the corners of her mouth lifting. She's been where I am; trying to give a boy a chance to spread his wings, but still unsure of how to let go and keep the baby she raised safe.

We turn the corner. Mr. Johnston wheezes, clearing his throat. He picks up a teensy forest green pot with a crippled plant in the soil.

"For you, my dear."

The majority of the flowers in my kitchen he's given to me in the same manner. It's the inevitable outcome of visiting a great old soul's stall when you can't help yourself but tend to the branches in need of TLC.

"What is it?" I ask like always.

"You'll have to wait and see." He shakes a finger at me, replying in his usual manner.

My cheek draws up. "Not even an idea of if it prefers sun or shade? Mr. Johnston, you give me too much credit."

"Have you killed one yet?"

"Well, no." I've over-watered a few trying to figure out what the plant needed.

"Then it's settled."

"Do you want me to return it?"

I politely inquire the same thing each time. I had brought the first, a plumeria, back to life and tried to return it to Mr. Johnston to a considerable amount of scolding about returning a gift and hurting an old man's feelings.

"Heavens, no. Just show me the picture on that camera phone of yours."

The way it comes out, I half expect Mr. Johnston to have used "newfangled". I've taken out my cell to show him my success stories since that I've posted on my private social media account.

This was supposed to be a quick stop at their market stall. I need a new pot for a plant that's outgrown its dirt home and to get Mrs. Johnston's opinion on her favorite ceramic. Per her usual, she chooses the brightest and most colorful. Mrs. Johnston would get a tattoo.

I place my new little treasure inside my purchase and Bhodi carries the two for me as we stroll toward the crosswalk for the next building, passing the fruit and vegetable vendors. The smell of strawberries accosts my nose and we agree to buy a bushel before going home when Bhodi leans into me and begs for spring fruit. It's too hot to leave any of this in the car. In the sun they might soon wilt too.

"Holly, wait!" Cece calls from behind us.

She and Sylvie Rhys scamper across the lot, giggling. Her tote bounces behind her, filled with green leafy vegetables.

Today, Dusty has a deck to build and Laurel's ex has Emory, giving her a much-needed day to herself. So, when Cece offered to meet us out for brunch—which is more akin to lunch given my sleep schedule

—and the rest of our girlfriends heard, they decided it was mill girls' day out at the Farmer's Market.

"Oh, good! I thought we were late," I say.

"I needed a few things for dinner, so we tried to plan accordingly. And you know what they say, better late than pr— uh, in Kimber's condition." Cece bites her tongue and blushes, glancing at Dusty's daughter. "I'm still getting used to this." She touches Sylvie's honey locks apologetically. She's new to parenting.

"Agreed… And you're doing fine. It's only been a few months since you and Dusty started dating for real, and I haven't once heard a negative comment from Sylvie Rhys—or Renata." I tack on Sylvie's grandma's name.

We continue walking to the farm-to-table restaurant. The kids are up ahead.

"It's the opposite." Cece tucks her hair behind her ear, biting her lip. "We're getting lots of questions from daddy's little princess."

"She's eager to move things along?"

"Pushy is more like it. I'm worried about Renata's feelings about her M-O-M."

"I know how to spell *mom*." Sylvie Rhys pipes up from a few paces ahead.

We go bug-eyed at one another, unable to tell from the inflection in the six-year-old's voice if she means she can spell mom or if she's calling Cece mom already. Beth, Sylvie's mother, died when she was a baby.

"See what I mean?" Cece whispers. "And Kimber having twins has given her baby fever."

"Careful, I've heard that's catchy."

Cece wrinkles her nose.

"Awe, come on, Cece. You and Dusty would make some gorgeous chubbykins."

I spend far more time with them than I do with Trig and Kimber, therefore I'm going to need Cece to have a baby I can hold to get my fix once Emory starts school. The one thing I won't ever be late for is my time of the month.

"Someday, but not now." Guilt and confusion lace Cece's voice.

She's fallen more and more for Dusty's daughter. They've established a great bond, and yet Cece wants what's best for Sylvie without sacrificing herself. I gave up a lot for Bhodi. It was tough, and he's my flesh and blood.

My son is lucky someone like Cary is still willing to stand in and model some respectability for him. It takes a real man to keep showing up on the weekends, despite sleeping with a kid's mom the way we did. *I'm lucky.*

I risked so much trying to let Cary down easy a few weekends ago. I'm not sure if he stays on the periphery of my mind because he's proven he's handled the situation better than I expected or the sex was amazing. BOB hasn't had the magic touch as of late. Maybe I need to replace the batteries or splurge on a new one?

What's more likely to solve the issue is leaving for my shift earlier so there are fewer awkward conversations when Cary brings Bhodi home. How many times can I respond to a polite, "How are you?" without saying, "Desperate to have your cock inside of me." The answer is *a lot* when your child is within earshot.

Inside the restaurant, the servers are pushing two tables together so there is enough space for all of us. Kimber is putting her toddler, Owen, into a highchair. His adult sister, Aidy, guides his feet through the leg slots and buckles him in. She rounds the table, noticing Cece and I have come in, and pats the seat next to her, making room for her boyfriend, Morgan's, sister.

On Aidy's opposite side is Hailey, who lives at the mill and whom I haven't seen in ages. I stop to hug her and then Sloan, who has the head of the table. After scooting around everyone's brimming sacks of fresh produce and country goodness, the remaining spot left for me to sit in faces Sloan with Bhodi to my left.

Our uniqueness has struck me before. Aidy and Hailey are in college, younger than Celine. Kimber is closing in on forty. In the grand scheme, Sloan and I aren't that far behind. We're all bound by the mill, or rather they are, and I am included in the friendship shenanigans in an odd sense of guilt by association. I'm also the only one of us who is currently unattached. I love how excited everyone is for Kimber and that they're all getting to the point no one minds children around or I'd find myself the odd woman out.

The kids color after we place our orders and pick at their food when the server returns, eating mostly the fries and bowls of fruit, minus the cantaloupe.

My girlfriends and I idly chit-chat and gossip about what we've been up to. I'm thankful when it's mentioned how gorgeous the TV mount Dusty made is that Cece leaves Cary's name out.

For Bhodi's sake, not mine.

Although Cece glances between my son and me, and her lip twitches as she remarks, "I could live off of what Laurel grills... and these." She pulls a hot-from-the-oven buttermilk biscuit from the extra basket we requested.

I reach in for seconds, tearing mine apart. The steamy bread melts in my mouth when it hits my tongue and I groan. Who needs a man when you've got a cloud of buttery carbohydrate heaven?

Bhodi leans into me with puppy dog eyes. I give him a smarmy face, pull off another small bite, and hand him the rest of the biscuit.

He's got it half shoved in his mouth when I barter a typical mom-exchange. "Trade me for your melon?"

My son plops the remains of his fruit cup on my plate, grinning. I'd do anything for him to stay as happy as he's been recently. He's even doing better in school.

After we settle the bill, everyone troupes back through to vendors to get what we couldn't carry before brunch. Kimber has an hour to burn before Owen's nap and suggests heading to the park for the kids. Bhodi and Sylvie Rhys glom onto the idea.  We wind up splitting off from Sloan, Hailey, and Aidy for the short drive up the road.

I leave my windows cracked so my Honda doesn't pressure cook the quality produce and park close to the entrance. Walking toward the gates, I can't help notice how many license plate holders advertise Cass-Stanton's auto mall. I decide I'm hit with so many subliminal messages and it's contributing to the madness I feel between Cary's visits. I shouldn't be looking forward to seeing him again, but something in my chest swells when regarding all these vehicles as a measure of his success. I'm proud of him in a way, even if I have no right to be. Even if I'm not the woman on his arm when he's my age and has come into his own.

"I'm not sure I've ever seen you smile like that, Holly. What are you thinking?" Kimber asks.

She pats Owen on the bottom, encouraging the toddler to join Bhodi and Sylvie Rhys on the slide.

"Who—wha?" I guess I'm not as clever covering my tracks with my besties as I am with my kid. "It's nothing."

"I have a feeling it's the kind of thing that explains why you were quick back at the restaurant to change the subject when I mentioned we'd had dinner with you and Laurel… And Cary Cass." Cece nods to the line of cars visible beyond the tall metal fencing of the historic playground.

I take a sharp inhale. I should've known my silence would be short-lived once Celine got me alone.

Kimber shakes her head, beaming. Her eyes widen with acute interest. "Is there something you'd like to share about Bhodi's 'big brother'?"

I cross an arm over my chest and use my other hand to cover my face. "Not here, Cece," I mumble, knowing full-well as she sidles up next to Kimber she'll ignore my plea.

"I'm pretty sure Holly would like to give him a bath and tuck him in. And from the way Cary watched her, I'm figuring he'd be okay with Holly getting into the tub so he can touch her all of the places her bathing suit covers too."

I fret while Kimber and Cece titter on about how attractive Cary is. "Oh, God! That's not a visual I need!"

Especially not when I can't get the sight of Cary touching me out of my head.

Cary

The jacked bouncer grants us entry and I pull Glen to the side, away from his groomsmen and the other men they invited to his stag party. Somehow my name got added to the guest list. I had no say in where it was being held since I wasn't in on the planning.

"Not to freak you out or anything, but Bhodi's mom manages this place."

Glen pales swearing, "Shit, dude. She's not going to..."

According to his best man, Glen's had a few cocktails to get over pre-wedding jitters. The ceremony is a week away and he thinks his fiancée hung the stars. I have the inkling Glen's either afraid of her reaction finding out he's been watching women take their clothes off, or Glen hasn't been to a nudie bar before. Could be both.

I'm less concerned with Holly seeing me at the club than Glen is about her reporting him to the parent of his mentee. I've also been half-hard each time I've thought about coming out tonight and, unlike the guys I'm here with, it has zero to do with the dancers.

I stop a boozy Glen from pitching a tizzy with a calm down motion.  "Holly's cool. I owed you a heads up in case she happened to introduce herself."

I'm hoping she does, if only to have her attention for a minute. Whenever I have downtime, I seriously can't get this woman out of my head.

If I'd believed taking over the family business while Rex was in the hospital was like herding cats, now that I'm officially in charge of the dealerships it's like I'm juggling the fluffy felines while they claw the crap out of me trying to escape. The only thing I need on a more consistent basis than some good pussy is a better night's rest.

We push our way through the extra thick crowd. Glen's groomsmen are at a table near the stage, pouring from a pitcher. I'm in the mood for something else to drink and want to start a tab to cover a round. I tell Glen to save me a seat and veer off to the bar.

A dense crowd has packed itself inside Sweet Caroline's. Despite this, there's an extreme amount of space surrounding a single booth on the far wall. It screams "keep away" to patrons similar to the way a hazmat or biohazard sign stops unauthorized entry. I'm mildly shocked Dusty is guarding the perceived bubble. Although Holly's nickname for him is "big guy", and it's an accurate description.

Celine spies me and waves me over. "Why are you here?"

"Bachelor party. We must have picked the same night as every other poor sap."

"I don't think so. Word got around that tonight's Kimber's retirement. A lot of our old clients came in. None of us expected it would be this busy either."

"Hold on, you're—" I stop mid-gaffe. Cece's hair is down around her shoulders. Her bright yellow top and red heels, which add inches to her stature, are a little more daring than the work outfit she had on the evening at Holly's condo.

Dusty slips his hand around her waist and pulls his girlfriend close. She reaches up and pats his mammoth chest as if she's taming a beast. There's a glow in her expression, attracting his attention to her mouth. Dusty's lip quirks and I see his body relax.

"I'm sorry," I say in earnest, realizing Cece is calming the palpable tension radiating off of Dusty. I was mere seconds from a possessive bear of a man mauling me.

It makes perfect sense now how Holly knows the couple. Cece used to dance here. She had a wicked performance with a rain slicker.

All of a sudden, my past rears its ugly head. Dusty is a solid, friendly guy and I've come to this place to watch the woman he's in love with taking off her clothes. The fun I'm here for tonight with Glen and his groomsmen seems a lot less innocuous.

A shrill whistle has us turning our heads toward the bar. Her victory rolls standing tall, Holly points to the door and unless I'm mistaken—which I very well could be because I'm so damn focused on the bright smile Holly flashes at me—the crowd parts to let a couple through.

A powerful grip tightens at my collar. "Mr. Cass, haven't seen you in too long."

"Carver Galloway, how is the car running?"

I may address Carver by his full name, but our handshake is strong and familiar, filled with levity.

"Well. But I'm *this* close to trading her in on a whim." He mimes before saying hello to Dusty and Cece. I get the impression they're all well acquainted.

The striking woman at his side lets out a light

sound, as if she's tickled by the idea of a new vehicle.

"Cary, This is my better half, Sloan." He's affectionate, pecking the fingers of her left hand that he's been holding.

"Cary Cass." I introduce myself. "I didn't know you had a… fiancée?" *wife?* I presume, glancing at the impressive rock.

"Sometimes." She evades the question. "When it's convenient for Carver and makes him look like an upstanding citizen."

The corners of Sloan's mouth perk deviously. She places her hand on Carver's chest in an identical manner to the way Cece had Dusty and taps lightly. Then she slides into the booth where the others have made a generous amount of room for her on the rounded bench.

"My wife thinks she's a comedian." Carver lifts his eyes to the ceiling. "Joke's on her. I'm going to replace the Maserati with a minivan and see how long she lasts after having a taste of the finer things in life."

The hair on my arms stands on end and it takes me a moment to realize it's not the lost profit between selling a luxury import versus a base model mommy mobile affecting me.

"From what Bhodi's told me, Cary's got some amazing pimped vans on the lot." Holly pipes up next to me. "He wants me to buy one and taxi him and his buddies around while they game in the backseats."

"I didn't see you there," I say, aware the shift was Holly's proximity. When she's in my bubble, my body reacts.

"I'm stealthy." She winks. "What can I get you, gentleman?"

As the new arrivals to the booth, we place our orders. I give Holly my card, signaling I'd like the drinks on my tab. Carver upgrades his ride once a year and has been loyal to Cass showrooms since before I was aware he was a valued customer. Popping for his bourbon is the least I can do. And, not to sound like a car salesman, but given Carver's financial resources and the way he looked at his wife and kidded, I can picture him buying her the top of the line Honda I drove Bhodi home in a few times— even if it is as a joke.

Holly lingers, chatting with the other ladies at the table while I talk Carver out of a Bentley. It's one of the few lines we don't carry. I can find it on the secondary market, but he buys new and I don't want anything unforeseen to creep up and tarnish my dealership's reputation.

"I'll send Kelsey, the new girl, back with your order." She tells Carver. "Better she gets to know your table before she's on her own." Holly blinks a few times when Carver's taken his seat and she's got my attention all to herself. Little does she know it never left her. "I saw you over here and wanted to say 'hi'."

"Hi," I repeat, making her red-stained lips turn up in another smile.

We're grinning like fools, and I shake my head. The fat tongue in my mouth proves Holly is under my skin. I tell her with few words why I'm at Sweet Caroline's.

"Too bad it's not a quieter night. Kimber's got a ton of people here who want to say farewell, and I'm still training the new assistant manager. Jake's supposed to be in later too." She gives me the impression she'd be more attentive if she could. "Is your party bar hopping or shutting the place down?"

"It could go either way. You have a break?"

"For a half an hour at eleven." Her tooth bites into the flesh of her lip.

I look at my watch. There are better than two

hours until then. I want her, but I don't want to push my luck.

"Can I entice you to come find me at five past?"

"It could go either way," she says coyly. Holly lifts on her toes and her nails sink into my abs. "Do you think I'm a sure thing, Cary? We agreed it was one time."

"You agreed. I wasn't in on the negotiations." My breath whispers past her ear. "If you liked the test drive, I'm certain we can strike a deal to get a newer model into you."

Her hesitation to meet me is obvious as she draws her hand away from my stomach. Holly's not so sure about the double entendre, but she's also slow to walk away.

I'm cognizant of the sway of her ass in those too-short shorts as she approaches the bar. Some patrons nearby get loud and Holly fakes interest, using the disturbance to glance over her shoulder to where she's left me. I may be drooling like a hound dog, but I've got her right where I want her and it won't take much to seal the deal.

By eleven, a level of apathy for the entertainment leaves me not quite as positive. I've lost count of the number of times the house lights have gone up or down and the instances the strobe lighting from the stage has blinded me.

Every so often a shrill whistle has pierced the theater that's not a catcall. Upon hearing Holly yell her catchphrase "sure thing" to a cocktail waitress, and seeing her standing on top of the bar, I become conditioned to seek out her form each time.

Fuck, the body the woman's got. The toned legs and innocent ruffles on her blouse concealing those high, tight boobs have other men looking too. I'd better be the only guy at the club who isn't left guessing about her full-body tattoo. I'd planned to trace my tongue all over those inked petals. Whether or not it's tonight or another night, now I'm thinking of how to make Holly my sure thing.

I'm fingering a pasty that a groomsman stuck to the front of Glen's shirt and I yanked off when he was distracted when eleven-twenty rolls around. Glen is three sheets to the wind. He's unlikely to remember the dancers his buddies paid to give him private shows. I'm starting to feel bad for the guy. When everyone at the bachelor party is absorbed by the deafening music and strippers, I've been secretly swiping the indecent garments they've caught. I doubt it will go over well if his fiancée finds any of this stuffed in Glen's pockets.

Slung back in my chair, I'm not enjoying the performer or the company I'm keeping. Holly's lateness is affecting my mood. I'm considering making a vanishing act. No harm or foul that she's changed her mind. Yet, it seems like Holly and I won't be meeting up. Her scheduled break time is almost over.

Nails scrape up the back of my neck, and the little adhesive circle is plucked from my grip.

"I would have been here sooner had I known you had this." She puts a hand on her hip.

"Worried I took it off a dancer?" I cock my chin, hoping she's jealous.

"No, two of them were fighting backstage over who stole whose costume accessories. I had to put the dancer set to perform again before we close into time out. The bigger of the two troublemakers is on their way home." Holly scowls.

She reaches out and as soon as we connect, she drags me through the crowd and back toward a long hallway.

A door swings open, and we make an abrupt stop.

"Here." She holds out the pasty to the woman

trying to leave. "Don't lose your shit in the crowd and throw shade on someone else. I don't come to work to play your goddamn mommy or babysit you. Kimber may be leaving—and I may not have danced —but I've been in charge of the club enough years that you know I won't put up with any disrespect."

"I didn't disrespect you." The dancer turns from Holly, putting on the same shameless act for me I watched her give Glen. "Aren't you a tall drink—"

"I heard you call me a bitch as I left and *he* is not here to quench your thirst. So, drag your butt out the back door and decide overnight if you want to dance at Sweet Caroline's. I can replace you in a hot minute with someone younger and tighter."

"Seems you know all about that." Troublemaker numero uno's hair swishes as she storms away.

We head in the same direction. I push the silver bar, keeping the back exit open. The night air is stale, but we're in an alleyway so there's no fixing it.

"That made me sort of hot for you," I compliment as the door clicks shut behind us.

Confidence on full display, she tugs my waistband, drawing me closer. "You were already hot for me."

# Chapter Eleven

*Holly*

The club employees wouldn't dare call me a pushover, but I'm not certain where the boldness I had in the hall when taking on the dancer came from. I thrive on kindness because I have first-hand knowledge of what it's like to be tossed aside.

Wherever the nerve to speak my mind originated, in this instant I'm terrified to let go of the empowerment it's given me. I don't have brass balls when it comes to men. Love's left me used and broken. I tell myself I won't get involved again and countless times I've stood my ground and relied on my intuition. But I'm stumbling around Cary, and it scares the crap out of me. No rational judgment will result from the way he's taken my lips in a scorching kiss.

Our hands are all over each other. Teeth gnash against teeth. His bite, tugging against my earlobe, and returning to suck my lower lip into his mouth. Our bodies respond in a frenzy, the result of anticipation and the tension of doing the right thing by staying apart.

I wish Cary hadn't dropped into Sweet Caroline's this evening—or any night—but as the hours passed, I realized how glad I am he is here.

I've been known to decline even the most innocuous sweet shot of liquor while serving to keep my wits about me. You never know when someone will need you to call them a cab. Cary's paced his drinking throughout the night. If we're bold enough to do whatever this is sober, this time will be different. My aim is to get him out of my system, stop worrying about if I look presentable when Cary picks Bhodi up, and wondering if the awareness lighting up my entire body when he looks at me is a bold-faced lie.

Sex with Cary won't be the same as the first time we were together. It will be a clean break, instead of his strong steady gaze meeting me in my room tomorrow morning. Finding one more excuse to stay. Hoping what we've done doesn't change our opinions about each other being otherwise decent people.

I won't be reading into why Cary cares if William steps up for us or not. I'll be able to get my wits about me and remember this man isn't in my life, he's in Bhodi's. Cary has volunteered to build my son's confidence, not add incendiary fuel to the constant thoughts of him keeping me awake and unfulfilled.

The more Cary touches me, the more my jealousy builds over the interactions in the hall with the dancer. She wasn't the first to pluck him out of obscurity in the audience and comment on his rugged good looks. I doubt she'll be the last. Tonight Cary's mine, completely. I want him to leave having wanted me more than he'll ever want one of my employees. I don't want to share, to the point where I regret shushing Cece's lighthearted ribbing each time

Carver's table ordered another round.

My head falls back against the brick and I pant as Cary's face dips lower, devouring the length of me like a starved man. He crouches on the asphalt with his palms slunk up the back of my shorts encasing my ass and his tongue swirling the vines on my torso as if he's tasting each sweet inch of some forbidden fruit. The stubble of his beard tickles my stomach.

I'm so wet. It wouldn't take much to get me off if his fingers explored forward to the throbbing spot at the seam of my shorts. I almost don't care if we're caught with my pants down and his mouth on my core, though I was cautious to move us to the spot where the surveillance cameras intentionally go dark.

"This is so trashy," I say, because it is.

It's daring and this man, whose reputation I'm likely sullying, is sexy as hell. I work in a strip club and don't doubt sex in public turns anyone on.

My breathless words halt Cary's hand from pushing up my top to pinch and pluck at the bouquet underneath.

He stands, pressing our foreheads together, kissing my nose. His rigid cock pushes against where his face was, leaving me with the distinct impression it isn't on board with his latest negotiating tactics.

"Cary?" I question whether he's come to his senses and is about to help me regain my own.

My palm caresses his cheek, drawing his hazel eyes to focus on my brown ones.

"You're right, Holly. We're literally surrounded by garbage cans and you're worth more than a back alley fuck."

"So that's it? We're not?"

"Not here, anyway. Later? Someplace a little less... smelly?" He alleviates my confusion and I reward him with a soft smile.

He shakes his head with a goofy turned serious

grin, caging my body against the exterior club wall. "You don't wanna know what runs through my head when you smile at me like that, Hol."

"There's a party afterward for Kimber. You could stay and tell me..." *Show me,* my voice trails suggestively.

"I'll stick around on one condition. I need a plus one for Glen's wedding."

"You want to take me on a date?" His tactic surprises me.

"I didn't sputter when I mentioned not wanting to fly solo." Lowering his mouth to my ear, the scruff of his beard sets me on fire again. "And if you're set on me fucking you tonight, I can guarantee the next evening we're together will end with my cock buried inside you."

My hard nipples scrape the soft cotton of my shirt when I let out a sharp inhale. It hurts, but not as bad as the unsatiated throbbing in my core.

He turns his face. "So, are you in?"

Rendered speechless, my chin bobs in agreement.

If I thought the last three hours on my feet were torture, the next are murderous. What's worse is my willingness to forget the warning signals flashing red to remind me Cary is out of bounds. He doesn't return to the bachelor party but takes up residence next to Trig and they strike up a conversation. It carries through Kimber's husband walking behind the bar to refill their drinks as customers slam us with orders.

Near the end of the rush, Morgan escorts Aidy up to the bar. He stands a few feet behind her while she asks for a water. Cary tacks on a second for himself and adds both of them to his ever-growing tab. My position is closer to the cooler, so it's an easy reach for the bottles. Aidy and I thank him.

Trig doesn't miss the lingering touch when Cary

accepts his drink from me.

He chuckles, thanking Cary for a third time. "Aidy lives in my house. There's nothing more important than taking care of the women in your life. Trust me when I say trust her."

I catch Trig pointing at me as I scurry away to fill another glass. I can't decipher the rest over the din of the crowd. However, aware I *am* a sure thing, I've also felt Cary's eyes lingering on every inch of my body and his agitation each time the club's patrons flirt with me. It's left me wondering how to prove to Cary it's him I want.

After last call, the club empties, and the house lights blaze on for the overnight crew to begin cleaning. I get to the job of stocking right away, so I can enjoy the party for Kimber. Cece rounds behind the bar with Dusty carrying the usual cases of liquor we go through like water.

"Go." She prods. "I owe you this."

I have no clue what Cece is talking about, but hell if I'm passing up the chance to sneak off while everyone is following her lead.

Cary's shuffling top-shelf rum to fit in the row. He must think it's normal to pitches in. He snags a bottle with an aged pirate ship and hums, "Have you tasted this brand?"

"Sure I have. It's the bee's knees. The distillery is smaller and in demand now, so we have a hard time getting it and don't let on that we serve it unless someone asks. The owner gets persnickety when we run out." I put the bottle back, motioning for Cary to come along.

Jake's office is in the same hall as the dancer's dressing room. It perpetually smells of Italian leather and expensive cologne… and sex.

In the middle of the room there's a desk with a closed laptop on it. A couch is jammed against the left wall that's been painted a dark wine. From one side to the other on the perpendicular walls old posters dating back decades cover the mirrors. They feature the dancers who used to perform here like Kimber and Cece, "Sweet" Caroline herself, and Carver's mother. The very center both in front and behind the desk is open and I can see our reflection.

I walk around the desk and move the computer. Cary is on my heels, so by the time I turn to face him, he's pinned my upper thighs to the desktop. I sit back, spreading my legs and letting Cary into my space. He's giving me a cocky-assed grin and I shoot one back.

"How the fuck did you figure me out?" His hardness edges closer, exactly where I want to feel it.

I stay silent. Cary likes to watch and, when the alleyway didn't happen, catering to his proclivities was the quick and obvious answer to reignite the mood. I'm glad the stars aligned to pull it off. The next best private space to choose from would have been a broom closet.

Cary tips my chin up and our lips meet. The kiss is softer than before. He takes his time exploring my mouth and caressing down my arms. The shivers it creates excite me. My grip pulls him closer. I inch his shirt up in the back to touch his muscles and my other set of fingers plays with the short hair at the nape of his neck. I love the way his body feels under my hands.

Between the possibility that I may ruin the best friendship my son has developed with someone good-hearted and our age gap, I should end this before it goes any further. However, the reckless part of my personality that developed when I found myself all alone eggs me on. Someday I'm going to be somebody's granny and, for the life of me, I want a scandalous, secret story penned in a worn journal with a cracked spine. One about a devilishly handsome young man, who finds me attractive enough to invite to a wedding, who treats me well, and who makes my toes curl once or twice before the quiet affair ends. That seems like an awfully romantic story to leave to my imaginary granddaughters, doesn't it?

I'm lost in the moment, the fantasy of possibilities we play out with our dolls when we're girls, and my growing infatuation with this man when the knob turns.

"Hol—why's my door locked?" Key in hand, Jake's barging in like he owns the place, which he does. "What the hell?… Stanton?"

"Cass." Cary's jaw grinds.

My boss and my—uh, sexcapade?—are locked in a stare-off. I've never asked why Cary goes by Cass only, but considering how hot my cheeks are flaming, now isn't the time to dig deeper. Thinking the coast was clear when Jake hadn't shown up at Sweet Caroline's, I'd brought Cary back here for all the wrong reasons. It's apparent there's some sort of bad blood between the two of them. This could cost me my job.

I give Jake my attention, ready to face the music. "I'm sorry," I apologize.

Kimber taught me two things when dealing with Jake. First, like in any other situation, own up to it. Second, when Jake flirts or expresses any semblance of innuendo, it's a test.

Years ago, I thought there was a flaw in Kimber's logic and sleeping with Jake would keep me in his good graces. I'm glad I took her advice because Jake has uncanny respect for the women he can't easily wear down and who'll say no to him. The only exception to this rule seems to be Sloan and I've always had an inkling that had to do with her control over Carver who is Jake's business partner.

Jake chucks the keys on the desk and they hit the laptop hard enough to etch the matte silver surface. His tongue rolls around in his mouth, measuring the combative words he directs at me. "Guess there were a few things Trig didn't uncover for you about your kid's upstanding mentor, huh? Like how big a dick he is. Oh, I mean has."

Cary's finger's on my stomach tense, and his arm around my middle loosens.

# Chapter Twelve

*Cary*

I've developed some pretty engrained opinions about Jake Ballentine, but have kept my shit locked down about Holly's boss. After all, he gave her a decent raise and the autonomy she has being in charge of Sweet Caroline's overshadows her grievances about Jake not giving a damn about his bar.

Spouting off that I have first-hand knowledge of the people Jake's screwed over to line his pockets— and that depending on how you look at the situation, I'm one of them—won't score me any points with this woman. It won't afford an opportunity to get to know her better. And more importantly, when I'd found out Holly worked at Jake's club, pissing about what a douche he is was a surefire pink-slip for hanging out with Bhodi. Grown men making shit choices controlled my youth. Holly's kid doesn't deserve the brunt of any bad blood.

I've avoided the golf club, dodging Jake's polite interrogations to see if I've figured out I'm Cass-Stanton family's dirty little secret. The likelihood I renew my membership is low. I'm not interested in being boxed into a corner. Someday, when it suits my purpose, I'll air my dirty laundry. Put it on the line. For me, refusing Jake's offer on the nineteenth hole, but buying a drink and a good time at Sweet Caroline's falls along the lines of keeping my enemies closer.

But now I can't help wondering how close I've let those enemies get, and perhaps if I have my arm around one of them.

My fingers splayed on Holly's stomach tense and the protective arm I'd wrapped around her midsection when Jake barged in and she'd turned to see who interrupted us loosens.

Trig pulled up things about my past and reported on them to Holly? And who else? Why?

Another figure fills the doorway.

"Jake! Leave it." Carver barks like Holly's a freaking dog bone.

"Shut it. I told you she was mine. You can't lay dibs on every woman who walks into *my* establishment." The brash words leave Jake's mouth.

Even mad, I don't like how dismissive either of them are of her.

"He doesn't mean—Carver didn't choose me as a mill girl." Holly pales trying to expand on something she'd tried to explain when we were drunk the night I stayed over.

I'm not happy Galloway is the Carver she mentioned. I didn't get the concept then, and I don't want to now. Holly told me because of her job most of her closest friends were these mill girls; Women who started out dancing on Jake's stage before being plucked out of obscurity and given a chance to fulfill their dreams and reach their goals. They abide by Carver's firm guidelines to live under his roof at the old factory across the street.

The only thing I do believe based on my experience with Carver is, under his guardianship, it allowed plenty of them to find more respectable jobs. According to Holly, there's no one clear path each has taken. Some are in legal or medical fields. There are teachers and real estate agents. However, everyone is fulfilled and living their best life.

*What else could you wish for them than to be truly happy? Holly said.*

Yet she'd never considered the happiness the other mill girls have found a possibility for her because she had Bhodi.

"Jake's not finished throwing a tantrum about Kimber and he's taking it out on anyone in a five-foot radius. It's a delightful part of his charming persona, and it's better if you go before Jake embarrasses himself any further." Carver's tone is brusque and laced with bitter sarcasm, indicating we should get while the getting is good.

"You're an asshole." Jake directs his comment at Carver as we pass into the corridor.

"Maybe it's the company I keep." The door closes, but Carver continues. "What the hell is wrong with you still that after all these years you can't ever be happy for anyone?"

I slow my pace once we're alone in the hall. The two men are trading loud insults. Holly and I stop moving at the same time.

"You did a background check on me?"

"Bhodi's my son."

"You had me checked out!" I repeat the phrase.

"Put yourself in my shoes, Cary! If you had the means, would you have let Bhodi go off God knows where with someone you don't know, blindly trusting they were an upstanding member of society? I'm his mother. You don't get to second-guess my choices. I'm the only one keeping him safe because his father took off before the day he was born. Without my son, you have a new Coupe de Ville to drive every day of the week. Your life doesn't change. But without Bhodi, I have nothing. Do you understand that? I'm sorry if it hurts your fragile ego."

I sag against the wall, massaging my temple. My brain is about to explode. If this woman deduced after one roll in the hay that I like watching and brings me into a mirrored room to get me off, Holly's gotta be smart enough to have figured out long ago that not everything Jake does is on the up and up.

I wipe a palm down my face, marring my features. My dick's as deflated as my pride. I want to yell. I want to lash out at Holly for the audacity. I want to drag out everything of her to find out if she's hiding that Trig told her the rest of the story… And most of all, I want Davina to have had the foresight to protect me the way Holly does for her child.

That's what hurts. My mom perpetuated fairies and rainbows and didn't step up for me. I'm prime to unload that indignation on someone else.

Like Ballentine is doing. *Fucking therapy.*

Holly's head hangs in shame, waiting for me to keep arguing, making every emotion shredding my insides ache a million times worse. She's standing there with the same defeated expression Davina got when Rex put her in her place.

"I get it," I say, understanding the way she's backed herself a few feet down the hall is something I don't get at all. Holly's no mouse. She's a damn lioness when it comes to her kid.

It dawns on me she'd also have run in the opposite direction if she had an inkling underneath the surface I wasn't who I appeared to be. Holly is unaware of Jake's dealings with Rex, but I'm more certain than ever Ballentine *knows*. The question has become what am I doing with that information? Oddly enough, the confirmation I've been seeking gives me a sense of power instead of feeling like Jake can put the screws to me.

I offer my hand as an olive branch and, as soon as she stops hesitating, I pull her close. She's shaking. Not with rage, but in inexplicable fear. I envelop her body almost as if mine can insulate her from danger and rest my chin on her hair.

"You don't owe me an apology."

"I do. I'd have been upfront about Trig offering his services if I had a freaking clue that Jake would ever wind up walking in on us in a compromising position. I'm not two-faced."

I huff, kissing her head. "While we're being honest, I didn't intend on messing this up so soon."

"Neither did I." She pulls her head away. A lock of her hair frizzes and she smooths it back. "And I wouldn't have survived here very long if anything had happened with Jake. Our relationship isn't like that."

The last band constricting my chest eases.

"I meant getting my whiskers tangled in your crazy hairstyle—how fucking long do you spend looking in the mirror?—but whatever this is between us too." I joke to lighten the mood. "Know how you told me you didn't bring men home a lot? Well, I follow women home a second time even less."

How do you say you're trying to turn over a new leaf without sounding like you've been a skirt chaser?

"Are you laying the 'you're special' line on me?" Her cheek goes back to resting against my chest.

My heart is racing and I hope Holly plays it off as remaining adrenaline from our argument coursing through my veins.

"Thicker than your winged eyeliner, Doll. But it's the truth."

She would have let me go for her kid. Like Holly said, Bhodi's all she has. He is her best life. The only one who makes her truly happy and who she can do the same for. And I'm starting to wish for better for both of them.

The first thing I notice when we're back in the theater area is Trig consoling a ruddy-faced Kimber. I may have been pissed Holly had me investigated, but this reminds me that my initial impression of Trig is that he's a stand-up guy.

He didn't balk when other men wanted Kimber's attention. He worked the bar during our conversation, doing more than refilling our drinks. Trig took it upon himself to take the pressure off of Kimber with the patrons who didn't care who served them. I don't think his comments were a warning about Jake, but to trust Holly's decisions.

Noticing we're here, Trig nods what I take as a silent admission of guilt. I doubt he'll offer a full acknowledgment, so I return the gesture and consider it over. If I want Holly I don't get to pick and choose the trappings of her life that are included. She'd fucking pack it in after judging my own indiscretions.

Holly is like a beacon to her tearful friend, hugging Kimber and patting her on the back. Whatever went down while we were in the office was bad enough almost everyone else has disappeared. Only Sloan remains, insisting they'll celebrate another night— without inviting Jake, whom I get the impression she thinks little of—before Trig and Kimber leave too.

Holly insists we walk Sloan across the street to the mill, so she gets home safely. Then I get in my car and follow Holly's back to her condo.

We wind up slipping into her room. Holly's suspended the Moravian star Bhodi bought her from the ceiling like a pendant. She clicks on a bedside lamp and the soft light reflects up through the prisms, casting overlapping triangular shadows.

It's past three am and I'm beginning to get the bigger picture as to why she sleeps where she does. Laurel, Emory, and Bhodi have been fast asleep upstairs for hours and Holly's movements won't cause any loud noises to wake them.

She flips through her phone. Another eighties tune flows faintly from the bluetooth speakers.

"Explain the music."

"Of all the weird things I do, say, or wear, this is where we're starting?"

I slide my fingertips to her waistband, unbuttoning her short shorts, and dip my lips to her neck, finding the sweet spot that drives her wild. "Not focused on what you've got on when my goal is getting you out of it."

"Another smooth line."

"Smooth... jazz?" I pull away, trying to place the music. "You don't dress up in spatter-painted lycra with leg warmers too, do you?"

"No!" She laughs, pushing at my chest.

My ass hits the mattress and I pull her down, parallel to the pillows, to lie next to me. We turn to face one another. I cup her cheek. Kiss her lips. Content that I'm free to explore her body unhurried whenever I want until the sun rises. Yet, it's not getting my dick inside Holly driving me. It's getting to know what's inside Holly that makes her tick.

"Why does Bhod school me on Fleetwood Mac?"

"They were one of my dad's favorites." She smiles, but there's a world of hurt hidden behind it.

I nod, encouraging "Oh yeah?" so she'll continue.

"My parents loved music. It's all stuff Laurel and I grew up listening to. A way of connecting to the past even though they're gone. They were desperately in love with one another, and the music they listened to was impossibly romantic in comparison to what's played nowadays. It makes us happy to remember."

"How long ago did you lose your mom and dad?"

"Long enough that them not being around is normal and not long enough that you forget you can't call them on the phone and ask silly questions… My parents flew out of Raleigh-Durham. Dad was an airline pilot and mom was a stewardess; a flight attendant just like Laurel and I were. They passed down the travel bug. Laurel is still infected." She lets go of a little laugh. "After retiring, my parents kept flying because they wanted to explore the rest of the world on their terms. They'd gone on a trip on their own and the twin-prop we'd traveled in forever as a family went down with engine problems. Neither survived their injuries."

"Damn, Holly, I'm so sorry you lost both of them like that."

"I'm not." She lifts a single shoulder. "They were so in love and they died doing what they loved. I can't imagine either having to go on without the other. The accident would have stripped them of who they were and all the joy they had. They got to meet Bhodi and Emory, and because of the schedules they kept while we were growing up, they'd raised Laurel and me to rely on one another. I sort of feel like no matter how difficult it is without them here, they understood we'd find a way of making it through."

"That's—wow. A lot more mature than I'd handle it."

"Don't worry. You'll grow up someday." Holly winks.

"Ouch." I wince. "Does my age bother you?"

"No." She focuses on my collar and says with dissatisfaction, "Mine might."

"I don't think any of the customers tonight would ever guess you have a nine-year-old at home unless you'd had Bhodi in your teens. You're beautiful, Doll." Like something out of a wet dream when she bends over the bar. "Do you have any idea how hard it is to want to cover you so no one sees you and simultaneously take all of your damn clothes off?"

Holly's nails skim my abs. "No, tell me about it," she remarks with a hint of sarcasm.

# Chapter Thirteen

*Holly*

Cary hasn't stopped peppering me with questions since we laid down.

We trade gentle touches. His fingertips skim my forearm. Mine circle the outline of his areola under his shirt. It would crush my libido believing Cary was never going to fuck me again, but I'm also tired. He's been patient and I need to study the page from his playbook and wait for the date he promised.

There's a familiarity to having Cary in my room again and something soothing about his company. I enjoy talking to him and listening to him speak. It could be Cary's job, running a big dealership—or that I've got early onset symptoms of senility—however, he doesn't act the way I expect of someone his age.

"The fifties thing?" He goes to drag a pillow under our heads and decides against it. Instead, we wind up pulling down the covers and lying in the bed the way normal people do.

"It was for fun at first." I cover my face, yawning wide. It makes Cary yawn too and we stupid-smile at each other. "I had some rockabilly dresses. Bhodi and Emory wore costumes to the grocery store when they were little and Laurel and I were just like, 'Why not join in?'."

We're both single moms and had nothing to lose by dressing up. The compliments are nice when you're struggling for a pep boost. The fun of it sort of morphed from there, expanding to the furniture and retro decor.

We drowsily keep up the conversation until Cary asks about my tattoo.

"I'm sleepy," I respond, rolling over on my stomach. "I'll tell you the story another time."

I have nothing to hide. I started getting ink after William left because he'd been against me doing it and I'd always wanted one. The size of my body art isn't me thumbing my nose at my ex. It's me embracing the ability to do something important to me. William's dirty feet aren't allowed in my mind while Cary is here.

Cary's thick arm tugs at my hip. He curls his body around mine. He doesn't make a move to leave or peep that he's going to go. I don't want him to either, even if it means coming up with a plausible excuse for Bhodi tomorrow.

Blackout shades are wondrous things. You have no clue if it's morning or night, rainy or sunny when they're drawn. Like an interior room on a cruise ship, you can lose all sense of space and time.

I'm drowning in extreme fatigue using my pillow as a life preserver. The only reason I know I'm still breathing is Cary's scent filling my nose. It changes depending on if he's been in the service center shop or has had motor oil on his hands, but the underlying tone is a woodsy sweet tobacco and fruit with a hint of vanilla.

I move my head, languishing in the warmth of the covers. My nose twitches, seeking out the smell that's not as pungent now that my face isn't buried in the pillowcase.

"Goooood Morning!" Laurel flings back the curtains. Light floods my bedroom, blinding me even with my eyes closed.

My arm flails, trying to hide my face from the sun, and my right hand hits something hard. It's not the body I expect to find there, which makes my "Mother of God, what are you doing!" screech at Laurel a little more palatable for my sister. She hasn't actually walked in on me in bed with Cary.

I rub my eyes as they adjust to the light and my hands become streaked with caked black eyeliner. I can't imagine what kind of a train wreck I resemble, and I've never been so happy to not be mortified with embarrassment.

"You've slept long enough." My sister informs me.

I want to hate her, though waking me is for my own good. The days I work are all over the map, but the time of day I go in for is consistent. Staying in bed throws off the cadence. I wind up late and forgetful. Laurel's doing her best to help me avoid that trap.

"How was the party?"

"Let's say Jake broke up the celebrations early."

"Oooh, that bad?"

I've told Laurel time and again I wish I understood what gets into Jake. He needs therapy.

Reaching for the object I hit, I bring a ceramic Tiki head to my lap. It's got one of those coils sticking out of the top to place snapshots in. In front of a silly picture of me and Bhodi is a scribbled note on ridiculous floral paper. I pluck it out to read the message.

*Had to run to a meeting. Didn't want to wake you.*

*Will call with the wedding deets.*

*—Be there or be square, Cary*

I giggle at the winky face and let out a girly sigh that piques Laurel's curiosity. She leans in and finishes the note aloud. There's a curved arrow drawn in the direction of the second sentence.

"*Ps. I have no chill when it comes to you, so don't freak if it's tomorrow. I need a nap first...* What does he mean about wedding details?"

"Cary's friend is getting married next weekend, and they were at Sweet Caroline's last night for the stag party. He asked me to go because he didn't have a date."

Laurel does a double-take between me and the note. She regards my rumpled clothes and breaks into hysterical laughter.

"Stop!" I demand she quit her cackling.

"Please, please tell me sex with him is good. You wouldn't give a crumb before, and I let it go."

"I'm dressed." I motion to my wrinkled shirt.

"You're also being no fun at all."

"Apparently, *you* are the only one who thinks that." I steal the note back, slipping it in a Moleskine notebook by my lamp.

What Cary and I are doing is a mystery to me. I'm persnickety about men. I don't date anyone in the military anymore or older guys, so crossing younger ones off of the list wasn't a hardship. Cary isn't what he seems at first glance. When he's around and attentive to Bhodi, I feel a little less alone. And I can't deny there is a powerful connection between us during our midnight discussions about everything and nothing. The ease of being with him when my son isn't part of the picture is unexpected and reassuring.

"Do you like him?" Laurel's expression softens and her tone is like one she used asking about a cute boy when we were teenagers.

I hear the remnants of loneliness in her voice. The ones she tries to hide when the two of us joke around about men and sex.

I pick at the sheet instead of answering.

"Hol, I think he likes you more than you're ready to admit he may. You can't close yourself off to love forever. We have to hold out hope there are more Carys in the world than Williams or we're doomed. And you've already jumped the biggest hurdle a single mom has with dating. Cary loves Bhodi."

I know my sister is right. Yet, the only thing that would hurt more than losing my heart is breaking my son's when a man I'm seeing calls it quits. I've never introduced Bhodi to anyone I've been out with for that very reason. I want to believe someone who leaves a sweet note on my pillow wouldn't let a romantic relationship's end ruin a friendship, especially one with the kid whose life I'm responsible for putting back together.

We're navigating such a slippery slope. For Bhodi, Cary is everything he lost out on; a mentor, a good male role model, a big brother, the sort of best buddy relationship with a father similar to what Laurel and I had with our mom. When we're together, I risk upending that. For what? In the light of day, my selfishness in the alley and Jake's office punches me squarely in the nose.

Laurel places her hand on mine before she gets up to leave. "Do me a favor? Don't think about what can go wrong. Focus on what's going right. So what if Cary's not what you had in mind for forever when you were his age? It doesn't mean he can't be your now."

The problem is, Cary is what I had in mind for eternity when I was his age, and my experience has taught me it's too late for forever.

I smooth my hands down the front of the dress I have on. Baby blue satin with a bateau neckline. The hem ends at my knee. I'm hoping it's classic enough to stand the test of time. My fingers are clammy and I inspect the rolls of ruching that bunch from underneath my chest to below my hips, making sure there are no sweat marks.

I've applied more deodorant than my son agrees to wear in a month. Although that's not saying much, seeing I'm the one to do his laundry and most of his clothes could get up and walk away on their own.

I've never been so unsure of a casual date before. I mean, Cary laid out his expectations when he asked me to go to Glen's wedding. We're  having sex afterward. So, why am I nervous when I'm not the one getting married?

The bell rings and my heart stops in at Baked Beans for coffee and a bagel before it resets its rhythm. I nearly faint waiting. And then the funniest feeling flows over me. I may think I've been freaking out about choosing the right dress so I don't draw undue attention away from the bride or leave other guests snickering behind Cary's back, but it was actually the fear he'd leave me high and dry. That I'd gotten my hopes up about someone wanting me for nothing. Because that's what I know.

Seeing his silhouette on the other side of the door, the anxiety fades. He's here.

"Right on time!" My red-stained lips curl up, likely giving away how thrilled I am when I answer his knock.

I'm pushed back into the hall by a bulk of rayon and stuffing. Cary's carrying three brand new sleeping bags with the tags still on them.

"Bhodi knows right?" Cary buzzes like a bee. If I didn't know any better, I'd think he was on something.

"Uh, yeah? He's in the living room watching TV with Laurel and Emory." I shake my head at Cary's goofy grin, unable to hide the way I'm smiling back.

We'd discussed the importance of being honest with Bhodi, but only giving him the information he needs and letting him ask questions if there are any blanks to fill in.

My son's response to me going out with Cary? A very blasé "okay" before turning his attention back to a Lego set. Emory on the other hand… Let's simply say I was cordially invited to Barbie's double-ring ceremony and she and Ken have renewed their vows several times this week.

Cary flits down the hall. His exuberance calls to mind the way Bhodi and his buddies scamper for the video game console when a new game releases. Cary's acting like a trick-or-treater on Halloween, eager to sort and share his stash of candy. I want to be upset that he hasn't said hello to me, but this child-like buoyancy is endearing.

I saunter in high heels to the living room, listening to excited voices. Leaning against the jamb, I cross my arms over my middle. For as lit as Cary is, I'm equally calm, enjoying the sight of him making my son his priority.

Bhodi rips the tag off of a navy blue sleeping bag

and has it out of the sleeve in record time.

"No pink at the store, Emory. Only purple. Think you can survive?"

"I love purple!" She hugs the roll, her still chubby arms too short to fit snug around it.

Cary helps her unfurl it the way her cousin has.

"Who is that one for?" Bhodi asks from the carpet. He slides in between the layers, reclining on a couch cushion he's using as a pillow.

"Me! We have to practice for the big brother campout. Test the gear!" Cary's level of enthusiasm makes it hard for the kids to sit still.

"Cool thanks!"

My sister voices how incredibly sweet it is that Cary included Emory by buying her a sleeping bag too. I couldn't agree more.

"What do you say, Emory?" Laurel prods.

"Fank you, Mister Cary."

"You guys will be out like a light when your mom and I get back, but you gotta save me a spot here on the floor." He points at the rug, continuing to talk a mile a minute.

"We will!" They shout in unison.

"We have to go." He turns to look at me. His face blanks and his eyes darken.

I peer at what I'm wearing. No visible stains. I'm not sure what— Ooh.

As he stands, Cary adjusts his dark dress pants and the lapels of a tailor-made jacket. It's the first full view I've gotten of him and my mouth goes dry. His beard is clipped and the nape of his neck trimmed. The double-breasted suit fits him like a glove.

"Have fun." My sister sings, and Emory waves.

I back step into the hall, unsure he's heard their goodbyes considering the heated way he's stalking toward me like a lion chases a gazelle.

When we're out of view, Cary's palms glide against

my hips. I let him draw me closer. We had the same reaction to seeing one another.

He brushes his lips against mine with a restraint I'm not sure I'd manage if he wasn't.

"No sleeping bag for me?" I ask, pouting my lip.

"I have other sleeping arrangements for you."

# Chapter Fourteen

*Cary*

I have never been so damn nervous about a date in my entire life. Even though I've texted with Holly, we haven't been around one another this week.

It's become normal lately for me to pick Bhodi up from school and bring him to the dealership. We tinker with whatever the guys have on the hood open for in the shop. This week, I'd been looking forward to a glimpse of her when dropping Bhodi at the condo afterward, but the shit hit the fan in the corporate office when one of our higher vehicle line's transport trucks got in an accident on I-40. The insurance adjuster has had Cass-Stanton Group jumping through hoops. Upon hearing my CFO reportedly signed off on paperwork for upwards of two hundred and fifty thousand dollars in destroyed secondary market inventory, I wanted to puke.

Still, that day my company was in the limelight and the responsibility fell on my shoulders. It was the first bad thing to happen on my watch. Nobody cared if I've only officially been in charge for a few months.

They would've used my age against me had I not done the right thing, inspected the damage personally, and drafted a statement about our transportation safety history and reliability in the communities we serve. There are a million people in the Research Triangle, and damage control for screwing up their afternoon commute remained my focus.

I felt like an ass for bagging on Bhodi and called Laurel's phone—a number I've had in case of emergency—later that night, asking to talk to him so I could apologize. The little dude was excited that he'd seen the aerial footage of the crumpled truck on the news. I didn't have the heart to tell him it was one hell of a headache for me. I was just glad he wasn't pissed.

I'm toeing a fine line with him and Holly and never want Bhodi getting the wrong idea. He wasn't a means to an end to get in his mom's pants. I want to spend time with both of them, separately and together. I hadn't realized two people could demand so much of my attention, nor the guilt of trying to split it evenly. Since the truck accident, the only thought running through my mind has been how not to blow it with either of them.

Wrapped up in the two of them, my playlists shuffled through bands I know doing covers of songs Holly likes on the way to the store this morning to get the sleeping bags. Picking them out, my mind replayed Bhodi's uncorrupted question about why we had the "sleepover" without him.

Fuck, Holly was on the ball with her reply. Nobody's fooling anybody tonight. I'm spending the night at the condo and waking up there in the morning. If I need to rely on my wits, then it's better to have a plan from the beginning to make them both feel special.

Amped, I pretty much barge into Laurel's place and power past Holly to get to the kids. Their reaction is as if Santa has come down the chimney in spring. It reminds me that while these kids don't go without, they also aren't spoiled. I'm starting to believe part of it is the throwback fun Holly and Laurel have living this way. The perception of values and morals of days gone by. Yes, Holly earns her living working for human trash like Jake Ballentine, but Carver Galloway defends her and I've never known him to be less than upstanding.

My counselor crams down my throat it's the sum of the parts—good and bad—which make a person whole. I couldn't contrast that to my situation before meeting Holly. She's given a fresh perspective to the way I feel about the man Rex tried to shape me into. The things I've done in my past don't determine my future, and I see how Holly's choice to work at Sweet Caroline's isn't as much about her as what she can do for her child with a good paying job.

I'll also admit, listening to the dancer shoot off her mouth, I had a little bit of pride when Holly stood her ground. She has backbone, and I'm not troubled in the least with anyone finding out I'm dating the hot manager at a gentlemen's club that's been around longer than I have.

Laurel prompts Emory to thank me. The expression Holly's sister doesn't hide well proves I'm a court jester, rambling a mile a minute.

I hadn't wanted to be late for the wedding. For Bhodi to believe we rushed out without him. Or Emory's feelings to get hurt because she didn't get a sleeping bag. Most of all, though? I've worried leaving a note on Holly's pillow appeared sleazy instead of a mild attempt at something she'd view as romantic, and I can't wait to get my arms around her.

Buttoning my suit jacket, I stand up, say goodbye

to Laurel and the kids, and turn my attention to Holly.

The word breathtaking doesn't do justice to what I'm seeing.

I pat my lapels down flat and hope I haven't screwed up all the freakin' ironing I did on my slacks by playing on the floor. It's for damn sure I'm going to be the man on her arm, not the other way around.

She's transformed herself into a classic movie actress and elegant fails to describe how drop-dead gorgeous Holly is. I finally understand why fans go ape shit over their icons, needing the tiniest piece of them to hold on to. I've never wanted to touch anyone so much and it is sheer willpower I'm able to walk over to Holly without falling at her feet.

Holly backs into the hall and the desire to show the world what I have is the only thing stopping me from giving chase into her bedroom. Especially when I've managed some restraint when I kiss her and she saucily asks, "No sleeping bag for me?"

If we ever go camping, I'm making her share mine.

Holly pouts her lip and I tug her close enough for my body to betray how affected I am. The way she responds, squeezing my biceps, I think it gives her a thrill. I'm conscientious tucking my nose to her neck and trailing my lips over her baby soft skin. Kissing Holly the way those lips deserve ravishing means I'm going to ruin her lipstick. I won't risk a simple smudge wrecking our night.

We make it to the ceremony minutes before the bride and find an uptight wooden pew on the groom's side. The ushers watched her enter the church. A few women have checked her out too, though it's possible they like her blue dress. What I don't know about women fills all twenty-six hardbound installments of the *Encyclopedia Britannica* Gramps had on his bookshelf, and I doubt any of it is available online.

Likely I'm biased, but I'm certain Holly's stolen the show.

"Maybe I should have gotten you a sleeping bag," I comment, uncomfortable with everyone's attention on her. *To wear* is implied.

"Jealous?" She teases, tickling my side.

"Nah, you're all mine." I wink.

"You seem awfully sure of yourself."

I am. I've calmed down and can feel the warmth of her next to me. I'm definitely more confident until the preacher gets to the vows. While my mind is wandering in one direction, Holly's tightly balled fists and rigid posture mean she's someplace else entirely.

I haven't asked why her marriage fell apart. It opens me up to having to be truthful about the nasty shit in my life. I reach for her hand and place it on my thigh, bringing her back into the moment with a gentleness I didn't know I was capable of. She's too pretty to be sad.

Later in the receiving line, Glen introduces himself to Holly and, like any good teacher, shares anecdotes about Bhodi. She's gracious, not letting on that they've already met. He was too drunk to remember.

Before leaving the church, the bride tosses the bouquet and two overzealous bridesmaids volley the roses back into the air. They're disappointed when it lands in Holly's hands since she was standing outside the circle, trying to give them ample room.

She brings the flowers to her nose before looking to where I stand on a granite slab. Her shy smile hits me where it hurts. While driving to the reception, I'm devising a scheme to reap more rewards than the dealership gives incentive bonuses to the salesforce.

There's a break in the dancing after the waitstaff serves the chicken when the DJ calls the single men to gather on the parquet. The groomsmen, who've enjoyed the open bar, push and shove. The calamity of elbows is all the encouragement I need to gain the upper hand. My grip furls around the bride's garter, noticing a blue ribbon running through it that matches the color of Holly's dress. It was meant to be hers all along.

I don't make a gaudy show of slipping the garter over her toes. I plan to treat this woman with respect. Always. But that doesn't mean the chance to lean in and kiss her is escaping. Every guest sees we're together.

We haven't gotten that intimate all night, and it opens the floodgates. I want to fuck her, but we proved last weekend we could wait. Holly's infectious laugh at my flirting and dumb jokes confirms she's enjoying herself and so am I. We shouldn't stop on my dick's account. All that does is bring midnight closer, Monday, work, and waiting for next weekend to see her again for a few minutes before she leaves for the club. I'll stay frozen here on the dance floor with my arms around her while she listens to my heart beat for as long as she'll have me.

"Cary?"

"Yeah, Doll?" I touch my chin to the top of her hair. It flows down around her shoulders in silky waves. My whiskers won't mess it up.

"It's late. The kids are probably asleep."

"Do we chance waking them?"

"I can be quiet, if you can… And if you can't, I know where my sister keeps her silk scarves," she says with the most innocent eyes.

Mine bug out and Holly spins. I catch her and drag her back against my chest, tucking my nose to her ear.

"You say the dirtiest things."

She stops wriggling and giggling and jerks a defiant chin. "Only to you."

I slide a controlled hand over her ass instead of

giving it a hard slap.

God, who knew a woman could be so much fun? The freaky clothes, the weird-ass music, the mouth. When I'm near her, I tend to forget we've only slept together once.

Back at the condo, we use my phone's flashlight to tip-toe into her room and close the door. Holly bends, switching on the lamp. I'm sitting in the shell chair near where I've dropped a bag of stuff I'll need in the morning and pull her onto my lap.

She snuggles in with her legs draped to the side, wrapping her arms around my middle. I fiddle with the straps and buckles on her heels and place them on the floor. When I'm done, I lift my hips, nudging her with my cock. Holly moves so I can lower the zipper on her dress while holding the front in place.

My palm is cupping satin and before she shrugs the top down, exposing her bare shoulder, it's apparent the layers of cloth have hidden her unbound breast. She can walk the walk. But underneath? Holly isn't changing who she is for anyone. It's sexy as hell and appeals to my other senses too.

Holly gets up with her back to me and I unzip the rest of her dress. She turns and lets it puddle on the floor, revealing a lacy white thong. Inches below is the garter. The panties may come off, but I'm fucking her with that perfect circle banded to her flesh.

"Gonna let me take care of you, Doll?" My knuckles skim her thigh, and I place a delicate kiss between the two separate ruffles of lace.

Holly cradles my beard in her hands. Her chest rises and falls. Her pulse is pounding fast. I glance up and she's licking those still red lips.

My question isn't about the here and now. If she gives herself to me tonight, I'll keep returning.

# Chapter Fifteen

*Holly*

Rising to my feet with my back to Cary, my heart rate ticks up. By the time I've turned, and the dress lies in a lump I have to step over to get closer to him, it's pounding outside my chest.

It may be the anticipation talking—after all, we didn't stop fooling around once, but got interrupted twice last weekend—however, I've never wanted someone like I do Cary. It's an odd sense of "what you see is what you get". He's not hiding anything. And if he is, it's trivial; Something that won't matter to me the same way my past won't change where we are in this moment. He can be my now. I've already proven I'm capable of picking up the pieces of a shattered heart.

Cary tucks his nose to my leg. His lips make contact with my skin. In a gravelly voice I feel at the apex of my thighs, he asks permission to take this further.

Flashes of the alley behind Sweet Caroline's flood to the forefront of my mind. Cary's so close to where

I'd needed him. Though, perhaps neither of us had the foresight to comprehend simply being together was exactly what we both needed. Whatever taut thread of passion holding us together won't fray overnight.

Cupping his cheeks, I lick my lips and nod.

Believe it or not, the woman who has been flirting back is an untapped part of my personality I'm trying on for size. I first met her at work, learning to mix drinks. She's never seen the light of day, let alone been on a date before. I like how her boldness matches the rest of me. She gives me the confidence to keep going with Cary while the wounded side of me screams to run the other way.

I'm strong enough to choose fleeting happiness. I've put my son first while nursing my wounded pride once. I can do it again. The distraction of making sure Bhodi is all right will make it hurt less. We'll cross that bridge when the road forks.

I steel myself for what's next, both physically and mentally. I heard the rumble in his chest as he asked to take care of me. I've agreed to more than sex.

Cary slides the lacy thong down my leg and is slow to stand, admiring every inch of my nakedness.

His hand goes to his belt buckle and mine to his collar, loosening his tie and unbuttoning each circular pearl. He stops my progress after I've gotten the second undone.

I look up at him and find myself shy. "I've never undressed a man in a suit before."

His dark eyes bore into me. "I'll give you a crash course." His grip tightens over my hands and he pulls them apart. I heard the tear of fabric and buttons scattering across the wood floor.

Our lips meet in a heady crush. I push Cary's shirt off his shoulders while he removes his pants. He lowers me to the bed, caressing the garter like it's a security blanket and refusing to remove it. Then he parts my knees.

"Wide," he demands, setting my heels on the mattress and dragging my bottom to the edge.

I blink, almost startled that something can feel so wrong and yet simultaneously so right.

Cary's form dips down to kneel. As if I'm unable to follow a simple directive, he needles his fingers into my ass, pushing his thumbs into the junctures of my thighs, and holding me in place. Pleasure and pain mix. My back arches off the bed at the sensation. Trying to get away. Trying to move closer. I understand the tension in his grip now. The way he licks and sucks erases all the false and judgmental reasons why dating Cary is wrong from my mind.

He can be mine for this tiny fraction of time. And I can be his.

My thoughts jumble and travel elsewhere with the consistent ministrations of his tongue darting in and out of my most private parts. I'm spread bare for him in the lamplight. But would he have done this in the alley? And if we hadn't gotten interrupted in Jake's office, what would those mirrors reveal about me? I've seen pleasure on Cary's face, but what of mine? And what's with his penchant for watching?

I tilt my chin and look between the valley of my breasts. Cary's mouth is on the tender bundle of nerves, but his eyes are on me. I search for something dirty to say to egg him on, but Cary moves his left arm and I feel the invasion of his thick fingers and the words get trapped in my throat. He needs no encouragement.

My splayed legs shake. Cary moves his right grip up toward my knee, bringing that limb closer to his ear as if he likes nothing more than burying his face in my pussy. My left hand rubs against the hard peaks of my nipples and my right hand dips low. I'm able to touch the hair on his cheek if I stretch my fingertips.

Our eyes connect, and I see the spark of the devil. Not a man out to do harm, but one experienced enough to bring me to the brink and for whom the sins of the flesh he's developed an undeniable fondness for.

I let this level of unabashed persuasion guide me to the point of no return, allowing Cary to steer me as I crash down and he wrings the last flutters from my body.

In a rush of pure male satisfaction, Cary has the condom out of his wallet and me shimmying to make room for him on the bed.

I brace myself for his swift infusion into my body, perhaps because it's what I want. However, Cary is slow to push inside of me. Along with him, I watch his rigid length disappear. It's as glorious as my misaligned expectations of rough sex.

Cary leans toward me. My nails rake his sides, trying to draw him closer.

"Not giving you a chance to forget any longer how good we are together, Holly." He kisses me and regains his position on his knees, pulling my legs over his shoulders and pistoning his cock into my slick core.

I meet him stroke for stroke. So close himself, Cary's unrelenting as the second wave of bliss makes the dirty words I reply to his with incoherent. And when I have nothing left, he holds my ass, using it to leverage how deep he spills inside of me.

Grunting, Cary lets go. My legs slide to the mattress and he collapses forward, panting. Neither of us can catch our breaths. He nuzzles my neck. We kiss with reverent touches. I hold him inside of me until we have no choice but to part.

Cary pulls something to wear out of his overnight bag and goes across the hall to the bathroom to clean up.

My eyes have drifted closed by the time he comes back. He pulls the sheet over me but doesn't get under the covers.

"You okay?" He lies on top, blanketing his body over mine.

"I don't think I can move a muscle."

He laughs quietly and kisses me. "You're stroking my ego, Doll. But I sort of like having you trapped. Means you can't go anywhere… and I have to leave."

My brow furrows, but my heart brims when Cary continues.

"I promised someone else a sleepover tonight." Cary lifts on his elbows.

"Thank you." I trace the line of Cary's jaw with my fingernail.

"For what?"

"For making Bhodi feel important. You didn't have to buy him anything. I could have done that."

"Both are why I did. The kid means a lot to me, Holly. I'm not taking this lightly. I have to come through for him to have a chance with you and vice versa. Don't think I'm blind to what I'm taking on—"

I stop his earnest soliloquy with my lips, our tongues meet with velvety sweeps, and the kisses end with little pecks at the corner of one another's mouths.

My legs have separated and my lower half cradles Cary's pelvis. We're not going hot and heavy, but the friction is building. The cocky smirk on his face proves I'm making it harder for Cary to do the right thing. He told Bhodi he'd sleep in the living room. Once more and I'll share.

The morning noises in the rest of the condo are louder than usual. I get up and walk out of my room, pausing long enough to swipe a clean washcloth over my face in the hallway bathroom.

I can't see the living room carpet under the forest of sleeping bags, couch cushions, pillows, and blankets. Whatever happened, I missed out on some serious fun while catching some Zs.

Walking into the kitchen, I spy a pajama-clad Bhodi and a shirtless Cary hovering over the waffle iron. They are happily chatting about their upcoming camping trip. Emory, in a princess nightgown, hefts a jug of milk on the table and sets out her favorite jelly jar glasses with cartoon animals on them for us to drink from. My sister's wearing a blush to go with her matching cotton top and bottoms.

"What?" I mouth, wishing we had telepathy.

Just then Cary moves out from behind the island, giving me a full view of why Laurel's shit-eating grin is so wide. The outline of his dick is visible beneath the flimsy running shorts. As he moves across the room approaching me, it bounces.

My sister smartly stays behind Cary. Her lips make an "O".

Cary looks over his shoulder as she goes still as a statue and her expression blanks. He laughs.

With burning cheeks, Laurel says she's getting ready for the day and to save her a plate. She heads upstairs. Honestly, if I could crawl into a hole and die for her, I would.

Cary greets me, chastely pressing his mouth to my forehead. I reach for an apron hanging from the nearest peg. Slipping it over his neck, I tie it and mumble, "You wouldn't want to get burned from spattered grease."

He adjusts the apron over his bare chest as if it's no big deal and cups my cheek. "Safety first. And you know, added benefit of your sister holding a discussion with me and not my junk. She does understand the one-eyed monster doesn't talk back, right?"

I snort, covering my nose. "You could have come in to get your shirt."

"I didn't want to wake you," he says in a tone sweet enough to melt me into a rambling puddle of goo.

"Laurel's not," I stammer. "She doesn't mean to make you uncomfortable. It's been sisters against the world—"

Cary puts his arm around my waist, cutting off my words with the lone action. He's cognizant of what I'm trying to explain without me needing to go on.

"It's ready!" Bhod calls as the waffle iron timer goes off.

"On my way, man." The corners of his mouth lift responding to my son. Cary is quick to give Bhodi his attention.

"I can do it."

"I know you can, but wait and show off those mad breakfast skills to your mom." Cary takes my hand, pulling me along to the waffle making station. "Safety," he remarks to me with a swagger in his step. Then he warns Bhodi, "Careful. It's hot," and I'm aware he's the one not ready to let my son do this alone.

With steady assurances from Cary that he's doing everything right, Bhodi's got the perfect waffle plated. My son dips the ladle into the batter, adding more to the iron like a pro.

Emory hippity-hops over to Cary. He jumps her

onto his hip and the three of them count down, waiting for the next waffle to finish cooking.

I tuck my upper half into the fridge, searching for the syrup, and when I pop out the nostalgic image of the three of them hits a place deep in my soul.

The players may not be what I'd envisioned, but this is what I'd thought my life would look like on a weekend morning.

Cary

"Take this. And this. And don't forget this." I load Bhodi's flat forearms with camping equipment from the trunk of my car. The pile reaches above his head.

He turns around laughing, trying to steady it all, and takes a few paces toward the front steps like a tightrope walker.

"I'm kidding, Half-pint. Get back here." I wave him to my side and pluck a few of the more precarious things off the pile.

Bhodi thanks me and yet somehow manages to drop three perfectly stacked items on the way to the door. With each goofy and apologetic glance over his shoulder to say sorry to me, I wind up tucking one more thing the kid has dropped under my armpit to bring inside.

I use the spare key to unlock the front door. By the time we hit the hallway, we're poking jabs at one another and joking about silly things that happened on the big brother camp out.

We had a ton of fun during the overnight at a local

lake. The boys swam and we played baseball, hiked, and fished off of a dock. There were s'mores around a fire pit before the dog-tired and grubby kids hunkered down in their sleeping bags. Which reminds me...

"Dude, hit the shower before your Aunt Laurel gets on you."

Bhodi's dumped his belongings on the couch and is on a return trip to the car for more. His lip curls in disgust, but I'm pretty sure he's nose blind to himself like all the other pre-pubescent boys were.

Was I like this? Probably.

Every-so-often I consider asking Davina. Then the idea goes away. My mother spends most of her time on the Outer Banks, squatting in my beach house. I concurrently flit back-and-forth between the condo and the house I was raised in depending on Holly's work schedule.

If I was a smarter man, I'd choose one permanent spot to live in, but coming up on three months of dating, my moving into Laurel's home is tacky. Even if Holly and I had been together longer, I couldn't let her and Bhodi stay at Rex's. There are too many fucked up memories there. Now, if I were an intelligent man, I'd boot Davina from my place and finally be able to suggest bringing them there for the weekend like I've wanted to since the days got longer and school let out.

My therapist alluded to me avoiding conflict when I'm happy. I hate the douche for being right. But why ruin a great streak of luck by dredging up the past? Am I supposed to pop every party balloon because one of them lost its helium and is a grounder?

Letting my mother's ridiculous assumption, that I need to know about the guy she screwed nearly three decades ago, get under my skin isn't going to help me move forward. If anything, I'll wind up acting like a jerk to my employees and letting that negativity seep into my personal life. No way am I fucking this up. Not when things with Holly and Bhodi are as good as they are.

I slide an incidental bag of mine that's made the trip inside next to Holly's door. I knew she'd be at the club already, but I hadn't anticipated missing her when I saw the bright space empty without her in it. The clutter of everything she owns cramming every nook and cranny aside, the bedcovers are pulled up. The journals she writes in are piled in neat stack on the nightstand and the clothes draped over the shell chair look intentional.

Bhodi and I head back out to the car to get the last of his stuff. Laurel's sedan pulls up in the spot beside my SUV. She gets out and walks toward us with a sack of groceries on one hip and Emory on the other.

"How was camping?" she asks.

We trail Laurel back towards the condo. At the steps, Emory wiggles to get down. I scoop the groceries from Laurel so she doesn't drop them while her daughter slides down her leg.

"The campground was awesome, Aunt Laurel!" Bhodi's on a high from the trip.

"That's great! I picked up ground beef for hamburgers. Are you hungry?"

"I'm starving." Bhodi twists in a mock faint.

"Okay, then. Hop in the shower and by the time you've washed all the smoke and grime off of you, I'll have the grill fired up."

The kid looks at me to save him.

"What did I tell you?" I raise a brow, taking Laurel's side.

"Stay for dinner, please?" He leans in, giving me a half-hug the way I've seen him do to Holly.

"Won't take much more than you scrubbing up to twist my arm. Laurel makes a mean burger."

"Mean like this?" Emory growls and pretends to

flex her hulking arms like a bodybuilder.

"Yes!" The brown grocery sack crinkles as I mimic her posture and the hulking sound she's making.

"No, mean like this." Bhodi roars, getting in on the act.

We all turn into grizzlies and then both kids wind up attached to my leg and stepping on my shoes as I walk around the living room. Forgetting the fact that middle school isn't too far off for Bhodi, they're cute together.

Laurel goes out back to grill our supper. It's informal, to say the least. Just beefy burgers with all the fixings, no sides but she's promised dessert.

I put the groceries where I think they belong and take kid duty. Emory's brought a big box of crayons to the kitchen table and we color together while we wait.

Through the window, I spy Laurel tapping away on her phone. She looks at me under her lashes, almost as if she doesn't want me to see what she's up to. Every time she puts her cell down, it goes off again. After the last flight of her fingers, it's silent for a beat before mine goes off.

Holly: Everything go okay?

So that's who she was texting. I should've been smart enough to figure out Laurel would let her sister know I was still here. Honestly, I appreciate it.

Me: It did. He's going to want to tell you about it, so I'm not spoiling it.

I hit send and start typing again.

Me: Hope you don't mind me staying for dinner. Bhod asked and I sorta didn't want to say no. I figured I'd stick around to see you when you got home?

Those damn little bubbles stay on my screen way too long waiting on her reply.

Holly: Wow—you really don't have chill do you?

She makes me laugh.

Me: Whatever I had left you've melted. I'm a

puddle now. I fucking missed you.

Holly responds with a video of her blowing me a kiss.

Part of me wants to tell Holly I love her. I've never said those words to anyone and I'm scared that, like the idea of moving in together, it's too soon.

Bhodi comes downstairs squeaky clean, but dripping wet like a spring rain drizzling off the oak trees which line the sidewalks surrounding the lots at the auto mall. He slides a coloring book out of the stack and chooses a crayon from the bin.

"Look, Mister Cary."

Coloring in the lines, I peek at the scribbles on Emory's sheet of paper and start to tell her what a great job she's doing. I wind up cracking up instead. Emory has a green and a yellow crayon sticking out from under her top lip like walrus tusks. When I look in the opposite direction, Bhodi's got two more sticking out of his nose.

"Dude, that's gross!" I'm falling over myself and clutching my chest at their goofiness, joining in by putting a red and a blue crayon in my ears. "Do not do this, and if you do, do not tell your moms I showed you."

Despite my warning, we wait for Laurel to come inside with the tray of burgers. She gets a kick out of us and when she asks us whose idea it was, Bhodi and Emory point fingers at each other and I point at them.

The kids are complete wild nuts while we eat. The way our trip to the woods was, it's awesome.

*Why didn't I have a sister?* I think. Well, that's obvious. Nobody in their right mind would want more kids raised under Rex Stanton's roof.

However, Bhodi's a different story. I've seen how amazing he is with someone Emory's age. He gets along well with Dusty's daughter Sylvie Rhys too. My protectiveness of Bhodi makes me feel like he's missing out on something important.

By the time Laurel serves banana pudding with vanilla wafers, they've settled down.

"This is my favorite," Bhodi says, around a mouthful of cut banana.

"Mine too. My mom used to make…" I stop with the spoon in mid-air.

The memory of Davina when I was a kid comes flooding back. My mother and I had late afternoons like this one once upon a time. She baked cookies and helped with homework. It hadn't seemed to be important or to have made much of a difference while it was happening. Yet, all of a sudden I see the intent in Rex's refusal to come home a decent hour and sit at the dinner table with us. He was the one who took the back seat in parenting until he'd laid the framework to make me think Davina didn't care. That she was willingly disregarding his licentiousness. The hitch is, I'm still too indignant when it comes to Davina to do anything about whatever this epiphany is.

# Chapter Seventeen

*Holly*

The television is still on when I enter the room. Cary lies on his back with the covers low on his hips. There's a hint of his cotton boxers and the trail of dark hair I love to explore peeking out from under the sheet. Shadows and tints of color play on his relaxed jaw and the skin of his torso the way they do on clients watching the show at the club.

Warm from the July heat still radiating off the blacktop in the middle of the night, I toe off my shoes and socks and pull my white tank top over my head, shedding my work clothes. Then I slide over the mattress like a sloth and reach for the remote beside him to turn off the TV. Too lazy to roll toward my nightstand, I tuck it under my pillow, planting my face in the fluffy cotton.

Cary shifts next to me. He kisses my still pinned hair. Worry laces his sleep-graveled voice over how late it is. "Good night?"

I mummer back something incoherent. I should have been home an hour ago.

Kelsey, the new assistant manager, is working out well. The issue cropping up is the dancer from before likes to make trouble on the nights I'm off. The lack of respect sends everyone else off-kilter. Most recently, she'd tried to get her claws into Jake. He isn't long for a solitary woman, but there's an occasional one who warms his bed more than twice and he's been busy with a cocktail waitress he hired.

This caused an uproar between the dancer and waitress and a series of catfights ensued. Feeling like the employee he was sleeping with had become a clinger, Jake has given me permission to let both of them go. Of course, now I'm stuck trying to be the best person I can be and waiting for a reason that's more legit than getting let go for sucking the owner's dick.

I keep having to put out little fires and appease frayed nerves. I feel like a failure compared to Kimber, despite her telling me on our last mill girls' day out how she slogged through the same scenario a dozen times when she was the manager.

She also reminded me that for every stripper who thinks they'll make the big time tied to Jake, there's a dressing room full of dancers trying to make ends meet, feed their kids, and use the cash they earn to build a better life. I've seen that firsthand, and it's part of the reason I stay.

"You okay?"

"Sure. Some nights I wonder why I do this, though."

"Why do you?"

"Complacency? Comfort? My closest friends show up when I least expect it. I'm not ready to leave it behind the way they are. Maybe I worry if I do, there won't be anything out there for me, and I'll have lost what I had."

"You've got me." Cary's fingertips trace the curved

lines of my ass. The feather-soft touch sends anticipatory chills up my tense spine. "I tried waiting up for you."

"Why?" I ask. Except his wandering fingertips make it obvious.

"I started thinking about how hot you always look leaving for work and if any guys you served tonight wanted to take you into an alcove and close the curtain. How many of them were interested in sticking their cocks into your honeypot."

Cary's hand dips between my legs, and my body tightens at his words. No one's talked dirty to me with the candor he does.

After we started dating, Cary and I made a deal for him to stay away from Sweet Caroline's. Unless I, Carver, or someone associated with the club invited him to a bigger event, Cary sticks to his world filled with upstanding citizens. Although, I'd never admitted my main reason behind it was I hadn't wanted to watch women looking at him with the same appreciation club clientele appreciates the dancers. Aside from female staff members, we have plenty of female guests. Tonight when Laurel texted to say he was staying for dinner, I was thrilled. But I also found myself wanting him closer and for Cary to sit on the stool Trig used to occupy. He can't do that at night and get to the dealership in time for him to do his job the next day.

It wasn't the first time having a third shift job put a crimp in my life. I'm falling for Cary, but I can't give it up. I put my future on the line for a man before. Bhodi and I need the security if Cary comes to his senses and finds someone his own age.

"Are you jealous?" I ask, hiding my misgivings.

"No." His lips flutter against my shoulder. "They can stare all they want. This sweetness is all mine."

I yawn. Cary moves his palm, caressing up toward

my spine, and rests his hands on my lower back. With the action, a part of me is disappointed. The massage had loosened my tight muscles.

"You're not going to put your cock in me?" I frown, missing the closeness of making love to him.

"I like active participation, Doll."

"Having an orgasm is participating."

Cary chuckles in the dark. "Rest. I'll be here when you wake."

The air in the room is still. I've got cottonmouth and the beginning of a dehydration headache. Curious, because I don't drink on the clock.

I kick the sheet off of my sticky legs and flop them over the mattress onto the floor. The wood under the soles of my feet lacks its usual coolness. I sneer, making an ugly ass face, wiping the sleep away from my eyes, and stretching. I'm not a morning person, I pretend to be one for everyone else's sake.

On the other side of the door, I hear wing-tipped footsteps and Cary's voice. I'm glad he hasn't left for the dealership, but I can't take comfort in his promise that he'll make love to me before leaving. He's already dressed for work.

I'm a sweaty mess. I throw on something cute so he'll ignore my bedhead and the bags under my eyes from working Friday through Sunday. Then I head for the kitchen, hoping there's coffee left in the pot to perk me up and time to have a cup with him.

Cary's begun spending the night here when I'm not on the schedule at Sweet Caroline's. Yesterday was the first time that he hung out for the evening while I was at work.

With the boys gone, there was no reason for me to sit at home. I'd juggled shifts and given Kelsey Saturday off and enjoyed the extra cash the clients passed my way. Normally, it's a day of the week I hoard for myself so I can see Cary more often on the weekends and enjoy a stretch of the summer. Unless it's a couples' thing, we take Bhodi wherever we go. I'm not included on big brother event weekends for obvious reasons. It doesn't bother me. Though admittedly, I was down in the dumps not being here when they got in from the campout to ask my boys about the fun they had.

With her cell to her ear, my sister is pacing by the kitchen table. Cary is doing the same near the sink.

"That's the soonest we can get a service call?" Laurel's jaw scrapes the linoleum. She ends the call and slumps defeated in a chair nearby my plants on the windowsill.

"I don't know when I'll be in, maybe lunch? Something's come up. Hold on." He covers the receiver to talk to Laurel. "What's happening?"

"Another company that's backed up. Two days to get out here to even look at the unit. Another seven to ten if it needs replacing."

Cary blows out a breath and returns to his call. "Hey, can you text me the name of our HVAC repair? The air conditioning is out at my girlfriend's place. Her sister has called three companies and is getting nowhere."

I notice the pit stains on Cary's shirt and that the temperature didn't drop when I walked out of my bedroom. It's got to be over eighty degrees in the entire condo. No wonder my skin is sticky.

"Where are the kids?" I ask Laurel.

She motions outside. "Filling the kiddie pool. It's a sauna on the second floor."

"As if it's not down here."

The crease in my sister's forehead proves she agrees.

We peer over the plants, watching Bhodi and Emory use the garden hose while Cary takes a second call. He hangs up and walks up behind us. Wrapping his arms around my upper shoulders and tugging me against his chest, he kisses the back of my head. We're quicker to part because it's stifling.

"Hot enough for you?" he jests before acknowledging a questioning look on Laurel's face. "Good news is my guy can be here this afternoon. Bad news is he's saying the same thing. If it's busted, you're looking at seven days to order and install a new system. Middle of the summer is not when you want your air conditioner to die."

"What was I thinking asking for the house in the divorce?" My sister throws up her hands in frustration.

"That you were keeping a roof over your daughter's head?" My right cheek bunches.

I feel awful for Laurel. She's responsible for everything that breaks, and the cost of this repair is mammoth. We'll figure out a payment plan with the service company. At least I can pitch in for more than I could have if this happened a few months ago. My son and I live here too, and I won't leave the burden up to Laurel.

"How are we going to manage the heat until it's fixed?" She's ready to cry.

"I've got two ideas," Cary suggests. "I can run out to get a bunch of window air conditioners at the hardware store. Dusty is over at Cece's. Laurel called him first for recommendations and he offered to help me set them up if I ran into any trouble." He informs me.

"We can't let you do that. It's too expensive."

Laurel balks.

In agreement, but seeing few other options, I run for my purse. "What's the second idea?" I question, searching my wallet for the hundred or so I made in tips Sunday night.

"How do you ladies feel about an all-expenses paid beach vacation?"

Laurel insists Bhodi and I go to the Outer Banks alone with Cary, but he won't hear of letting my sister stay behind to swelter. It takes a lot of smooth-talking on Cary's part and coercion from me to get my sister to call in sick. She also has to contact Emory's dad to adjust my niece's visitation schedule.

Laurel's ex, Bennett, doesn't offer to help with the air conditioner repair bill, but he also doesn't stand in my sister's way when she lets him know the reason for the impromptu trip. What Bennett's most concerned about is seeing his daughter, and they agree he can have Emory an extra day each of the next few weeks to make up for it.

Amazingly, there are men like my former brother-in-law who give a damn about their children.

Cary leaves us to pack and I log onto Sweet Caroline's scheduling system. I put in for my vacation time and flip a few of the stronger employees around so Kelsey has good back-up if anything goes awry. Then I call her about the changes, whip off a text to Morgan and the guys who hang at the mill asking if they'll check in on her, and finally hold my breath as I hit dial on Jake's number.

"Is she able to handle it for the entire week?" a

groggy Jake demands about Kelsey.

I'm sure Jake asked Kimber this same question when I was the new assistant manager. Kelsey hasn't been around long enough to have earned Jake's seal of approval.

"If she can't, she has you on speed-dial." No different from me. "You could, I don't know, show up and help?"

"That's what I pay you to do."

I huff. "You also give me paid vacation, Jake, and like hell am I letting it go to waste. It's the middle of the summer for heaven's sake and I'm pasty because I live the life of a vampire."

"So Cass is taking you away?" he grumbles.

"For a few days. I'll see your bright and smiling face before you'll notice I'm gone."

"Doubt it."

"Anyone ever told you that you're a pain in the ass?"

"Kimber. All the time."

Hence, how I knew I could get away with it.

"Fine." Jake blows out a breath, making me wonder if he's smoking. "I'll see if I can make it into the club some day this week."

"During operating hours," I clarify.

"Yes, mom," he quips sarcastically.

Jake pauses and I hear a female voice on the other end of the line. He covers the receiver, muffling what he says to her before returning his attention to our call.

"Do me a favor, Hol. When you get back, fire both those bitches. They're driving me insane. And figure out a way that if this happens again, I don't have to worry."

Why do I feel like taking time for myself, and focusing on my happiness is letting him down?

## Chapter Eighteen

*Cary*

"Is the XL in the lot ready to roll?" I ask the head of my service team.

The black extended SUV with chrome package came in on trade. I've learned not to ask why the owner trades in a vehicle they've taken pristine care of and take advantage instead. It's a current model year, gorgeous, freakin' mammoth, and fits the bill to get three adults, two kids, and a week's worth of bags to the Carolina coast.

"I'm about to pass her info onto sales to add to the online inventory." He shows me the paperwork.

I check the mileage and a few notes the tech made. "Hold off. I'm going to put it through the paces."

"As in, you want it?" His brow quirks when I shrug. "Sales will want to know where it disappeared to."

"Grab me some plates and tell them I'm taking it on an extended test drive."

The thing I like best about my job is I rarely get car envy. I have two registered under my name. The one I use daily is a run-of-the-mill mid-size SUV with the same body style most of the manufacturers are sticking to. It gets me where I need to go, but I can't say it's fun to drive. That's why I pilfer from the lot when something comes in that attracts my attention.

Bhodi is developing the itch to do that too. Since his mom is with us more often on Saturdays now, I block a few hours after school on Friday for us to tinker with what customers have brought into the shop and search for cars online that might become our next project. It's our guy time and I feel like I'm making up for all the moments I lost out on with my grandad.

Bhodi picks something different to drive away in when we leave. On the way home, we bond over the automotive company's history or what other cool models they sold back when. He's becoming less obsessed with the entertainment systems than what's under the hood and has even blown the service center guy's minds with what he's picked up. I hope he likes this one because he hasn't ridden in anything this ostentatious.

Key in hand, I glide back toward my office to finish up a few lingering tasks. I haven't had a real vacation for months and am amped to get out of Brighton. So much so I'd immediately rescheduled my counseling session to help Laurel when the air conditioning busted and began formulating the plan to swoop in and take everyone away.

Not that Laurel or Holly need me to rescue them. They fared fine before I waltzed in. But that's the point, isn't it? If Holly's putting her paycheck to the repairs, then I can do my part too. I mean, Dusty hadn't flinched offering to install the window units.

Holly's running behind when I get back to the condo later in the afternoon. God love her, the woman will leave me waiting for her in perpetuity.

And Lord bless me with the patience to deal with it. The other side of the coin is Holly isn't the kind who cuts out early or shirks her responsibilities. Glen's bachelor party, when we disappeared into the back office, is the only instance I clearly recall.

Her tardiness gives me time to hoist the rest of the bags into the trunk and install Emory's car set in the second row. Bhodi takes command of the entire third, but not until he's gone over every spec and thumbed through the glove compartment to investigate what's in there. He absconds with my cell and, tapping away, brings up everything he can find, including the coming soon listing sales put on the dealership's website.

"Do you know how much this car is worth?" His eyes bug out and he clutches my cell like it's a gold brick.

Putting Emory's sippy cup in the holder, I laugh under my breath and wink at the kid. I do. And yeah, I chose it to create a first impression of what this trip will be like for them. Deep down I want to prove to Holly I can take care of her more than in the bedroom, and even if she doesn't need me to. I believe she's aware I can, but not by how much. This vacation will erase any doubts.

Three hours after Holly gets her ass in gear, we're pulling onto a private road. Laurel gasps from the seat behind me and both of the kids let exaggerated wows fly. I'm not satisfied until the woman beside me reaches across the console and her nails dig into my forearm. We may both have chills, but for very different reasons.

I pull the SUV into the short driveway of my house with the nose emblem up close to one of the garage doors.

"This is…" My girl's words falter. She stands on the running board, taking off her dark glasses, and looking up the three stories.

"It's a castle!" Emory supplies, princess doll waving in Laurel's face as her mom tries to get her out of the five-point harness.

I walk around the rear of the SUV, popping the hatch so the ocean breeze blows in to keep it cool while we unload. Bhodi scrambles over the back of his seat to where the luggage is and I keep moving. On the passenger side, I take Holly's hand, helping her down, and pulling her tight to me.

She slides down my trunk and I claim her lips. Resting my forehead to hers, I get an up-close glimpse of the bewildered yet happy expression plastered on her face.

"This is all yours?" She squeaks.

I spin her a hundred and eighty degrees, making her squeal.

I've never wanted to share this place with anyone the way I do with Holly, nor have I ever wanted to show off to anyone as badly as I do right now.

Does it make me conceited? Fucking yes, but I'm owning that shallow emotion because I haven't cared what any woman thinks of me in the past.

I bought the beach house as a party pad on a whim when I was in college with cash Grandad left me. My father reeled on and on about how stupid I was to blow the wad and what a shitty investment it was buying property this close to the ocean because of the damage hurricane season brings. My mother took a different approach. She waited until I tired of the drive from Brighton and got bored with the place. Then Davina called in her interior designer, had my cheap-ass furniture hauled away, and decked the place out in soothing beach tones that match the views from the large winndows.

Previous to meeting Holly, Davina and I had the go-around about me selling it. Like an ostrich, she buried her head in the sand and refused to hear me out. And considering my mother's car is parked next to us, she's also dug in and not listened when I told her to get out of my house.

"Lovely of you to join me." Comes her voice three stories up from the mid-point on the widow's walk between the master bedroom she's commandeered as her own and the kitchen. Holding a towel, Davina wiggles her fingers. "I'm on my way to the pool. Come say hello when you're settled!"

Holly looks up and her jaw drops.

"So, ah, my mom is here." I cringe and stiffen, bracing for the worst. "I'm sorry. I asked her to leave."

Holly's head falls to my pec. I drag my chin over her hair before kissing it. My scruff drags strands from her ponytail. I really need to be better about not ruining her style. She expends so much effort on her appearance. I like the way she looks. I freaking love her hair pulled back too when she lets me mess it up.

Holly's eyes fill with a million questions.

"Does it bug you she's here?" I ask.

I don't talk much about my family, and I hadn't expected to make a game plan to discuss the reasons.

"It's only that I hadn't expected to meet her… Today," she tacks on.

"You and me both, Doll."

Holly cups my cheek, and something about the action soothes my soul. She's so damn forgiving when I've put her in an awkward position. I kiss her again, unable to utter the words I want to say, and hoping whatever happens while we're here is enough to prove them.

We unload the car, bringing the luggage to the second floor. Laurel and Emory unpack in the room across the hall from Holly's and mine. One door down, Bhodi is bouncing off the walls excited over having his own bathroom and a slider to a porch overlooking the backyard.

"Get your suit on," I tell him when he sees the pool below. "And don't hang over the railing, ya goof. I'll kill you if you fall in from all the way up here."

"Not if mom kills you first." Bhodi smarts.

I put up a finger in warning. But this kid, he's got me… And so does his mom.

I jog the few steps to the bedroom Holly and I are sharing while we're here, slowing at the threshold to watch her taking it all in.

She's pulled the sheers aside, checking the view, hoping for the glimpse of the shoreline that we had on the drive and boats bouncing on the ocean waves. Her bright red bandana print halter top and the deep navy of her denim shorts make her a focal point against the white walls in the room and the soft colors of the bedding.

Damn, she's beautiful.

I shut the door. Walking behind Holly, I slip my arms around her waist, using my nose to move the bouncy ponytail she's sporting, and running my lips over the soft skin above where her top ties. I'd give anything to slip the knot, but settle for skimming my palm up under the fabric, cupping her breast, and rolling her nipple between my fingers.

Her soft moan makes my dick jump. Holly's hand drops the curtain and lifts over her head, grasping the back of my neck. My other palm skates up, exposing her stomach and massaging her painted breast.

We're interrupted by a knock at the door. She tries to step away from me, but I use leverage to clutch her close.

"I'm changed!" Bhodi raps a second time.

"Stay here," I whisper in Holly's ear, leaving her tits exposed to the cool air as the working air conditioner in my house clicks on. Before moving away I tug on that ponytail so she's aware of exactly what I'm about to do to make her come.

I crack the door enough to see Bhodi in the hall and Laurel and Emory leaving their room. All are suited up. "Holly needs to lie down. We'll be out in a few."

My fibbing is improving. Holly does need to get on the bed. Maybe not to lie down. I'd like her ass in the air and my hand wrapped around her long blonde hair. It's taken me a few months to figure out sometimes she and I get to come first, and I'm allowed to need her coming all over my cock.

The kids skitter down the stairs. Laurel's brow arches as she turns to follow them.

"Just talking," *dirty. See, not lying.*

"Whatever makes you feel better." Sarcasm laces Laurel's reply. "Oh, so you're both aware. My loyalty to my sister ends if this isn't *quick*."

Guess Laurel isn't interested in getting stuck entertaining the *lovely* Mrs. Stanton either.

*Holly*

Cary slams into me from behind and my pussy quakes. I call out his name, glad no one is inside to hear my gasp between the broken syllables. He grunts, falling forward, his front against my back. Then his nimble fingers trace forward, skimming my lower belly and massaging the last remnants of pleasure from the tight ball of nerves that wield control over the pulsing around his cock.

Cary is a man who loves to fuck and, crap on a cracker, if I ever needed a quick roll in the hay this was it. I was already high-strung  packing and tying up loose ends for a fun, but impromptu trip. I hadn't realized how tense I was about meeting Cary's mother until he touched me, and then all I wanted was for him to ease my nerves. "Lucky girl" doesn't even begin to cover his attentiveness in and out of the bedroom.

When he's certain I'm satisfied, Cary pulls out, grabs the waistband of his unbuttoned jeans so he doesn't trip on the way, and uses the attached bath to dispose of the condom and wash up. I slip my halter back over my breasts and find my shorts kicked under the bed frame. I smooth the wrinkles in my clothes in an attempt to look presentable and mess with my haphazard ponytail in the mirror.

"Stop," Cary commands.

He tucks his cell in his back pocket and takes my hand to lead me out of the room.

"You look beautiful. I won't let her not love you," he pauses as if there are more words on his tongue and rushes to hurry up with, "and if we don't get down there soon the delivery guy will have to make a second stop here because they will have eaten it all the pizza I ordered while you were getting dressed."

"You really think so?"

"That Bhod will fucking devour all the pepperoni? Damn straight. Have you seen the way the kid is putting away food lately?" He notices every foible my son has.

Ignoring how serious things are between Cary and me is a losing battle. He's gone from some guy my son goes on an adventure with once a week to the man we're coming to depend on. Since my past has taught me reliance on anyone but myself is stupid, a part of my personality prefers perpetuating living in a little bubble, taking it day by day, and not hoping for a future which isn't mine to share with Cary.

I have a feeling the woman out by the pool would intimidate anyone Cary brought home. But for me? I'm not simply a silly someone who dug her nails into Davina Stanton's baby boy. I'm almost her age, and I'm dropping a kid into Cary's lap, asking him to care for a child that's not even his. I'm more unprepared for this intro than Cary would be if I was asking him to change a diaper.

My feet stall on the staircase, causing Cary to tug my arm. He steps back up a few stairs. Still standing below me, but able to bring me close to his chest. I smell me on him and him on me. It's my favorite comforting scent. But I've also abandoned my nine-year-old when I should have been out there putting my best foot forward. What if my son has been awful?

"Doll?" His voice is low.

"Hmm?" I play with the collar of his shirt.

"Don't lose sight of the fact that I started everything up there. I wasn't letting you down these stairs until we had a little of the 'active participation' we talked about. And my mother is a guest in my home, not the other way around."

There's a slight edge to his words I haven't heard before. Not during a spat, which we've had, and not once since I've begun deferring to Cary and allowing him lay down the law if he sees Bhodi acting out.

Maybe Cary's as anxious about going outside as I am?

God, what if he *is* worried about our age gap? It's not as if he can pretend he's oblivious to it forever. I mean, some things become obvious the longer you look at them, like gray hair, crow's feet, and the effect of gravity on your boobs. I may need to start wearing a bra STAT.

Outside, Laurel and Mrs. Stanton sit at a patio table. Davina's pushed out her chair and Emory wiggles on her lap. Bhodi has on goggles and a snorkel. He ducks under the water lapping at the pool's edges as soon as he spies us.

"Nice of you to make it out here before the sun goes down." My sister taunts, rolling her eyes. "How was your nappy-poo?"

"Aunt Holly takes naps with me so she can go to work at night," Emory informs Cary's mother.

Davina is about to ask where when Cary supplies the answer.

"Holly is the manager at Sweet Caroline's."

"That must be interesting." Davina smiles.

"It's a challenge, that's for certain." I try to let it drop, though my niece makes it difficult.

"There's dancers there, but not ballerinas."

Davina laughs at her innocence, but a hint of concern crosses her brow. "Did the two of you meet there?"

"I'm Bhodi's mentor with the big brother program. It's safe to say he introduced us." Cary cuts me off before I say anything.

A flash of animosity I don't recognize crosses his face. I squeeze his hand and when Cary looks at me it fades, replaced with a sorrowful look I haven't seen from him since the week after his father passed.

Emory takes Bhodi up on a cannonball challenge. Laurel spends the next few minutes catching me up on what we missed while everyone else was out by the pool. By the time the pizza delivery guy shows, handing our order over the pool fence, and the kids grab towels, I'm starting to think things have settled. We may have a good vacation, despite the added guest.

Davina insists I call her by her first name and is as cordial to me as she is to Laurel. It is obvious Cary's mother has taken a liking to Emory. She also listens in earnest when Bhodi finally has my undivided attention and I can hear the stories about the campout. When Davina asks about the other trips he and Cary have taken, Bhodi recounts the events on the day they went to the living history museum.

"It was fun. This guy had leeches—"

"The apothecary." Cary supplies with a toothy smirk.

Cary hasn't stopped beaming while Bhodi tells the story. This is the first time he's interrupted, letting my son have the stage. I love how patient he is with

Bhodi, how much their friendship means to him, and the little moments he steps up to boost Bhodi's self-confidence when he doesn't even realize he's doing it.

"Yeah, him... and Glen said it's the name of the guy and the place he works."

"I thought he'd be too bored to pick up on a detail like that." Cary turns to whisper in my ear. "Guess it made a bigger impression on him then I gave credit for."

"Bugaboo," I caution. "Miss Davina may not be as inclined to discuss leeching over dinner as we are." I have a little boy and some of the grosser subjects make me queasy.

"It's fine. I'd like to hear the rest of the story. All of it," she encourages.

"The apothecary was saying all this gross stuff, and I started feeling really sick. Cary crawled across the floor and he took me outside. He got me a drink and he helped me pay for the star."

"The one hanging in my room?" I touch Cary's bicep, unconscious of the action and suddenly aware of how many times when I'm not around there must be when my boyfriend steps up to be the dad my son needs. The trip was months ago. No wonder they have such a strong bond.

Cary cups my cheek when my eyes shimmer with a silent "thank you."

The sentiment is short-lived.

"I'm not surprised." Davina folds a greasy paper napkin as if it is cloth, placing it on the table next to a thin paper plate. "You have a big heart."

"Whatever." Cary stands.

The metal legs of the chair he was sitting in scrape against the concrete decking. He quickly gathers empty plates, snatching Davina's when she lifts it toward the stack.

The metal gate clangs hard, slamming behind Cary

as he exits the enclosed pool yard. Laurel and I sit in stunned silence. There is a loud thump from the trash bin lid falling shut and Cary's footsteps fade. He doesn't return.

My sister takes the hint and picks up the conversation, asking Bhodi more questions.

"If you'll excuse me," I apologize to everyone.

I'd rather hear the rest of what Bhodi says. I sense Cary needs me more.

Collecting my soda can, I use recycling it as an excuse to go out the fence and stroll along the length of the house. I toss it in the bin and keep walking to find Cary.

In the driveway, the tailgate of the SUV is up. Cary's sitting in the trunk with his legs hanging. He stares off in the distance. The view at this level between the other tall houses is identical to the one from the bedroom we are sharing this week.

"Go back. You shouldn't be here," he says as if I'm invisible.

I'm standing with my thighs to his knees, so it makes the sinking sensation drag me down.

I've fallen in love, drowning in its murky depths before. The one thing it taught me was to kick back and fight to reach the surface. Not necessarily to cling to things that weren't meant to be, more to prove I can continue on.

"Am I supposed to go back inside the fence or back to Brighton?"

Cary reaches up, his fingers fall before he allows himself to grasp my elbow. He refuses to meet my eyes, staring instead at where our bodies connect.

Men come into Sweet Caroline's for their own reasons; fun, fantasy, to leave the stress behind, escaping from a girlfriend or a wife they no longer have deep feelings for, or grieving a lost lover. Over the years, I've listened to every story under the sun.

But I doubt any will ever be more important than the one Cary is about to tell me.

I also understand his unwillingness to share, and that I have no way of placating him with alcohol to hurry his words along. But he craves what's real. The things he can see.

So I square my shoulders, take a step back, and show him inches instead of miles divide us. He can widen it and run. But I have faith in the man who put my little boy first before considering what his life would be like juggling us both and becoming a part of a ready-made family.

# Chapter Twenty

*Cary*

"Your mother hasn't said an unkind word to me, Cary. On the other hand, you've found every reason to cut off her questions, jump to conclusions, and treat Davina poorly. You're not the man who brings out the best in my son right now."

Underneath my crawling skin, I'm aware of this. Davina could have mentioned Holly's age, disparaged where she works or insinuated she's using her son to lure me in.

Holly's honesty stabs me in the chest. She's disappointed because she counts on me to show Bhodi how to treat women with respect. This woman had a purpose when she enrolled her son in the mentoring program. I wouldn't linger in Holly's bed, let alone in their lives otherwise.

Yet, as soon as Davina and I were in the same vicinity, the shell fell off, exposing the genesis of the person who Rex was trying to groom me into. Underneath it all, I'm a kid who unwittingly watched as his mom deserted him. It happened slowly the same way the rest of what Rex put me through came to feel normal. But it wasn't and the wedge is still there because I've been so focused on making Bhodi's childhood something he'll want to remember that I haven't made peace with my own.

"You don't know her or what my parents did to me." My pulse pounds in my ears.

"Obviously not, if you haven't mentioned it." Holly's palms fly to her hips.

We're silent for a tick, the same awkward way it was in the beginning when I fumbled for reasons to stay and she looked for polite ones to send me away.

Her voice comes down an octave from the antagonism she drew out of me. "I don't want to fight with you, so why don't you tell me what you're fighting against instead?"

I've pushed her away, but she's not so far that I can't bridge the gap. I nod to the empty space to the right since I don't want anyone touching me. All the shit Rex paid women to teach me—the things I do to Holly—make me feel dirty and undeserving of her.

"My grandparents were married for ten years when my grandmother called it quits and divorced Grandad. Nobody gave me the reason she left, but he never spoke poorly of her abandoning him with a child." The same way Holly acts for Bhodi's sake. "He told me loving her was a choice he made when they said their vows." Grandma was allowed to change her mind, but Grandad never did.

Davina was young when she met Rex. He worked for Grandad. My mother's mother discarded her marriage and Davina had nothing to compare her relationship with my dad to. No one to look up to, admire, emulate. Being married was harder than Davina thought. After a few months, she walked out.

One day she went to the dealership ready to come clean to Grandad. Davina slipped around a corner to avoid Rex. She ran into this guy named Powell. He was a business associate from up north who Grandad wanted Rex to foster a partnership with. One thing led to another. Davina and Powell shacked up while he was in Brighton and until the newness of it petered out. It was easy to keep the affair hidden. Davina had been staying in a hotel, too ashamed to admit to her father she was like my grandmother.

Eventually, Davina moved back in with Grandad, lying that she and Rex had just had a fight. Soon later, she found out she was pregnant.

Even though Grandad lost his wife, he was a romantic deep down. He saw me as some sort of divine intervention and a way for Rex and Davina to reconnect.

But the timing didn't add up and, as soon as Rex put two and two together, my dad was faced with the fact that my mom was carrying another man's child. She was bold-face lying to her father and, without mom, Rex had nothing to tie himself to the dealerships. He'd be out of a job and my best guess is he didn't want his reputation ruined as a laughingstock who couldn't keep his wife out of bed with the competition.

So, he canceled the deal between the companies and yielded what little power he had over my mother. She'd been as concerned about people's perceptions, especially her father's. They agreed to stay married, Rex would raise me as his own, and no one would find out about mom's indiscretion.

Pretending a bouncing baby boy was the outcome of reconciling with my dad and choosing to love him made sense to Davina. That's what she was taught.

Holly's brows knit together with intensity. In the recesses of her mind, I was Bhodi's age in an unhappy household. She has no clue.

"My dad pretty much left me alone until I was in

middle school. Spending time with Bhod and Emory, I actually remember it was more like your house. Gradually Rex was home more often and things changed. I'd find porn tucked between the books on my desk. Women would be nice to me, compliment my clothes, or tell me how I was maturing." I shrug. "All stuff I passed off as normal until it became that. He started paying prostitutes to abuse me over the next few years under the guise of turning me into a man."

I lean forward, my elbows grinding into my thighs and my back bowed so all I see is the loose gravel on the driveway.

I can't even look at Holly. I don't want her to see how ashamed I am that it was a woman her age I lost my virginity to when I wasn't much older than Bhodi. I don't want her to think the feelings I have for her are disgusting or that I'm a masochist seeking some sort of perverse gratification. I worry about the humiliation she'd feel.

If I had an any-older-woman proclivity Laurel could have fit the bill. It's not. I've dated enough younger women to understand the connection Holly and I have isn't based on sex alone. It's that she isn't shy about showing me who she is. Like she said, the only thing she has to lose in this life is her son. I'm almost positive the tether to him and only him is what allows her to live free.

"How did your mother not know? Not say a word?" The comparisons between her parent's marriage and mine are visible in her expression.

"I'm not sure she figured out how bad it was until I was in high school." By then Rex used girlfriends to cover up my earlier exploits. "It's not a crime to build your son's confidence with a pat on the back and a wink. Davina didn't like it, but she shrank to Rex's will whenever they argued over it."

"And when Rex died, she told you who your father was." Horror laces the words as Holly sums the why up quietly. "Rex used you to teach Davina a lesson for having the affair. He tried turning a child into a deviant. Someone who didn't have any emotional attachments when it came to sex. Someone who would have an affair like your mother had with Powell to prove you weren't any better than they were… and make her wonder if her mother was the same way."

"She maintains he also conned her into a bum deal with Grandad's company that left her with nothing if she brought any negative press to the dealerships. I've seen the legal documents, but I don't comprehend why she agreed to sign them other than it was in my grandfather's best interest. Save the business and sacrifice the kid." I pause. Now that it's out, I owe Holly for listening without bolting, and I want her to know how proud I am of her choices. "At least, you got out of a crappy situation for Bhodi's sake."

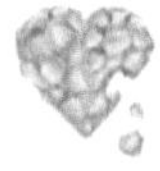

# Holly

"Is that what you think happened?" I laugh caustically.

I've heard the sorrow in his voice. I saw his confident presence shrink as his shoulders fell. He's worried his past will define him in my eyes. I can't blame him. So much of the truth he's shared is information he's still digesting. Rex Stanton's death was just this winter.

I hadn't wanted to own my story either. It took a long while for me to sort through the lies. And so much of the truth reinforced the feeling that, even as a victim, I was a bad person because I was too immature and naive to see the writing on the walls. I should have been stronger, for myself and for my child, then to have let Bhodi's father have the gall to trample and use us for his own vanity.

"William went back to his wife and daughters: A family I didn't know he had. He left me with a diamond ring that wasn't worth stepping into a pawn shop to cash in, sky-high rent, a mountain of hospital debt, and a newborn whose birth *he missed*."

William hid an entire part of his life from me. One that, approaching his forties, had become too stressful. So, when the Army transferred him across the country, he abandoned his first family and took up with an unsuspecting blonde from a background where cheating spouses were secrets people like the Cass-Stanton's kept. Raised by parents who quite literally couldn't live without the other, I knew nothing but rainbows and fucking sunshine.

The man who ruined me wanted out of a similar white picket fence life he'd built. He was starting over. Until he decided he'd made a mistake and was too old for the responsibilities a baby brings.

I was William's mid-life crisis and my son was never wanted by his father.

"I never got a choice to stow what remained of my pride in a bag and hit the road. What I had was some other woman's sloppy seconds: A man who lied to my face and told me he loved me. Promised to marry me. And, with every ounce of my being, I believed him. I blindly believed my baby was going to grow up in a house with two parents, a front yard, and family vacations every summer." My eyes burn, but I can't cry over it. Not anymore. Emotion. Tears. Those I reserve for happy occasions.

I've raised a wonderful kid on my own so far, and I'm plumb out of pity for the stupidity I'd shown in my youth. I don't have the luxury of looking back and wondering if I could have done something differently.

With what money? What resources?

And, even if I'd had to choose between parenting alone versus putting a roof over my son's head with someone as vicious and abusive as Cary's admitted Rex Stanton was, where was the other man? Because yes, there are days I could sure use an ego boost knowing I'd been too proud to take that kind of offer and have made it on my own.

But I don't know Davina's side of the story, and the level of deviousness Rex Stanton showed to Cary seems premeditated. I can't fault Davina for believing she was doing her best for her infant son either. No one foresees a reprisal to the extreme Rex went to.

For better or worse, people hide the scariest parts of who they are and you have to dig to find the roots. That doesn't mean they're all rotten. The bulbs I plant wither after the spring and a year later there are new green shoots growing up from the earth. You're supposed to prune back the dead boughs so healthy branches can feel the warmth of the sun and grow stronger in their place.

"You told me your grandfather said love was a choice."

Cary nods.

"But you've been struggling and hate yourself for loving Davina, don't you? You don't know how to stop those memories from when you were a child and things seemed perfect from seeping in, and you want to forget the person Rex needed you to be. Your father isn't a man you'd admire like your grandad who gave his heart to one person forever and always."

He covers my hand with his. "My shrink and my bartender girlfriend see things I can't."

"You can. You do. Or else you wouldn't have trusted me with who you are." I turn my palm up and we lace our fingers together. "Cary, I don't talk about William because I won't carry a cloud that affects my mood. This life is my parade, and he's an unwelcome guest. Is Davina? Hate is a choice too, and until you both figure out where you stand with one another, you're giving Rex the power to rain buckets on your heads."

"Are you going to be here?" Cary lets go of a heavy breath, and the weight of his concern hits me.

"I don't see why they're mutually exclusive."

"Are we, still, exclusive?"

"Nothing you've said changes the way I feel about you."

"There's something else that may."

I bite my lip, nodding for Cary to keep speaking.

"I need you to keep what I've told you on the down low until I figure out when and how... *if* this is something that I want everyone else to be in on. It could affect the dealership's reputation and more than the business, I'm worried about what it means for us."

"Because dating a strip club manager already sullies your impeccable character."

"No, because I don't want anything coming between us to ruin what we've started. I love you, Holly."

# *Cary*

Holly's thick lashes blink a few times and her cheeks pinken. I've taken her off-guard.

"Too soon?" I ask.

*Talk about bad timing. She's going to think you're using your feelings against her.*

Her lips form a little "O". "No, just unexpected."

"You don't have to say it back. I wanted to try it on for size."

"Does it fit?"

"Perfectly." I smile and her wide grin bursts my heart. "You may not be the only person I say it to."

Her happy expression falters.

I lean in, kissing her cheek. "That kid of yours. I need to be the kind of guy who can show him it's not weird to say it aloud before he's too grown up to hear it. I want to be around, Hol, for you and Bhodi to count on. He deserves more than what I got."

A tear spills from her eye, trailing down Holly's cheek.

"That bad you'll risk ruining your makeup?" I joke.

"That good." She reaches, running her fingers through the short hair at the nape of my neck, fusing our mouths together.

"I'm in this, Holly. Seriously, I won't treat you like William did. I won't let anyone do to Bhodi what was done to me. You don't have to worry I'll throw you away and you don't have to say—"

I tell her that all I need is a little more time. Other people finding out about Davina's affair shouldn't include banners like a Presidents' Day sale.

Her index finger presses against my lips, taking me

by surprise. "Shut up. All your white knight professions are ruining my opportunity to say, 'I love you too'."

My surprise turns to shock. I thought Holly was solid as a rock, smarter than to give herself to me freely. Intelligent enough to walk away so she could protect her child from a monster when I revealed my pain. But she's here, teary-eyed, with a wide smile that fills every hollow spot inside me.

"Although my love comes with a string attached, Cary. You say you don't want Rex to reach beyond the grave, yet you're giving him control over your anger. I won't allow my son to see you treat Davina the way you have this evening. You need to apologize to your mom."

"I'll do it." My words rush.

"Stop." She catches my arm as I stand. "You don't understand. It's not me or Bhodi you are doing this for… It's you. You can't say we're your priority unless you make yourself one first."

# Chapter Twenty-one

*Holly*

I won't tell Cary he's wrong. Loving someone isn't a choice. If it was, we'd have been doomed from the start because otherwise there is no way I would have let my guard down and the spark between us ignite.

If I've learned anything from my mistakes, it is: hearts are foolish. They want what they want and controlling emotions is far easier said than done.

My mom, dad, and Laurel would agree, I was a hot mess working through the aftermath of William. If there was the ability not to love Bhodi seeing how a part of him is William's I might have taken the coward's way out of motherhood.

Love doesn't work like that. Honestly, the only worse emotion is grief since in some regards you can beat hate with logic.

There's not a damn thing logical about falling in love with Cary. Falling out of love with him when I'm up to my elbows in how deeply he cares for us is a huge reality. Staying in a relationship with him until our time is up? That's absolutely a choice I'm making to be his now, knowing he's not mine forever. All I can do is savor the moment, even if a hidden spot inside of me wants a different outcome. It's the same secret place that wishes I'd met Cary when I was younger and that he was older or that wonders if I was born too soon. When Cary isn't next to me and my mind wanders, it is to all the things I can't change about the situation I'm in with this wonderful man.

I'd have never imagined the pain Cary hid. The utter devastation on his face when he confessed—as if this man was worried I'd think less of him for situations his father led him blindfolded into as a child—was terrifying. I hadn't feared he'd hurt my son, but if he'd ever done anything in the past to himself out of fear and self-loathing. I also worried he'd turn the small space I put between us into a cavern we couldn't bridge and each one of us would wind up on the losing end when this trip started out as Cary trying to save the day.

We lie on our backs in the trunk of the SUV, holding hands, and slipping in and out of discussing the pain Rex put him through. Each time Cary opens the door more to what a life of privilege had actually been like for him.

I realize he felt he was a disgrace long before Davina released his parentage. Whether the insight makes it easier for him to come to grips with and move on from, I'm not as certain. Unlike the man I've fallen in love with, I have a decade of experience on Cary to have bested my demons. There are milestones, but no standard roadmap for recovery.

He's within his right to ask for my silence. Cary doesn't want his life defined as the bastard who broke up what Rex led others to believe was a happy marriage. I understand that level of misery. William's wife was quick to cast me as the home wrecker. As if my actions were intentional, though I was as in the dark about William's cheating as she was.

We continue whispering as the moon rises and the stars come out. I have enough trust in those I surround myself with that I'm not scared Cary will turn into the monster his father was. I'm also positive Laurel safely tucked my son into bed.

I can't wait to see Bhodi in the morning and a little of that is knowing how much Cary means to him and that we'll be doing it together. If I'm lucky enough to have Cary for another month, next year, or a few more after that, the one thing I want is for Bhodi to have had a taste of the perfection I did growing up. Even if it is fleeting, my son deserves to see two adults loving one another through thick and thin. Cary? He's worth showing he can love and be loved in return. He's been open and honest with me, and if he can do it once, he can do it again with someone else.

I won't push Cary to tell Davina he's sorry for his caustic remarks tonight. I'm not his mother and he needs to approach her on his own. I can only stand on the sidelines encouraging the way I'd do for any of my other closest friends.

The heat of the day finally escapes into the darkness and we are left with the damp sea salt-tinged humidity of overnight settling on our skin. Emotionally wrought out, we're exhausted and need a rest. Though it's well before when I'd turn in, Cary takes me upstairs to our room and we slide between the sheets.

I'm used to Cary being up by the time I'm awake, so the only unusual thing about waking the following morning is being someplace new. I find my short housecoat before padding to the third floor to join everyone, glad I haven't slept too late. The sun streams into the open space. It's a beautiful day.

Cary and Bhodi are bonding over bowls of cereal at

the breakfast bar. Emory has Davina's full attention on a couch. My sister sits reading nearby. When Laurel notices me, she winks and I wink back, mouthing "thank you" for her help last night. She puckers, blowing me a silent kiss.

"What are you reading, Laurel?" I ask, strolling by my men and making my presence known. I drop my lips to Bhodi's head and then peck Cary on the cheek while he munches.

"It's all about the Wright Brothers."

"We'll hit the memorial tomorrow." Cary swallows. "The crowd should be thinner mid-week and the weather's supposed to be great."

"The two of you have the whole week planned before I'm even out of bed."

"You snooze, you lose." Laurel flips the next page.

"So what's on tap for today?" I ask, pouring the remnants of the coffee carafe into a mug. The first sip hits my palette and I'm in heaven. "Oh my goodness, this tastes even better than smells."

Davina turns her attention from Emory and smiles at me. Yet she doesn't respond that she's the one who made the pot. My cheeks bunch in appreciation. This morning could have been a huge ugly scene, and she's being gracious about Cary's lack of manners. I wonder if they've talked already, but when I look back at Cary, he's stretching with an imperceptible shake of his head.

He places a hand on Bhodi's shoulder, nudging my son to bring his empty bowl to the sink, and getting up from his stool.

"Here's the deal for today; First y'all need to get dressed. Then you and me, Bhod, are taking a drive out to the fish market to get spiny lobsters for everyone for dinner."

Bhodi's nose wrinkles. "Fish smell."

"So do you, but we love you anyway. And you're

going to love fish, of all kinds, once it's buttered up. You'll have to if we're hanging out here more often. Spending time at the shore and not eating seafood is a sacrilege."

"What's that?"

"It's like going to a baseball game and not eating ballpark frank."

"What's that?"

"A hot dog, dude."

"Oooh, I get it. Like tradition."

"In a sense… And once you have a taste for them, we can charter a boat and go diving and eat the ones we catch. Sound like fun?" Cary tugs Bhodi toward him. My son rests his head on Cary's stomach. "When we get back with the lobsters, Aunt Laurel is bringing you and your cousin to the beach for a few hours, since Emory wants to play in the sand, and I'm taking your mom out for lunch. Just us."

"This time." Bhodi insists.

Then Cary does something unexpected. He snags Bhodi under the armpits and hefts him up, wrapping his arms around my son's legs so they're eye to eye. "When have I ever gone back on my word?"

"Never. So far…"

"So far. You wound me!" Cary tosses his head back. "Bhod, I'm always making time for you and me, know why?"

Bhodi shrugs.

"'Cause you're the reason I met your mom. That makes you top tier. You're like my wingman. Who else can I ask for advice on what songs to play in the car that she'll like?"

I blush, ducking my head. How did one simple application for someone to hang out with my son change our lives this much? My heart melts. I'm so in love with the way Cary loves Bhodi. How he always returns to making my little boy feel special and like he's an essential part of *us*.

Lifting my eyes, it's hard not to see Davina watching the two of them and the wistfulness in her expression. She wanted her son to have a dad like this too.

"Come on, I've got something to show you." I think Cary means Bhodi, but he tugs me by the hand as well and drags the two of us down two flights of stairs to the first floor filled with exuberance.

"Ta-da!" he exclaims, letting us into the garage and punching the overhead door button.

The narrow room fills with light and Bhodi yells, "No way!"

I codfish, realizing as the girlfriend of a car enthusiast I'm supposed to know what I'm looking at, though all I'm sure of is the rounded lines of the antique white roadster are stunning.

"It's a 1960 MG MGA." Cary's already got his cell out of his pocket, handing it over to Bhodi. "I didn't know much about it until after I bought it. I'd lost out at an auto auction bidding on a replica of a 1962 Shelby Cobra."

Bhodi's jaw drops lower than mine. He's not sure what's more important, searching the specs or clamoring into the convertible and gripping the steering wheel while Cary takes the black ragtop down.

I'm beginning to think I need a crash course in cars. But all I can do is stand back and take in the scene the way I had the evening Cary flew in the front door of the condo with the sleeping bags.

"I was looking for something to restore and sort of got ahead of myself when I saw the Cobra which was already road-worthy. I could have tinkered with that car and driven it fast, but I don't think I'd be as attached to it as I am to this one. It wasn't an original either." Cary jumps into the passenger side.

He runs his fingers over the dash, citing the differences between an MGA and MGB, the history of this particular car, and how he fell into the deal with the previous owner. He's proud of the effort that went into this car.

He has Bhodi's full attention while he recounts how many man-hours went into restoring it.

"What are you waiting for? Go get dressed, half-pint." Cary makes a salty sailor's growl, needling his fingers in the air in a way that reminds me of anemone tentacles. "We have to get those lobsters before the fishmonger sells out."

"We're taking this?"

"Uh, yeah." I hear the "what did you think?" inflection in Cary's voice.

He doesn't have to ask Bhodi twice. My son whips past me for the opportunity to ride in Cary's roadster.

"This car is so beautiful," I say as Cary rounds the hood and pushes my back against the wall's open framing.

"So are you."

"Hmm…" I hum after he presses his lips to mine. "For a second, I doubted either of you noticed my existence."

"Doubting your importance? Doll, everything I do for you is for him, and for him is for you. I wouldn't have it any other way."

"I love you so much."

"I. Love. You." Between words he pecks me on the mouth. "I gave Laurel the keys to the truck so she can explore wherever she wants. It was her idea to take Bhodi. I want to do something nice for her, Hol. I'm not blind to the fact that she saved my butt last night."

The twinkle in Cary's eye has me agreeing. He's a good man who wants the best for us. "But," I plead. "In all the excitement, don't ignore what we talked about?"

He drops his forehead to mine. "I'll figure out the Davina situation. Give me a little more time? There's more to it than being sorry for last night."

# Chapter Twenty-two

Cary

I mean what I say to Holly about patching things up with my mother. She's not the only person who's been after me. My therapist had to have seen something like what happened last night coming from me keeping my emotions bottled up. Perhaps I did too, and it's my own fault for trying to turn a blind eye. I was keeping my past and my future separate and the possibility that things would come to a head when Davina and I weren't alone hadn't crossed my mind.

I came off as an ass and, in some respects, I regret not telling Holly about my childhood sooner. She's the one person I can say almost anything to without fear of judgment. I suppose that's because she's either heard it all or experienced some of it firsthand. The perspective I get in counseling makes perfect sense—in hindsight. But Holly's outlook is the second opinion I needed.

I am prioritizing. Not exactly how Holly suggested, but I'm taking credit for baby steps. The first thing that occurred to me when I woke up was my girlfriend walked out on what should have been a relaxing poolside evening with family to attend to my needs. We left Bhodi high and frickin' dry with no explanation, and it was damned presumptuous on my part to expect Laurel to step up for us.

Besides watching a grown man throw a fit, what did that show the boy I agreed to mentor? That more men than his father aren't dependable and he can only rely on the women in his life, that's what.

We have a convo in the car on the way to pick up our lobster dinner. I tell Bhodi I was a turd. Scuttling around the subject by saying, no different from when he and Holly don't get along, sometimes Davina and I don't. Though, my actions were disrespectful to everyone.

Bhodi took it with ease and—spotting a flock of seagulls on the return trip—made fun of me, which was cool. Everyone likes a good bird turd joke.

When Bhodi and I return, the rest of the house is ready to get a move on. Laurel's packed a picnic for the beach and invited Davina along. I don't make a huge deal of it as they make a hasty departure, cocking my chin and commenting, "Have a good time."

I'm distracted by my cell while Holly's in the driveway, reminding Bhodi to be on his best behavior.

"Whatcha got there?" she taps the top of the screen.

"It's nothing." I flick the app closed quickly. "Checking in on work," I lie like a complete shit head, hoping she'll forgive me.

"Well, I'm ready."

"You?" My brow quirks. Holly and on-time aren't synonymous. "How did I get so damned lucky?" I slip my arm around her and she beats my chest for making fun.

Really, how did I? I'm living a life I hadn't considered wanting a year ago with a woman who proves she's too good to have to wait on a guy learning to growing the fuck up. Holly's stolen my heart. Is it any wonder my sole motivation is proving giving hers to me was a safe bet?

I tuck Holly into the MGA and hop in on my side. It's the middle of the summer at the coast and approaching hot as Hades midday. But getting the engine purring, I shift the car into gear and set my hand on Holly's covered knee anyway. On the short ride, I can't stop my eyes from shifting over to her. Holly looks like she was made to sit in the passenger seat.

Narrow cat-eye sunglasses have replaced her thick eyeliner. She's got on this demure, thin-strapped dress. It hugs her chest. I no longer wonder if she's wearing a bra underneath anything and the starched fabric hides anyone else's suspicions. Her floral ink complements the dress to a tee, stealing the show. She's wrapped her head in a scarf to keep the wind out of her hair. She's also only this naturally beautiful to me after she's woken up in the morning.

Holly licks the watermelon pink gloss on her lower lip and it has the same effect on me as the ruby red does when her mouth encircles my cock.

A few miles down the road, we zip into the parking lot of the cozy restaurant with amazing porch side views of the sound.

Our entrance catches the attention of a bunch of college girls. Used to people staring at the lines of the MG, I'm ignoring the group so I don't get sucked into answering inane car questions. My experience is twenty-something-year-old girls in a gaggle are more interested in a fast ride. The guys who like their ego stroked by it are curious about what's under those girls' hoods, so to speak.

I'd rather waste my time shooting the shit with an any-age biker's old lady. At least they appreciate chrome and horsepower.

Holly's taken off her glasses and has unwrapped her scarf by the time I get to her door to offer her my hand. I'm so focused on making the few hours we have alone thanks to Laurel count, and doing something special for Holly to show her how much she means to me, that I don't hear the other women cackling.

Holly stiffens. She looks up at me in shock and then down at the pavement as what they're saying registers in my ears.

"Guess it's granny's day out of the nursing home, ladies."

"Think she has dementia and doesn't know what year it is?"

"Well, the car doesn't help much, does it? What is he doing with her?"

"So hot. He's definitely out of her league."

We go out to eat all the time in Brighton and even into Raleigh. My girl's confidence attracts attention. Our fingers intertwined while we've been dining, I've gotten more than a few kudos from older gentlemen, telling me not to let her get away. This is the one and only instance I can recall anyone reacting loudly to our age gap.

Infuriated, I set out to show these stupid chicks that they are immature brats. Holly's in a league of her own.

My hand presses to the small of her back, and I pull Holly close. When our bodies are flush, I dip her so she rests atop the MG's hood. My touch protects her delicate skin from the heat of the engine.

"I want you in every possible way," I say before thoroughly kissing her.

Our audience gasps, hurrying on. I've got a million-dollar grin on my satisfied mug. Holly's expression falters. I guide her to a sitting position, standing between her legs. Then lean in, so we're on the same level.

"Doll, I—"

"Shouldn't have done that. Lust fills those girls' heads, not commitment. They aren't thinking about if you're in love with me. They're imagining what you'd do to them. Kissing me would have been romantic on a deserted beach." She cups my cheek.

I push it against my scruff, not wanting to lose the connection and drop my gaze to a headlamp.

"I haven't heard anyone dare speak about you like they did."

"Then you haven't been listening, Cary."

Whipping away, I pace, scrubbing my beard in frustration.

Holly doesn't move. She watches me as it sinks in.

"Who?" Which assholes have had the audacity?

"It doesn't matter." She shakes her head, bunching the scarf into a ball.

I can tell by her actions it's not anyone, it's *everyone*. And it wears on her.

I've been too caught up in the safe parts of our relationship to notice. This is no different from me not addressing my problems with Davina head on because, with Rex out of the driver's seat, I hadn't wanted to stand amongst the wreckage. Moving forward is what I aimed to accomplish. And to glimpse contentment along the way. Feel valued, instead of someone simply telling me I should believe they loved me. I can't do that unless I'm willing to check my rearview.

I do want Holly any way she'll let me have her. Yet, I've never explored how people view us. If I don't admit how flawed other's perceptions of us are, we can't actually be perfect for one another. We won't have the tools to see it through, lift each other up when the road gets rough.

I flop my butt onto the hood of the car. "I'm sorry I blew it and embarrassed you. Again."

The sigh I let go of is like a deflating tire. Fucking awful, wondering if I'm stuck by the side of the highway alone.

*Damn.* I huff, ready to kneel to kiss Holly's painted toenails so she won't be mad at me. *I don't even have legs as nice as hers. Nobody's going to stop and pick me up.*

With trepidation, I link a finger through hers. Holly squeezes back.

I wish she'd told me. I feel more foolish than I suppose people have been implying we are as a couple. And I don't have the first clue how to make it up to her.

Twice in twelve hours I've let her down. She's got to be tired of my stupid ass. Holly didn't get into this to turn me into a man or for any salacious reasons. I'd always thought we connected on a certain level beyond our ages. Maybe I was wrong. The fact that I needed to show off my house to her and show her off in the car is proof.

I tug at her knee and kiss her blonde hair like it's our last goodbye. I'm unsure how we'll make it to the weekend. With the condo's AC still kaput, Holly can keep the SUV and stay at the beach house. I'll tell Davina we have to go back to Brighton.

"Figures from where I came from that I can't even hold my own family together." My voice begs, "How do I fix this?" I'm at a loss and I'm not too proud a man to need her to lead me.

She's quick to move, staring at me in shock.

"You guys, Doll." My voice cracks and I clear my throat, saying in all honesty, "I'm not ready to give up on you."

Despite Holly saying she doesn't cry, her eyes are

misty, giving away the hurt she feels inside.

"Cary, this is who we are. I forget too, and then someone says something to remind me. It can be as innocent as Dusty commenting about Cece's birthday that jogs my memory that you should have more in common with her."

"Dusty wouldn't like that."

"Neither would I." Holly harrumphs sadly. She rests her head on my shoulder. "If you're still hungry, we can get takeout."

Something stirs inside me akin to what I'd felt dipping Holly to the car's hood to kiss her, but deeper. I can't force negotiations with Holly to go my way. However, I'm unable to retreat. Seeing exactly what we're up against opened my eyes, and it will help me broker a deal so I, *we*, won't lose what we have together.

I stand and hold out my upturned palm, wanting to face the low note of the music playing.

"If you can manage it, I'd rather go inside and act like the man you needed a few minutes ago." I'm pulling another mulligan, asking to start the weekend over when I don't deserve to. "I may not get it right, but I want the chance to try."

# Chapter Twenty-three

*Holly*

"Let's go! Let's go! Let's go!" Impatient, Cary kneels and brushes my hands away from my sneakers, pushing the laces inside. "You can tie them in the car, Doll."

I glare up. My brow raises. My lip curling in disgust, my nose scrunches at how perky he is this early. Inhaling his cologne, my body remembers how late we fell asleep and my nipples become tight. Stupid body.

I curl into myself and roll onto the couch.

My sleep schedule is a mess and I'm so freaking tired.

Yesterday evening made up for the afternoon. The kids tracked sand straight to the pool where they soaked up the rest of the daylight hours. We had cocktails on the patio and, when I started deadheading the petals and leaves on the potted plants, Davina and I had a long conversation about plants. Cary prepared our late dinner using the burners on the grill to boil the lobsters in a large stainless steel stockpot. He'd wisely purchased premade side salads in the deli case at the market that were divine.

After eating, Laurel and I marched the dishes back up three floors to the kitchen to wash and rinse. She filled me in on the little details about the beach that she couldn't share in close company, saying the kids were on their best behavior. They'd had a wonderful time with Davina. I told her about the lunch fiasco. My sister hugged me before we rejoined the rest of the family.

Family… Cary thinks of us as part of his, and it wasn't until he said it aloud that I recognized he's as important as any of the mill friends I've got. Maybe more since we're attached at the hip.

I'm sure I'll react the wrong way to something he has to forgive me for at some point.

Today doesn't count because I hate that our normal life includes me working the graveyard shift and him being this bright-eyed and bushy-tailed businessman.

Don't get me wrong. I love his bushy tail. The man has an incredible ass. But drinking in the sun, and a late bedtime, followed by not going to sleep since we couldn't keep our hands to ourselves, has me wanting to call him one.

"You're being a big baby about this," says Cary, bringing me back to the moment.

"*Waa,*" I moan, taking a page out of my son's book.

He laughs at me.

"I swear Holly, it's a few hours at a National Park. Then you can come back and sleep the day away." He brushes some hair off of my face.

My eyes are closed and I snuggle into his touch.

"Let's go before it gets too hot." Unwilling to let me argue, Cary's arms go under my body and he heaves me over his shoulder.

I shriek as my boyfriend carries me like a sack of

potatoes down the flights of stairs to the driveway.

We're a few paces from the running SUV. I'm dangling head down and all I see when I open my eyes is the back of his legs and our shadow on the concrete. Cary slows to a stop.

"You awake, Doll?"

I make a garbled sound. Blood is rushing to my ears and I may puke from bouncing around. I haven't eaten and my cup of coffee is in the SUV to entice me, like dangling a carrot, to get a move on.

"Would you mind if I took my mother to dinner tonight?"

"Uh, no?" The question lit a spark in me.

I'm excited Cary wants to take this step. Yet, I don't want to seem overeager.

"I'll make it up to you." He places me down in the front passenger seat.

"You already have. I'm going to bed early," I joke.

He kisses my forehead and Emory's feet go wild against the back of the chair, reminding me we have an audience. Davina is sitting next to her and Laurel's taken the empty spot in the third row next to Bhodi.

I tuck into my cup of coffee, polishing it off by the time Cary pulls up to the gates at the Wright Brothers' Memorial. He doesn't wait to open Emory's door and has her on his hip, pocketing the key fob and reaching for Bhodi's hand. Something has him amped and all the rest of us can do is follow along with whatever mission Cary is on today.

We bypass the visitors center, hiking up to the monument first. The National Park has just opened and as the sweat beads on my skin, now I understand what the rush was. The sun is beating down on us and the humidity is rising. Even the ocean breezes don't seem cooling as we parade up the sloped pathways. But the views once we are up at the top make the trek more than worthwhile.

"You'd swear you could see all the way to Carolla, even though you can't." Davina stands next to me, admiring how breathtaking it is.

I sigh in agreement, as Cary's mom walks away, leaving me to stare out at the Carolina Coast and looking out over Kill Devil Hills. It's lush and green, making the world seem filled with possibilities and giving a keen awareness to the sense of how big the opportunities out there are.

"It's like a view from heaven. Do you think this is what Dad and Mom see?" Laurel asks, brushing up against me.

"Every hour of every day," I reply with certainty.

My gaze follows the flight line markers down the hill. I sling an arm over Laurel's shoulder and we allow ourselves to feel the weight of emotion, the ethereality of what flying meant growing up, and how grounded it's made us since because of how close our shared experiences keep us as sisters.

I would literally do anything right now so Laurel could get back in the air and travel. Instead, in our similar retro-inspired outfits, we link arms and watch our kids giggling along with Cary while he reads them every plaque and sign.

"Bennett loves Emory," my sister says in a whisper about her ex. "He'll do anything for his daughter. But I'll murder you if you let Cary get away."

It's at the same moment Cary looks at me. The grin on his face broadens, a distraction that warms me all over and makes it easier to ignore Laurel's caution.

Our parents were the same age when they passed. I'm sure, if either of them survived the accident, the wait to get back to the other would have lasted an eternity. It's another reason why Cary is my now. Forever is a long time for a young man to commit to.

He checks his watch, hustling Bhodi and Emory towards us, and beckoning to his mother who's been strolling the perimeter.

"Did you see that?" Bhodi points to the sky.

I hadn't paid much attention to the airstrip until the whirr of propellers broke through, capturing my other senses. A biplane emerges from beyond a line of trees.

"Cool with going over there?" Cary directs his question at Laurel, looking for her permission to take Emory with him.

She agrees and his short-lived seriousness dissolves. My boyfriend is back to being the excited kid. The man who restores the childlike wonder to the world and gives the impression that this was the way Bhodi was supposed to grow up; alongside a guy who encourages fun and laughter. Even though Rex Stanton did horrible things to his son, Cary hasn't lost the ability to be enthusiastic.

There have been times my mind has traveled to before the holidays when Cary hadn't been a part of our lives. Had Laurel and I brought this much joy to our kids? I hoped we had—we made our fun—but perhaps I was mistaken. Whatever this is, I like it more.

I was in my mid-twenties when I settled down with a baby. I was ready for a white picket fence, hearts and roses family. Yet I wound up a struggling single mom. I guess, having rapidly progressed through the stage of life Cary is in, that there is an appeal to his charm. I didn't know very many men his age when I was his age, and I explored being twenty-something with trepidation instead of excitement.

I'm realizing as much as Bhodi needs Cary, I need him too to show me what decent men are like, and that you can care and be carefree.

I have so many regrets that my poor choices about who I trusted mean my son will never get the type of father who signs up as a T-ball coach, or root for him from the bleachers at a soccer tournament. Try as I may, I can't replace what Bhodi missed out on. However, I'm still his one-hundred-percent-there-to-support-him mom. Having Cary along for the adventure with us makes me feel like I haven't totally let Bhodi down and, selfishly, as if I haven't lost out on as much as it seemed like I had.

In a long chain, Bhodi, Emory, and the man I love are skipping—*skipping*—the paved walkway to the airfield. Emory stops to pick a milk thistle and tries to blow the seeds off the top. They're still purple. Cary tucks the weed into a ribbon loop on her top, pretending it's a beautiful flower. My ovaries ache. He's incredibly sweet with my niece.

She runs to catch up with her cousin and Cary jogs along after her. They wait for us in the shade of a tree. The heat has kicked up another notch and the moms meander at a steady pace, making small talk.

Cary holds up a hand, waving at a woman approaching them wearing aviator glasses. She greets him with a handshake. The next thing I know, a commotion ensues and the kids are jumping up and down, yelling, "Me!"

"No really, who is going to be my co-pilot?" the woman asks as we meet up with our group.

From behind, Cary puts both his palms on my sister's shoulders. She glances at me bewildered.

"This is Laurel and she gets the hot seat," he remarks with a breezy air.

"What? I can't fly. Bennett flies!"

The pilot startles but is swift to recover. "Did you not want the controls during flight? It was what Mr. Cass requested. I've got thousands of hours teaching and was under the impression you'd flown before."

"She has. Laurel's not licensed, but we both flew under our dad's supervision. He was a commercial pilot," I say in reassurance. Turning toward Cary, my heart is about to explode. "This is why you've been taking calls and hiding texts since yesterday, isn't it?" He'd been planning a surprise thank you for my sister.

She's shaking, on the verge of tears, staring longingly at the line of aircraft.

Cary blushes under his trimmed beard. "You're not scared, Laurel?" He thinks he blew it again.

What Cary doesn't realize is for Laurel there's no more fear in getting back in the air than there would be for anyone who lost someone in a traffic accident. Flying is in our blood. Laurel wasn't grounded for any other reason than it was what was best for Emory.

"No," she whimpers, hugging him and using the backs of her palms to wipe her cheeks. "This is the nicest thing anyone has ever done for me. Thank you."

"It's the least I can do." He rubs her back.

"Oh, God! Don't say that. Else, I'll expect you to top this at Christmas!" She bubbles with laughter and utter disbelief.

We move down the tarmac closer to the private planes and stop in front of an adorable prop. Exactly the way my dad did, the woman caresses the plane's nose like it's her most prized possession

Inside, it's bigger than I expected. There's ample room for all of us.

"Well, are we ready for takeoff?" Cary claps his hands together, winking.

The kid's faces light up and Cary is officially the best boyfriend ever.

# Chapter Twenty-four

*Cary*

There's no formality in the way I pull the chair out for my mother to sit and push her back in. It's the same natural action I'd do for my girlfriend when we eat out. The only reason I'm aware after doing so is that I want to start out on the right foot with Davina this evening. To be proud of the effort I'm making from the start and for everything to go well.

My mom's got on the same outfit she wore on our trip to the memorial today. It's less chic than her country club society norm, which is why it captured my attention. But I'm in jeans and a tee with leather thonged flip-flops.

It's a good thing we're at a casual beachcomber restaurant. I'm not sure I could do this back in Brighton at Royce's over Lobster Thermidor and Steak au Poivre. We need the ability to get as messy as we had teaching Bhodi to crack the lobster tails the night before this. Not that I expect a scene. Davina is a little too refined for public displays of aggression.

Paper placemats are stamped with the menu. There's a laminated beverage list stuck between the salt and pepper shakers. My mother orders a white wine and I get a draft beer.

Even though I planned the day's surprise with Laurel in mind, my mother hasn't stopped thanking me for the plane ride this afternoon. She stops short of expressing the meaning behind her gratitude, but I understand it has more to do with us including her.

Bhod and Emory excitedly clapped taxiing down the runway. Got the adults into the action as Laurel took over the controls. And we cheered again at touch down. When Davina and I left the beach house, the kids still hadn't stopped talking about how high off of the ground we were. Peering out the tiny windows, the cars looked like lines of ants. It's an experience they won't forget. Me either.

The way everyone reacted to the surprise had my chest swelling. It wasn't an ego stroke the initial way bringing them to the beach to spoil was. I feel like... a family guy. A normal human who does nice shit for the people he cares about because he can.

It's one more check in the column of things I've done right. The list is growing. The overwhelming feeling that I've sucked at relationships—connecting with anyone, not only women—isn't as pervasive as it had been.

"I like Bhodi. He reminds me of someone." Davina winks, taking a sip from her glass.

"Don't say me." I cover my brow, sliding my hand down my beard. Heat rises from my collar. I turn my head and swig my beer.

My mom chuckles. "He's a good boy. Seems attached to Holly. From what I've seen she's a good mother."

"She is." It comes out more boastful than I expect.

The corners of Davina's lips curl up. She hasn't

taken the statement as pretentious as it sounded. "You were worried I think less of her."

There's no sense beating around the bush. "I told Holly about you and Powell the other night, so it was more she'd think less of you." *Of me.* "But my girlfriend has been through her own rough patch and people have spilled worse secrets to her."

"The boy's father isn't part of the picture?"

"He's gone. She's raised him by herself. That's why they're so close."

"We were too. Then you grew up. Stopped being my little boy."

"Yeah, I suppose I did." I huff. Looking back, I went from manipulating Transformers to women in the blink of an eye. "Listen, Mom, I wish I'd known what he was doing to you, to us."

"Had I recognized it sooner, we both would've been better off," my mom scoffs.

A lot of what Holly's said about the choices she had runs through my brain. We're here hashing it out, so why not place my cards on the table?

"If you had to do everything all over again would you have gone after my real father?"

"Hell, No. I would have had the courage to reinvent myself and raise you on my own the way Holly's doing with Bhodi; Gotten a full-body tattoo. Not worried about what clothes I wore. Stopped trying to impress people whose friendships were fleeting. Learned all I could about your grandaddy's company while he was still alive and been the one to take the dealership in a new direction.

"Nothing Rex accomplished was all that complicated, Cary. He brought in the right people to assist him; The ones with the true insight. I could have done the same had I had a modicum of confidence in myself as a young woman. It wasn't a God-given talent your father had. Grandaddy taught

Rex the business. My father was a good man who traded in kindness, even if it wasn't a fair trade."

It's true. Rex may have stunted Davina, but she's not stupid. Neither am I. I'm flipping twenty-five and in charge of billions of dollars a year in inventory. Behind closed doors in the corporate offices, it's the executives Rexy hired to manage the things he couldn't who are now showing me the ropes.

A cocky grin slides over my face.

"What?" Davina asks, unsure unloading the baggage up front was a wise decision.

"You could have done it."

"I should have. Perhaps then you wouldn't have stopped being mine—even now that you're grown."

I stand up from my chair and squat back down in front of Davina, leaning forward to wrap my arms around her. She clasps the back of my head as I hug her.

"What was that for?" Her palms surround my face.

"I'm sorry for the way Rex treated you, Mom."

Holly was in her twenties when William duped her, but Davina? She had barely a chance to mature when Grandad married her off.

For all intents and purposes my mother was a teenager when she had me. I can't hold a grudge against Rex for pulling crap on me at that age and give him a free pass for doing something as underhanded to Davina.

"There's no need to apologize, Cary. We were the parents. It was my job to protect you." Her eyes water.

"I didn't say I absolve you entirely." I laugh. "But after spending time with Bhodi, I understand why me having two parents was important to you, and how Rex led you to believe he'd come through for us. I'm sorry he duped you into trusting him. I wish he'd been the man you deserved."

"We deserved. *Us.*" Davina corrects me.

"I love you, Mom." I never stopped. Even in my anger.

"Oh, sweet boy, I loved you from the moment I knew you were on the way."

I get that now. Going back to Rex had been my mother's biggest mistake, not me.

"I have a million regrets, Cary, and I don't want you to have any. This is the last time I'll bring it up because I don't want to fight. Consider meeting your sister. Had I been honest all those years ago, you would already know Adelaide already."

The server interrupts, clearing his throat. I go back to my seat, leaving Davina's request hanging between us while eating our meals.

"Can I ask you a question?" My mother folds her napkin in her lap. It's a bracing move, giving off the impression she expects me to tell her to mind her own business after she asks it.

I swallow and nod.

"Why her?"

"She's…. Holly's not interested in being anyone but herself. She doesn't care how people view her." Or she hadn't until I came into the picture. Hence, why I needed to be open to Davina's tense question. I'd assumed until the parking lot fiasco everyone interpreted Holly's confidence the way I had. "With Holly, I can be me and I like that. She doesn't expect gifts, which makes them more fun to give. She doesn't hold my past against me since she's made her own mistakes. I didn't plan on dating her when I volunteered to mentor Bhodi. As a matter of fact, I was tongue-tied around Holly for months and freaked out she wasn't as attracted to me as I was to her. We'd hardly spoken to one another for the exact same reason."

"You were both looking out for her boy's best

interests."

I nod. "Now, the three of us are a weirdly constructed unit."

"A family."

"Yeah," I agree, running my fingers through my hair.

"What you wanted, but didn't get."

"Is that so wrong?"

"Not at all, Cary."

"You think she's too old for me."

"It's more likely that I'm a little jealous that she gets someone like you, sweetheart. Someone a little more noble and selfless like Grandaddy."

"Gross. We're not about to have one of those Oedipus moments, are we?" I rely on a joke to lighten the mood.

My mother tsks, rolling her eyes. She points a finger dangerously close to my nose. "Stop being awful and hear me out. I will tell Holly you're being rude to me."

My lips twist. I don't doubt it. My girlfriend and her sister have taken a liking to my mom. Their subtle approval of Davina makes it easier for me to accept there are things in the past I can't change. They help me to recognize I can move forward.

Mom pushes her plate to the center and leans her crossed elbows on the table. She's all ears wanting to embrace the story of how I fell in love with someone who brings light to every dark place in my soul.

I can't fathom that I'm about to confide in Davina what I've only said to my shrink. "I think about marrying her twenty-four seven."

Holly's not a woman I'm trying to figure out what bucket to place in any longer. Not only is she the whole damned bucket, she's also the person I want to cross off my bucket list with. I want to give her the feeling she talks about when she mentions her own parents and how they lived for one another.

Does that make me a sap?

Hell, yeah.

Holly wants to slap a fugly fifties rockabilly print shirt on me with  stars, hula girls with ukuleles, and horseshoes on it?

I am down with that. As long as she's there with me.

My mom grabs my hand.

I panic for a sec that I shouldn't have been as honest about my intentions. "Does her age bug you?" I ask.

"Are you happy?"

"Yes."

"Then don't worry about whether I approve... I can find common ground with Holly, especially where she loves flowers."

We stay for another drink and Davina orders dessert. So I'm stunned after breakfast the next day to see my mother's bags by the door. There are a lot of them in addition to a large box of her things in the second floor hallway that make it seem as if she's moving out.

I find Davina hauling her towels to the washer. She hits start on the machine as I look on, stunned.

"Fold these for Holly when they're tumbled dry. She agreed to water the plants and I hate to put much else on her plate," my mother says.

"Where are you going?"

"Home, darling. Where I belong. You all should enjoy your vacation without having your mother around." She juts out a hip. "The master bedroom is empty. I left a few things in the event I'm invited back."

I note my mom's not surrendering her key to my house. She'll be here again.

"You don't have to—"

"I want to, Cary. And the best part about Rex being gone is I get to do what I want. I would like it if you brought Holly and Bhodi over for dinner soon."

"I'm not sure." I don't like the idea of them anywhere near the house I grew up in.

"Cary." Mom embraces me. "Placate me and say you'll consider it."

"I'll consider it." I mumble into her hair, hugging her back as if I'm seeing someone I hadn't in fifteen years.

Cripes, when did Davina get so small? My mom had been a tough negotiator, getting me to clean my plate. Isn't she the person who I had to look up at when she placed a platter of cookies on the kitchen table?

It's a beat before I change my mind. We'll be over. First, I need to digest. Prepare. Ask Holly if she's willing to go to Rex's house.

"You enjoy the rest of your time alone... Oh, and Cary?"

"Yeah, mom?"

"I'd be ecstatic to have a granddaughter at some point too."

# Chapter Twenty-five

Holly

"You sure about this?" Cary asks, warily.

We're standing in Davina's driveway, so it's about half past late to send our regrets. My boyfriend takes the cake I've carried in my lap on the drive across Brighton.

"It's fine," I repeat for the bazillionth time since Cary asked if we'd go to dinner at his mother's home.

Cary's refusal to let me walk toward the front door is getting on my nerves. It isn't like the beach house hadn't made it apparent the Cass-Stanton's are part of a significantly different income tax bracket than me.

"I wish I understood your reservations about Bhodi and me—" My voice trails because I don't want to admit I'm worried he's embarrassed by us.

"This was his house." Cary means Rex's.

"Oh," I say, regaining a little confidence that I'm not white trash. "It was yours too."

I know Cary moved out and I've gleaned it was his concern for Davina that had him moving back in.

"You stay here when you don't stay with us."

I step toward a hedgerow. Cary has to follow.

"I don't want to wear out my welcome at Laurel's and I can't move you and Bhodi in here. If we get someplace it'll have to be in a different neighborhood."

"Uhm, I'm not looking to move anywhere." I'm smart enough to figure it's Davina's house and her rules. However, I can't resist the tiny seed of curiosity Cary's planted and stop short. "But why? Or, uh, why not?"

"I don't want you guys where the things Rex did can touch you." The glass cover of the cake holder rattles. Cary's nerves have the best of him.

I cock my head, taking the cake plate back so we don't wind up cleaning sticky shards of glass covered in strawberries and cream off the concrete.

Then the root of his hesitance hits me. "This is about bad memories."

Cary flopped in bed last night and didn't want to touch me. I hadn't thought much of it since we're exceptionally good at patience when it comes to sex. The build-up makes the waiting worthwhile. Why accept a quickie trying to time it between kid interruptions when you can have it long and leisurely.

Who am I fooling? I'll take it both ways.

The reality is, Cary likes to make up for the absence of sex with lots more sex and an abundance of orgasms. I've decided this has far more to do with dating a man in his prime than Cary's past. Yet, he's cautious about using sex to mask his doubts.

"I did things here I wasn't proud of."

"Intentionally? And let me be clear; were you aware while you did those things of your father's intentions?" There are better places to set the cake stand than on the scorching hood of the car, but I put it there anyway since it's the closest flat surface that isn't the ground.

"No." He scrubs a paw down his face, tugging at the front of his hair. His beard is a little longer and due for a trim. Cary looks rugged… and strung out.

I wrap my fingers around his and bring them to my lips.

"Are you guys coming or what?" Bhodi yells from the doorstep.

"Ring the bell and let Miss Davina know we'll be right in." I flash an award-winning smile at my son to disguise our conversation. Turning my attention back to Cary I say, "Show me the mess your mom made."

When Cary opened up about Rex, he also talked about his troubles with Davina after Rex's death and how she'd spilled a bucket of paint in the living room.

"That's cleaned up. She hired a contractor to do some of the other rooms too."

"So it doesn't look the way it did when she tried to paint it herself." It's not a question.

He paces in a circle with his hands on his hips. "No. None of it's the way it was before." His hands slap to his sides as I push on with my point.

"Do you think she's erasing bad memories?"

"I think she's got nothing to do and is spending money." He quips.

"It seems to me she's stuck in a house she hates as much as you do and she's trying to make the best of it."

"She can sell it."

"Not with a dated living room in this neck of the woods, she couldn't. Your mom has nothing but you —and that's *when* you let her into your life. You said she redesigned the entire beach house. Perhaps this is a project she needs to hold on to, or maybe to let go."

Cary tugs me by the neck, putting his firm lips

against my forehead. "I don't know why I pay so much for therapy when I have you."

"Don't stop going on my account." I laugh.

It's okay to need help. Everyone does now and again. I journal my thoughts to make sense of them. Going back to read what I've written during the toughest times, I wonder why I'm so hard on myself or how I could have taken small events so personally when I've lived through larger ordeals. But hearts hurt easily, and this family endured an unusual type of pain. One I couldn't have begun to fathom had I not fallen in love with this man. It's insane expecting them to be over it in a matter of months, and I grant Davina grace because it's what Cary needs from me. I hope someday if I'm having a rough go, he can do that for me.

"Can I tell you a secret?" My voice is muffled by the soft cotton of Cary's shirt while I continue to hug him. "I'm older than dirt, and I've never been brought home by anyone before. Even having met your mom, I'm anxious and excited. I want to see where you grew up, have your mother show me embarrassing baby pictures, and maybe sneak up to your room the way I didn't get to do when I was in high school."

Cary's chest rumbles. He rests his clasped hands on my lower back, fiddling with the bow on my dress. "You want me to kiss you up there?"

"Only if you want to." I roll my lips between my teeth. "That may not be the person you need me to be for you today. But if I wasn't open about my own insecurities, I'd be afraid my behavior would make you think I wasn't able to be that person, anyway."

"I love you, but I'm not ready to bring you up there yet. Can I kiss you someplace else?"

"You can kiss me anywhere you want." I wink.

"Here's a good spot," Cary moves my hair and

pecks between my jawline and my ear, chastely.

It sends shivers down my spine and he winks, promising more when his battered heart can handle it. Then he grabs the cake and we make our way inside.

Davina is warm and inviting. I get the grand tour downstairs on the way out to a covered porch. Bhodi sits there, having gulped down half a glass of lemonade, and is helping himself to the entire plate of crudités.

We're in the shade and an overhead fan pushes the heat of summer back into the bright yard. Davina points out a few new plants she's purchased since the weekend she stayed with us in the Outer Banks.

"I'm bored," Bhodi announces after we've eaten. I made him leave his video game at home. "Can I play on your phone?" He holds out a palm to Cary.

"I'll do you one better. My laptop is in the house and we can go search the online auctions for cars?"

Bhodi fist pumps. They're off and I'm alone with Davina.

"They're cute together." Cary's mom hums. "Thank you."

"For what?"

I should be the one thanking Davina. Dinner was delicious. I don't hate the kitchen, but people underestimate how spoiled it feels having a decent meal cooked for you.

"Bringing Bhodi into Cary's life. Being there for my son. Not believing I'm a harpy." She lets out a self-deprecating laugh. "I overstayed at the beach. Cary makes himself scarce. I've hardly seen him at all since the funeral, and when I have he hasn't been overjoyed that I'm around." She leans back in her chair. "He'd called and asked me to leave that morning, but he sounded lighter and it made me curious. I'd apologize for intruding, but I'd be lying.

It was nice to see a spark in him. I dare say beforehand it was a relief when he argued with me instead of shutting me out. I am sorry if I did anything to make you uncomfortable. And I'm grateful you came today."

"You're welcome. It was awkward at first, but that was all on you." I wink and tease Davina. I like her company.

"It was on me." She laughs, somberly. "I made the mistakes and appreciate that you aren't holding them against me."

"You're not my mother. And I love Cary. He doesn't need me against you to take his side."

"You aren't at all the girl I expected my son to bring home."

"I sort of figured. What part has you?" I count off on my fingers. "The clothes, the job, the kid, or the age?"

"The acceptance," she counters. "How truly happy you make him. Watching you two… three," Davina pauses to include Bhodi. "It's like Cary found something he didn't think he'd get. Perhaps even that he wasn't aware was out there."

"I know what you mean. Cary's that person for Bhodi. I could watch them for hours. How goofy they are together. If you take me out of the equation as it stands, Bhodi's never had a man in his life that he didn't have to share. My friend Dusty spent time with him, but he has a daughter. My former brother-in-law, Emory's father, did what he could with Bhodi while he and my sister were together," I remark, wistful. "I do like it when Bhodi and Cary include me. Though, the car stuff confounds me," I admit with an eye roll.

"But you know flowers, and we could make our own gardening club. "

"I'm no expert, but I haven't killed a plant,

recently."

"You could whip this place into shape in no time." Davina gestures to the yard.

"Is that a challenge?"

Davina's yard is green, but it lacks other vibrant colors.

"No, sweetheart. It's an invitation. Give me something to look forward to by coming back another time. If it's not too much to ask, let me see my son enjoying being in love.

"I can't change the past. And since I realized what Cary had been through, I've been embarrassed by the way I acted and terrified he'll be judged because of my indiscretions. He didn't choose to be born into this mess. No child would. I've given him space, holding my breath for the moment it all implodes and the world finds out what a horrible person I am. I'm tired of the distance and feeling like I'm still failing him. So, when that happens, I'd like a few good memories to hold onto."

# Chapter Twenty-six

*Holly*

Tired.

The energy to say exhausted isn't even available.

I peer down at my cell, thankful for Cary's patience. He's sitting in the dark parking lot outside. I've kept him on standby an extra half an hour past when I promised my shift would finish.

He hadn't sent a message saying he was here right away. I'm unsure if that means he built in extra time to accommodate my general lateness or just what. I do know I love him for the lack of text-based foot tapping. There's enough guilt eating me. However, this is the first time since we've been back to the beach house this summer that I've knocked us off schedule.

It will likely be another ten to fifteen minutes before I can reassure the cleaning crew they can lock up after me and leave. Having Jake around is compounding their nervousness.

"What are you going to do?" I ask, wishing I cared more about Jake's response than hearing he expects me to handle it during my days off.

Beyond the bone-weariness, I don't give a hoot: A problem in itself.

My boyfriend is rich. I'm not. I need this job, with its sucky hours that force me away from the people I love. I have bills to pay and a son to finish raising who has gotten a taste of the finer things in life. I have too, but it's different and has reminded me of the world of possibilities I had for Bhodi before he was born.

Out in her garden, Davina's been chatting me up about the private high school Cary attended. It was never an unknown institution. Bennett went there. If I start saving now, I should be able to afford the tuition, assuming nothing catastrophic happens. Bhodi deserves the option of becoming a businessperson or a pilot. Although my heart soars when he says he wants to work with his hands the way Dusty does, or doing all the mechanical things Cary tutors him in at the service center.

I had dreams once upon a time. Uncomplicated ones, filled with babies and sunshine and flowers, that hadn't seemed like much of a stretch when I was younger. It wasn't as if I hadn't intended to go back to work for the airlines after Bhodi was old enough. Now years into this job, I'm realigning my goals, and making my son my "mill boy" for lack of a better term. I may not have been a mill girl, but Carver invested in my friends. So why can't I in my child?

A custodian skitters through the theatre, trying their best to remain inconspicuous while the owner and I discuss business at the bar.

See no evil, hear no evil. That's been my motto as well whenever I've been in the club and questionable issues have cropped up.

Jake shrugs, downing a shot of rum and pouring a second. "She's not the first dancer to quit with short notice."

I'm aware of this. I simply hadn't expected after tossing the waitress Jake asked me to let go and the dancer who was causing so many other issues that a third employee the dancer fought with would hand in her notice.

Maybe I'd become too complacent where things have been going so good outside of the brick walls of Sweet Caroline's. Perhaps I'd enjoyed the occasional visits from friends here too much. It's hard to balance work, family, and friendships. My girlfriends don't keep vampire hours like I do anymore.

Overwhelmed by fatigue, I miss having Kimber behind the bar at my elbows while we served, and think back to Cece's retirement when I fixed where Dusty smudged her lipstick before her final performance on the stage. They've all gone on to better... The dancer who quit tonight is too.

I'm still hanging around, making the best of it. Except my melancholy mood leaves me wondering when my turn is. I know it's after Bhodi is grown. I have to survive the tribulations of the graveyard shift until then. I hope Cary's willing to hang out in a deserted parking lot in the middle of the night that long.

I blow out a breath and the end of the kerchief tied around my French roll lifts. "Think she'll show for the performances this week?"

"From past experience, we both know that's doubtful." Jake swirls the droplets of brown in his shot glass.

I'd called him in before closing time since I'm supposed to be gone the next few days. Needless to say, Jake wasn't thrilled.

"You hate it here as much as I do, Hol?"

My eyes widen, and I blink fast. I don't know how to answer or if he needs to talk something out.

There was a single instance years ago when Jake asked me that very same question. It was after hours and I was behind the bar pouring him shots. A drunken Jake, with his head lowered and inspecting every layer of varnish the bar had been sealed with, offered me a glimpse of his history. It was a snippet and I haven't puzzled where it fits in to make sense of why Jake generally couldn't care less about the club. But I'll always remember Jake's sobering recount and glimpse into his history. And how my listening—to something I'm not even sure he's revealed to Kimber —built a measure of trust between us.

Inebriated or not, the fact that Jake believed enough in me that I could keep his secret is why I can find kindness for him when our friendship isn't necessarily a two-way street.

Jake is skittish. Like a wounded animal in search of comfort, he's unable to let his guard down and he bites out of habit.

He's also predisposed to piss on things, marking them the way a dog does, which is super-fun. Case in point: His territorial fight with Trig over Kimber.

Unfortunately, I can't be his grief counselor now, and sharing my current feelings on him being my employer isn't going to get me out of here any faster.

"I'll log in tomorrow and rearrange the schedule in case."

"Nice way of avoiding a lie." He clicks his tongue.

I consider telling Jake I loved it here when I first started because I did. The sliver of truth that the club was lively and appealing back when my biggest excitement was potty training won't placate him. Nowadays, I'm chained to it both to maintain connections and monetarily. I'll never find anyplace else that pays me this well. This is the first instance I'm a trapped mouse to Jake's cat. He's aware of how difficult the situation makes it for me to leave.

I stand up from the stool, grabbing my oversized purse off the bar, and sliding a glass to Jake. With a fluid motion, he places it in the sink. Retreating inward, I tell Jake I'll take responsibility for calling the dancers who need to cover shifts and placing ads for new talent while I'm gone.

Cary doesn't deserve me leaving him on permanent pause. We have a three-hour stretch of road in front of us and he's the one driving so I can sleep.

"Cass still dragging your ass to the beach?" He confirms wanting to know if he can count on me to be in if things go downhill.

"I enjoy having my ass dragged to the beach, thank you very much. And yes, we're leaving as soon as I walk out the door."

"I need to rethink your vacation allotment if you're spending it with him."

Having never gotten to the middle of Jake's animosity toward Sloan, I don't latch onto caring about the history behind his opinion of Cary. Managing strippers and persuading drunk clientele to take it outside is enough drama. I have a headache from tonight already.

"Is there anything else?" I roll my eyes. One hand is on my hip and the other on the exit.

"Bring me rum? The distillery is there." The request is brash, yet Jake's body language is bashful and resigned for me to excuse myself from the task.

"Cash." I walk back toward him, holding up my palm. I pocket the crisp bills Jake counts out of his wallet. "We have a distributor rep, you know."

"And I also have you," he mocks, forgoing a thank you.

Jake's attitude has changed to an edgy pride in ownership that I hate because it reinforces how stuck I am.

I lumber to Cary's SUV. The little one he drives

around Brighton, not the massive XLT. Laurel's stayed home since the air conditioning got fixed. Bennett's a stickler about visitation, and Laurel prefers not to be a third wheel.

We had Dusty and Cece to the coast overnight. The guys went deep sea fishing, returning sunburnt and exuding male pride with their catch. Cece and I exchanged looks at how chummy they were sitting around the beach house with kids on their laps, drinking beer together. It was as if over the course of an afternoon they'd become brothers of sorts.

Cary's invited Davina to come tomorrow afternoon. Sometimes she joins us wherever we're going from north of Nags Head all the way down to the Cape Hatteras Lighthouse. Others she suns herself by the pool, or tends to the plant pots, and has appetizers and wine set out for when we return.

Consistently, she scoots Cary and me out the door at least one evening, insisting we need a few hours alone, but cautioning us not to fill up on dessert. While we're at a restaurant, she and Bhodi concoct something delicious in the kitchen, and I'm happy to say my son is growing attached to Cary's mom.

At the beach, everything about us and the fun we have feels like what a normal family does.

"Hey Doll, you look beat. Everything okay?" Cary and I lean toward each other, giving a brief kiss hello after my bum hits the leather seat.

I wave off his concern, hoping sleep will come easy, and I won't feel as weighed down once my toes are in the sand. There's no sense in complaining. I chose this life whether it was obvious what I was getting into as a single parent or not.

I made the decision to date Cary too. So, I won't be too hard on myself. He covers me with a blanket, places a horseshoe-shaped travel pillow in my lap, and shifts the car into gear.

"Thanks." My smile is weak but genuine and his broadens. "I'm sorry for the delay."

I yawn, looking back at my son fast asleep in the backseat. I chuckle a little because he uses the sleeping bag every chance he gets and has burritoed himself inside of it.

We're hardly out of town when the company and the road soothe my frayed nerves. My eyes drift shut. Though I'm desperate to hear about what they've done together before bedtime, it has to wait.

"Hol, sweetheart, wake up or I'm carrying you up the stairs."

I lick my parched lips and hum, cautiously pressing my fingertips to my eye sockets so that I don't smudge black everywhere.

"Hey, you." Cary coos, using the same tone I do when I call Bhodi "bugaboo".

He's standing at my open car door. The sun's coming up over the horizon and the salt marsh air has me inhaling deeply. I unfasten my seatbelt and slide onto the cement, rolling the blanket over one arm and hugging my boyfriend with the other.

My bushy-tailed child is upstairs, raiding the pantry for cereal and hunkering down to watch his alien animals in flashy balls cartoon for the next few hours.

I love his routine at Cary's house and that he isn't sitting around bored, waiting for me to perk up so that we can go build sandcastles and fish off the pier. He has a new wakeboard and wants to practice to show Sylvie Rhys he's as balanced on the ocean as she is skiing the slopes.

I lean into Cary's shoulder.

"Gonna make it?" he kisses my temple.

"Maybe. Maybe not." I joke.

The stress of my job rushes at me like the incoming tide on a stormy day. An anchor is tethering me, only allowing the boat to drift so far. I wish like hell that the mooring would snap so I can set an alternate course sooner.

# Chapter Twenty-seven

*Cary*

I take a minute to look out over the sound before closing the curtains in the master bedroom on the third floor. The house's views are astounding—a reason I bought it—but none more than the one gazing out this window. From this vantage point, I can see everything clearly.

The rising sun paints the world in pinks, purples, and golds. The moon is beautiful. Almost translucent as it fades into the sky, giving an almost ethereal feeling that makes you feel how insignificant your problems are—or would be if you took the time to get past them.

There's a whole incredible world out there waiting to be explored and the person whose hand I want to take and explore it with is by my side.

I stare at the retreating space between the sun and the moon. The place I've been stuck waiting for my future to hit me like daybreak.

Maybe it was my level of maturity, but I'd naively thought the answers to my problems with Rex, my mom, and my teenage years were going to be dropped in my lap. I hadn't realized I had to grow through those experiences. Step into the future, reach toward the things I wanted most, while not even fully conscious of what they were.

Step one: counseling.

Step two: Did I have what it takes to care about a kid when the man who was my role model failed miserably and with every intent to do so?

Step three: Find someone to fall in love with who saw past the physical things I could provide and accepted the flawed emotional side of me without running in the other direction.

Holly steadies my rocking world by the way she loves me. Forgave me without hesitation for not explaining why she had every right to second guess letting me mentor her kid. Everything about her makes enduring my past worthwhile.

No. That's not it at all. Finding Holly makes up for it, though. She's a reward I won't ever deserve. I didn't understand love could be like this.

She makes me feel unsullied and, in my weakest moment, she treated me like an equal. Holly is my favorite confidante. The one whose opinion matters the most. She gives me the ability to be patient with myself and I've come to the conclusion that's what allows me to ignore her aberrant lateness since there's never any ill intent when Holly makes anyone wait.

Holly's always trying her best for someone else. It's not my place to like or dislike that tonight she directed her kindness at a jackass like Jake Ballentine, merely accept it was his turn. Holly doesn't take her own turn often enough. I need to make up for that by not bitching about waiting a few extra minutes for her.

*How's that for growing the fuck up and not making*

*everything about me, my past trauma, or giving power to the people who damaged me?* I wordlessly fist-pump.

At my most recent therapy session, I asked my shrink if I could have had an ideal upbringing and still found Holly.

His response?

"Cary, there's not a man in Brighton who doesn't know what block Sweet Caroline's is on. Anything is possible."

I noticed he stopped short of saying he'd been there too. Maybe it was out of respect for Holly. Maybe his bachelor party had been there like Glen's. I can assure you mine won't be. It would be fun to do something unique. The deep sea fishing I'd done with Dusty last month was a pretty enjoyable trek out.

Somewhere deep down I wonder if the reason I made it so awkward with Holly when we first met was because I hadn't been ready to step forward yet.

Not that for a moment I grieved Rex Stanton's death. Quite the opposite, I needed time for it to sink in that those chains didn't bind me. The more they've loosened, the clearer I've resolved that I'm free to love whoever I want and have them love me back.

I close the shade and draw the curtain. Three hours' sleep isn't enough for Holly to function on, but I find myself pulling back the covers and curling around her body with lustful, eager intent. My heart knows she's mine. My body wants a tangible reminder of the way the soft skin between her thighs feels beneath my fingertips.

Half awake, she adjusts, rolling onto her back and arching toward each caress as my hands wander up her stomach, cupping her breasts.

I've had my fair share of amazing sex, but not all pussies are created equal. Some you get lost in for the moment and others you know you could live in.

The little flutter Holly's pussy makes when I enter

her is as if it's welcoming me home. Sometimes, I pull out just to slide into her entrance a second time to feel the sensation again. The more I fuck her, the more I'm coming to realize how unlikely it is I'll move on and screw around with anyone else. I don't want anyone but Holly, and I want to prove it to her.

"Doll," I say, covering her with my body. "I wanna feel all of you soon. Fill you with my cum."

We're both aware I don't mean spilling into the condom. I'm ready to take down the last barriers and embrace the consequences of skin on skin. It's time for me to truly be the man I needed who put family first. The man *they* need.

What I've got with Holly is the beginning of the rest of my life, and I won't lose the chance at being there to see Bhodi grow up. Bit by bit, I'm claiming them as mine.

I have her caged in and Holly's index finger traces my lip. "No," she responds quiet but firm as I'm about to kiss it.

"It doesn't have to be tonight."

She's on the pill. I can get tested. I have been, but I get it if she wants proof in writing.

"No, Cary. Even if I wanted to, I can't. I'm not ready. I may not ever be ready."

My expression betrays, *But we love each other.*

She sees it, and yet Holly is steadfast. "I won't raise a second baby alone, Cary. Not if I can help it."

"If that happened, I'd be there."

Her eyes dart away and I realize what I've said to her honestly is the same lie William told. He'd promised to marry her before she was pregnant and backed out.

My fingers brush Holly's cheek and, when she has no choice but to look at me, every broken promise she's endured is staring me in the face.

I can't believe William took her for granted, missed

his own son's birth, and left Holly to bear the burden of his awful choices. Who does that and can still call themselves a man?

True, the consequences of having a kid might've been an afterthought before meeting Holly. But I wouldn't have shirked it—or I hope not entirely anyway—because I see the effects it has on the people I care for the most.

"Okay," I whisper, brushing my lips against hers. "I won't ask again. You tell me if you're ever ready. But, I'd love *it*, you know. If twelve layers of protection failed, don't think I'll run. I'll stay and sing bad eighties covers and be scared alongside you."

"You'd be afraid of becoming a father because of Rex?" She shudders as if chilled.

I hold her tighter.

"No. For you, since it'd remind you of everything you went through on your own. I'm fine with playing it safe a little longer." Right now all I know about being a dad is pretending I am one to a kid. Hell, I've never even held a baby before.

"You still want to make love to me?" Holly lets out a ragged breath.

I reach for my wallet on the nightstand, pull out protection, and hand it to her.

"Sure thing." I grin, catching Holly's lips with my own.

She hits me with a soft smile. It's the one where her jaw loosens, the corners of her mouth lift tentative, and I lose my shit wondering if what's running through her head is as dirty as I think it is. The first time I saw it, we were nothing to one another. The last time? Before she left for work yesterday afternoon and had slipped to her knees, surrounding my dick with those sweet red lips. And she's slain me every time in between when she's called out my name, like I'm the sole man to have ever worked her body into a frenzy.

If I have my way, I'm the only one who will ever again.

Both her palms push at my chest, rolling me onto my back. Holly pushes my knees apart, settling between them. She plays with my balls and dips her head. I take a sharp inhale when her tongue connects with my hard cock. Before she can take me to the back of her throat—be the giver that she is and leave me with the impression like she hasn't asked me to concede something I really, really want—my knuckle tilts her chin.

"Up here." I tap her hip.

She tugs on my dick a few more times ahead of my fierce negotiations that she should instead brace her hands on my shoulders. Her legs splayed, I grip her ass with one hand, spreading her folds with the other.

We train our eyes on my fingers dipping into her core, spreading the sweetness over her cunt, and the way my thumb glides through, gathering the slickness to pinch and press and pinch again at the nub I love to suckle when I'm tongue fucking her.

Holly grabs her tits, moaning, "Don't stop. I'm so close."

Not that I need an owner's manual to figure out this beauty, but I ask her what she wants anyway and do exactly as she says. Sometimes it's better to be on the giving end because of what the universe decides you're worthy of receiving back.

I got her and I'm going to give as good as I get to keep Holly. Even if she fights it at every mile because it's so ingrained that she can't make herself the priority.

Pushing two fingers inside of her, I curl them, adding a gentle tug back-and-forth to the slow rhythm of her hips. She detonates, and I rise, capturing her lips and her cries of pleasure. This moment is only for my heart to hear.

"Show me more of what you want," I whisper, biting the shell of her ear when the quaking subsides and her pussy releases its grip on my fingers.

My girl suits me up, making sure my attention is rapt on the delicate stroke of her thumb and index finger rolling over my shaft. We both watch as she lines me up. Her knees spread farther apart and she sinks down. My erection disappears into her heat. And then she rides me while my hands caress the landscape of her body. There's no view more spectacular than this.

# Chapter Twenty-eight

*Holly*

I take a bite, laughing while trying not to drop crumbs from the brownie wedge. Once again, Davina baked with my son while Cary and I were out at dinner.

Bhodi is wiping the chocolate Cary smeared on his face off with a towel. My son's belly shakes as he does it. Taking the joke in stride, Bhodi pulls a fudge-laden red M&M off of Cary's desert and puts it on my boyfriend's nose. They constantly behave this way together and, where Cary now resembles Rudolph, the two launch into all things Christmas.

Davina gleefully talks about the traditions they had when Cary was little. Some are so close to the things that happened when I was a girl that I can see them playing out in my mind.

It's August and my son's holiday list is short, but not cheap. It has more to do with his age than his current surroundings. Although my gut tells me that unless I'm careful, there will be a lot of unnecessary gifts under the tree this year.

Smudge of brown still on his nose, Cary pulls Bhodi to his stomach. He flashes me an expression as warm as the brownies are gooey when Bhodi's arms wrap around him. Bhodi steps on Cary's feet and the two maneuver to the sink.

"So what now?" Cary asks after washing up

We're dressed. Not to the nines, but the restaurant we'd gone to was lovely and new to me. It felt good to get cleaned up, wash off sweat, sand, and sunscreen, after spending the day on the beach. I'd put work worries behind me for the next few days following a call with Kelsey, who offered to rework Sweet Caroline's schedule for me. Giving Kelsey the task in a pinch and her willingness to send an SOS if the changes took on any water was reassuring.

It's normal for Bhodi to want to go for a late swim. He's picked up his hand-held gaming system instead, engrossed in the same game as he watches on television. There's no sense in urging my son away. Bhodi's been active all day.

Davina holds up a paperback and puts on her readers. "Don't get any older, Holly. It's a trap. My crow's feet are from squinting at the page." Her humor is self-deprecating, yet Davina hardly shows her not-quite fifty years at all.

And while we're on the subject, my ass does Cary's mother have arthritis. We've hacked out more bushes in the gardens here and in Brighton this summer than I can shake a stick at.

"I guess it's you 'n me then. Let's go sit outside." Cary pours us wine, carrying the glasses down the stairs to the pool.

He gives me mine and sets his on a side table next to a lounger. Cary grabs a spot on the long part of the chair, elbows on his knees and hands clasped. I settle beside him, sipping the tart, bold red he's chosen.

He kisses my temple and we sit in absolute

stillness, listening to the sounds all around us. Cars on the road out front. The rustle of birds and animals in trees. Security lights switch on in another backyard and there's a splash from the neighbor's pool. We're in the final stretch of summer vacation and I don't think I've lived a more perfect year.

I shouldn't love the way Cary loves me so much. Alone with my thoughts, it reinforces the time will come when the other shoe drops and all this ends. Nonetheless, I'm grateful he treats me like I'm precious to him. I don't know if I'll ever be back to spend another season here—vacationing in the Outer Banks seems like a rite of passage; something that happens once if you're lucky and with every intent on coming back whenever possible.

I'm resigned to that not happening, but I also want to believe that at least Cary and I will still be a couple come Christmas. Not for anyone's sake but my own.

"So, I ah—I gotta ask you something. Where do you see things going from here?" Cary boldly presses.

Contrary to any idyllic notions I've been toying with, my brain dives into mom-mode, toward Bhodi and school and their big brother field trips.

I set my glass on the deck. He shifts then slides something warm onto my pinky, it's weighty and dangles loose. The action catches my full attention.

"This is where I see it headed, Hol." Cary's fingers twirl the stone upward and I gasp.

The facets glint in the moonlight.

"That's a mighty big diamond." My words rush out.

"I want to move it here." He touches my index finger. "Permanently," he says with conviction.

"So why didn't you put it there to start with?" My heart beats fast.

"Good things come to those that wait, so to speak." His chuckle isn't as undaunted as the courage he showed a minute ago. "If I promise you this will be the least prophetic, most pathetic attempt at being romantic I make, can you listen to me with an open mind?"

"Sure thing," I whisper.

Or maybe I blink with my mouth hanging open. He's proposing and I can't breathe. Tears prick my eyes.

He wants us forever.

Cary laces our fingers together and I hold on tight. I've been drowning in him for months, kicking to the surface to stop from submerging entirely. From wishing for things he can't give. Hiding those effervescent bubbles that he'd want to make a promise like this to me in the wondrous secret caverns of my journal's pages.

"When Dusty and I were out on the boat, we got to talking about how long he's been with Cece and learning not to rush her. Sometimes it's hard for him to watch Trig and Kimber get ready for the twins since he wants that with Celine, you know? I want that too... *with you*. And I guess I get that you've waited for someone and might worry that time will slip away while you're being patient. On top of that, you'd be ready if the right man told you he was committed to you. Every damn day for the rest of this life."

I'm hanging on every word, captivated in a way that makes my insides tremble with shyness, and the excitement that accompanies being young and inexperienced fills me.

"There are expectations you have of me, Doll. To be a decent man to you. A role model for your son. A good son to my mother. It's made me set the bar higher for me. I've been caught, unable to take one last step. I suppose if I go through with putting my house in order, living up to who both of us need me to be, I also need the reassurance you're waiting here to love me just the same. I know you will. But I want us to have something to look forward to." He turns his head, gazing up at the moon, openly unsure of himself while amazingly confident in this negotiation.

"Are you going away?"

"Only long enough to miss you like crazy." He nudges my shoulder. "Takes about a split-second if you haven't gathered that yet… I have a ticket to New York to meet my half-sister. While I'm there, I want to tell her about my fiancée." He shrugs. "Be able to invite her to the wedding."

I have so many questions, but the first that slips off my tongue is, "When did you want to move the ring to the other finger?"

*Good God, did that sound anxious?*

Cary gives me a nervous chuckle, taking in my blush. "I was hoping now?"

*Don't think about what can go wrong. Focus on what's going right.*

The man I'm in love with placed his flaws at my feet instead of hiding from the things that scare him.

I hold up my hand expectantly and Cary moves the diamond over one digit. It fits securely like Cary had it made for me. He fists his fingers around mine, bringing our joined hands up to kiss my knuckles.

"I want to marry you, Holly."

I cup his cheeks. "You were wrong," I say, brushing his lips with mine. "Opening your heart makes this the most romantic thing anyone's said to me."

Unable to keep the news to ourselves, we go look for

Bhodi, finding him planted on the couch. His nose is pressed to the screen of his video game and Davina has tucked into the thick novel she's reading near the window.

My little man gives us the same aloof response as he had when I'd told him about my first date with Cary. Cary's brow furrows, and we exchange concerned glances. I worry my lip and leave the room, trying to hide my disappointment.

Davina is hot on my tail. She grabs me by the elbow. I about-face and she's hugging me.

Over her shoulder I see Bhodi launch himself at Cary with the biggest bear hug from my cub I've ever witnessed him give any other adult.

That's when the tears of happiness that I thought I had a handle on renew, streaming down my face while Cary's mom and I spy on their private moment from behind the threshold.

With the patience of a saint, Cary answers Bhodi's barrage of questions the way a parent would until Bhodi asks him "when" and my fiancé doesn't have a straight answer for my son.

"Girls like Valentine's Day." Bhodi supplies. "Sylvie Rhys got a hearts sticker book for Valentine's last year. She put stickers everywhere, not just on the pages."

"You need me to get you a hearts sticker book?" Cary joshes.

"No!" My son wrinkles his nose in absolute disgust. He leans back against the arm of the couch, putting as much space between them as possible. "I was only saying it because I noticed. Emory wants one. You can get that for her."

"I will take your suggestion to heart." Cary winks. "But I have a bigger issue than what day because I can't get married without a best man. If there's nobody to stand up for me then there's no wedding."

Bhodi panics. "Where do you find one of those guys?"

"I was thinking since you were my wingman, it could be you."

"Me? I'm not a grown-up."

"Doesn't have to be an adult. A best man is someone the groom trusts. They're someone who likes the bride and takes responsibility for getting him to the church on time."

"Well, I like the bride." He cups his hand, whispering, "When she's not yelling up the stairs to use soap in the shower." Bhodi rolls his eyes as if everyone knows to scrub up.

I stifle a giggle. He needs the reminder. Davina smirks, tugging at my side.

"They have to do other things too: Not forgetting the rings. Making sure I remember to brush my teeth," Cary continues, slouching on the sofa.

"Why?"

"I have to kiss her, dude!"

"You kiss mom all the time. I saw you kiss her after eating a jalapeño, so I don't think she cares if your breath smells. And, like Aunt Laurel says, 'this is a woman who can smell a skunk a mile to the east when the breeze is blowing in from the west'."

Cary erupts into laughter.

"Point taken. Okay, what if I'm standing up there in front of everyone and my fly is down."

"I'M NOT ZIPPING IT!"

I snort, giving away our position to the men of the house, and we're all howling with mirth.

"Not the point, half-pint. You gotta be there so I don't embarrass your mom. There's a lot to remember and it'd be your job to make sure I do everything right."

"You already do everything right for mom. It's why she looooves you." My son rises on his knees and belly flops on the cushions. The top of his head lands against Cary's thigh and Bhodi talks into the couch.

"I can't hear you." Cary ruffles his hair.

"I said, 'I'll do it'!"

"Knew I could count on you. Put 'er there." He holds out a firm hand.

Bhodi shakes it, his arm a limp noodle.

A tickle fight ensues with raucous laughter. Bhodi suggests we celebrate with seconds from the tray of brownies. To which Cary agrees. This man knows how to communicate with my son. When to push and when to keep it light.

The whole while, Cary's words echo through my mind. I knew I could count on him too.

*Cary*

Holly and I lie in our bed later, touching gently after she lets me make love to her. It's the kind of moment we had when I'd brought her home after our first date, except this time the level of intimacy skyrocketed, understanding we're dreaming about our forever instead of on the sidelines watching someone commit to a lifetime together.

We doze and talk and doze some more, not able to come down from the high. Each time my hands dance over her body, my chest constricts tighter than it had when I'd sat her down by the pool.

In all honesty, after Holly gave me a flat-out "no" about scrapping the condoms, my chances of hearing a "yes" fall from her sweet lips seemed slim. We haven't been together long, but when it's right you know it is deep down inside of you. Holly will be my wife a solid year after she came into my life. That's how everything feels right now: solid, rooted, unwavering.

Counseling has provided me every chance to look

at us sideways. Pick apart how we came to be. The difference in our ages. If getting involved with her was some silly fifties sitcom notion that my subconscious was fooling myself into because I have unresolved issues with my teen years.

It hadn't taken much for me to see both sides of the coin and realize if I was legitimately in search of a white picket fence scenario to fix all the fuckups I'd endured, she'd be younger, I'd be older, and Bhod would be a sparkle in my eye, not a flesh and blood kid. I could have somebody else's ideal life, but it wouldn't be with *her* and she's who I want.

Holly was meant to be mine. Half-pint was too.

Unable to sleep, Holly calls her sister as the sun is coming up. Laurel breaks into sobs learning our news before Hol has the chance to ask her to be her maid of honor. She's got Laurel on speaker and the waterworks gush through the phone. Laurel is so happy for us.

Davina has an event planner on speed dial. Apparently, Isobel keeps as unusual hours as Holly does. My mom has already managed to set up a meeting for the day we get back to Brighton. I do appreciate Isobel's willingness to squeeze us in. I guess in the social circles Davina is still a part of, setting up a wedding in six months is short notice. I also like how Holly's asked her sister to tag along. I'm deferring to the ladies for this one so that I can get ahead of things at the dealership. However, the timing means Holly won't be able to adjust her sleep schedule, meaning she'll be dead on her feet going back to work and I tell her my concerns.

"We can do a smaller ceremony, or change the date," Holly suggests with a shrug.

"No, Doll, we stick with Bhodi's choice of February fourteenth." I won't compromise to suit other people's expectations, and I'm adamant her son needs to feel he's a part of this.

Though I may have gone too far, and need to dial "fun dad" back. I allowed Bhodi another brownie for breakfast since I'm positive it had as much sugar in it as his heaping bowl of fruity cereal. He was bouncing off the living room walls, and now we're burning off the excess energy in the pool instead of letting him watch the TV or gaming.

Davina brings down bubbly mimosas for the three of us. Holly once again pipes up about decadence. My mom insists we're entitled to  keep celebrating. Holly deserves to be spoiled and I follow Davina's recommendation up with a matter of fact "get used to it."

"I don't think I ever will." Holly's struck recognizing there's a heck of a lot she's about to get a crash course in as my wife.

She and Davina are like two peas in a pod in the garden. I'm trusting Davina to walk my fiancée through the rest of it. Above all, I don't expect Holly to change for me. With me in time. But she's worked for everything she has and altering that seems unnecessary. I understand there is a sense of pride in it for her.

Can I afford prep school tuition? Well, that's a stupid question. Of course, I can. But she wants to be the one who pays for Bhodi to go to the same private high school I attended. I want him to see she was the one who did it too. There's a bit of feminist girl power in that statement and stroking her own ego involved. Let's not forget Hol labored alone, birthed him alone, and has cared for him every day since, making choices about who gets to be a part of Bhodi's life—like me—All. On. Her. Own. She's entitled to celebrate her accomplishments.

Bhodi is her son, and until now he's been her responsibility to raise. There was zero malice in her heart getting into a relationship with a well-off businessman or any intent of shirking those financial duties off onto me. For fuck's sake, I'd tried to give her cash for a lawyer and she turned me down and booted my ass out of her bedroom. I'll be damned if anyone tries to call her on it.

That doesn't mean I'm not haplessly in love with the woman and won't try to lay the world at her feet. Although I make quite a few complimentary suggestions of my own about the big day, every idea Holly bounces off of me I meet with the phrase, "You can have anything your heart desires."

I do.

Bhodi is swimming and I'm sitting on the concrete pool deck with my feet dangling over the side, enjoying our lazy morning. I refill a squirt gun and wait for the little boy we both freakin' adore to aim and fire.

Holly scoots up behind me. "Wedding or not, my heart desires the sexy as sin man acting like an absolute dork while having a water gun fight." Her knees hit my back and her hands push my shoulders.

Having been dunked before, I catch onto what she's doing and grab Holly by the wrist, using the power to propel her over my head so that she lands in the water around the same time I do.

My shorts and her pajamas are soaked, and her expression is pure shock.

"C'mere." I tug her to me while she's shaking out her arms.

Any other girl I've met would fuss. I ruined her prank, her hair, you name it. Holly's biggest concern is that she's lost the rock on her hand.

I double-check along with her, twisting the stone upward for her to see it shimmering in the sunlight. The facets catch the rays the way they had the moonlight last night.

"Did I tell you this is the most gorgeous ring ever? Thank you." She cups my cheek.

"You're welcome. I should be thanking you for saying yes." It would have been an awkward getaway otherwise.

Her nose gets closer to mine and Bhodi yells, "You guys are so gross."

I laugh and Holly snorts.

"Oh yeah, what do you know anyway?" I toss back.

"I'm in fifth grade, so a lot—like that you never had a sleepover."

*Crap, the kid was onto us in the beginning?* "That so?" Dead. I'm dead. And now I'm wondering if the boy played us or if he said something on the playground to another kid who helped fill in the blanks. Guess I have to plan for the birds and the bees talk, and soon.

"Sure is," he says with amusement.

"So, best man, if you're so gosh darn smart then you know I can't kiss the bride without practicing."

My lips seek Holly's, pressing to them with a kiss. She smiles and that tightness in my chest is back, but it has a halo of lightness I hadn't taken note of before. Whatever this feeling is, it hadn't existed for me before.

I understand now why you shouldn't throw around the word love lightly. It's weighty, and I've only begun to discover half of how meaningful.

She pulls back and her brown eyes dance with mischief. She's distracted me and found another water pistol floating nearby. All of a sudden, the three of us are at war. No choosing sides, no rules, no cares, just fun. The damn perfect last weekend of the summer. I swear it'll go down in history. *My family's history.*

It's finally when normal people are moving about for the day when our skin begins pruning. I wrap in a towel around my waist and cover Holly with another, rubbing her arms to dry her off. Bhodi's earned some gaming time, and Davina disappeared thirty minutes ago into the house.

"You ready?" I ask, swiping my cell from the porch table.

"I am!" She wipes off her left hand and pulls up her phone's camera, pausing long enough to turn my face to hers and gives me a real kiss.

We'd schemed after making love last night. I'm sure the endorphins all around are what's keeping my girl awake and making her wild. After this, I'm putting her to bed. Hell, we all need a few hours of shut-eye.

I text Dusty that I've popped the question right before Holly posts a snapshot of  her engagement ring to her private social media account with the caption: *I said yes!*

She was awestruck finding out Dusty and I'd had a man-to-man about where we saw our futures heading. Holly and Dusty's friendship has carried over to mine with him. I don't exactly lack in the buddies department. Nevertheless, having someone who gets where I'm going from to share stuff like proposing with is huge. Also, Dusty never uttered a peep to Cece and that counts for something. Holly's girlfriends are all finding out the same way, so there's no pecking order and every one of them is thrilled for her.

We're a combo of exhausted and giddy as our fingers fly over the individual screens, showing one another reactions and trying to keep up with responses.

When it dies down, Holly shoots me a shy, seductive smile.

"You know better than to look at me that way."

"I do." She smarts, squealing when I place my arms under her.

Lifting her off of the seat, I toss her over my shoulder.

"Where are you taking me?"

"It's nap time." I slap her ass. "And about time I hear you scream my name when I ask 'who's your daddy'?"

# Chapter Thirty

*Holly*

The rest of our time at the beach passes in a love-struck blur.

Cary and I agree that after both of us have rings on our fingers, we'll see if we can make someone else who calls him daddy. From what I've seen of Dusty with Sylvie Rhys and the glimpses of my former brother-in-law, Bennett, with Emory, Cary's going to be an incredible father. If all I bring to this marriage is the ability for Cary to see it in himself, then that's the gift I'm giving my husband.

Him. He is what made the wait worthwhile. He's perfect for us. Genuine. Loving—and getting better at firm. Flawed but willing to patch himself up and stand tall instead of running from what wounded him. Ours is a love I'm willing to drown in because I love Cary. But if the bonus is watching him raise up my child into a strong man? Don't bother throwing me a line. I'll ride the swell of every wave.

Minus a message from Kelsey that's half congratulatory/half *Jake wants to see you ASAP,* I'm chipper when we finally get back to the condo.

Laurel cuts my morning nap short, shooing me out the door to get to Sweet Caroline's before lunch. Our appointment with Davina and the wedding planner is later this afternoon. Bennett has Emory.

"I hope this doesn't take too long," I say to my sister.

Laurel insisted on tagging along as an insurance policy so that Jake won't act up too much. A carbon copy of a lethal predator, he plays suave around people he doesn't know until he's trapped them in his good graces.

"I'm sure it won't." She waves off my fear.

"He could be firing me."

"Doubtful. Look at the marquis." Laurel lets go of the steering wheel, motioning to the large sign in front of the old building.

*Congratulations Holly and Cary* is spelled out in big black letters.

"Think he's using this to his advantage?" Laurel mocks with veiled reproach.

"With Jake anything is possible," I sigh, grabbing my oversized purse and heading toward the entrance.

Kelsey greets us as we reach the door. "Bad news. Jake's not here."

"How is that bad news?" My sister retorts.

I glance at her, confused by the flat tone she's using, and step into the dark theatre. Something's off. Kelsey isn't on the schedule. Why is she here during the middle of the day? And why are the house lights off? I squint from the halo of the sun shining behind me toward the red emergency exit light, trying to get my bearings.

My sister pushes me forward and the heavy door thuds closed. A metal echo breaks the eerie silence, making my shoulder blades draw together and my spine straighten.

"Surprise!" The thunderous cheers have me jumping out of my skin.

My mill girls swarm around the cocktail tables along with some of my favorite dancers and Sweet Caroline's employees throughout the years.

"OhmyGod!" I shout, my words running into a jumbled screech. "What are you doing?"

"You've refused to let us celebrate you. So do you think we were going to let this pass us by?" Kimber rubs a hand over her burgeoning belly.

Sloan holds me around the middle, agreeing.

"You were in on this?" I ask Laurel, stupefied.

"Good things happen, sweet sister. It's okay to acknowledge them."

"Every one of us reacted the same way," Cece takes Sloan's place, hugging me and laying reality on the line. "If you thought for a minute we'd plan an engagement party, bridal shower, or bachelorette, you'd be certain things would go wrong and go as far as finding a reason to get out of marrying Cary."

"I would not!" I insist.

But as my bones resettle in my body, I know my friends are right. I appreciate them even more for understanding this about me. I can do life's little wins. I can live, accept love, and be loved in return on the simplest of terms. But the big stuff? That's harder for me.

Between William and then my parents' death as I was getting back on my feet, I expect life will pull the rug out from under me. So, I roll the rug up before that can happen.

It took months for me to accept I'd proven I could handle the job, and I'd earned my role as manager here at the club. I still have fears that my age holds Cary back from a future with someone else. Although, I'm challenging myself to see that now that his eyes are open. We're a team that can slow at the yield, look left and right and then keep moving.

I would have put an enormous red stop sign in front of my friends had I foreseen any party. Not because I don't love Cary. Making a big deal out of anything seems precarious to me. Each time I've felt the slightest bit deserving of anything there have been expectations of myself I haven't been able to live up to.

I should be mature enough to flip the sentiment on its ear. One man did this to me, and it was *he* who hadn't lived up. Except it still feels like my failure that I'm trying to overcome.

Taking a deep breath, I do what I do best. I give. I hand those few hours over to my sister and my friends. I let them celebrate the way they need to. They regale stories of our shared past. At first, I put on my bartender's hat while listening. After a while, I have an uncanny awareness that I've become intent on hearing what these women have to say the same way I sense Cary does whenever I talk to him.

Somewhere along the way, the dread at being the center of attention subsides. I'm honored by their extreme efforts to cut off my worst inclinations. And for the next few hours, instead of being an honorary mill girl, I am one.

"I'm so sorry we're behind schedule." It's one of my biggest faults.

"It's a tick past the hour." Davina admires her diamond-encrusted watch. "You're not late at all. And Isobel gets paid to wait when we are."

I blink. It seems rather rude.

"Holly, the whole point of a bridal consultant is to take care of all the little details. Their idea of a glitch and yours is very different. I've worked with Isobel on several occasions. She's padded those extra thirty seconds it took you to leave Sweet Caroline's into her fees along with the ten—make that twenty—minutes late you'll arrive to the ceremony. She's a professional. This is her job."

It's only after explaining that Davina hurries us into the storefront.

"It feels like a lot for a little wedding," I whimper.

"I know it's your big day, but I'm hoping it's also the only one my son has. I can't help wanting to do it right for both of you. Little... or big," she tacks on, hoping I've missed the comment.

"But we don't need anything ostentatious."

"You don't know what you want until you see what you can have, now do you? You didn't know Cary was what you needed." She points out.

"I'm not marrying Cary for his money."

"Who said you were? And who said I wasn't footing the entire bill to make my son happy because you make him happy and that's what *I* need?"

I swallow. It took a lot to get comfortable when my friends showered me with attention today. This makes me uncomfortable.

We stand in a greeting area surrounded by swaths of beads and crystal chandeliers. It's all very elegant, but not me by any stretch. I'm out of my element.

About the time I snicker to Laurel that Isobel makes me look punctual, she appears as if gliding on ice. She's a tad older than Cary's mom and fuck if her ass doesn't have southern pedigree branded on it like *Xavier Roberts* stamped his name on a Cabbage Patch Kid. How do I know? Because I serve the husbands of women like Isobel at the bar.

Isobel takes Davina's hands in hers, air-kissing her

cheeks, and exchanging pleasantries. I'm itching for introductions to be over so we can get the heck out of this place. It's giving me hives.

My sister shrugs, capturing Isobel's attention. The wedding planner dismisses me and focuses on Laurel, whose lack of full-body tattoo, a bra that conceals her headlamps, and slightly more conservative appearance today matches the rosewater aura of the office. Though, Isobel's genial smile slips recognizing Laurel is not a twenty-something coed sporting a flirty ponytail and carrying thousands of social media followers on her cell with the propensity to drive more business her way.

Okay, so late-summer pinup couture is *out* along with my six followers.

I blow out a breath, glancing away. Cary and I could have a backyard wedding? Have it up on stage at Sweet Carolines. *In the alley where he first showed me I was more to him?* Anywhere but the cliffside this woman wants to punt me from.

"Holly's our bride-to-be." Davina acknowledges Isobel's apprehension in assuming which of us is marrying into the family.

Isobel looks at me like I'm the before image of *Sandra Bullock* in *Miss Congeniality.*

I may dress differently, but I'm not *that* bad. And I'm older than Cary, but I'm not *that* old. I don't like how Isobel has my hackles up, or how my fists scrunch defensively like I want to take a swing at her. However, I won't embarrass Davina by causing a scene, so I bite my tongue and play nice.

I can tell Cary we don't suit later. I mean Isobel and me, not him and me.

"Let's get down to brass tacks, shall we? How many guests are you expecting?" Isobel settles us at a round table stacked with thick binders of swatches and samples. There are flutes of champagne and a small bottle open on a sterling silver tray that we are encouraged to take.

"I'm not sure Holly and Cary have gotten that far yet, but they'd like to do something outdoors. A tent large enough for two hundred will be sufficient." Davina tilts her glass to sip from.

*Two-hundred?* I mouth to Laurel. "I don't know that many people."

"I do, but it also doesn't matter." Davina insists.

"Do you have a location in mind?"

"No," Davina says, not suggesting anything further or asking me for input.

I take it finding potential places is Isobel's duty.

"And you are positive about February the fourteenth? Colors? While it's not spring yet, a soft pastel palette is acceptable. There are lovely trends; heart-shaped macaroons in pinks and teals. Perhaps a Parisian theme?"

For once, Davina defers to me.

"It's Valentine's Day. I was thinking about keeping it simple. I love bold cherry red. Maybe alternating with white swags to decorate inside?" I've stumbled over my words and am quick to bite my tongue.

Isobel is regarding me as if I've asked her to plan a three-ring circus, not a wedding. Given all of the extras Davina and Isobel go on to discuss, like favors, place settings, and the fabric the cloth napkins are cut from, it may be.

I lock eyes with Laurel. Her neck strains when Davina gives an obscene dollar amount she's willing to spend on a single party.

"Seeing how we have a budget in place, is there anything else I should be aware of?"

"Yes," I say. Unwilling to hear Isobel's denial, my voice still wavers. "The officiant should have a jumpsuit on."

It started as a joke, but Cary agreed.

"Elvis?" Isobel's jaw hangs.

"Elvis," the three of us repeat in unison.

This is the moment I realize Davina has a little devil in her disguise. "You'll also find a limo service with pink Cadillacs. For Cary, of course, you know his love of classic cars. We wouldn't want to dismiss something he's interested in when the two ideas mesh so perfectly."

"Yes, nothing shouts 'perfection' like velour and Naugahyde." Isobel's misgivings slip.

"Do you have a problem with the requests? I hoped you'd be up for an exciting challenge, but if that's not the case, I can take my business elsewhere." The lilt in Davina's voice doesn't match her body language. She produces her checkbook, swirling her signature on the paper.

"I do elegant parties, Davina. You're aware of that."

"I am. And this right here," she tears the hefty check from the perforations and slaps in on the money down, "means I have confidence in your ability to turn our unusual requests into something unique and refined. Now, do you want to be the bridal consultant who organizes our ostentatious requests into something cultured, or do you want to be the has-been consultant who lets an opportunity pass by?"

Davina slides the deposit toward Isobel, who brings it closer to her chest. I don't catch a glimpse of anything except a wild number of zeros.

"I thought so. We'll be in touch, Isobel." Davina rises from her chair. "Oh, and if I were you, I'd get the photographer in touch with Carolina's Bridal Magazine to set up a photo shoot. I can't wait to see what you come up with. We'll see ourselves out. Enjoy your evening."

My face is as white as a ghost when we get to the parking lot.

"I'm no pushover," I say to Davina, "but I'm not sure how I'd ever pull that off with the level of tenacity you had in there."

"You have all the confidence you need inside of you. Knowing when to bring it out is an art form. I don't mind showing you how, though I may need you to do something for me in return."

Davina winks and I'm uncertain if I should be wary of her offer.

*Cary*

My fingertip traces the line of a Porsche Cayman. The metallic luster makes my already erratic heart thud in my chest. It sits in the showroom, protected from the city grime, pollution, and likely from theft, a few feet away from this year's Continental GT. It's the car I've been hesitant to let Carver Galloway test drive.

My dealerships stock some of the best high-end automotive lines out there, but my older sister has shown me up before we've even met. Pulling up outside between the customer and service lots it was obvious luxury motors are a profitable business for Adelaide Powell. There aren't keys for a vehicle with an MSRP under a hundred k within grabbing distance.

High heels clip-clop coming from behind me.

"She'll be a few minutes more, sir. Is there anything I can get you… Sparkling water? Espresso?" The receptionist keeps her manicured hands clasped at her middle like she's in a chorus.

I shake my head. "I'm fine. Thank you."

"Who are you with again?" She cocks her chin, trying to remember.

I'm not here representing Cass Stanton, so my company isn't something I led with for status and to get name recognition when I'd approached her desk. My business here is private and meeting in a public space was at my half-sister's request. I assume she wanted it to be on her turf for a reason and won't judge Adelaide for needing the advantage.

"Me." Comes a firm but sultry feminine voice to my left. "Mr. Cass, I apologize. My meeting ran over. Some things you can't rush, even when you're in a hurry to wrap it up."

My sister and I apprise one another. She's got long, medium-brown hair with bronze streaks, rounded eyes that are blue, and her skin tone is as if she's never missed an opportunity under the sun. Hard when your place of business is in the cool shadows of one of the biggest cities in the world. It's fall in New York and my mind is thinking parka, but her turquoise dress has no sleeves.

She takes in my appearance. Dress pants that thankfully the hotel had an iron to press and a button-down with the collar open. I have a jacket in the crook of my arm. It has the Cass-Stanton logo on it, but I'd taken it off in the cab on the way here since the heater was on full blast. I guess the driver prefers a warmer climate too. The strap of my laptop bag, which is inconspicuously filled with everything I'd needed for an overnight trip, is slung over my shoulder.

Adelaide smirks as if she likes my presentation, but not in a sexual sense. More that I'm not some bonehead off the street who is laying a line on her that we're related. It's more as if we're on a level playing field, and my response to her introduction confirms that.

"Ms. Powell. Understandable. I've been in the same situation a time or two." I hold out my hand, grasping her palm.

"Call me Addie. Come along. We can talk in my office." She's friendlier than she'd been on the phone when we agreed to this meeting.

The whole out of the clear blue, *hey, you don't know me from Adam, but your dad fucked my mom* situation probably had her tires screeching to a halt.

"I didn't see it, did you?" Addie turns her squared shoulders to me, pushing open the door marked with her moniker. She gestures to a chair and, like the lady she is, takes her place behind her desk.

"The resemblance? Nope," I answer back.

"Must be that cars are in our blood. I look like my mother. The second, Mrs. Powell."

Addie tangents telling me she only goes by Ms. Powell at work and uses her married name otherwise —in case I was curious. I respond by informing her I legally dropped Stanton, preferring Cass, leaving off it's not because it's my Grandaddy's name *or that Rex was a complete asshole who doesn't deserve for his family name to have a legacy.*

"Did you have me checked out, Addie?" I flash her a cocky smile, rubbing my chin, and getting comfortable in the seat.

I never once mentioned my background when I'd contacted her.

"Of course. You've got a nice inventory, Cary. I'm beginning to see what our father saw in your mother. That's nothing against your mom, by the way, mine fell victim as his prey too," she scoffs.

"Mrs. Powell number two." I phrase my question as a statement.

"He didn't do *alone* well. He didn't do together well either. Eva's mother wasn't the third Mrs. Powell. Though, at least my mom had divorced him before you were born. And to her benefit, Eva's mother never became wife number four."

She hasn't once said his name. Interesting.

I'm getting a clearer picture of my family. The father who didn't raise me was a womanizer. My sister doesn't seem god-awful, though. She lays it on the line and I like that about her. No hidden surprises. Okay, minus the younger sister. At least from my mental calculation, she is younger.

"Eva?" My brow raises.

Addie leans forward, placing her elbows on the blotter, and talks with her hands. "Long Island. Mother of two. We don't interact much. But I've got nothing against her. It's the opposite. She seems less fond of me, so I keep my distance unless she reaches out. She's a former college professor. Married to another intellect. With smart babies. It's a Christmas card exchange relationship."

"I know you exist and acknowledging it lessens the internal guilt."

"Exactly."

"And you and me? We play in the same sandbox?"

"Possibly. I could always play the role of the horrible older sister who flaunts her success." Addie flops back in her seat, becoming soft and contrite. "Why are you here, Cary? It's not for the money. I'm sure of that. You do well enough on your own."

My chin furrows. Then my cheeks puff out and when I open my mouth, I'm not sure where to start.

Addie opens a desk drawer, pulling out an envelope and a piece of paper.

"Let's get this part over with. Sign here." She opens the flap, showing me a wad of bills, and points to a thin black line.

"Thought you didn't think I was here for money?" I act aghast.

"You aren't." She rolls her eyes like I'm ten and

she's twelve. "That doesn't mean there isn't any. He knew he couldn't keep his pants on, so there are conditions that anyone who shows up gets the same inheritance. Now sign the damned paper and take me to lunch."

"No DNA test."

"Seriously," my sister deadpans. "If you were broke, showing up here wanting a reunion, maybe. But I'm willing to bet whatever you have to say is worth the cost of admission... And I know you're good for it."

I look at the standard contract. It's short but has a layman's terms. A TL;DR that cuts out the jargon and says if I take the cash it's all I get. I scroll my name, figuring Adelaide's lawyers have her back and she's entitled to keep her business. *He's* been dead for years. So she's the powerhouse behind the dealership's current prosperity.

I feel a kinship with her. Fixing cars is where my passion lies. However, when Rex died, my end game became building Cass-Stanton bigger to show the asshat up. Addie's inventory is filled with makes and models I don't have manufacturer's contracts for. Given that the deal between Rex and Powell fell through around the time Davina fell into bed with Powell, it makes perfect sense.

And whether or not Addie had as tumultuous a relationship with my biological father as I did with Rex, she's proving to me she's been able to make her own mark. A joint venture with my sister, expanding her territory to the south while increasing what I can offer my customer base, could be profitable for us both.

"Where are we going? Do I get to drive?" I ask, feeling like I'm sixteen and have just passed my license test at the DMV.

"Do you have a car?"

"Not with me. But you seem to be flush." Fuck acting cool. I have car envy and the only way to calm the itch is to get behind the wheel.

Addie throws her head back, hooting. She gets it. "Which one?"

I forget the Cayman and my sister tosses me the keys to the Bentley, giving me directions to where I'm treating her to eat at. The car is a beaut, drives like a dream, and I've gotta negotiate one of my favorite customers out of it unless I can get my paws on the line of cars.

Being with Addie is far different from what I expected when Davina dropped her bombshell. I'm uncertain if I believed she'd had a perfect upbringing, or she'd scorn me, or if last winter I was in a place where I was scorning myself, and the scenarios playing out in my head made me defensive.

Rex wanted me to be the demon. The home wrecker my biological father was. I reminded him of the man who destroyed his happiness and stifled Cass-Stanton Groups' growth. I didn't deserve the things Rex couldn't achieve. And it hits me that perhaps guaranteeing Davina's silence—gaslighting her for decades and hoping she didn't have the balls to reveal Addie was my sister—was another sinister motivation.

I've got everything he hoped to hold me back from and there's no way in hell I'm taking that for granted.

Over lunch, Addie and I get to know each other better. I don't say much about my mother, figuring someday her name will roll off my tongue. I plan to put my best foot forward until then. I do tell her I have a fiancée. Addie is charmed hearing about how Bhodi's love of cars mirrors ours.

"You like weddings?" My ask is to test the waters so to speak.

In my enthusiasm, I haven't forgotten Adelaide

Powell is a businesswoman. Her gears are grinding about potential contracts and connections exactly the way mine are. If she's shrewd enough to get where she is, she's smart enough to play me.

Let's not ignore the fact that we were both raised by narcissistic egomaniacs.

"I love weddings. Ask the third—and final—Mr. Mizz Powell. He'll set you straight… Don't look so shocked, Cary. In between liaisons, our father married four times. My mother did twice. That kind of showing made it easier for me to choose wrong— and boy did I ever—until I got it right." She swirls the ice and liquid left in her cocktail glass. "I'm happy for you. That you figured it out earlier," she says into the drink before looking back at me. The forlorn expression fades, replaced with a genuine smile.

There's more to Addie's story. I won't pry, but the hint of vulnerability gives me  a bit of comfort. It's almost as if Addie battled similar demons, making her question her roots. My best guess is even without enduring the crap Rex pulled on me, my sister has a shit-ton of relationship phobias that our father's philandering hailed down upon her.

I tip my cup in her direction, thanking her for the compliment. "You know, you're the only one who knows we're related besides the obvious." Davina. Holly.

"My husband and our lawyer." She supplies on her end. Eva isn't mentioned. "Do we keep it that way even if we join forces?"

"Who said anything about joint ventures?" I chuckle.

Are we more powerful teaming up, or does the industry's knowledge of the undercurrent make the bond impenetrable? Do I trust blood when I nearly decided meeting this woman wasn't worth my time? I'd initially written her off before Addie had the chance to impress me with her accomplishments. Was her instinct the same when I reached out?

All of this is something I'll need to strategize if and when Ms. Powell's name is added to the final guest list. My mother has her event planner in a tizzy for how fast Valentine's Day is approaching, so I'm glad when Addie cuts to the chase.

"Oh, *baby brother,* We're reading each other's minds. Curiosity about who the other was is working to our mutual benefit."

"What you're saying is we are playing in the same sandbox."

"And I'll lend you my shovel for your bucket if we can find a way of ensuring both our castles get bigger."

# Chapter Thirty-two

*Cary*

"Where's Holly?" I bend—almost in half—placing a kiss on my mother's cheek.

Davina's lying on her stomach on the couch in the formal living room of the house in Brighton. A tumbler of alcohol is within reach.

"Out back. Digging. Her favorite spot to be. No wonder she's still sporting a tan."

I'm not sure why I was so hesitant to bring my fiancée into the home I grew up in. More than the paint and the flooring changes that Davina made after Rex's funeral, Holly's presence here lightens the entire mood.

And it's no lie that it takes a lot to call Holly out of the backyard. My woman is constantly pruning and trimming, potting, and planting. It feeds her soul. Even if on a technicality the garden is not hers, I like to think of it as being so. Like she got the one she mentioned wanting again.

"How was your trip?" Mom asks.

"Good," I respond.

*Incredible*, I should say. But part of me doesn't want my mom to know that she was as right as she was about me needing to meet Addie. I also don't want her to learn all about it before Holly does.

My mom sits up straight to pick up her drink and winces.

"Are you okay?"

I place a palm on her shoulder and Davina lurches away as if me touching her is agony.

"I'm fine. We had our own fun while you were gone."

"What kind of fun?"

"Shopping, gardening—I went to Sweet Caroline's! —got a tattoo…" she mutters the last three words.

"You what?" My refined mother spent an evening watching strippers and, "What kind of tattoo?" Please, make it be the temporary kind.

"It is none of your business is what it's of. They really do hurt, though. Do you have one?"

I scrub my beard, wondering what other trouble they've gotten into while I was in New York. "Yeah, I do."

My mother hums, her curiosity appeased.

"I'm going to let Holly know I'm home."

"You do that, son. I'm going to sit here and sip my gin and tonic." She lifts the glass in a toast. "By the time you wind up back inside, I'll be ready for Holly to make me a refill. She's an excellent bartender."

I half expect Davina to be slurring her words. Mom looks haggard. From the dirt on her kneecaps, it's obvious she's been out digging in the garden too. I hope she's been smart and kept the new design on her back well covered and out of the sun.

I have the slider open when Davina stops me. Mom's lips twist. "Cary, Holly's had a long day. Go easy on her?"

"Yes, ma'am." I wink. Whatever, I'm not coming

down on Holly for taking my mother to get inked.

Tall hedgerows trap the heat of the day between them and the southern-bred boy in me is thanking fuck it's warm out. I'm going to need Addie to meet me down here if we join forces.

Holly is leaning over a shrub with clippers. Of course, she's got the pin-up girl red bandana taming her long upswept hair. I don't think the woman owns a pair of shorts that she can't put on for a shift at Sweet Caroline's.

She stands to wipe her brow and that's when I notice how soaked with sweat the ribbed white tank she's wearing is. Holly looks like a wet t-shirt competition contestant, making me instantly hard. She's damned sexy. But my body's reaction is also because I haven't had her in a few days.

"Christ, Doll. You're killing me." I tent my hand like a visor while shaking my head.

It's too fucking bad I can't knock my mother's new gardener up yet. I want to see her breasts stretch the material and for it to rise above the swell of her stomach into a crop-top.

Misunderstanding my meaning, Holly looks around the yard, making me grateful for the tall hedges that act as a natural fence. Her gaze drops her sweat-soaked shirt.

"Oh that," she says, lacking embarrassment. It's slicked to her wide, flat nipples. "They're tits. I don't see why everybody gets so worked up about them. For Heaven's sake, mine are smaller than yours."

I choke on my laughter as I approach her. "Holly, your breasts are exactly the right size and I have a genuine appreciation for them, but—"

"Don't you dare tell me to go put on a bra, Cary Cass." She wields pruning shears in my face.

Oooh, she used my full name. I'm in trouble now, but can't help poking the beast.

"Do you even own a bra?"

"Yes," she replies in a tone that resembles Bhodi with a chip on his shoulder.

Her answer makes my brow arch.

I want to see this bra. Is it silky? Flexible so that I can pull the lace cups down and feast on Holly? Or will the fabric scratch my skin while I fuck her? Inquiring minds never realized, when your woman doesn't wear lingerie, what I goddamn turn-on it is thinking about her wearing it.

I grab Holly around the waist, cupping her lush denim-covered ass, and drawing her lower half straight to mine. I'm as unashamed of the rock-hard wood I'm sporting as she is about showing me what God gave her.

If some neighborhood perv has been watching her, they can look all they want. I'm not freaked that anyone's staring at her chest. Holly's gorgeous and, if she caught my eye, she's definitely someone else's wet dream.

"I'd love to see you in that bra. *Nothing but it.*" I whisper, wiping a tiny sweaty curl off of her brow. "I missed you."

Holly sighs into me, wrapping her soil-stained arms around my neck and leaning her forehead on my shoulder like I'm an anchor. She smells like she's been out here for hours. The fragrance is a mix of sod, flowers, and the scent of our bodies when I've ridden her hard.

"How was New York?" she murmurs.

"I'll tell you and Davina about it at dinner. Right now, my mother is calling for her favorite bartender."

Holly snorts. It's the first time tension has left her body. Dampness soaks my shoulder. She turns her face from me, brushing wetness off of her cheeks.

I cup her face. Fat tears brim in her eyes. Uncontainable, they tumble down, connecting with my knuckles. The awareness that these are not tears of joy is overpowering.

"Hey, I'm back. It's okay," I say with my heart in my throat.

"It's not okay, Cary. I got served today. William left his wife. He's back in North Carolina and he wants visitation until the court grants him custody."

It's then that I see the manila folder sitting inside an empty plant pot. It is dirty with black fingerprints, as if Holly has read and reread the legal documents trying to make sense of them. The papers have been shoved back inside—by someone who is beyond frustrated.

Large pruners, twigs, and full limbs filled with beautiful blooms lie on the ground not too far away. I have a sneaking suspicion Davina left Holly out here to work out a little aggression. My mom understood my fiancée needed a little peace and quiet to reflect on her troubles.

"Joint custody or full?" I growl, not at all liking where this is going.

"It says joint, but I don't know. William's also petitioning for me to pay him child support."

"How can he—He hasn't even paid his fair share!" I roar in disgust.

Holly shrinks and I catch her belt loop, drawing her back before she can make that cavern between us too wide. *My wife.* Mine. *My family.* He forfeited.

Holly's shaking her head like it's all unbelievable. She's breaking down, and I'm goddamn livid on her behalf.

"Look at me." I grab her chin between my thumb and forefinger, forcing her red-rimmed eyes to meet mine.

Those lovely black wings she paints around her lids have gone missing. She's cried alone amongst the flowerbeds that held so many promises of better days ahead.

A sorrowful expression has replaced the one that must have been sheer anger. Holly's regrets are like sharp, evil spades, cutting into her roots and tearing her to shreds.

She's already mourning the things that haven't even happened between us; our marriage, our babies, our future. The picket fence and the suburbs and the summer vacations in the Outer Banks. Bhodi's graduation from prep school. Everything that filled her heart with hope. All the dreams she'd given up when William Mayer cast her aside. Every one that bloomed anew and even bigger when we met.

"I'm so tired, Cary." She cries, snapping her head away. "I'm so tired of this!"

Holly throws a trowel I hadn't realized was in her hand. It smashes against a ceramic pot, shattering the side. In frustration over breaking something that wasn't hers to begin with, she shucks her gloves, flinging them onto the lawn.

The fight's not gone from her.

"I know, Doll."

I drag her back to me again, letting her bottom bump my groin and lowering us to the ground. I slip her legs over my lap, cradling her. My palms caress her soft arms.

She'd given herself permission to be happy when the mill girls threw her that impromptu party. Holly doesn't like it when people fuss over her. It's as if she sees outcomes like this as inevitable once her guard is down. My mother gave Isobel the earful she deserved. Yet, I know between the outlay of cash for the wedding and the event planner acting like a bitch to test how much she could get any with, Holly's reaction will continue to be that she's beneath the threshold of good fortune.

Holly doesn't take my mother's wealth or my

community status lightly, and she's the least entitled woman I know. What she expects from herself is to do her best for everyone else. That's why doing things for her makes me happy. She's never bargaining for anything.

I let Holly let it all out, wondering when the last time was that someone had. Was it her mom before the plane crash? Laurel?

I'm here and I'm not going anywhere. Not without Holly, anyway.

# Chapter Thirty-three

*Holly*

The court gives me little choice or time to accept what's happening. The proof of William being behind on his support payments doesn't matter at all. I haven't fought to get the money my son deserves or attempted to terminate William's parental rights. My stance—that William isn't worth anyone wasting their breath on—has come back to bite me. As Bhodi's biological father, he's allowed to see his son.

After hearing Cary's trip was to visit his sister, Bhodi has developed a morbid interest in where he came from. I can't blame him. My son has settled into the fifth grade. The world he lives in now differs from his universe this time last fall. It's filled with adults he never knew, experiences he hadn't had, and the anticipation of the changes to come when we move in with Cary.

Bhodi only balks hearing his Saturday court-appointed—and supervised—visitation is the same day as a big brother group outing. There's been a level of fearfulness since Cary and I started dating when Bhodi's joked the two of them were going to get kicked out sooner or later.

My son doesn't want this to be what makes it sooner. The friends he's made mean a lot to him, and I've noticed over the past week he's clinging to stories of past field trips.

Over the summer, The Cass-Stanton Group became an official big brother program sponsor. In private, Cary told me that whether they can still participate or not, he wants to ensure there's a viable organization for the community. He'd like it if Bhodi saw to follow in his footsteps and become a mentor to a kid himself.

I'm surprised when Bhodi takes both Cary's and my hands entering the building where the meeting is taking place. All of the boastful things I've spoken about my son seem to float away.

He's little and quiet. His reaction to seeing his father is one-hundred and eighty degrees different from the bubbly anticipation he had meeting Cary. Does Bhodi think his father is a monster because I keep my feelings about William to myself? Is he afraid to hurt ours? I want to buckle him into the backseat and drive home in reverse to the point in time that everything went awry.

*How far would I rewind if I did that?*

I've agreed to an advocate named Marie Grant chaperoning this visit. Marie takes Bhodi into a room where William is. The single small window is covered over with a poster about adopting kids in foster care. Cary and I sit on a low bench outside. He turns his palm up and we lace our fingers together.

"I'm sorry for this," I apologize for the hundredth time.

"You don't need to be." Cary shifts in the seat. He puts his arm over my shoulder, kisses my temple, and reassures me again, "You didn't do anything."

But that's the problem. If I had the legal sense to cut William off, my boys would be on their field trip and I'd be at Isobel's flushing out wedding details.

Even Davina's snarky event planner—who I shut down in no uncertain terms when she alluded I should consider a panel in my gown because our nuptials were awfully rushed and "being decisive beforehand is better than risking the dress not fitting as you begin to show"—is a more positive experience than this.

Tucking myself under his wing, Cary scrolls his phone, answering work messages, and giving me the mental space I've needed to deal lately.

The last time William saw Bhodi he was an infant. He said he wanted things to be amicable between us. By that, William meant he wanted my son to still be named William Mayer Jr.—fat fucking chance—and for us to leave him alone so he could go back to his former life.

His wife had forgiven his cheating. She couldn't abide the reminder that William had another child out there somewhere. William didn't want me to send pictures. It would upset her.

William never touched a gurgling, happy Bhodi or asked to hold him. My beautiful baby stayed strapped in his carrier in a cold office conference room. The whole while lawyers haggled over how much William's lack of self-control would cost my son in love and monthly payments. My child's existence alone had more value than the bargain struck. And over the years, William had the nerve to whittle his contributions down.

As my reality was cracking me square across the jaw, I'd held out hope that even if William didn't love me, even if he changed his mind, he'd have some attachment to his child. Who am I kidding? I had hoped he'd have loved me enough when we were together that he'd care about my feelings after we were apart.

My parents had the occasional loud, long shouting matches when life became stressful that sent Laurel and me skittering to our room. *Too much togetherness*, they'd apologize later on. They always found their way back to one another. That was my naive version of love. Between midnight feedings and diaper changes, I'd believed for months that William could have remained married and still respected me enough to love Bhodi.

When he'd initially disappeared I'd said to my family I did not want William back as a lover, a fiancé, or a husband. It took until that day for my heart to stop bargaining for my future and understand what my logical head already knew. From then on, I never looked back. William did not exist in my world unless he inserted himself in it. There was no other way to be enough for Bhodi and to do the job of two parents. There was no other way to regain my confidence and be enough for *me*.

That moment I was as broken as I'd ever been... until now.

The same strategy that we've survived by is the one William is employing against us, dredging up old feelings of how he hurt and used me.

The initial hour ends and Marie holds the door for Bhodi, who bee-lines to rest his head at my belly. William follows them.

My ex is thin in the chest. His shoulders hunch forward disguising a rounding paunch at his midsection. He has more salt in his salt and pepper hair. His pants and collared shirt match but there's nothing that distinguishes him as handsome the way I'd admired him a decade ago in his military uniform.

He glances my way, looking me up and down. The telltale signs he doesn't approve of my outlandish wardrobe and my full-body tattoo are noticeable to me by the same way his left eye squinted ever so slightly when I'd mucked up a meal.

William was never mean to me, but I'd forgotten he was critical of appearances. Almost like he stuck little needles under my fingertips to see if I'd squirm while he molded me into the person he needed me to be.

In all likelihood, it was a younger version of his wife. But who the hell cares now?

Obviously not William if he left her... twice.

Cary's gracious enough to shake William's hand when Marie extends introductions. I have no desire to and remain cool and polite when Marie explains things went well. We're given reminder cards of when the next time is that I have to produce my son for these ridiculous sessions.

On the way home Bhodi tucks into his gaming system. The sole peep from the backseat is to ask if we can have stir fry bowls for supper. I send him and Cary off for a late lunch to satisfy the craving. I have to nap because I need to come through tonight to cover for Kelsey.

The days tick by. I scoot between Davina's house and Laurel's condo, forgetting things in both places for both Bhodi and myself.

Bhodi brings the first true cold of the season home from school. The symptoms hit me late in a shift. I oversleep the next afternoon and miss picking up Bhodi and Emory, who is now in kindergarten, from the bus stop. The kids walk home. Bennett has to wait for me to get the last of Emory's clothes from the laundry basket folded and into her overnight bag when he arrives to get my niece. I scamper back to Sweet Caroline's with a drippy nose and a pounding headache.

Cary picks up the slack with Bhodi. It makes me

feel awful that he does, and that I have zero reserves left in me to give to others what they need.

Jake happens into the club. He takes one look at me and tries to send me home.

"You can't be a corpse bride in front of the customers," he balks when I refuse to go.

Snotty isn't sexy. It's bad for business.

Unable to stand up to my boss. I wind up with my head propped on the arm of his leather sofa, glad my nose is stuffing so badly the room's aromas won't penetrate my sinuses.

Jake shoves his cell in his shirt pocket after calling Cary to fetch me. Apparently, being a cunt about leaving Sweet Caroline's during my shift—something I've never done—renders me incapable of driving.

Though, perhaps that's a smart move. My addled brain can't figure out if Bhodi is at Davina's or with Laurel.

I shiver, and Jake throws a blanket *at* me.

"Get yourself together," he reprimands, shutting the office door behind him.

My cheeks grow wet. I lie to myself it's migraine pressure. Since Cary found me in the garden, I've hidden the moments I've cried out of anger and desperation from him. More times than I can count the tears haven't come at all as frustration swallows me whole.

A racked sob leaves my chest and I pull the thin blanket up, clutching it to cover my body, using it as a shield.

Distraught, I cry the way I had when I knew for certain William had always intended to abandon us, and when my mom and dad soared into the sky together. My sister may have been there. My friends. Even so, I've kept myself in an obscure pit of loneliness because I was too inept as a young woman to open my eyes to the imminent signs of danger and it sealed my fate.

I've taught my mistrustful heart to head unnecessary warnings. It doesn't know any better anymore.

The things I tell myself—the words I've lived by that William is not worth wasting my breath on—are getting drowned out by my fears. I'm seeing every fatal flaw in what I've done, and what I haven't done, to protect Bhodi.

I can't organize my thoughts. I'm never on time. The rockabilly clothes—were they to make me happy or was my original intent to ward off strangers? Testing who to let into my inner circle and revealing the people who couldn't accept me if I wasn't their version of perfect. I've never considered that before. I was too busy pointing out that the way I dressed wasn't attention-seeking.

The mix of emotions is the most tiresome I've endured. I'm being dragged in one direction just to be pulled back in the other. My internal gyroscope can't right me. I'm less than good enough for my son, my sister, my niece. My friends shouldn't have thrown that party. There are better people to fawn over.

There's a woman out there that a stupid society woman like Isobel should be planning Cary-freaking-Cass's wedding to.

But I want him to love me.

I don't know how to make him choose me *forever*. Is it selfish that a small part of me wants Cary to give up so that I'm not the one who failed?

*I'd thought he'd have walked away by now.*

Before he'd proposed, I hadn't seen into next month, let alone next week without him by my side. I don't want his side of the bed  cold when I wake up tomorrow morning. I want the silly scribbled notes on the pillow telling me he'll be back before I can miss him. That's not the faintest bit true. I notice when Cary isn't by my side. Like a wartime bride, I wait each Friday afternoon by the window for my men to come home safe and sound.

I can't force Cary to stay. I can't force him to go. I can't give both my son and me the one person we both need because the one we hadn't still holds the power to break my will.

The door to Jake's office slides across the carpet.

I sit, grabbing my forehead to bring my addled brain along. The soft blanket falls to my lap in a heap.

*Compose yourself.*

Cary kneels, putting his hands on my knees. "You can't keep this pace up, Doll."

I hear the concern in his voice. The anguish marring his features.

Yet, I tell myself I have to. I have no other choice.

# Chapter Thirty-four

Cary

Two months into the biggest friggin' nightmare.

Two months of putting our excitement on hold, despite our wedding day approaching on schedule.

Two months of loving Holly through it... as if not loving her was even a choice.

Sparks of Holly's spirit emerge every now and again. The toll it's taking on her I see every day. It was supposed to be the three of us. William was never part of this picture. We were a unit and no one had reason to consider we'd be dealing with a custody dispute. Not to mention William's request for support from Holly has her convinced she has to work herself to the bone to keep up with the demands of her job.

If it was this easy for William to get visitation, what stops the court from denying him anything else? She's put herself back on the club's schedule for the weekends, lying that it gives me and Bhodi back the time together we deserve to spend together on Saturdays.

It's not her fault her ex has waltzed in after a decade of being a deadbeat. Nevertheless, she takes it personally.

I'm no fool. The tips are bigger and she's saving every penny she earns. She shuts down any conversation about me covering any legal bills. Her stubbornness is becoming a detriment instead of a habit I treasure.

From what little Holly's lawyer has mentioned, these negotiations won't be equitable let alone in Holly's favor because of past precedent. She had less incentive to go after William when it was going to drain her bank accounts. That was cash she needed for them to get by.

The funk she's in is hard to pull her out of. I need her to count on me, and she's reticent to accept that she can. Saying it's not fair to me seems immature. It's not, though.

I'm almost mad that Holly taught Bhodi such good manners around strangers. The initial hour-long Saturday visits went smooth enough that, well before I'm ready, William's at our doorstep, interrupting our family time.

I wish Bhodi would have fought like hell to get out of seeing his father. But I can also tell by his sullen attitude about missing out on a third monthly field trip with program friends that my half-pint's not into having to act the grown-up.

Holly and I promised him next weekend we'll go to the beach house if the weather holds out. He's allowed to bring any friend he wants. I can't believe we're in a position where we have to make up for the time he's forced to spend with his father.

I insist to Holly that William needs to pick up Bhodi from my house in Brighton. It's a prick move, but I don't trust William and I want him to see the power Holly has standing behind her.

What's that saying? Walk softly? Yeah, we're playing the game by the fucked-up-and-ridiculously-skewed-in-biology's-favor rules. However, William needs to see how big a stick I can hit him with if I decide to. I flat out asked my therapist if that made me as bad as Rexy. Got a straight answer from the counselor this time too: A big fat no.

We're outside in the driveway with my palm encased on Holly's waist for comfort. William glances between us and the second floor bedroom window where Bhodi has stuck cartoon character clings to the glass.

William placates me with "nice place". He'd come off as sincere if dollar signs weren't flashing in his eyes. Although, perhaps it's the reaction I was looking to gauge for myself.

From the get-go, my car salesman intuition has been tossing some big red flags up. Something is off about this guy.

It's not that I'm pissed William's taking up Bhodi's time that used to be mine—and, yes, I am. I'm simply calling that jealousy what it is and setting it aside—or that Holly's having a hellish few months. William is tearing apart the person she created in his absence. He's hitting one of the strongest women I've ever encountered right where it hurts.

"Without Bhodi I have nothing," she once said.

But if I don't have either of them, then what am *I* left with?

Holly's working overnight, compartmentalizing her feelings so Bhodi doesn't see, collapsing inward, and maintaining that, for as much as I love her, I shouldn't have to deal with any of this. Meanwhile, we're trying to plan the rest of our lives together. I'm worried if we halt the momentum—any and all excitement about getting married—then *we stop,* and it's over. So, all I can do is encourage her to focus on the wedding.

While Bhodi is gone, Holly and I run an errand to find out about flowers for the tables. Holly pulls up the map app on my cell and we arrive at a ramshackled old nursery on the outskirts of town where a grizzled old man named Mr. Johnston greets us.

He's hunched, is as weathered from the sun as his faded Battleship North Carolina cap is grayed around the edges, and his demeanor is as affable as any agent on my lot.

Mr. Johnston has employees, though it's a small operation. By the looks of the greenhouses without any translucent plastic roofing stretched over the framing, the offerings they've grown have condensed as the owner has aged. Customers bring their purchases to a woman in a wheelchair. She has a cannula in her nose and my gut reaction is that the dust the cars entering and leaving the lot are kicking up can't be good for her health, let alone the pesticides. Then again, her makeshift desk is a stack of four flat white organic manure bags. She's dressed as vibrant as any granny who retires down to Florida, complete with royal blue polyester pants and a printed fuchsia top. The white-haired woman waves in Holly's direction about as fast as a snail runs, pleased to see her.

The wave Holly returns is enthusiastic, genuine. However, she's knee-deep into her conversation with Mr. Johnston already.

"Not going to happen. Too cold in North Carolina in February, girlie."

Mr. Johnston gives me the impression he would rock back on his heels if he were about four decades younger.

Holly came to him specifically for advice. Her hopes for simple low pots of decorative plumerias on each table at the reception are dashed.

"Hibiscus, like that perfume you wear, is sketchy too. Now orchids with good winter care, those are sure to bloom." He offers some sympathy. "Season is right. Your florist could source them."

"Could you?" Holly asks, wanting Mr. Johnston to have the business without a middleman's interference.

"Any other year if it were a potted plant, sure. 'Cept I can't make promises this year, Miss Holly. My wife, Doris, isn't as well as she used to be and I'm not sure we'll be around come spring. I gave up the stall at the farmer's market when the rental agreement came due. It's too much for us anymore, lugging the inventory. Keeping up with the credit card chips and readers that need the internet."

"You can't retire." Holly bites her fingernail. "Where will I get my plants from?"

He tosses his chin toward a quaint bungalow across the street where I presume he and his wife reside. The paint is chipping and there are colorful lawn ornaments scattered over the grass.

"That's my garden. You visit and I'll send you home with clippings." He winks.

"Will you tell me what they are?" My fiancée side-eyes the war veteran.

"What difference does that make if you can care for them? You done fine so far bringing my plants back to life," he compliments her green thumb.

Holly makes it a point to chat with Mr. Johnston a while longer and when Mrs. Johnston is customer-free she leans to hug the quiet woman, introducing me. Mrs. Johnston wiggles her eyebrows, and I get the impression the ladies have a quiet connection they both enjoy.

Our task lasts less than an hour. We leave the nursery, Holly conceding in a text to Isobel that plumerias are out. She still wants a low plant as the centerpiece so that the guests at the round tables have no problems conversing over it. It should be colorful and Holly prefers a traditional terracotta pot.

That's likely the most mainstream of anything we've directed Isobel to do. She found us a location: A drive-in that's closed for the season. The Cadillacs —some pink, some blue—are going to be lined up with the tops down on the convertibles and we've licensed movies to play on the big screen. And, God bless the woman, when she found us a red and white striped circus tent and I followed it up requesting for an animatronic fortune teller machine, she sourced other carnie games without me asking. Isobel's gotten into putting our personalities on display instead of fighting it. Thank fuck for small miracles.

Exhaustion mars Holly's features, and I tuck her into my bed for her nap. Then I shoot off my own text to Isobel. A man has to keep a few surprises up his sleeve for his soon-to-be wife.

Not soon after Bhodi returns.

My entire body vibrated the first time Half-pint was alone with the guy. I have the same reaction watching a sullen Bhodi walk up the driveway.

Something's wrong.

I've always been aware of Bhodi's features that match Holly's. How unmistakable it is that he and Emory are cousins. I don't like the similarities he has to William. I'm glad William's shit personality is not mirrored in the ten-year-old. Yet, neither looks as if they've had a fantastic time.

I ask anyway, rubbing it in.

Bhod shrugs. William holds onto his shoulders tight as if he's a proud papa. All the while he babbles on about the batting cages, baseball being an All-American pastime, and how "the boy will learn how to keep his eye on the ball."

"You get hit?" I ask Bhodi, hunching down to his level.

"Only in my leg." He rubs his kneecap.

William sucks in his cheek, giving me the impression he not only doesn't appreciate my presence or my concern. And also that I should have made the kid a bigger baseball fan.

Whatever, not every kid is going to win the *Little League World Series*.

Bhodi is good at tinkering. We do cars in our house. He's excited when a new model has the hood open in the service garage bay. I get to foster his interest. It's called bonding. If William only takes the kid to do what he wants, they're never going to have a decent relationship.

As soon as Willam pulls away, a glum Bhodi mentions a car show in Raleigh. I swear the kid can sniff them out since we've been to at least four since the summer. On Friday nights, when we're at the dealership, he shows me the flyers for muscle car clubs that have monthly cruises in the area.

This is Bhodi's idea of fun. It wouldn't shock me in the least if it's what he'd told William he wanted to do before getting locked into a batting cage, pelted by baseballs, and degraded by callous remarks of what he's lacking instead of encouraging his skills.

We're in my nondescript SUV on our way before Bhodi second-guesses suggesting it to me. He sticks close when we arrive, taking my cell to find out specs on vehicles he's too shy to ask about.

One owner draws out his curiosity over a Shelby GT 3500. Didn't take the kid for a Mustang enthusiast.

"Does your dad like cars?" The man regards me, standing to the side.

Bhodi turns his head but doesn't take his eyes off the line of the white stripe lines and lettering near the wheelbase.

"He knows a lot about them." Holly's son says, almost inaudible. "He wanted a Cobra, but he got an MGB that he restored."

"You help him with it?" He opens the door, letting Bhodi sit in the car and allowing him to explore the interior.

"No, he let me help with a Colony Park. It's not his, though." Bhodi smooths his hand across the worn leather the way he does with the cars we practice on.

"You do engine work on the side?" The Mustang owner eases me into the conversation.

Eventually, I admit who I am. He knows a guy who knows one of my service center guys.

"So your dad put a car you restored in the front window of his dealership. That's a colossal achievement for someone your age. You've got to be awful proud."

"Yeah." Bhodi toes the asphalt, his sneaker circling out in shallow arcs, moving a loose black stone.

A few more minutes go by and the man shakes both our hands, encouraging Bhodi to keep up the good work, and saying he's going to drive by to take a peek at the Mercury.

"Cary?" Bhodi tugs my elbow as we walk away.

I look down at him. My full-on fucking grin fades. Guilt radiates from his slumped shoulders.

"Don't tell Mom I lied about who you were, okay?"

"I won't." Because he didn't.

The moment Bhodi refused to explain to the man I wasn't his dad was the moment I became his dad. I want this and it's obvious Half-pint does too. I take Bhodi's hand and don't look back.

This afternoon it was me and my kid. Letting the limelight shine on him. Showing Bhodi how fucking proud I am to be the guy Holly trusted enough to bring into his life. With her by my side, nothing stops me from giving *my son* everything I didn't get.

# Chapter Thirty-five

*Holly*

"Did you have fun with your father?"

Asking Bhodi anything should be simple.

*How was your day?* shouldn't have any underlying meaning. But confirming he's okay spending time with a man whose trustworthiness I'm concerned about makes me squirm like a worm about to be plucked in two. I loathe every piece of me that needs to know beyond the broad generalization; the parent who can't accept my son responding "good" at face value.

"I guess." Bhodi stabs a trowel into the ground over and over again. Flicking small piles of dirt a few inches out. "Can I ask a question?"

"Sure thing."

"What does 'robbing the cradle' mean?"

"Where did you hear that?" I turn quickly from the spot I'm digging in, blinking fast.

I couldn't have heard him correctly. Cary and I are conscientious about using that particular phrase.

"He said it. He said Cary is stupid, and you're

robbing the cradle."

"Oh, I see." I place the shovel on the ground and fall onto my bum, mirroring my son's crisscross position. "Did your father say anything else?" I press, knowing full well it is a rocky slope.

"I dunno. He asks me about you guys a lot." My son moves so we are side by side, leaning in, and wiping his nose on my shirtsleeve.

He'd like me to say it's gross. To tell him to stop. I won't.

He's scared to admit how torn up inside he is. There's more Bhodi isn't confiding in me. Everything that has to do with the ever-changing custody situation is confusing my son. I think he's brought this up to arm me against any attack. The last thing that shocks me is William's intent to turn Bhodi against me.

"Does it make you uncomfortable when he brings up Cary and me?"

My son nuzzles against my shirt. I kiss his head and pull him close.

We finally have a wonderful man, an amazing role model in our lives, and William is out to ruin it again.

Why couldn't Cary and I have gotten married before this mess began? Why hadn't I sought to terminate William's rights?

"You're allowed to tell your father that, Bhodi." I try explaining he can say as little or as much about what he wants to talk about in a way a fifth-grader can comprehend.

All the while, I'm not surprised William has been digging for information while I've been holding cards close to my chest, keeping my negative feelings about Bhodi's father from my son. It's not fair to put a child in the middle. The worst part is I don't understand why Bhodi is even part of this tug-of-war.

I'm not entitled to anything of Cary's and won't be

until we're married. And that's if I don't follow through on pushing the idea of a prenup on Cary. He's viciously arguing against it unless the deal leaves me with far more than I'm willing to accept.

Other than indulging his apparent jealousy, what does William have to gain by making me—or Cary—out to be the evil ones?

I've been there from day one.

Cary volunteered to brighten a child's life. The fact that it was my son and we've created something more is dumb luck, not nefarious design.

The writing on the walls is clear. William is going to use this relationship against me in court. I literally gave him a *give* by forfeiting years of child support and William can't even be a decent human and not accuse me of doing something wrong by becoming romantically involved with someone younger.

Pretty comical since there's an age gap between William and me and I didn't leave anyone during a mid-life crisis. Funny how it wasn't a huge deal when a man did it *and left me pregnant,* but adding that child back into the equation as he's about to hit puberty is appalling.

My anger spikes along with my resentment of the double standard. I did everything I could to take the high road and prove I was the better person and still a man with his dick hanging out has control over my destiny.

*How can anyone be blind to how the system keeps others down?* I want to demand, spitting my outrage at the judge who agreed to this travesty. This charade, parading around like it's justified.

My stomach sinks. Maybe marrying Cary isn't a wise choice. What if William succeeds in driving a wedge between us? I'm torn between protecting my child and the man I love. And I'm back to wondering if it was smart to make Cary my now. If he isn't my forever, then breaking it off will hurt less doing it sooner rather than later.

It'll save his reputation and his wallet too.

What if we could have survived anything *but* this? I guess we'll never know since my depression has me ready to sabotage our impending marriage to keep Cary safe.

I take off my garden gloves and run my fingers through my son's hair. He places his head in my lap. He was entitled to have a great dad. He deserved Cary.

The problem is that I actually don't.

It's slow midweek at the club. I have the night off and am lying on Cary's bed in Davina's house. I like it here.

Cary's mom comes and goes the same way my schedule ebbs and flows. She's either at the beach or out in the garden. The landscapers mow the lawns and my pruning to rid myself of pent-up aggression has left them little hedge work. Davina's keeping Mr. Johnston in the black. She's been planting bulbs for spring.

Her issue before? Definitely not arthritis. I asked.

Her flowerbeds were for therapy and kept her sanity when she couldn't reveal to anyone what an enormous mistake she'd made by not divorcing Rex. As if someone has unkinked a water hose, Davina chatters to me while we tend the backyard about what those years were truly like for her.

Bartending I've learned to listen with an open mind as people share their stories and try to break the chains binding their hearts. Since William mucked everything up, I've been using her open emotions and the regrets she reveals as a distraction from my own.

All the while, I doubt our kinship will survive the frost.

We toiled, soaking in the last of the autumn sunshine today. Although the season is short-lived, rain will keep us inside during the winter months. On nights like these, I've become accustomed to sapping my energy to go to sleep early. The schedule I keep makes it easy for Cary and me to be passing ships. We so rarely tumble into bed together, both ready to pass out after a long day, and being able to do so seems earned.

Normally I'd slip my arm around him, splay my fingers over his chest, and lay my cheek to his warm back. Tonight my back is flat to the mattress. My dowdiest pajamas hide my legs and arms. The sheets add a second layer of protection.

My intentional wardrobe malfunction is not the deterrent I anticipate it being.

Cary rolls onto his side and slides his hand below the waistband of my pajama pants, stroking his fingers through my curls.

"What would you do if I shaved that all off?" My nose is in this month's issue of *Carolina's Bridal,* the magazine that's supposed to photograph our wedding venue for their spring edition. It was the closest thing on the nightstand I could find as a distraction.

"Buy a cat. I'd need a pussy to pet."

I roll my lips between my teeth. His joke is funny, but we can't get along the way we used to. "Some of the mill girls are bare down there."

"There's a visual of your friends I didn't need. Also, I suppose I understand in Cece or Kimber's situation. Maybe dancers are used to that? But why do you need to do it? Is there something you aren't telling me? You wanna dance for me?" His knuckle provocatively rides my landing strip.

"I thought you might like something... different."

"I got different when I landed you, Doll. Don't go changing to try and please me when what I've got is perfect the way it is."

"Cary?"

He hums, kissing my neck.

Wetness pools between my thighs. Cary knows what he's doing when he shows me the things our bodies do to each other's, bringing the siren out of me that sings his dirty praises and makes me beg for him to take me harder.

"What happens when you're ready to blend in and this version of perfect starts to sag?"

His palm skims up toward my belly—a place I'm conscientious about toning and moisturizing, since the skin there wasn't so stretched before I had my son—and he cups my too small for my liking right breast.

"Feels perky enough to me," he says, weighing it in his hand. Flicking a thumb over my nipple, he sends chills down my spine.

Cary turning me on isn't helping me use my age to my advantage. It's time for him to have a realistic view of what a ten year's difference means a decade from now. I won't be in my prime. Hell, the prime of my life likely came and went.

His humor is him trying to lighten the mood but, "I'm serious, Cary. I was last year's model before we even met. Give it a few more years and I'll be broken down by the side of the road with two flat tires and my engine block scraping the highway and not enough ground clearance for the track at Le Mans."

"Oh, fuck. It cranks my jack all the way up when you talk cars to me, Doll. Let me oil your chassis and remind you what a damn talented mechanic I am."

He tries to kiss my fears into submission, but I move my face and his forehead hits my pillow, pissing Cary off. I won't talk dirty back. He flings the covers onto the floor and jumps to his feet.

"What the hell is wrong with you tonight? What? Do you want me to offer to pay for you to get new double Ds? A nip here and a tuck there, like Davina's had? Will that make you happy? Will it wash away all the concerns you have that I won't love you unless we're the exact same age? Because fuck me, I've wanted those tits in my mouth since the day I met you. I've wanted *you*. The past twelve weeks, I've fought for *you*."

He paces between the wall and the bed, not averting his gaze from me. Clothed from head to toe I've never felt so naked and ashamed.

"What you're terrified of isn't your birthdate or mine. It's not some stupid chicks in a parking lot gawking at me in public the way *I* conceded I wouldn't watch men do to you at Sweet Caroline's. Or somewhere down the road, me growing a beer gut and having a midlife crisis and cheating on you with someone younger. It's that your fucking ex ruined your version of perfection.

"You're acting too stubborn to see another man standing in front of you, ready, willing, and able to put the pieces back together. It's not that you don't trust my love for you, Holly. You don't trust any man could love you, would want better for you or Bhodi... And that leaves me with shit end of the stick."

He reaches for the comforter, pulling it the rest of the way off of the bed, and heaves the bedroom door open. The knob sticks in the drywall.

"Wh-here are you going?" I swallow.

All of a sudden, I'm conscious that I don't want Cary to leave. I don't want him to give up on me so easily.

"To sleep on the fucking couch!" he yells.
What did I just do?

# Chapter Thirty-six

Cary

I don't wind up on the couch. What I do after storming down the living room is roll the king-size comforter into a lousy ball and throw it, not caring where the heap of fabric lands. Then I grab my cell and keys and find myself sitting in a booth at the Wafflehaus at ten o'clock at night across from Dusty of all people.

I feel like a shit grumbling about Holly, but I need Dusty's advice. They were friends first, and that's why I called him.

It's gotten so bad that Holly won't even let me buy Bhod a pair of shoes. She wants to take care of everything herself, and it's killing me. I have lawyers and resources at my disposal. I could find a way of making this all go away. But Holly won't let me.

I unload all the stuff I'm taking care of unbeknownst to Holly; From the wedding surprises I have planned to how Laurel and I are in cahoots.

We're only splitting time staying at Laurel's when Emory isn't with her dad, Bennett. Holly still watches her niece each afternoon before she goes to work at Sweet Caroline's. The shuffle contributes to Holly's exhaustion, and her reluctance to move before we find a home of our own is driving me nuts.

One of the reasons Holly keeps giving me about waiting until after the wedding to move is that she doesn't want her sister stuck with daycare bills or on the hook for the condo's full monthly mortgage payment. Laurel has actually tried to persuade her that the kids are better off at Davina's after school. They'll have a bigger yard to play in and, more often than not, my mom is around.

Holly's douche ex aside, she and I haven't been together long enough to understand how either of us would react to the big changes we're going through. I can live with Holly being stressed. But tonight she intended to cause a fight.

"What's bugging you is she's nnot acting like herself." Dusty sums it up succinctly when I finally stop dumping every stupid detail of her recent change in behavior on him.

"Yeah."

"Hol-ly is what I'd want my Bbeth to be if-f we'd never met." His stutter, which I'm rarely tuned into, is thick with emotion talking about Sylvie's mom.

Dusty lost Beth a few years back in the same car wreck that gave him the TBI that affects his speech. Not only was Dusty not married to Beth at the time of the accident—they were waiting to do so, taking into account other people's feelings, and trying to appease Sylvie's paternal grandmother—he's also Sylvie's real dad through an adoption that happened this year.

I have hella respect that while recovering from a major auto accident Dusty never wavered, let the court of public opinion sway him, bowed down to the legal red tape, or other family member's grief when it came to claiming his daughter.

This is a guy I want on my side. A man I want to show Bhodi he can be like.

Dusty pauses, forming his thoughts so he can speak them clearer. He backtracks when he begins talking again.

"When I worked for Jake and Carver, the guys ribbed me that Holly and I should get together." He puts his hands up, stopping me from getting defensive. "We got along because we both had kids. Morgan, and the others our age, don't." He motions between us. "They don't get it… I stand by my comment before. Holly's w-what I'd have wanted Beth to be for Sylvie Rhys if she'd been all alone. But, because of that, Holly's not my dream girl." He scratches his brow. "Mine was shaking her ass up on stage. I watched like an asshole. Thinking Cece only wanted me for my dick. Pissed when she didn't act the way I wanted her to and forgetting she had her own baggage to unpack."

"Holly's is unpacked."

"Is it? Sure seems William is taking her on a nasty trip down memory lane."

I toss my palms up so Dusty will enlighten me.

"You're pissed she manages everything—except putting herself first. Let me ask you this: How many guys do you think Holly dated that never got introduced to her kid?"

My tongue presses into my lower lip, pushing it against my teeth. I don't think about Holly and other men who may have been around Bhodi. They're mine. What's more, my fiancée doesn't let shit-for-brains near my son unless she's got a fucking court order taking her choice away.

Dusty takes my concentration on my water glass as an answer.

"The woman does two things well. Protecting the

people she cares for."

Dusty speaks slowly. However, this time he pauses long enough I'm uncertain he'll keep going.

"And?"

"Instead of dealing with her feelings, what any bartender is best at. Building other people up. Make them happy. Not a fucking front since it fills her up. But she's depressed. William picked an old wound. It's festering. You gotta give Hol time to feel all the shit she is. Process it."

"You don't get over ten years of hurt in a few months," I reply.

*Hell, I proved that this summer by blowing up at Davina at the beach house.*

My friend taps his skull.

"She takes care of everyone else first." I wish I said it with pride. My words come out dejected. "Since I understand, I can save her."

"No, you fucker." Dusty gets agitated. "You need to st-top using happy coincidences to ssave her... Follow a-long here since I have a little princess at home and you don't. The kind of chivalry Hol wants is for you to give her the sword to slay the dragon. She's been through battles without you that she can save herself."

"Trust her."

That's what Trig said to me.

"Once you do, she'll begin trusting herself again." Dusty gives a new perspective to what I thought I knew.

Dusty and I shoot the shit for the next hour.

He emphasizes that after everything Holly's been through, she doesn't know how not to work harder. And no matter how hard she works, the custody battle with Willam makes her believe it won't ever be enough.

I guess she's even got it in her head that the cash Jake's been throwing her way since she became the manager at Sweet Caroline's belongs to her by default. Holly's boss is PO-ed at somebody else, and she's the beneficiary of Jake's foul mood.

The thing is, I always do things for Holly because she doesn't expect it. This woman isn't out scamming anyone for a free ride. The blush on her cheeks is a giveaway that she appreciates me being thoughtful, whether that's toward her or anyone else. Uniquely enough, Holly is far happier sprinkling kindness on others than comfortable accepting a shower of accolades.

She's entitled to be happy too.

It's past midnight when I leave the twenty-four-hour breakfast joint. Dusty's perspective lifted a weight and gained me the big guy as a groomsman. I hope the tailor makes Incredible Hulk-size suits that come in more colors than green and purple. Although the wedding has a carnival theme, so he could don a cheetah print loincloth and go as the strong man and fit right in. Nah, Dusty is more like the Hulk after Banner exposes them both to more radiation and their personalities merge. A rocket scientist before his accident, Dusty's still genius enough to pull that trick off.

Wedding on the brain, I've assigned each of my groomsmen two alter-egos: a superpower and a circus-themed one. The latter makes me want to ask Isobel to shake it up some more and search out funhouse mirrors that stretch and widen and distort bodies. I'm running that idea by Holly once I've apologized to her.

She's going to love it. Holly's the yin to my yang. I need her maturity and she needs my goofiness to emphasize she's not over the hill yet and that she can recapture her youthfulness.

But I have to say I'm sorry first for yelling and making wild accusations about her not trusting me. For making it about myself when I should have freely given what she actually needed from me; a reminder that she has the power within.

I worried she was giving up on us, and my outburst might have given her a reason to. After all, Holly stayed when I lost my shit at Davina this summer. She didn't make it about how I embarrassed her. Holly wouldn't have ever brought up William all those months ago if I hadn't been so rip shit over the way my mom had acted. And Holly accepted that she'd never understand Davina's motives, yet hasn't once held them against her.

I love her for that and for showing me I can have a relationship with my mom and my sister.

Since we began, our conversations have always come easy. That level of intimacy is something I've never encountered with any woman. I want it back. But I also want her confessing every heartbreak instead of hiding it from me. I should have pushed more for her to confide her deepest darkest fears so that Holly understands I can be her bartender and listen the way she does for everyone else. I could have reminded her she rebuilt my confidence when I'd given Holly every reason to doubt she should let me be responsible for the most important person in her life.

She's proven she trusts me. She needs me to show her I trust the person she is.

Dusty is right, Holly doesn't need me to be her savior, but she does need to know I have her back.

With the chinks in her armor exposed, it's apparent I wasn't doing near good enough a job of proving that. We've both sort of been stumbling through the unexpected, haven't we?

I jog up the front step, certain we're halfway over the speed bump.

The light is on in the formal living room. Davina's folding the comforter I left on the floor.

"What are you doing up?"

"Holly woke me when she left. She didn't want me to worry in the morning if neither of you were here."

Sounds like my girl but, "Why did she go? Where did she go?"

"I'm assuming to Laurel's. Holly had her and Bhodi's things packed. I know you argued. I heard you leave…" Mom's voice trails. She lifts an envelope from the coffee table and hands it to me. "It's not my place to butt in."

I gauge the weight of it in my palm, knowing at once there won't be a letter explaining why Holly left. I tear the corner and tilt the envelope. Her engagement ring slides out.

My mom inhales. All my breath has left my body.

*Holly*

Raising my hand to knock on the door, I notice my bare finger for the umpteenth time. Someday I'll stare at my hand and my throat won't close up. Yet, I know my sadness is only a part of the doubt I have that I'm making the right decision.

I've survived a relationship ending before. My heart didn't stop beating. Well, not the organ. The heart currently ruling my emotions hasn't been ticking since I slid the diamond off my finger.

It was important to me to say goodbye to Davina. She spends so much of her time alone at the beach house. I've gathered Cary's mother doesn't have many true friends to count on. Sneaking out like a thief in the night would make her believe I wasn't one either.

Giving the envelope to her seemed an immense burden to bear. However, the ring needed to be safe, and I knew she'd return it to its owner instead of Cary overlooking a small item on his nightstand, or worse, throwing something that valuable away by accident. It's one of the most beautiful things I've owned and what it may have cost Cary exceeds the limits of my imagination. The rock was the size of Sloan's and Carver doesn't spare a penny on his wife.

I hesitate a moment longer. It's before lunchtime at Sweet Caroline's. Only a fool pretends they don't know what that means.

Me.

I've played the fool the whole time I've been employed here.

But today I'm expected. Jake's car is outside. I've asked for an audience with him.

I'm opening Pandora's Box because misery has already found me. I don't know how to combat it on my own, so why not let evil in too? We may be more deserving bedfellows than I'd previously considered.

What if he wants more from me than I have to give? What if Jake notices my engagement ring is gone and he expects Cary's secrets in return for his help? I can't do that. I'd rather cross the line with Jake than divulge Davina's affair.

I finally summon the courage to rap. Jake barks at me to enter. He sees me and his eyes flash. His smile is sinister as he pulls at his collar, adjusting the top button.

His private bathroom door opens and a sheepish young woman slinks out. He ignores her attempts to claim his attention. Shooting him a glare, she says something about waiting in the theatre at the bar and leaves the office door ajar.

Jake rolls his eyes. I have a feeling the woman is about to become my problem.

"To what do I owe the great pleasure of your visit?" he asks as if I hadn't begged on the phone for him to meet me here.

"Shut up man, and just... Just shut up!" Trig walks in with his dog, Tallulah on his heels. He aims his frustrations at Jake. "Give her the fucking file, jack-off. He snags a manilla folder off of Jake's desk, shoving it my way.

"What is this?" Morbid curiosity gets the best of me and I flip it open.

The file is full of what I'm here for. Things I've intentionally kept my distance from. See no evil, hear no evil, and especially speak no evil.

Trig flops down on the sofa next to me. "I started pulling everything I could find as soon as... As soon as Kimber mentioned your problems. Let me know if you want me to dig further. But most of what you need is right there." He taps the papers and photographs.

"You've had this... for months?"

I watch as Tallulah places her head on Trig's lap and he strokes her short, dark fur.

"I figured where you were hot to have Cass checked out before he got near your kid..." Trig shrugs.

His explanation makes perfect sense. Except.

"Why didn't you give it to me before?"

"What stopped you from asking for it?" Jake says with haughty reproach.

But Trig's explanation hits the nail on the head. For me, there's a huge difference between asking a guy with a security company to do a simple background check as a favor, compared to digging up  evidence intended to ruin a person.

Is that actually what I came here for?

A little voice inside me calls out *yes*.

If Bhodi's big brother was a bad guy, I would have simply asked for another. This is information I need to ensure my son's well-being, but it's also damning. It's meant to be used to hurt someone else. Even if that someone else caused me the biggest pain I've felt in my life, I still deal in kindness. I don't like rushes to judgment. Although, all along my gut told me William's motives hadn't changed.

I swallow and look at Jake who is leaning against his desk. His arms are crossed, his head tilted, and there's a hint of compassion in his features that he's quick to wipe away.

"Read it." Jake tests me. "We don't have all day. You're *on* tonight."

The way it comes out, you'd think I was dancing up on that stage. It's my likely future. I've left my fiancé and come to a man who dabbles in the criminal for help. My pride has nothing to lose.

Trig has found every seedy detail of the decade William hid from his responsibilities.

In a bitter voice, Jake narrates each slip I look at.

"Retired. Sole source of income is his military retirement. Divorce decree and alimony payments to his first wife. Younger daughter gets two more years of child support."

"This is more than he owes Bhodi each month!" I'm nauseated.

Trig swears, his annoyance like an aura. He must know how little my son has actually received.

"The older daughter's arrests for shoplifting began four years ago," Jake continues, making me wonder if he was ever a lawyer as he lays out the facts. Perhaps it's his dead delivery. This scenario may have played out so many times in this office that Jake seems to take pleasure in being a great big jerk.

Don't ask why I won't call him a mobster. Underworld criminals are dark and broody. Jake's more of a sharply dressed Viking out to pillage in his crisp linen pants and a light blue shirt that matches his icy eyes. Maybe because I love Jake in my own weird, forgiving way and I don't want to see him as the bad guy... And that's another reason I couldn't convince myself to come to Sweet Caroline's when the lights were on. I didn't want to believe he's a man capable of doing anything illegal.

*Unseeming* I've given up on.

Ungentlemanly too, when he lacks politeness and prods me to keep going. There's credit card debt and the foreclosure of his house.

"But I thought his wife got that in the divorce?" I question.

"She did, but he'd drained the equity."

"This isn't the man I was involved with."

Bhodi's father was in the military. He wasn't a spendthrift or a gambler. When we were together, he never struck me and anything less than a decent boyfriend. William's issue was his midlife crisis and his wife not wanting to move to North Carolina when the military transferred him here.

He'd gone back to her. She'd won—lousy prize as it was—but for William to console her, agreed to forgo a relationship with Bhodi.

Or do I have it wrong?

The person in this file is in financial ruin. The life he went back to wasn't as perfect as he'd led me to believe. He said he loved his wife and missed his kids.

He never missed my kid. He hadn't loved me. William is the most selfish man I've ever encountered besides Rex Stanton... And I manage a strip club owned by a criminal for Christ's sake. If anyone's interacted with her fair share of questionable men, it's me!

"When your mill girls fixed the marquee, Kelsey mentioned a guy was in who asked if Cary was a guy or a girl. She told him it was Cass. When he didn't know who that was she said, 'the guy who owns all the dealerships'. Most customers wanted to know when they could congratulate you in person, but this guy's ears perked. He hounded her to the point that

Kelsey freaked she wasn't supposed to say you were engaged to Cass."

"Who I was dating was common knowledge. Bhodi practically lives at the service center."

My son asked me recently when he could call Cary 'dad'. I put him off saying we'd discuss it after the wedding. He won't be able to now. I haven't figured out how to keep Cary in Bhodi's life if I'm not in Cary's. The road has forked and that's a bridge I'm about to cross.

"We pulled the footage from that night." Trig shuffles through some grainy photos, showing me several views of the same man.

"William," I mutter.

Cary's money did play into this somehow.

The final paper in the folder is actually three clipped together; A birth certificate for a baby girl who is Emory's age. The spot marked father is blank. Underneath is a court order for a DNA test that's a year old, but no test results, and finally an injunction to garnish William's wages. Both of those were filed in another state.

"Did he—"

"Have a kid with someone else?" Trig finishes my sentence. "Near as we can figure. She got pregnant before Mayer's divorce... Might have even been the cause, if he got caught twice with his pants down... He must've persuaded her not to list him as the baby's father. In my digging around, I found one instance where a William Mayer cited this other woman's residence as his own on a single document after his wife had filed for dissolution. So they had to have been together after the baby was born. But they aren't now, and without proof of paternity, she can't get child support. William's been living in Raleigh quite a while, avoiding the mess he made."

"He has three kids he owes money to?"

"Holly, he has two other child support payments he's behind on. He's trying to weasel what he can from you to *give* it to them," Jake explains. "This isn't about Bhodi at all."

I think I'm going to be sick. I believed I was playing by my rules, but I hadn't fought William at all. He expects me to roll over the way I have. He's counting on it.

"What do I do?" My voice waivers as I shut the folder and stare at it on my lap. What I really mean is "what do I do next?"

"Take it with you. Give it to your lawyer to present to the judge."

"What if that's not enough? None of this says William is unfit. That he's abusive. The judge disregarded that William hadn't held up his end of the bargain before. Why would the court care now when William has two more kids clear across the country?"

"Get it to the judge and I'll take care of the rest."

I startle. "You're going to bribe a judge?"

"Pipe down, Holly!" Jake demands. "I run a respectable business here."

Trig snorts. "Respectable my ass." He winks at me and tosses a thumb in Jake's direction. "The fucker has done far worse than call in a favor to get your ex's rights terminated."

"Don't involve her, Trig. She doesn't want to be involved." Jake gets angrier.

"Are you here for help?" Trig pushes on.

"Uh-Yes," I respond. *But what happens to Bhodi if I'm charged with a crime?*

"She's involved, Jake."

"Cass has the resources to do the same," Jake says about convincing the judge to see my point of view.

"He's not a party to any of this." I'm steadfast.

I don't want any of what we've discussed touching

Cary or his business. It's why I left last night and why we aren't getting married.

"You heard her, Ballentine. *Any of it.* Let's keep it that way… For Bhodi's sake."

Trig departs after a hug. I'm left with Jake, who tucks behind his desk, focusing on the scratched silver laptop, clicking away on the keypad. I wonder if the thank yous I've gushed to them come close to being enough. Unsure what the correct next step is, I wait a beat. Accepting my boss intends to ignore me, I get up to leave when the air gets thick and awkward.

I'm about to close the door when Jake pipes up with his instructions.

"Hol, the girl out there. Get rid of her before you leave. And be back here on time tonight to go over next week's schedule with Kelsey."

"Sure thing."

This is my life, and I'm now indebted to more Jake than I ever was.

# Chapter Thirty-eight

*Cary*

I pull into the lot at Sweet Caroline's. Taking the space closer to the entrance and next to Holly's Honda, I use the Colony Park to hide her car. She can't duck out without me knowing.

I picked up the car Bhodi and I worked on from the dealership this morning and switched the title to my name. Not because I'm giving it to anyone, but because it's special to me the way Holly and Bhodi are and I want it. Also, I needed to fill time and the registry motor vehicles seemed like the best way to waste it waiting for Holly to make her move.

I had a feeling she'd go to Jake. She trusts him. Why I'll never understand since his reputation falls a peg lower on the outlaw scale than the drug pushers and gun runners he's guilty of associating with. But Jake's been good to Holly and I'm not jealous, even though I could have done whatever she's decided to ask him to do.

It's like Dusty said: if I wasn't around, I'd trust Holly would protect Bhodi at all costs. She took me out of the picture last night because it protected me.

I spent a good part of my life too young and too spoiled to understand what it's like to fight for the things I wanted. They won't just land in my lap. Now, the things I want aren't things at all. They're people who make their own choices about their own destinies. I can't make Holly accept me as her hero. She has to be her own. And yes, heroes get knocked down and they bleed. And they get back up and fight.

I get out of the Colony Park and lean against its brilliant trim. A woman   is storming out of the building. It's not Holly. Trig finger flashes me a wave a few minutes later, jumping on his motorcycle, crossing the street, and entering the open fence to park in front of Carver's mill. He gets why I'm here. We don't need to speak. Trig's given me all the advice I'll ever need about my future wife.

I don't know what deal Holly's striking in there, but this is where she works and she'll leave when she's ready the way Kimber did.

Holly keeps me waiting another ten. The glimpse I get of her knocks me out. She's still so goddamned beautiful all I can do is take her in.

Her wrecked expression doesn't match the flouncy pony. She's got on a cream-colored crewneck sweatshirt. It's the traditional kind that has the little upside-down triangle under the center of the collar. Her capris are a deep navy. What little her tattoo is showing disappears under lacy bobby socks. Then there's her Chucks. Holly's an innocent picture of days gone by. You'd never assume she'd been inside Sweet Caroline's, let alone asking a favor of a snake like Jake Ballentine.

Fuck, she's amazing.

There was a moment when Davina handed over that envelope last night that I worried I'd never see Holly again. My mom told me that my grandfather never got past the crushing torment that he hadn't done enough for my grandmother and that's why she walked away. He chose guilt and grief over finding a new love. Davina doesn't want the same outcome for me.

The change in Davina in the year since Rex has been out of over lives is amazing. She can't get enough of the kids and—minus the tat, which she still refuses to let me see—acting grandmotherly. I no longer see my mom giving me advice on what to do as overbearing. She's been through the grinder too, and she only wants what's best for me. Davina's words resonated. Yet, the space I gave Holly overnight and this morning was to prove to myself if this all falls apart I tried to do exactly what she needed.

"Why are you here?" Holly asks, approaching me with caution.

As soon as she's within my reach, I pull her close. I gotta admit. Wondering what Jake wants from Holly in return put me on edge.

Her fists raise between us, which is perfect.

"You forgot something." I unfurl the tight ball of her left hand, sliding her engagement back where it belongs.

She looks at it. Really, really, looks at it and tears threaten her eyes.

"I can't marry you," she chokes out, smashing her lips to grind them between her teeth.

I tip her chin. When she focuses on me, her cheeks dampen.

"Did you do something in there you don't want to tell me about?"

"Yes," she whispers.

"Was it for Bhodi?"

The one thing I'd bet my business on is that Holly does nothing if it doesn't benefit her kid. That's the kind of mom she is.

"Yes."

"If you had to do it all over, would you do it again?" I rub her arms as she shivers.

"Yes," she replies for a third time with conviction.

"Okay." I toss my shoulders back and hit my girl with a megawatt grin.

Her brow creases and I kiss her forehead.

"Wh-hat do you mean 'okay'?"

"As in; Fine. Good. No problem. Sure thing," I tease her with the last word and then I get serious. "I trust you, Doll. You didn't want to do what you just did. You don't plan on cutting me out or keeping secrets again. But you also don't want any of this coming back on me. Am I right?"

She nods, my words sinking in.

"I was thinking February the fourteenth still works." I grab both of her hands before she can move away and bring the big rock up to her nose so Holly sees what's right in her face.

Cary—" Holly sighs.

"I want to marry you. I want to marry you because you don't need me to save you, Doll. You were doing fine before I arrived on the scene. Hell, you scoped me out. You opened the gate for me to be a part of our boy's life. There's not a damned good reason why you can't put the barriers back up that William is trying to tear down. Not only won't I stop you from doing what you think is right to protect Bhodi, I will stand by your side and love you while you find a way to put William in our rearview. And we won't look back."

I kiss her slow and leisurely. We've got the rest of our lives. The more gentle I am, the more insistent Holly's lips are moving against mine. She opens, so I can sweep my tongue inside her mouth, tasting the sweetness.

Her nails on one hand cut into my abs. The other palm flattens against my pec and my calloused thumb slides up, grazing the bottom of her unbound breast as I clutch her to me. Her teeth snag my lower lip as she breaks away. I chase her with pecks, not wanting to break the kiss, but aware of the free show we're putting on for the traffic passing Sweet Caroline's.

"For however long this lasts, Holly. I want it. And when it's over, I'm hoping we get a story like your parents had, because I don't want to live this life without you in it."

"That was definitely the most romantic thing you've said. Seeing you here, when I was leaving the club—"

"Sort of the angle I was going for." I tuck an imaginary loose strand behind her ear and kiss her again. "I'm sorry I got upset last night. It's been harder than I imagined watching the two of you hurting."

My girl smiles and I wipe away the last of her tears as her face flushes.

"Come on." I push away from the Colony Park, guiding her to the passenger seat. Holly's never been in this car before. "We're going for a ride before I tuck you in for your nap."

"Is this car a stick-shift? Don't you want to teach me how to drive it?" Her lips twitch.

She's got a lot to learn about cars to catch up with the rest of the family.

"Automatic. And the only stick you have to worry about is mine."

Holly tucks into the seat, running her manicured fingertips over the dash. "You know, there's room in the back to go parking… If I were that kind of girl."

The wedding planner's been on us to check out the venue. So instead of bringing Holly home right away, we head to the drive-in to find out how roomy it is.

# Chapter Thirty-nine

*Holly*

"That one's pretty too." Davina's nicety doesn't reach the level of enthusiasm we're searching for.

I knew we were in for a long haul at the bridal shop. I've put off finding the perfect wedding gown, and it's getting down to the wire. I've been trying on dresses for an hour already. I'm not sure what magic I'm supposed to be feeling, but the spark's not there, even while I'm pretending, fucking exuding, that the spark is there. With every ounce of me I love these dresses right up to the instant I open the fitting room curtain.

"No," Hailey and Aidy voice at the same time and in identical bored tones.

They're here for moral support. As is Sloan, who sips champagne next to Kimber on the damask couch.

Kimber and Celine are in the wedding, as is Laurel as my maid of honor. Choosing one friend over another felt odd since they are all dear to me.

I look hopefully at Laurel's reflection in the right

panel of the floor-to-ceiling mirror. My sister is quiet too.

This is the third dress I've tried on. Isobel has gotten each one right. I mean, she's bagged my style one-hundred percent correct. Each of these dresses I'd wear on any given day of the week.

The first was a sleeveless A-line with a slim satin belt and a tiny bow in the back. The second, a fifties-inspired swing dress. The sweetheart bodice had a built-in bra. I guess to guarantee I wore one. A soft ivory mesh of honeycomb tulle overlay gave the impression the gown was strapless. It was a lot like this third one with long sleeves and a row of delicate buttons at the ruched cuffs. Though, the one I have on has sequins and a diagonal floral appliqué from the knee over the shoulder makes it appear to have a single strap.

I play with the cuffs in the mirror, wanting to have liked this gown more on than I had on the hanger. Each of Isobel's selections has taken it up a notch, and all have been short and playful. They are exactly what I asked her to find.

I turn and the skirt flares. We go back for round four. Another full skirt of satin that lands mid-calf. It's simple with a few adornments. Twinkling clear beads and crystals cover the lower half of the bodice. A bow at the left hip sits over the belt. It has a folded boat neck collar and v back.

It's beautiful. It's me.

But I don't get bride vibes from it.

Once again, everyone stares.

"I'd wear that." Cece stops worrying her lip, making me glad someone has broken the silence. "I'd do it in a different color and pretend to be you."

I groan, buckling at my midsection. We haven't even discussed what my bridesmaids are wearing. If no one can come to a consensus on my dress, how are the mill girls and my sister going to agree on theirs—especially since it has to complement whatever I chose.

"It's actually better than the rest," Kimber agrees. "I'd wear it too, but only for you." She must have felt my angst.

I whisper my thanks.

"It does come in a peach." Isobel contributes to our conversation.

The flowers she found for the terra-cotta pots have delicate white centers with peachy-pink edges. The tips are incredibly vibrant. Bold like the circus tent, red stripes.

"Okaayy," I blow out a breath. "So you all are wearing a bridal gown and I'm attending my wedding naked."

Isobel puts her palm on my upper chest, tipping my shoulder back, and saying something about practicing good posture. She spins me around, marching me toward the fitting room.

I'm unzipped, standing there in my altogether while the wedding planner futzes getting the third gown back on the rack.

"Are you going to go with your friends' suggestion?" she asks, taking out her notepad.

"I don't see why not. At least, it's one more thing you can check off the list since I'm late making decisions."

"You're among the most interesting, but not the most difficult bride I've ever worked for," she chortles, moving the dress to the opposite side of the room under an embellished script sign that reads: I do.

The first two dresses are on the "I object!" rack. Pretty funny. The rest of the black garment bags hang from a much wider "maybe" pole. I keep trying to come up with a more appropriate sign for it in my head. Having it called the "'do you?' pole" makes me think about the pole on stage at work. I don't think Isobel would appreciate my humor.

I stand there cupping my breasts and it hits me that my toplessness isn't the least bit provocative to this woman. It's her job to dress and undress me until we get it right. Isobel has probably seen lots of uncovered boobs and her fair share of panties that don't cover a gal's assets. We've sort of got that in common.

She goes to the maybe rack and starts unzipping the next bag in line. She zips it back up and shuffles to the end of the row.

"I was going to pull this one out last. It's not what you asked for."

"Then why did you bring it in here?"

"It was something Cary said when I'd spoken to him. He mentioned you attended a wedding on your first date and how stunning you were. Like an old Hollywood starlet. He said sitting next to you at that ceremony he had a feeling someday he was going to marry you."

"He did?" My hand creeps up my neck.

Having never been married, I wondered while watching Glen and his wife say their vows if the bride still got the tummy-bumps Cary was giving me. My fingers balled in my fists, digging into the flesh of my palms, I pictured Cary up at the altar. I'd attended my fair share of weddings before Cary asked me to Glen's. However, I hadn't superimposed the groom with any face I knew. I chastised myself for being silly. William had promised we'd walk down the aisle and it was stupid of me to get swept up in and forget the heartbreak I'd been through.

Isobel unzips the bag. "I want you to close your eyes for this," she says as she's taking out the swath of fabric. "It won't look like anything until it's on.

And you need the full effect."

I drop my boobs and cover my eyes, keeping them closed as Isobel slides the silky wrap over my bare skin. The garment covers my legs and tickles the tops of my toes. I hear the teeth of the zipper catch. She tells me to hold still. She's not quite done and there are several snapping sounds at my back, followed by lots of tugging as she's draping.

My anticipation is getting the best of me.

"Do you think you can keep them shut a little longer?"

"Sure thing."

With my hands to my face, I'm led back out to where my girls are at. I feel the kick pleat in the back give as I walk.

"Oh, my god!"

I hear it repeated. Shushing sounds intersperse with squeals.

Isobel gives me the go-ahead to look. I gauge my friend's reactions in the mirror's reflection first. Sloan's not interested in her drink anymore. Aidy may bust off of the couch if Kimber didn't have a grip on her. Cece's fists are under her nose, hiding a wide grin. Hailey isn't hiding hers at all. Davina might have seen a ghost. And my sister, Laurel, is wiping her cheeks.

I finally drop my gaze to the floor, slowly bringing it up. Holy crap, this dress is amazing!

The mermaid design flares at the ankle and is tight through the knee. The bodice panels are form-fitting. It's strapless. The satin over the right breast is cut higher at a dramatic asymmetrical peak. The seam is crisp, flowing over into a cuff, making my chest seem rather impressive without the extra undergarments needed for maximum lift. It fits flush and I can't see down my top at all. Instead of a traditional veil, soft tulle waves attach at my back. The edges are a boa of more tulle that resembles ocean foam before the tide takes it back out to sea.

My face is clean of makeup and my hair is loose around my shoulders. Yet, I haven't ever felt this beautiful. This glamourous. Not even when I've tried. And I can't believe this is how Cary sees me.

"I know it covers your entire tattoo," Isobel concedes.

Showing it was never a concern of mine.

I grip her forearm, steadying myself. I'm unmoored, shaking so hard my knees buckle. My friends and family surrounded me, leaning in as they hug me individually.

Tears tumble out so fast I can hardly wipe them away before the next falls. I'm glad I intentionally didn't wing my liner so it wouldn't rub off, ruining all the delicate, expensive layers of fabric.

"Those better be joy or I'm going to clobber you with a can of beans." My sister smarts.

"They are," I gush, eating up the attention lavished on me. The whole moment feels right. Magical.

# Chapter Forty

*Cary*

A throng of half-pints rush by so close I have to raise the two round glasses of champagne high in the air so as not to spill them.

The boys—many of them Bhodi's friends from the big brother program—have carnie costumes over their dress clothes. Sylvie Rhys and Emory bring up the rear, skipping in white frilly frocks. Sylvie has colorful sleeves on her arms; the tattooed lady. My niece has a scraggly black beard attached to her face leftover from the strong man costume another kid's got on. But the bearded lady works just as well for what the photographer has asked them to do.

We're at the drive-in early to make the most of the light for photographs. It's a beautiful mid-February afternoon for an outdoor wedding. We'll have to turn on the heaters in the tent once the sun goes down, but every peculiar wish we've made, Isobel has granted. Funhouse mirrors included.

The wedding party has arrived, along with the mentors of the program boys. Glen and his wife got a plus-one invitation, as did all the other guys Bhodi and I went on field trips with. This is our last official outing and when *Carolina Bridal Magazine* found out about our story, they opted to make it a feature. The boys are also going to have their pictures taken as a group and individually and the moms are all getting reprints at no charge.

I walk away from the bar, out of the tent, and pass Trig one of the champagne glasses. Hearing a roar, I toss my head back and laugh. Dusty's got a kid hanging off each bicep and the rest are mugging for the camera. The photographer is eating the scene up, letting the kids be kids.

"That's going to be you one day. Kid hanging off each arm." Trig comments.

"Not soon enough. How are the twins?"

"Eating. Pooping. Definitely not sleeping… Wouldn't change a minute." His contented grin widens when Kimber rounds the corner.

The mill girls are pretty passionate about portraying Holly's look for a day. Their support extends from tip top of their over-sprayed bouffants, down to winged liner, sassy lipstick, pearl chokers, ending at the toes of wedge heels.

I'm impressed. By the hungry way his jaw ticks, so is Trig.

"It's good to get out without the kid, though. Remember that," he says.

The sun will have gone down in the next hour. I consider telling him there are plenty of convertibles with the roof up in case he and Kimber need some privacy to go necking. But I bite my tongue. It's my perverted fantasy Holly acted on when we were here last.

"I'll keep it in mind," I say instead since Trig's advice hasn't led me wrong so far.

Holly got a call from Marie Grant twenty-four

hours after her meeting with Jake. She wanted to reschedule William's visitation. A few days after that the session Marie canceled altogether.

Almost immediately the judge also contacted Holly requesting an appointment with her in his chamber. He asked Holly why she never sought sole custody of her son and listened to her side of the story. The court gave William the option of paying his back support or relinquishing his rights. He had a month to choose and he conceded within the week, breaking all ties to Bhodi. I don't think the responsible option was anything William  planned to follow through with anyway.

At Holly's request, we asked as few questions as possible about what was happening with William's other legal woes. She didn't want the other side of the story to hamper our happiness. Ignorance had a certain bliss to it, and we focused on moving on and planning our lives together.

Bhodi took his father's second disappearance in stride. I guess that's all he's ever known of the man. Holly also told Half-pint that he has a sister and that, when he was ready, she'd help him contact her. My boy asked a lot of questions about what it was like for me meeting my sister, Addie. And then he changed the subject to how much longer before we were back at the beach house.

He's a resilient kid. I hope he gets when he's older that all the thanks for that goes to his mom.

"Ready?" Kimber directs the question to me.

I clap my hands, rubbing them together. "As I'll ever be."

This is the moment I've been waiting all day for. The photographer and wedding coordinator have been rotating us around the big top. All of Holly's pictures have been taken on one side while mine have been on the other. I hadn't been anxious that I haven't seen Holly yet, but seeing the mill girls dressed like her makes it all kick in.

Kimber leads me away from the tent and into the clearing where Dusty and the kids were. I'm sweating when she hugs me, darting backward on her heels to get out of the picture. The photographer is on his belly, shooting upward. When I turn to see my bride, the picture he'll snap will make it look like we're on the big screen.

All. The. Stops.

I'm in for a dime, I'm in for a dollar if we have a daughter and she wants a lavish wedding. How do you top a big top?

I feel Holly's fingertips dance against my sleeve. Little sparks underneath cause the hair of my forearm to stand on end. Her breath catches and she goes to pull away. I clamp mine firmly around her hand, holding onto it as I turn for the first glimpse of my bride.

I was a fool to believe she was breathtaking on our first date. Nothing does justice to this. Holly's fucking perfection from the swish of her skirt up to the top of her head. Her victory rolls are half up, half down. The arch of her darkened brows emphasizes her cat-eye liner surrounding her bright brown eyes. Bold cherry red lips dare me to make an early escape toward our honeymoon destination. She's a knockout.

"That was amazing!" The photographer shouts, scrambling up off of the ground to take more candids of us reacting to one another.

Amazing isn't the half of it. I stumble for words and pat my lapels down. Pressing my front pocket, I frown.

Dusty claps me on the back. "I got the rings, man. Safe-keeping until it's time to give them to the Best Man."

"Th-thanks." I stutter and Dusty shakes me to get the word out. Or maybe he's playing with me. I don't care. "You know you have a cape on?" I ask Holly.

She turns and fluffs at it. "I do, don't I?"

"Rescuing anybody today?"

"Maybe me."

I like the sound of that. "I'm going to kiss you."

"Don't mess the hair," she teases. "Not yet."

I lean in, soft and gentle, and pull away in a flash. "Flowers? Flowers? Isobel where are they? Cripes, we got you here in plenty of time, but I keep losing things."

"Know where Bhodi is?"

"Uh, yeah." I glance around before I actually find him and point him out. Holly assures me that means everything is under control.

It doesn't feel that way because I have a bunch of surprises for Holly. Starting with the box Isobel is giving her.

"It's cold!" Holly lifts the lid and is outright stunned.

I've had a bouquet arranged for her. It's the colors she's wanted for the table centerpieces and the plumeria was shipped in from a warmer climate where the gardener could force the blooms. We've had to keep it refrigerated so the petals didn't wilt.

"You didn't have to do this!"

I don't have to do a lot of things she doesn't expect, but I'm going to do them anyway. Sort of like… now.

"This, too." I hand over an envelope, having to take the greenery from her while she reads the document inside.

"I don't even know what this means?" She's looking peaked.

"I signed a lease for Johnston's Nursery beginning this fall." Old man Johnston was ready to hang the for sale sign. I beat him to the punch.

"I have a job!" her mouth makes a cute little "O" that begs for another kiss.

"And now you have options." I puck the letter back, refold it, and slide it in my breast pocket.

I know what Holly is thinking and that everyone witnessing this is aware of too. She owes Jake… And maybe we do, but Jake Ballentine isn't ruling our lives. I won't be indebted to him for the next fifty years or let my family be a pawn in the snake's sordid games.

"Cary—" Holly argues.

"Not today, Doll. Work as long as you want at Sweet Caroline's. Partner up with Davina to start your own business. Heck, just go there and dig in the dirt! You got a garden big enough to fill with whatever plants you want."

"You'd be okay if I just planted?" she asks, sheepishly.

*Mm-hm.* I press my lips to her forehead.

"Thank you. This is the nicest thing anyone's ever done for me."

The next time I pull my lips away from Holly's we're standing inside the big top underneath a crystal chandelier that hangs from the apex of the tent's frame. The camp of our fun surroundings combined with the elegant touches, like the fine black-rimmed china that makes each place setting look like a stack of old 45s and LPs, is as outstanding as my bride.

Holly didn't walk down the aisle. I escorted her to the center of the room because once I had her in my sights, there was no letting go of her hand. Our wedding party surrounded us until Laurel took Holly's bouquet and we said our vows. Then they joined our guests seated at the round tables leaving us at the center of the dance floor along with a guy in a dazzling white jumpsuit and his dark as midnight hair sprayed slicked into a pompadour.

"I now present to you, Mr. and Mrs. Cary Cass. Thank you, thank you very much," he announces.

Holly covers her mouth, giggling at his snarl and accurate impression of The King. She squeals, throwing her arms arming my neck. I grab her hips, lifting her heels off of the parquet.

"Treat her right," Fake Elvis instructs me.

"I will," I say. As if all of this craziness we ordered for our wedding day isn't a dead giveaway.

Bhodi darts up from where he's been sitting at a table next to my mom. He ramrods his head into our stomachs. I *oomph* at the impact, my hand automatically going to the back of his head to pull him closer. He's grown so much since I met him last February.

Holly cups his cheek and pecks him on the nose. He *ews*, wiping it away.

His friends are around. I'm sure he wants to get out of here with them and go watch movies. We could hardly keep the kids away from the Cadillacs lined up. Every-so-often a whiff of hot buttered popcorn travels inside from the machine set up outside. If I were in fifth grade, I'd want that for dinner too, not the fancy-ass meal the caterer is serving.

"Can I say it?" The kid is bouncing on the balls of his feet.

"Go ahead." Holly gives him permission.

Bhodi looks up at me. "Love you, Dad."

Struck dumb, since he's never called me that

before, I grab Bhodi under the pits and lift him up. He gives me the biggest bear hug and Holly's given me the biggest gift by trusting me to raise her boy into a man. I'm not ready to let go when I kneel, placing my son back on the wood floor. The protectiveness I have for this kid means when he's ready to leave the nest I won't be then either. My kids are getting the childhood I didn't.

"Who is dancing with your mom first?" I ask him, fixing his suit jacket.

"Uh, you." He uses the duh voice. "Do I have to stay?"

"Nah. Go have a blast with your buddies."

He missed out on too much fun with them during the fall. There will be plenty of weekend mornings making pancakes when we crank eclectic tunes and he'll get to watch me twirl his mom in the kitchen.

Bhodi ringmasters the boys with a wave. Chairs scrape against the floor and their shoes thud, racing to leave the tent, ditching the grown-ups.

I reach, plucking a flower from Holly's bouquet and tucking it behind her ear before leading my wife back to the middle of the room.

Elvis has grabbed a microphone. The twelve musicians in the big band have the brass and the rhythm section at the go. The band starts out like a tinkling music box and Elvis croons that some things are meant to be.

# Chapter Forty-one

*Holly*

The big band was Cary's idea. He and the best man poured over my playlists, searching for perfect songs. Elvis, and the crooner who replaced him after our first dance, have sung marvelous covers of my favorites.

Although my son keeps slipping out of the big top before he'll let me spin him around the dance floor, I've cut a rug with everyone else. I've kicked off my heels, sliding in time with my girlfriends and swayed to a sappy song with Laurel. And now I've found my way back to my husband who holds me close, brushing his soft beard against my temple as he whispers lyrics in my ear.

Aside from my mom and dad not being here for my big day, today is perfect. The only point that my heart struggled was when Cary gave me the gift of Mr. Johnston's nursery. It's difficult for me to fathom someone doing something that enormous for me.

My past still is still doing a mental catch up to align with where I am today. It doesn't feel earned, but I want to take the out.

I swear Jake became harder on and more critical of me since  meeting with him last fall. After the wedding invitations went out, it got worse. Jake started showing up during my shifts and telling me what Kelsey does better than I do. Last week, I walked into the building on the hour and got an earful about how he's finished tolerating my lateness. He'd been so unbearable and on edge that I'd considered quitting if it were an option.

After laying awake on too many of my nights off, worrying Jake believes my staff doesn't respect me as a manager, I'm astounded he bothered to come today. However, I'd also have half a mind to call Jake if he didn't since pain in the ass or not, he's been such a huge part of my life. I've given years to Sweet Caroline's and I don't know what I'd do if the club weren't around. I don't know what I owe him for taking care of my custody issues either. Jake has yet to call in any favors or ask for repayment.

"Still happy?" Cary lowers his forehead to mine.

"I'm thinking about my parents." I white lie. It feels true when my heart pangs a little in my chest.

He tugs me in tighter as if we're one whole person and his body could envelop mine and reminds me how wonderful our family is. When Cary pulls away, he looks past me, and a look of curiosity replaces contentment. My gaze swings over my shoulder to Jake.

"May I cut in?"

Cary concedes without question. He may not be Jake's biggest fan, however, my boss coming through for me went a long way toward changing my husband's perspective.

Jake places one palm in mine and the other rests in a gentlemanly manner on my hip. We sway stiffly at first. My tongue sticks to the roof of my mouth. My happiness is overshadowed by wanting to choose the nursery over my current job. No one else would blame me. But Jake isn't a nobody in Brighton. He's an established businessman. Since those activities aren't always on the up and up it makes him dangerous. I also didn't put up with his antics for this long without coming to love and appreciate him in my own weird way.

"Word is that you are leaving me." The blunt words tumble out with an unexpected nonchalance.

"I—uh, I haven't made my mind up."

"I've trusted you not to lie to me, Holly. Don't start now." He pegs me with a hard glare, making me swallow. "You're fired, anyway. I don't want people thinking Cass has me in his back pocket. A close association with a pillar of the community makes me look soft." A devil-may-care smirk breaks over his features.

"Since when?" I scoff, certain Jake's knocked more than one pillar off of their pedestal. Quite intentionally, too. "You wouldn't really fire me." My follow-up remark comes out as a soft question.

I stare at the pearl button on Jake's shirt. My vision goes in and out like I'm on the ocean and a boat is moving away from me. Waves crest and I realize it's the haze of tears.

"Listen, Holly, mill girls aren't meant to work at Sweet Caroline's forever." Jake shakes his head, letting out a sigh that's more of a huff.

"I'm not a mill girl, though, am I?" I blink fast, hoping my eyeliner doesn't smudge if the wetness spills over and hits my cheeks.

He takes the handkerchief from his suit pocket and drying my tears. "Why don't you think you wouldn't be one? Because you didn't live on the third floor with the rest of your bat crap crazy girlfriends?"

I smack his chest with the back of my hand. He

snags it, holding my palm like we've made a deal, and gives me the piece of cloth. I look up into his blue eyes. Never having sat down with Jake to be on the same level, I've never realized how sad they were. There were things he lost in life too.

Jake's an enormous pain in my ass. His idiosyncrasies are on par with those of my very best friends. I stayed for *him* when everyone else left. I get that now. Whatever Jake had to give, that's what I needed. Not because he was a man who could take care of me, but because he was the only man with a measure of predictability to him. I knew when I could rely on him and when I had to rely on myself. He taught me to be stronger.

It suddenly strikes me why Jake's been meaner. I thought I'd been the one waiting for the other shoe to drop, but it's been him all along trying to delay the inevitable: The day I left him.

"Can we be honest here?" he questions.

"Sure, what do I have to lose? Other than my job which you've already taken from me."

"When you started at the club, I would have fucked you in a hot minute—or several of them—given the chance. I'm glad I didn't."

"Uh, gee thanks?" I pull away, my lip curling in disgust.

Good god, should we be having this private discussion surrounded by my wedding guests? It isn't exactly starting my marriage off on the right foot when one of them can run to Cary with this kind of gossip.

Jake chuckles at my loathing, drawing me back into his flat Nordic chest. Tall and broad-shouldered, he wraps his arms around me, so my head is close to his heart. It takes me a second to realize Jake doesn't want me looking at him.

"Carver is all about giving mill girls a second

chance. I knew the moment I hired you, he'd never tap you to live there because of Bhodi. Where was he going to put a kid at the mill? My endgame was using your fashion backward get-ups to give my clientele some variation in their eye candy. When they'd had their fill of *Rosie the Riveter*, I'd have a taste of Americana myself before sending you on your merry way."

"You don't say?"

What most new dancers and waitresses at Sweet Caroline's don't know until it's too late is the reward for sleeping with the owner is a pink slip. I've never seen Jake in a relationship that's lasted. I'm not even sure he's built for monogamy. The only strippers who amounted to more than one-and-done were either too oblivious to know better, or smart enough not to rock the boat if he was sticking his dick in anyone else.

"Then Kimber pointed out what a dedicated worker you were. So, I feasted on the girls she hadn't cared as much about to keep her happy. The clock had been counting down with her since the first time Trig saw her on stage. I don't like it when people I've grown attached to leave, Hol. But, since I'm a little rough around the edges, I had to have her train someone she trusted to take over when she bowed out. You became my replacement mill girl. Before you ever became the assistant manager, I had to treat you better for you to stay on, pay you more, *not bend you over my desk*—which come to think of it now, had I'd known the two of you would both call it splitsville so close to one another, I might have changed my mind."

"You're such an ass." I snort.

"You're right. It comes from growing up in a strip club."

"That's a lie, Jake Ballantine. Miss Caroline told me

herself that your daddy kept his pants on until she said, 'drop em'."

"Can we not do visuals of my parents getting it on?"

"As long as you're willing to concede you didn't inherit your, ah, reputation," we're both aware I mean his manwhore ways, "along with the keys to the club."

"Fine. Caroline was the love of my father's life and led him around by the balls. Can I get to the point?"

"Sure thing."

"And also, what the hell am I going to do without you?"

"Damned if I know," I joke.

Being in charge of an establishment like Sweet Caroline's is fraught with challenges. It's not as if I have years to train a new manager, but Kelsey is coming into her own.

"As I was saying. In the meantime, I realized why Carver offered my best employees a room at the factory. I wanted the best for you too. That's what you wound up with… I may not have as many mill girls under my belt as I have notches in my bedpost. But the one mill girl I had? I wasn't screwing up helping while she was finding a better life than the one life had dealt her."

"That is about the sweetest thing I've ever heard come out of your mouth."

Jake nudges my shoulder. "If you tell anyone, I'll deny this conversation happened."

"It'll stay between us. Wouldn't want anyone thinking you've gone *soft*." I wink.

"Low blow, Holly."

"The only type I'm giving you, Jake."

We both smart. Innuendo aside, sex and the two of us was relegated to the absurd a long time ago.

"While we're being honest, can I ask why you

never held me over a barrel for information about Cary when I turned to you for help? You knew I'd broken things off with him. Why didn't you use that against me?"

"The Holly I love doesn't ask questions about my business dealings," Jake pauses mid-rely. "And what I know about the Stanton's I promised I wouldn't use because it would hurt you more than I'd ever gain from it."

Jake Ballentine—for as many instances as he was a thorn in my side—did all he could to protect me.

"Tell me you're happy," Jake whispers ardently.

"I'm happy." I wipe a fat tear away with Jake's handkerchief clutched between my fingertips.

Jake tips my chin. His eyes are shimmering with an emotion I can't place. Pride? Love? He used the word, but did Jake love me? And if he did—*if I'm head over heels for Cary*—why am I figuring that out now?

"There's a place for you in the reserved booth whenever you need it." He presses his lips to my forehead then takes two steps back, bowing to me before turning to head outside of the tent.

"You okay, Doll?" The hands of the man Jake's allowing me to replace him with as my protector come around my waist.

I turn, reassuring Cary that I am.

There will be time later to tell my husband that Jake has let me go and perhaps that my boss kept Davina's affair close to his chest. I won't wait on it forever, but after our honeymoon sounds right. Over the next two weeks, Cary and I are soaking up the sun in Mexico. By the time we return, I'm hoping to have turned my vampire tendencies on their ear. And not going into Sweet Caroline's might make more sense to the tiny part of me currently struggling with Jake being selfless enough to abandon me.

___________

*Cary*

"What are you doing here, Doll?"

The clip-clop of Holly's heels caught my attention coming down the hall of the dealership.

Since we got back from our honeymoon, I've been knee-deep negotiating preliminary contracts for Cass-Powell Motorcars. The deal Addie and I are attempting to strike brings her high-lines to North Carolina. Our first location is a ways off, but I own property  next to Cass-Stanton's Mercedes location, and I'm hoping to build there.

Up in a borough of New York, Addie's got her own lawyers managing the process. Surprisingly enough she's more interested in getting into a few upper midlines than having access to Maserati—a line of cars she doesn't sell but I do.

It was Rex's loss that he couldn't close the deal and never went into business with my biological father and brought Bentley to Brighton. My sister and I have a great symbiosis and are using the other's reputation to our mutual advantage.

Addie's been a frequent flyer down here since the wedding. We spent Memorial Day weekend at the beach house with her husband. They'd like us to join them in the Hamptons later this summer.

My wife is all for it—as long as my sister and I talk shop during Holly's nap time. She says watching the two of us giddy and acting like Bhodi had when he was three with a new Hot Wheels car is both thrilling and exhausting. Back in May, I took my wife for a drive along Route 12 in the MG, and then up to our room at the beach to show her the meaning of thrilling and exhausting.

I push out my chair as Holly rounds my desk. She sits on the papers I have scattered on top. The pink skirt she's got on creeps up her sun-kissed legs. She's got a Jackie O look to her today. Pillbox hat. Big buttons on her suit jacket.

Why she's wearing a suit a week into July I'm not sure, but Hol's style is her own and she fits right in because she's not afraid to be herself. We've been to a few charity banquets and everyone wants to meet her. The spread in the bridal magazine made her a bit of a celebrity. It also saw an influx in donations to, and mentorship applications for, big brother programs across the state.

My eyes travel to the panoramic image on my office wall of Bhodi and his buddies camping for the camera. All pose atop the row of blue and pink Caddies at our wedding. Then I refocus on my gorgeous new bride.

"No complaints, but aren't you supposed to be at the nursery?" I ask, rubbing my hands along her thighs.

"Your mom is interviewing an agricultural student from Pinewood State today. She's got it under control."

I tip my chin, agreeing.

Holly's passion is the flowers. At least once a week, Mr. Johnston crosses the street to bring her something new to revive.

Davina? My mom could've run circles around Rex Stanton if she'd taken the chance. She's using her connections to hire students in the university system. The next step in mom's total-horticultural world domination is getting the lease back on the stall back at the Farmer's Market and finding a staff to manage it. After that, she's planning to source their flowers to the local florists and start a small roadside shop of their own.

"You two are going to be going gangbusters by the time Dusty and Cece's wedding comes around."

They actually don't have that long to prepare. Dusty popped the question and since Cece only wants her mill family in attendance they are getting married soon.

"And I'll be back in action once Aidy and Morgan tie the knot." Holly toys with my open collar. Then she adds coyly, "I'm here because I'm in the market for a new vehicle. One with a back seat."

My brow quirks. "I have a lot of cars with back seats. What other specs are you looking for?" I stand up, pushing my legs between hers. My cock growing harder, I whisper, "Talk cars to me, Doll."

My office door is open and I blithely wonder how long it'll take my admin to clear my calendar so I can get Holly in for a lube job.

I bite my wife's earlobe, pushing her skirt higher and she groans.

"Third row. Safety features. An entertainment system for Bhodi if he pulls As this semester. Definitely need LATCH."

My hand stills as it reaches her damp panties. "Lower anchors and tethers are for a car seat. Are you —" It hits me.

"One of the seeds *you've* been sewing took root," Holly licks her lower lip. "I'm pregnant."

I back away from my wife, have my office door slammed and locked, and am closing the blinds before Holly can react.

"Uhm, Cary?" she says in a panicked voice. "We talked about having a baby."

My belt is off and my zipper is down by the time I'm pulling Holly's ass to the edge of the desktop and setting back between her legs.

"Yeah, but one can never be too *sure*," I say, taking her lips in a scorching kiss.

"Oh!" Holly moans as I enter her, hissing, "Yesss. Let's make sure it's a sure thing."

# Holly

"Slow Down!" I yell, reaching for the *oh-shit* handle.

My weight shifts as Cary corners the road. Given his lead foot, the seat belt is useless.

Stopping short to get in line behind another car, he grits his teeth and slams a palm to the steering column. Cary's glare—meant for me—could crack the windshield. He won't take his eyes off the other vehicles waiting for the traffic signal to change. If we were in the roadster, he'd have one foot on the brake and the other on the gas, revving the car to jump through the intersection as soon as the light turns green.

Happy for the standstill, I breathe out and rub my distended abdomen.

He's mad… No, he's anxious. I tell myself.

I toiled at the nursery yesterday, getting everything ready for my maternity leave. I waved away the college helpers when moving seedlings from one side of the greenhouse to the other. Nesting at its finest, I even went crazy with the pricing gun, tagging all the birdhouses in the roadside store, and made sure the refrigerator cases for bouquets were to the exact temperature.

My I-can-do-it-alone moment extended this morning when I got on my hands and knees to scrub the shower tile. My husband very nicely called me out, saying the fumes were enough to choke a man to death, and I wasn't putting myself or the health of our child first.

Cary didn't understand why I was tired and irritable and still running, uh waddling, a mile a minute. He chased me between rooms in the house. I may have instigated an argument, nudging it along by not having my bag packed.

I can do labor and delivery. I'm looking forward to it in a masochistic sense because I can't wait to see Cary holding our baby. And Bhodi holding his little sister. And Davina to *finally* get her hands on her granddaughter.

What I don't want is to not be pregnant.

And it's apparent my lateness in life isn't working in my favor. A touch beyond thirty-nine weeks, I wasn't past due when my water broke all over the master bathroom floor. I guess my body had its reasons why I was more tired than usual, but I couldn't quite seem to slow down.

My husband—a man who is so over the moon ecstatic about his role as a dad he's had an infant carrier base installed in the backseat of every car we own for the past three months—was not amused that in all my preparations, I hadn't prepared for the hospital.

"I'm sorry," I say, meaning it now that I can see what I was doing the past few days a little clearer.

Cary trusts in my protectiveness. He understood my reasoning for keeping him, and Cass-Stanton, out of anything having to do with him taking his rightful place in our son's life. I didn't want any fallback to tarnish his reputation or for the man I love to be indebted to Jake. But Cary also needs me to let him safeguard his family, and he's quick to remind me I'm no longer alone. I have a partner I can trust too.

His tight features loosen a smidge at my apology.

It's short-lived when the next contraction peaks.

I groan loudly, letting the air out of my lungs like a balloon deflating as it subsides.

"So help me, Doll, if you have the baby in the car I'm going to put you over my knee," he threatens as he coaches me through my breathing exercises.

My mind, clear of pain, wanders to how our little darling wound up inside of me.

"Don't make promises you can't keep," I quip.

"Did you proposition me? Now?" Cary does a double-take. "What has gotten into you?"

I point to where my lap used to be. "Hormones are unpredictable things." I shrug. Then I twist my wrist, admiring the watch Davina got me at the holidays. "According to this, you have about four more minutes to talk dirty to me." A horn beeps behind us. "Or you could drive us to the hospitaaaal." My words stretch as his foot hits the floorboard again.

That's the last flippant comment I'm allowed to make. It's also the last one I want to make because the baby decides she's the one not arriving casually late to her birthday party. We no sooner have a parking spot than I'm up in the room, my knees to my chest, and pushing.

Shelby—her middle name is not Cobra, much to the dismay of her big brother—Cass stops wailing as soon as she's diapered and swaddled. My baby girl is staring wide-eyed up at her daddy. Cary is a mushy-mess. Tears fall over his cheeks that he doesn't bother wiping away.

My mind is a hazy mix of lethargy and euphoria, yet all I can think of is when Bhodi called Cary "dad" for the first time at our wedding. If the way Cary embraced fatherhood for Bhodi is any indication, Shelby got herself a good one.

And I guess I did as well.

Tucking Shelby to his chest, Cary leans and places a congratulatory kiss on my lips. Outwardly it's soft and sweet. I didn't miss the sweep of his tongue. Something tells me we'll be back in the hospital soon for the very same reason.

I just hope when we get here next time we have found a better name than "Chevelle", which tops Bhodi's list—along with "Gremlin" if he ever gets a little brother.

Lord, help me.

As fast as the nurses set up to welcome Shelby to the world, the flurry of activity subsides. Cary eases into a rocker, returning Shelby's affection like she hung the moon. He scoots them closer. I watch them as I doze.

A light melody fills the air.

"Is that—the *Arthur* theme song?" I ask Cary, reaching to lace our fingers together.

"It's a good song," he says. "Seeing as the best thing I've ever done was fall in love with you."

*Cary*

"I can't—" Bhod runs a hand over his thick dark hair.

The kid needs a haircut, but parenting a teen, it's all about which battles you choose. Besides, he's an adult and the only control I have over him is at the dealerships, threatening to cut his hours or banning him from the service center altogether. Not that any one of the other mechanics would rat him out if he showed up anyhow.

My son? He's a fucking good kid with a decent head on his shoulders. He gets along great with everyone. Most of the time. That right there is his mother's influence.

After his sophomore year, Bhodi sat me and Holly down and explained prep school wasn't for him. He'd spent enough hours in the bays that he developed a passion for cars. The boy negotiated—a tactic he leveraged watching me—going back to public school so that he could finish school and get CTEs in automotive.

It was a brilliant move. As was my counter that

graduating with enough credits towards a certification Bhodi could fill up his schedule at the community college with business prerequisites to get into Pinewood State. That last part has yet to be determined, but Bhod works part-time for Cass-Stanton and is doing well balancing school. He's got options for careers on two sides of the automotive industry. Sometimes he likes the business side. Other times his classes are as ignorable as Bhodi's mom and I are to any nineteen-year-old out there.

"Sylvie Rhys just got her license. She's excited," I remind him.

"Okay, then maybe it's 'I won't'. I don't want her crashing my car."

I catch my hazy reflection in the hood of Bhodi's Mustang while scrubbing my hand over my beard. It's longer now, and raising kids and running the motor group has me noticing how much salt it is peppered with.

"She's not going to wreck your car."

"Dad, it's my baby." Bhodi spreads his gangly arms. A hint of bicep peeks out from under his short sleeves.

I chuckle. He's attached to one thing. The Ford. But I also figured out about six months ago why he's not attached to *anyone*.

It's Sylvie.

The more she's grown up, the less comfortable Bhodi is around her. It makes perfect sense. She's a pretty girl. And there have been plenty of times I've been proud of him for keeping his distance. After all, Sylvie Rhys is sixteen. But it's affecting their friendship and to a lesser extent ours with her parents. The four of us walk on eggshells trying not to encourage a relationship between them, but are as aware of the inevitability as Bhodi was about the sleepover Holly and I had when we first started dating.

We're at Sylvie's birthday party. Or what's left of it, anyhow. Cece and Dusty invited Hol and me to stay late so our younger girls could play with theirs. It was like pulling teeth to get Bhod to show up for cake. And I have the distinct impression Sylvie stuck around to see him. Her girlfriends left about twenty minutes ago. She told them she'd *think* about meeting up with them later tonight.

The puppy dog eyes go both ways with these two. Nobody's playing anyone.

"Listen, dude." I put my arm around Bhodi's shoulder and we lean against his car. "I'm proud of you, you know that?"

"Gahd, stop already." He shrugs off my arm. "I gotta go."

"Where are you going?… No actually, what I want to know is why did you come?"

"Because it's her birthday."

"And you didn't want to let Sylvie Rhys down."

"Well, yeah." Serious *duh* tone.

Was I like this? Probably worse.

"Here's the thing I need to explain to you, Bhod: I'm not dumb. I know you care for that girl. And I have hella respect for you keeping your distance because she's—"

"Jailbait?"

"Glad we're on the same page."

"Then let me go." His hands fly to his face and he mutters something about not being able to believe we're having this conversation.

But it's an important one. I wish someone had been upfront with me at his age about women and sex. I also know the only reason Bhod hasn't jumped behind the wheel, gunning the engine, and flooring it is that I used Holly's rulebook and hadn't shied from answering his questions as honestly as I could. My son and I have always been close, and he's open to genuine advice.

"I'm not done speaking." *Crap, I need to cut the dad voice.*

"So speak."

I grab the back of Bhodi's head, pushing it forward and letting it go when he chuckles. He looks at me and his face blanks. He really isn't sure how to handle this.

"Years from now, you'll regret not taking Sylvie Rhys for that drive. Not because you kissed her, because if I hear that you did, I'm backing off while Dusty gives you the royal treatment." I bring my fists up, mock-punching his gut. "You'll hate yourself because you'll wonder what would have happened if you had taken that chance. The more space you continue to put between you and Sylvie now, the harder it'll be to bridge it later on. You're missing out on what that friendship is supposed to be while she finishes up school. Losing out on getting to know one another as adults. If you can't show her she's important to you today, you'll miss out on tomorrow. A girl as pretty as Sylvie Rhys is won't have trouble finding a boyfriend."

He but-but-buts me.

"What is stopping you from a friendly drive?"

Bhodi eyes Dusty warily. "You backing off when her father uses me as a punching bag."

My chest rumbles.

"Then go ask his permission. Tell Dusty how long you'll be gone and where you're going. Be respectful about it."

"She's three years younger than me."

"And Dusty's at least that much older than Cece. And your mom—"

"Don't go there." My kid cuts me off.

It's been a decade and while our life is as normal as

anyone else's, comments about cradle robbing set Bhodi's teeth on edge.

"Her age only matters for a few more years, and being conscientious about it proves you have a conscience. Show her dad you're a man and can handle it appropriately."

I finally persuade him to ask.

Dusty's sitting in a chair. His jaw twitches, measuring what he wants to say. I think he likes keeping Bhodi in suspense. Sylvie Rhys can't contain her excitement over driving the Mustang Bhodi restored for himself. Cece places a hand over her husband's and Dusty nods. He looks away too.

Makes sense. I've got daughters I'm protective of. You want them to find men who will treat them like gold.

Dusty's chest heaves and he stares at me. We're both thinking the same thing. *Did I make the right choice?* He points at me and then at the beer cooler. I bring him a cold one and pop the top on one for myself, sitting down between him and my wife.

"We're so screwed," Dusty says, lifting a beer to his lips.

"How so?" I take a swig of mine.

"Both of those kids were at your wedding. Think I'm footing that bill on my own and you're stupid, brother. They'll want fireworks or to ride in on camels or something crazy like that."

"Camels?" Holly questions.

"What? It's a car ride." I shrug.

"Yeah, and none of us ever did *anything* in a car. I want a fishing trip for going along with this cockamamie bullshit." Dusty tips the bottle he's holding in my direction.

"You're bartering our daughter for deep-sea fishing?" Cece blinks at her husband.

She and Holly exchange looks. My wife hides her

sheepish smile, pretending to wipe dirt from her skirt.

"Christ." Dusty rubs his thumb and index finger into his eye sockets. "Whatever happened to sticker books?"

The kids are back from the test drive sooner than the half an hour Bhodi told Dusty they'd be gone. I'm impressed. Sylvie Rhys is all smiles. They're both acting the way they had a few years ago when none of the boy/girl nonsense was an issue. Everything seems fine when Bhodi backs out of the driveway to go back to his apartment.

We'd offered for Bhodi to live with us as long as he liked. He's tight with his baby sisters, but I understood when my son opted for his own place with a roommate. That might bother me more if I didn't see him so often at work and have the chance to slip him a few bucks when his mother isn't looking.

It's getting late and a short while later, Holly and I pack it in with our daughters to get them home for bed. When the toothbrush in and tucking in is all done, I take my dad hat off and focus on the most important person in the world, Holly. She's laying in our basket bed in the house we built up the road from the Johnston's so that my wife was closer to the nursery.

Davina sold the house I grew up in and renovated the Johnstons' a few months after Doris died. Mrs. Johnston outlived the old man, believe it or not. Mom and Holly made Doris a fixture at the gift shop, enticing her to stay to hold mill babies and arrange flowers, but mostly it was to keep an eye on the woman and shield her from loneliness. We were all devastated losing someone who'd become special to our family.

I kneel on the bed and crawl over to Holly's side,

trapping her underneath the sheet with my body. She cups my cheek and pulls my face closer.

"What can I do for you tonight?" she asks.

"Not sure. The truth is I'm feeling old."

My son is nineteen and I'm thirty-five. My brain hadn't gone in the direction of weddings until Dusty mentioned it. Now I'm gobsmacked with the idea I could have already become a grandfather. Meanwhile, my forty-five-year-old wife cannot get her fill of sex, and my one-track mind—that is ready to pull into the station, so to speak—thought any more infants were going to be our *oops*. I'd gotten the snip so that I could keep up with Holly and not a toddler.

"I'd like to feel how old you feel." She kisses me, swiping her tongue over my lip.

I did mention Holly's libido, right? I used to think we couldn't get enough of each other, but we fuck more now than we did when we first met.

I grab Holly's hip, rolling her on top of me and my head on the pillows. She twines her fingernails through my chest hair, her eyes seductive and dancing when she pinches my nipples. I groan and my wife leans forward, licking the stiff peaks, her wantonness making me harder than a rock. Then Holly rises to her knees, pulling her nightshirt over her head, while I shimmy off my boxers and kick the tangle of bedsheets.

I watch Holly fist my cock as she hovers, straddling my hips.

"Put it inside you, Doll. I'm not as young as I once was."

Holly's head falls back as her laughter lights up the room. She smiles at me, knowing all the other ways I'd be glad to make her come. This one, allowing her to be in control as her pussy slides down the length of my erection, is my current favorite.

She grinds onto me once I'm seated inside of her.

Rocking with her, I sit up and grab the back of her neck, fusing our lips. Chasing her orgasm, Holly's having none of that. She pushes my spine against the mattress, using her palms on my chest to hold me flat. I feel the build and my skin censors a muffled cry when she leans in as she comes.

I use her bliss to my advantage. With a fluid motion, my wife is underneath me. I hitch her leg up over my shoulder, driving myself in deeper. Pushing her over the edge once more, I grunt a hard release.

We lie trading pecks on one another's lips with our bodies still connected. My dick twitches inside of her. Whispering and giggling, we goof about which one of us was louder, which of the kids could have heard us all the way down the hall, if we embarrass them, and calculating how long until our nest is empty.

The intimacy is second to none.

"Still feeling old?" She teases.

"No. But Christ, Doll, you're going to kill me one of these days trying to satisfy you."

"I'm content… For now." She yawns, stretching like a cat.

"Oh yeah?" I check the clock. "How long do I have?"

Somebody once told me that our age gap makes us well-suited and she'll slow down about the time I'm not interested in dipping into her honey-pot anymore. So what have we got fifteen, twenty years without medicated assistance? Hell, I'd get past my embarrassment over being the guy who has an erection lasting more than four hours, so long as Holly's needs are satisfied.

"Let's say I wouldn't be upset if both of us fell asleep and I woke up in the middle of the night with your cock inside of me."

"I'll do my best, but be more specific about where I'm putting my cock?"

If it hadn't been such a long day, Holly would keep our dirty banter going. She giggles instead, tucking her head to my chest. Our breaths even out, but Holly keeps shifting uncomfortably.

I'm about to ask if she's okay when she says, "I need to tell you something."

I roll toward her and tuck her blonde hair behind her ear, ready to start an all-night chat. We haven't had one in a while, though it's never stopped being our thing.

"Things were tense between Bhodi and Sylvie Rhys at the party because he'd already kissed her."

"What? When?"

"Cece found a text string between Sylvie and her best friend. It happened on her actual birthday. He'd gone over to give her a gift."

"That's why he fought us about showing up for the party, and the two of them were so awkward once he got there." I groan, covering my brow with my forearm. "Crap on a cracker. I shouldn't have had that talk with him." I blew it.

I give my wife the short version of what we'd discussed. "I didn't want him to be so concerned about their age difference that it made it an impossibility later. I wanted him to be her friend and have a chance when it mattered."

None of us are playing dumb. If Sylvie Rhys were nineteen or Bhodi were sixteen, they'd have been each other's prom dates or planning for the dance.

"And Bhodi needed to hear that, Cary. He understands the technicalities of the situation, but he needed someone to validate his feelings and let him know they weren't wrong... They're—ill-timed?" Her shoulder raises in a shrug. "When it comes down to it, I think he wanted to be her first kiss and he knew if he waited he'd lose the chance. But taking the risk changed things, and that's a lot of pressure on them both. Your son realizes they're in very different places in their lives." My wife smooths the crease in my forehead.

"I hadn't seen either of them so stiff around one another since the summer at the beach house when Bhodi realized Sylvie had boobs." This elicits a snort from Holly. "God, bad choice of words. I'm sorry... The only worse situation could be if he, you know, fell head over heels for the mom of the kid he's mentoring."

"That didn't turn out so bad." Holly hits me with a megawatt smile.

That's what I wanted to impress on my kid. I don't like imagining what my life would be if William had been a better man. The Colony Park wouldn't have broken down when and where it did, and Holly would have never offered me the drink.

"Nah, you're right, it didn't." I use a knuckle to tip Holly's chin up and place a chaste kiss on her lips. "So now what do we do?"

She places a hand over my heart. "We don't do anything. It's their own story, and it will have its own timeline. Maybe they will. And maybe they won't. But I'm glad you were there for Bhodi and that he wound up with a dad could trust to go to for advice."

**_Thank you for reading Home Wrecker!_** I hope you swooned over Holly and Cary's age gap romance as much as I loved writing it.

Enjoy this excerpt from **Deep Gap**, a deeply emotional, lonely hearts age gap workplace romance!

# DEEP GAP

## Greer

"Let me drive you," Karen offers.

I pause, shrugging on the thin coat I bought at the donation center before the winter weather set in. The collar has gotten stuck underneath the back of the jacket and my shirt sleeves have ridden up to my elbows. I should either take it off and try again or find a mirror to un-bunch everything.

"Please, Greer. It's cold out." I hear my mom's voice in Karen's reminder and see her concern that I'm not protected from the elements.

Turning from the soulful expression that I'm still unable to handle, I decide I'll be going back to the thrift shop for a thicker coat before Karen runs to the mall to buy one for me. I've taken too much from her.

*You took everything from her.*

"I walked here. It's no big deal. I walk everywhere." I stop fiddling and pull up my shirt, exposing the mismatched tank top I'm wearing underneath. Another donation center find I'd worn all summer when it was sweltering in Brighton. "See layers!"

For Karen's sake, I keep it cheerful and walk toward the front door without meeting the worrisome crinkles at the corner of her eyes. She was kind enough to feed me a huge breakfast before I go to work. I refuse to take advantage of her hospitality. The whole reason I agreed to come over was that I'd spent Thanksgiving with my mom and dad when Karen had wanted all three of us here. I hate disappointing her.

When I glance into the mirror there, my own face betrays the act I'm putting on for Karen's benefit. I don't recognize the detached woman who is staring back at me with her stringy blonde hair secured in a thick ponytail at the base of her neck. My outsides and my insides don't match.

Or maybe what's left on the inside is reflected on the outside. I couldn't smile if you asked me to. With the exception of everything Karen's husband, Mac, does for me, I haven't had many reasons to smile in years.

I flop my long hair out over my coat. The end smacks between my shoulder blades. As I'm buttoning up, it happens. Like a moth to a flame, my gaze finds the eight-by-ten Karen keeps on the mantle.

Senior year. God-awful mottled blue background that I guess is supposed to resemble the wide sky and all the possibilities in the world. Tan sport coat, white button-down, and red-bordering-on-burgundy tie because that's the  kind of momma's boy Ellis was that he allowed Karen to choose his outfit on portrait day. Although Ellis practiced for days trying to master tying it himself. He was so proud of himself. Heck, I was proud of him.

I feel the elation of his laugh from over a decade ago, when Ellis showed me how to do it, ring hollow inside my empty chest. My windpipe collapses and the parts of my heart that had begun healing since the last time this happened once again show the telltale marks of how threadbare my life is since Ellis died.

I miss his smile. His gleaming white teeth. How he towered over me from the moment our mothers introduced us. We had so much in common. There was never once I hadn't trusted Ellis. Whether that was showing me the secret of how to ease forked vegetables underneath the dinner table and feed them to one of his family's many animals, or slipping me the correct formula for a problem during a math test. Ellis was a constant. At seventeen, I couldn't envision my life without him. At eighteen his life was over.

So was mine.

Karen's hands rub my shoulders, breaking my trance. "He loved you. *We* love you."

"Thank you." I hug Karen, repeating the same response I've given to her and her husband whenever they've reminded me over the past few years.

What else do you say to the parents of the boy you killed?

*"I love you, too"* seems superficial. But *"Thank you for forgiving me for the unforgivable"* I can get behind.

Aside from Karen and Mac and my parents, I think I've lost the ability to love anyone. Some days I doubt I ever knew how to begin with.

I clear my throat and chirp, "Breakfast was wonderful. I appreciate you feeding me, but I don't want to be late!"

If Karen and I reminisce about Ellis now, we won't stop. Or she won't. I mostly let her talk out her grief and answer any questions she asks as frequently as she asks the same ones, albeit in slightly different manner. I refuse to hold things back from my best friend's mom and dad that they're entitled to know about their son. All the same, Karen and Mac own the dog training facility that I work at and she deserves an employee who doesn't shirk their responsibilities.

"It will only take a minute to get my keys?" She presses.

"It only takes a few minutes to walk that mile. The fresh air will do me good."

"The November cold has your cheeks permanently pink, sweetheart."

"Some people call that healthy."

She releases a wry laugh. "Promise me you'll be safe. Call if you need a ride."

"I promise to be safe." We both know I won't call.

Outside, I put my earbuds in my ears, letting the music play softly so I remain aware of my surroundings. I tuck my hands inside my pockets and am down the driveway, passing the house when Karen finally goes back inside. My lips move to the lyrics and my feet fall rhythmically, landing on the wet pavement. It rained last night. I avoid the craggy puddles where the worn road dips and water fills the potholes. The weatherman says it will be sunny and thirty degrees warmer tomorrow afternoon. North Carolina's early winter weather has a serious case of ADD.

The wind whips with an icy chill as I get to the rise where the four-foot white estate fence for the training facility comes into view. A car is traveling the rutted dirt and gravel road from the building's entrance. I recognize the man in the toque who salutes me as drives past at a snail's pace. Returning his greeting with a stiff wave, I appreciate Byron's friend kept the wheels of his SUV from splashing through the nearest puddle, dousing my jeans.

There isn't much glamor in scrubbing kennel floors, but I'd hate having to explain my appearance to Byron. He's a decent guy, but even the nicest man could read between the lines and hear, "your jerk face buddy nailed me with a wall of water."

Sighing, my stomach muscles release the corded tension that builds whenever I think about the possibility of having to defend myself to him. When it comes down to it, I rarely know what to say to anyone. So, I do what I learned to do when the judge sentenced me to six years at the women's penitentiary after my best friend and I didn't make it to our high school graduation. I put my head down and hope others see it as me respecting their privacy.

But the truth is, it's really that people in general haven't stopped making what sent me to prison in the first place their business.

*Byron*

Week after week, Tallulah is becoming increasingly attached to Trig. I'm thrilled the Plott Hound puppy has gotten the point that he's her person the way I'm Jovie's. However, I have to keep the dogs outside a bit longer than I expected, hoping the extra playtime provides a good distraction while Trig disappears in his car.

"Good girls!" I call, clapping as Jovie mouths the ball toward Tallulah.

They're great at sharing. Tallulah takes off running with Jovie hot on her tail. I have a decent amount of concern about how my animal will react to being alone.

It won't be much longer until Trig puts a lead around Tallulah and they drive off into the sunset together. Her training is going well—and it's a heck of a lot more education than she needs as an emotional support animal—but since I started training service dogs for vets, I've become a little finicky about animal behavior. I won't let Tallulah go until she's as dependable as Jovie became after we'd dug into her drills.

Jovie's come a long way from the starving roadside mutt I rescued and then petitioned the government to let me return with from my final tour of duty. Even before Mac offered me this job, she wasn't misbehaved. Yet once you see what these dogs are capable of, it's easy to fall into the mindset of expecting more from them. The more you love them, the more they live up to those expectations. All my dogs want in return for a job well done is praise and maybe a treat now and then.

I toss a final ball across the wide expanse of lawn. The girls go barreling after it, unaware the three of us have been the only ones playing for a good ten minutes.

My cheek sucks in on one side. My old Army buddy's stealth reminds me he has a toddler at home and he's used to leaving unnoticed. For as great as Tallulah is, any animal is unpredictable. That's another reason why she needs to be near perfect. Trig's got a family who depends on him. His wife, Kimber, agreed that a dog would go a long way to helping Trig with the PTSD he suffers from. I won't let Kimber down by expecting her to accept a dog I wouldn't consider safe enough to be around my kids. If I had any.

I whistle sharply. Jovie and Tallulah plop their behinds on the stoop at the back entrance. As soon as I open the door, they are through it. Tallulah stops to look around. She's finally figured out that Trig is missing. Her nose hits the tile floor, and she's searching for his scent. All I smell is a strong odor of disinfectant. A mop and sudsy bucket are in the hall, which means Greer is on-site.

I should correct Tallulah and the both of us should follow Jovie into my office. I'd planned on making use of my time by filing paperwork while I was here. Instead, I trail Tallulah through the hall. The pup won't find the person she's after. But I always make a point of bumping into Greer.

Greer is quiet and mindful. Impeccable at her job. Not that custodial work is hard, but it is labor intensive. I've never heard her grumble. Hell, I haven't heard a single complaint about the cleanliness of the facility since she started working here two years ago. Greer is the sort of employee that takes care of things before Mac has a chance to ask her to do it. At moments so efficient that there have been instances I've wondered if she's the ghost and not the son Mac and Karen lost ten years ago.

Any flippant remarks are best kept to myself. The three of them, Karen, Mac, and Greer, deserve to heal in peace without a big mouth butting in. It's probably why Greer's hours are odd; Early mornings. Late nights, after the vets and their service dogs have long since hunkered down to rest.

I'm about to bark at Tallulah when she crosses into the staff's break room, but become entranced by the quiet way the pup approaches Greer. The dog licks Greer's fingertips for attention. Greer turns from whatever has had her attention outside the window.

"You aren't supposed to be in here," Greer coos as she kneels down. She rubs Tallulah's ear and head and then brushes her nose against the dogs. "We need to get you out before Byron finds you."

Tallulah offers a paw.

Trust. Comfort. Whatever Tallulah sensed Greer needed, she's providing it. I'm proud of the pup. She's so close to having a loving family.

"Oh, thank you." Greer shakes it. "But I don't have any cookies to share."

Tallulah licks her snout while looking up into Greer's face. Then she inches forward to snuggle.

Good girl.

"Maybe I could take you to Byron. He's probably got plenty of treats." Greer presses a fingertip to her lips. "I won't tell him where you were. It's our secret." She shushes.

"I'm right here." I lean into the door frame. "No bones, though. How are you, Greer?" I firmly believe she's the type who needs a friendly hello or a kind word—even if she isn't keen on relying on compliments.

"Shoot, he caught you, Tallulah. I guess you'll have to face the firing squad."

I nicker, sticking out my index finger. Tallulah rears on her hind legs, sitting straight. I aim and *"Bang!"*

Tallulah rolls to the floor and Greer's giggle tinkles in my ears.

"I shouldn't laugh when you do that, but it's so adorable." She tickles Tallulah's belly.

I join Greer where she sits criss-cross on the floor, hauling the skinny pup onto my lap with her belly up like I'm holding a baby. I rub her belly while admonishing her for being in a room that we are conscientious not to let any of the dogs in. Positive reinforcement of negative behavior isn't my go-to.

But kindness matters.

"You aren't mad, are you?" Greer asks.

I'd never expect anyone on a cleaning crew to wear a ball gown. Yet it strikes me, in comparison to Karen's laid-back style after being married for thirty-odd years, that for a young woman Greer hides how pretty she is.

"Nah. I let her in, but I am going to have to make sure I keep her out so that she doesn't make a habit of it. What were you looking at?" I clear my throat. I've just given away that I've been watching Greer.

Greer's brow twitches. "The hives. Mac split two of them last summer. I'm not supposed to disturb them. Curiosity has the best of me."

"Those bees are plenty fine." Mac's voice comes from behind. "But I'll make you a deal. You can go check before you leave for the day if you let Byron drive you home," he says to Greer.

"Deal! I don't have much left to clean, Mac. I swear it won't take long." Greer jumps up from the mat she's been sitting on. She hugs Mac and scoots down the hall toward her mop and bucket.

I'm guiding Tallulah toward my office when Mac pats me on the shoulder. "It's okay I volunteered you? Greer has a proverbial bee in her bonnet about accepting a ride from Karen and scattered showers are passing through before it clears up."

"Yeah, no. It's fine. I have stuff to keep me busy until she's ready. No rush."

"Good. I hadn't found much that made that girl happy until she started helping with my bees. I'll do just about anything for Greer to smile every now and again. I appreciate your willingness to do us a favor."

Ready to read more?
Deep Gap is available now!
www.jodykaye.com/deepgap

# Author Notes

---

At the beginning of every book there is a disclaimer that reads something akin to "names are a creation of the authors imagination." And that's where I want to start. If you know Raleigh and the surrounding area, there are definitely names in this series you'll pick up on. Cary and Holly Springs are towns. There's a Nash Park downtown (Dr. Nash from Shred of Decency) that had just reopened prior to Covid. I won't say I don't choose character names for reasons, but I never choose them with malicious intent.

Seriously, let's go back to Covid for a sec... One of the things MJA and I did to stop going stir crazy during the initial lockdown was to go for drives. You'd be stunned how many Triangle roads and neighborhoods have the prefix or suffice "Glen" to them. More often than not, I'd be staring out the car window watching signs pass and think, "*ooh*, that's a great good guy/bad guy/baby name."

On the days writing was even possible, I was lucky my mind could wander into this alternate universe akin to the one I'd created for Kingsbrier. The difference is there's a little bit more somewhere than nowhere when your characters go to recognizable places. And, given the shittastic events of 2020 and early 2021, there's always a concern someone will accuse you of revisionist history or just generally being an asshole since everybody seems to have a reason for getting upset about something nowadays. Point: I don't write things to be a shitty person or out of malice.

Now that we've got that settled...

One of the things I love best about our move to North Carolina is how the newness of it all brought back old memories. My own family's roots originate in Southeastern, MA and Providence, RI. The checkerboard of the Kent Heights water tower was a beacon guiding us back in between my dad's military assignments. We shopped the mills for back to school clothes. When it was an ice cream stand, my grandparents owned "The Bucket" across from the Seekonk Speedway. That grandfather, a mechanic and antique car enthusiast, used to start his MGs for anyone who came into his shop and drove them across the Bourne Bridge to the Cape on the weekends.

The more conversations our family has had about our history, local history, and the nation's history, the more two distinct locals mixed and mingled in my mind to create Brighton. It's not perfect, no place ever is, and the people there are as flawed as any of your friends, but it's as close to hopeful as I've been able to make it so far. Yes, there's even hope for Jake.

I've mentioned in the past that there were several Shattered Hearts of Carolina Books that weren't part of my original plan. Home Wrecker is one of them. I'd been offered an opportunity in early 2020, and while hemming and hawing over whether take it, I plotted the basis for the book in two distinct ways, plucking Holly from Sliver of Truth (the book I was writing at the time) as the main character. When I opted to keep Home Wrecker as part of this series, I'd intended for it to be short, but it's actually one of my longest books. I'm unsure if that's why it took so long to finish... or if it's that I spent a lot of time on mental health car rides. ;)

I actually think I enjoy writing single parent romances because the kids are such an integral part of the equation. Their quirks and opinions, utter embarrassment or need to embarrass their parent make for livelier storytelling that's relatable to anyone with children in their lives. Plus parent and kid are a package deal. The love interest has to fall for both or the story won't work. Bhodi was such an innocent person as compared to the way Gracyn was as a child, when she first appeared in Colton, that I had to ask other parents and observe boys his age who weren't quite as worldly. Yes, those kids DO still exist.

I love that Bhodi was the link between Holly and Cary. They wouldn't have met one another without him because Cary's no longer interested in the trappings of his own youth—like Sweet Caroline's. After he spends the night, Cary's thrum of antagonism toward Holly and his immediate worry that perhaps the way she handled the situation allowed an adult to persuade Bhodi to do something wrong is one of my favorite subtler moments. This guy reacts because he cares about this kid. But subconsciously Cary is also already aware that Holly's child remains the focus of everything she does.

Holly's mind was interesting to explore. She knew what love was and being burned by it—and missing out on being Cary's age—developed her own set of rules. If I could change a single thing about what you know about her, it is that there was an opportunity to include her journals in more than passing. I keep wondering if she wrote down all of the wild stories she'd heard serving drinks over the years and if that's what allowed her to be less judgmental of Davina. Even without falling for Cary, I think Holly would have had a wonderful life because she approached it with an air of romanticism and ability to reinvent herself. I can't say that any other main character I've written could forge a life uniquely independent outside of their love story. Holly is someone who actually doesn't require a man because she's fulfilled and killing it on her own. (Since I know the follow-on question I'll get: No, Holly would never settle for Jake because Jake puts his needs first.)

Home Wrecker is my seventeenth book. I may have teared up as I typed that. The only goal outside of publishing a single book was finding a lone reader, outside of my small circle of friends, able to palate my writing style. Unlike the characters in my imagination, according to Goodreads and BookBub *you* actually do exist... And there is more than one of you, which is quite stunning! From the bottom of my heart, thank you for coming back time and again, for the reviews, the personal messages, the tags on social media, but most of all for the encouragement to keep writing. I would not be here to entertain you still if you weren't willing to read the next story. <3

Kristina, Alicia, Amanda, and Molly, thank you so much for sharing the highs and lows of this business alongside me every day. It's made the journey a million times better.

Jennifer, I drank every bottle of Mommy's Gold Juice you brought to my doorstep while writing this book. Hopefully, it didn't make the characters slur too much. Thank you for introducing us to the OBX and for the special deliveries!

Sarah & Kate, I'd probably lose what's left of my mind without either of you. So thanks for helping me keep up the daily illusion to my family that I'm generally sane. Friends like you are hard to find.

Kim, thank you for thinking of me. Somehow you always chose a day when I need a pick me up.

Jill, I swear someday I'll get you a draft when I say I'm going to. Thanks for being patient with me and for all of your feedback. It means the world.

MJA, *forever* and ever I know you do!

Also by Jody Kaye

---

Shattered Hearts of Carolina
*Splinter of Hope*
*Shred of Decency*
*Sliver of Truth*
*Holding Onto Hope*
*Home Wrecker*
*Deep Gap*
*Bleeding Heart*
*Shattered Soul*

The Kingsbrier Legacy
*Love Thy Neighbor*
*Gray Sin*
*Going Down*

The Kingsbrier Quintuplets
*Eric*
*Brier*
*Daveigh*
*Miss Cavanaugh*
*Cavanaugh*
*Adam*
*Colette*
*Colton*

The Canvas Duet
*Canvas*
*Imprint*

To view more great titles,
sign up for Jody Kaye's newsletter,
or find her on social media
go to www.jodykaye.com or

*Scan Now!*

# About the Author

Jody's husband asked what she'd been doing all day. After five years she finally confessed, "When no one is around, I write."

Okay, it was more like a bunch of stammering and trying to get out of saying a thing. Jody's a writer. You want it pretty. Let's compromise.

"Just finish one," he said, challenging her to complete a story and share it. Little did he know that those words of encouragement meant they'd return from a family vacation with a wild and defiant set of quintuplets stumbling their way into adulthood. Wasn't raising their three sons enough?

A native of nowhere, Jody settled in New England for 17 years before agreeing to uproot her brood of boys and move to North Carolina. She's a part-time graphic designer and marketeer with over twenty years' experience, and full-time writer. If Jody ever gets lost, you'll find her reading, all the while hoping that her ravenous children haven't eaten all the ingredients before she's cooked dinner.

Add your voice and help readers discover
this love story by writing a review!